To Kristen and
Mike Scanlin —

THE LOST INNINGS

A BASEBALL REDEMPTION

Warm Regards,

ALEX MURPHY

Alex Murphy

A Baseball Redemption

"A ballplayer spends a good piece of his life gripping a baseball, and in the end, it turns out that it was the other way around all the time."

Jim Bouton (1939-2019)

Major League Baseball Pitcher

Won/Loss 62-83

Cover photo and graphics by Ken Myers

Cover photo actor Ryan Schrock

Cover photo courtesy of Kitley Farms

Back cover photo courtesy of the Cincinnati Reds

Editing by Ms. M. Productions

DEDICATION

This novel about loss and redemption is dedicated to my father. When he read stories and poems or played catch with me in the backyard, he launched me on a baseball and literature journey that refuses to release me.

In Memory: Some of the characters in this work of fiction are named after high school classmates who have passed on.

"Puer autem amici tui in senectute bona."

CONTENTS

Prologue 1

1. An Easy Out 3
2. Thanks For The Memory 7
3. The Future Beckons 12
4. The Past Is Close Behind 18
5. Let's Make A Deal 20
6. Take Me Out To A Small Game 27
7. Please Allow Me To Introduce Myself 33
8. A Series Of Random Events 39
9. Meanwhile Back At The Farm 41
10. He Jests at Scars That Never Felt a Wound ... 46
11. The Baby Named Cake 54
12. When Accidents Happened Way Back When ... 61
13. Painting Therapy 65
14. Name That Tune 71
15. You Gotta Trust The Pitch 80
16. Down On The Farm 86
17. Pitching Is Upsetting Timing 94
18. Heard It In A Love Song 106
19. The Best-Laid Plans Often Ain't 114
20. Opera Meets Baseball 118
21. It Feels Different Until It Doesn't 130
22. Sorry Seems To Be The Hardest Word ... 139
23. The Lawman Cometh 147
24. The Confession And The Godfather 161
25. Sitting On A Pitch 169
26. Back When I Was A Player 176
27. When Push Comes To Score 182
28. Ice Cream Solves Everything 187
29. I Always Wanted A Neighbor Like You ... 195
30. And Ridley Shall Lead Them 211
31. Do You Know Mustang, Sally? 218
32. Hope Springs Eternal 227
33. Put Duncan In, Coach 235

34. Shoeless Joe Was Framed   255
35. Have You Ever Seen The Rain   264
36. Night Time Is The Right Time   284
37. A Try-Out Would Be Nice   294
38. Miles To Go And Promises To Keep   301
39. There's Only Three Lawyer Jokes   309
40. When Cute Goes The Distance   319
41. New Perspectives & New Projections   339
42. The Big League Beckons   349
43. Baseball's Redemption   361
44. A New Tomorrow Starts Today   370
45. The Ridley Return   380
46. Now Batting, Number Nine   390
47. Ridley To The Rescue   398
48. A Walk On The Wild Side   422
    Epilogue   445

    Teaser   447
    About the Author   451

PROLOGUE

There is always a moment in baseball that reminds you why it's easy to love the game. It's not always a long home run, or a monster strike out, or even an impossible double play. It might be as simple as a competitor congratulating an opponent on a great put-out. Perhaps it's a record-breaking hit that is etched in your mind forever. Maybe it's a sweet moment between a ballplayer and a fan, or even a fan's child. You never know when it will happen, but when it does, you are reminded that baseball is a reflection of what is best about being human: Certain moments coalesce into a patchwork of beauty that completes the allure of being alive and part of it all.

That's what drew Jack Ridley to baseball as a child. At first, it was a pathway to moments with his father. In time, baseball grew to be a part of his identity. The subtle approval of an 'attaboy' was Jack's perfect benediction. He was fulfilled by the rush of team competition and camaraderie. In short, he loved the game and everything about it.

Jack found success at every level. His teammates liked his relent-less competitiveness, and opponents liked his unfailing sportsmanship. When the college scouts came to see his high school games, Ridley made sure his teammates and opposing teams were noticed. The scouts came to talk to Jack, but he managed to finagle the conversation toward other players. He helped them get offers, which endeared him to everyone. By the time the pro scouts came calling, Jack was adept at sharing the moment. Everyone was happy that Jack Ridley received scholarships from several large schools.

No one was surprised that he was drafted by the Cincinnati Reds, but there were a few eyebrows raised when he decided to skip college and sign a pro contract. Predictable comments crept into conversations. Jack had finally made an error - not getting a degree from Notre Dame or Stanford.

Still, those same doubters were quick to say they knew all along that he'd find success in the big leagues. A catcher of his caliber was destined for greatness. When Jack was called up to the big club midway through his first season, a few said they saw his success as inevitable. And the general consensus was that his prowess at hitting the ball and handling big-league pitchers would someday land him in the Hall of Fame. Everyone knew that his talent would take him to the top and beyond.

But no one saw it coming when everything that defined him came crashing down.

1

AN EASY OUT

'Thousands of times,' Jack thought. He must have seen this sort of thing thousands of times. Jack Ridley didn't know the player swaggering up to the batter's box, but Jack could tell that there was more show than go in this guy. Why he thought it made a difference to strut in this meaningless game, in an almost meaningless town, told Jack that this game was about over.

It wasn't that Jack thought the game was meaningless. Baseball had been his constant companion all of his life. He was about four years old when his father gave him his first baseball glove. The boy was hooked from the start. Smelling the oiled leather made him feel like an all-star. The hours spent forming the glove to the curve of the baseball were never enough.

Jack loved the strategy of the game and he loved the graceful arc of a well-hit ball. Loping around the bases was euphoric. The amiable competition with the other players fascinated him, and it didn't matter if they were on his team or not. Jack had fun with the game and all the players. But mostly he had fun outsmarting batters and chalking up outs for his pitcher.

All these thoughts blasted through his brain as the batter settled in. Swinging for the fences was the only thing on this guy's mind, Jack could see. The tying run was already on second, and this guy would be trying to win the game with one swing. The young pitcher was rattled because the final out had reached second on a throwing error. A timeout seemed like a good idea and Jack eased out to the mound. Calming the kid's nerves was second nature for such a seasoned catcher.

"Just one easy out and we're done. I've got an idea about this guy."

This batter was just a bit too eager, and sizing up the opposition was Jack's forte. He decided to go with off-speed pitches. The change-up came floating in, and the batter swung when the ball was halfway home. It only increased the guy's frustration, so Jack called for a curve.

That got another early swing and Jack put the batter's anxiety to good use. Figuring that the batter would swing at about anything just off the plate, Jack called for an outside pitch. He was slightly surprised that his pitcher dropped one down the middle. The batter swung at what he thought was his home run chance, but he only chipped the ball in front of home plate. Jack swooped on it like a happy golden retriever, and fired the ball to first.

Game over. Chalk one up for the Jason Crushers. Jack trotted back to the dugout. He kept away from the Hooters' coach who was jawing with the umpire and losing ground. Jack noticed someone watching him approach. She was an attractive blonde, about college age. Her steady gaze signaled a hello and she met Jack by the steps with a useful greeting.

"Hey, trouble, you going over to the Zone with the guys?"

Planning for the evening hadn't entered Jack's mind. This young lady seemed friendly enough, but Jack felt his life was in disarray. He wasn't averse to a friendly face, but he didn't expect to find true love from any baseball connection. Still, Jack knew everybody had a story, and he was a good listener.

"See you there," Jack grinned.

Heading to the parking lot, Jack chatted with a few other fans. He arrived at his five-year-old Mustang. It was out of warranty and starting to run a little rough. For once, it fired up just fine. Jack knew the way to the Zone. He had been in Jason a few times. Baseball was now a benign avocation. Jack's real life was part owner in a sporting goods store back home. It kept him off the streets in the off-season, but when the small leagues started warming up, Jack still wanted to play. It had turned out that baseball was pretty much through with Jack Ridley, but Jack Ridley wasn't quite through with baseball.

Jack saw a couple of the Crusher players already there. They were young fellows, mostly recent high school players, working for the veneer plant that sponsored the team. They were happy to see Jack. Even though he was five or six years older than all of them, they liked the way Jack treated them as equals. They all knew Jack was an outstanding ball player, but none of them knew why he basically wasted his time playing with them.

When the players waved him to their table, Jack made a general announcement.

"Boys, no late night tricks. We have a game tomorrow night and I'm too old to help all of you."

Jack had an easy way of needling his teammates and they all liked him for it. He was halfway through a glass of beer when the young lady from the baseball game appeared. Jack had seen moments like these become sleazy, but this occasion seemed perfectly innocent. She started with a friendly curve.

"Jack, I know your name, but you have to introduce yourself anyway."

Her off-speed pitch made him grin.

"I'm Jack Ridley and I have one beer here with your name on it. Except it's blank."

His ready affability got a laugh.

"Write 'Patty Patterson' on it and you've got a deal."

They sat with the team and Jack kept the conversation away from his past or his future. He steered toward talking about Patty. Jack had learned long ago that people wanted to be asked about themselves.

They gabbed about Patty's college classes and her roommates, and when she was returning to school in the fall. She lit up when she talked about becoming a teacher. Jack mentioned that his mother taught English in his hometown. Patty was chatting about her favorite books and movies when one of the players from the local team approached. Her mood became cautious. She seemed to expect the yammering that the newcomer brought to the table.

"What are you doing with this jerk?" he threatened.

Patty's exasperation was evident.

"Jerry, why don't you just go away?"

The charmer thought he was in some sort of negotiation.

"Why should I? He ain't going anywhere."

Patty was rapidly losing her supply of tolerance. Jack figured she had seen this sort of thing before, but he tried to stay on easy ground.

"How about I buy you a beer and we all just hang out?"

"Ain't gonna be any beer with you, jerk wad."

Jerry leaned closer for emphasis. Jack was never inclined toward fighting, especially with drunks and their friends. His general preference was to just get along. He wasn't interested in exchanging punches with this guy. If the new-found Patty thought less of him for it, things were just going to have to be that way.

The result was that Jack was passive until Jerry grabbed him and tried to wrestle him away from the table. Jack had a blurred glimpse of Patty backing away, as he gave Jerry a healthy shove over a low wall that separated the servers' station from the bar. His attention was briefly diverted toward Patty. He wanted to make sure that she was clear from any damage this troublemaker might cause. Unfortunately, at that moment someone launched a bottle into the side of Jack's head.

The foam exploded around Jack's face and the lights in the room exploded along with it. He had a brief glimpse of the players who were sitting with him springing to grab Jerry and his friends. Then Jack saw a giant murky wave start to crash down on him, and he tumbled into darkness.

2

_____

THANKS FOR THE MEMORY

J ack could hear the dim roar of the major league crowd as he
approached the plate. He always went into some sort of strange
Zen-type of mindset in these moments. Besides keeping his focus
on the type of pitch he could expect from a given pitcher, he also
remembered whether this particular thrower had given him any past problems. Hearing the announcer's voice during his walk-up gave him a charge.

'Now batting, number nine, Jack Ridley.'

The rumbling voice echoed through the big ballpark and the roar of the
huge crowd bounced in his head. Still, there were certain voices that cut
through the din. He always heard "C'mon, Jack," as he settled in the batter's
box. This helped him center his thoughts and concentrate on the ball spinning toward him. Jack was sizing up the pitcher amid the crowd's calling
as one:

"C'mon Jack. C'mon Jack."

_____

For some reason the noise was fading and Jack was having trouble
hearing the crowd. He tried to adjust his uniform and get into his

usual stance, but his legs and arms weren't responding. The crowd noise ebbed and all he could hear was one voice.

"C'mon, Jack."

Jack's sensation that his arms weren't working right was replaced by the feeling of a hand stroking his shoulder. He heard and felt a warm breath.

"C'mon, Jack," was repeated.

Jack slowly realized that he wasn't in a ball park at all. He was wrapped in bedsheets, and what he heard was the young lady from the bar. She gently murmured.

"C'mon, Jack."

He had no recollection of leaving the bar. His head had a nice bump from the spot that met the beer bottle, and the room was a bit hazy. Jack was truly embarrassed that he had ended up in this strange woman's bed. It wasn't his style at all.

"How did I get here?" was all he could manage.

For the moment, he couldn't place a name. He remembered that she had mentioned hers last night. She giggled, as if she had just told a joke to herself.

"I drove you here, silly. You were out on the floor."

Jack just watched her, hoping there was some good information about to be revealed. Gathering details in a roundabout way was a possibility.

"You got me in your car all alone?"

Again, she gave him a giggle.

"The guys on the team helped me get you out of there. I told them I'd take you home but I had no idea where that was. So, you're here."

A look at the trees outside the window told Jack they were, at least, up on a second floor.

"You had help getting me up the stairs?"

She giggled a third time.

"You were kinda out on your feet, so I just walked you along like an usher at church. The whole time you kept asking me if I was the trainer. Whatever that means."

She was genuinely entertained by the story. Realizing that he was in bed with no shirt, Jack gave her a quizzical look. She got right to the point.

"Don't worry. Your shirt had beer all over it, so I rinsed it out. It's hanging in the hallway, all dry by now."

He was relieved. A night visit of this sort would only complicate things for him.

"So we never..." was all he got out before her giggling continued. It was a likeable giggle and he felt better when she spoke.

"Your reputation is safe, Jack. You mumbled a few words about some announcer and then you were out."

The relief on his face was obvious.

"I'm glad you helped me out of there and cleaned up my shirt," he admitted. "The guys probably would have left me on a bench somewhere."

He was genuinely grateful and she knew it.

"Let's just say you owe me another evening that doesn't end in a bar fight. That wasn't your fault. Jerry has been following me around for a while. I guess he was jealous that I was talking to you. Plus, you beat his team."

This reminded Jack that he was scheduled to play that night.

"So, I get to see him again," he deadpanned. "I won't mention your name."

She was not to be outdone.

"I won't tell any of the girls how I lured you into my apartment and took off your clothes."

They both smiled and she continued the joke.

"Well, it's partly true."

Jack was about to extend the kidding and ask which part she meant. Outside her window, unmistakable evidence of a baseball game interrupted the moment. He swung his legs out of the bed and found that his pants were missing. At least he had on his underwear, he gratefully realized. At that exact moment, for some reason, he remembered her name.

"Now, Patty, what's up with this?"

She was hiding her face behind one hand and Jack saw a blush in her cheeks.

"Well, there was beer on your jeans and I thought I should...."

Her voice trailed off, leaving the rest of her explanation hanging in the air. Jack wrapped the top sheet around his middle. He could hear the satisfying plunk of a baseball hitting a glove on the receiving end. Under any conditions, anywhere, he would know that sound. He'd heard it all his life.

Jack short-stepped his way to the window, in the sheet, to see who was playing. There were two teams warming up at a baseball diamond directly below Patty's window. Both teams were tossing balls back and forth, working out the kinks in their arms. A coach from one team was starting an infield drill by hitting balls to each position.

The other team was in the outfield, starting to shag fly balls. Another coach was huddled with two umpires. On each baseline, pitchers and catchers were loosening up. It all appeared, to Jack, to be a run-of-the-mill beginning of an ordinary high school baseball game. Just like any other in any community. There was nothing remarkable to be seen, and Jack turned to ask Patty for his pants and shirt. He was quietly pleased to see that she was already coming back into the bedroom with both items. She handed the clothes to Jack, helpful as ever.

"I'll get you some O.J. while you get your pants on," she smiled. "To keep your virtue intact, right?"

She was needling him again and Jack didn't mind. She had been fair to him. He leaned toward the window to see more of the warm-ups.

"Do you know who these teams are?"

He could clearly hear her answer from the kitchen.

"Sure, it's the local high school and the team from the next town over."

Jack's attention was naturally drawn to the pitchers and catchers. That was his part of the game. He spied another kid dressed in a t-shirt and blue jeans, standing with a pitcher. The clothing showed he wasn't part of either team. Still, he seemed to be showing the pitcher a particular grip.

The kid began to demonstrate a throw. Jack turned to see Patty walking back into the bedroom holding two glasses of orange juice. So, Jack didn't see the pitch. While reaching for one of the glasses, he heard the ball strike the catcher's mitt. It was loud and explosive and there was no mistaking what the sound represented.

Jack had his hand on the glass and shifted his gaze back to the window. He was looking intently at the boy in the blue jeans to verify what he had heard. The kid received the return throw from the catcher and spoke briefly to the uniformed pitcher. Jack was still standing by the window, draped in the sheet. He watched the windup as the kid prepared to throw the ball once again.

The ball smacked into the catcher's mitt with a crack that was audible anywhere on the field. Some of the players stopped their warm-ups to verify what they had heard. So did a couple of the coaches. Jack downed the juice and set the glass down on the window sill. He unabashedly pulled on his jeans.

"Thank you for helping me. I'll see you tonight," he told Patty.

He was putting on his shirt while he descended the stairs. His shoes went untied as he went out the door. Patty watched the exit from her doorway.

"See you later," echoed in the hall.

A closer look at the kid in the t-shirt and blue jeans was all that mattered. Jack Ridley had just witnessed one of the fastest pitches he had seen in his entire life.

3

THE FUTURE BECKONS

Jack crossed the short strip of grass between the apartment and the ball diamond. He had quickly dressed in a fog as he contemplated what had just happened. Jack had a highly developed ability to judge a multitude of details about a thrown baseball. He had done it all of his life. The average fan might think pitches appear identical, but there are differences. Sports commentators, players in a previous lifetime, are able to describe a variety of variations. Most observers are unaware of the differences between a curve, a slider, a cut fastball, and even a change-up.

But not Jack Ridley. His knowledge of baseball pitches would qualify as expert testimony in any court. He could tell a lot about a pitch based solely on the sound it made when it smacked into the catcher's mitt. So, he had no doubt as to what he had seen. The pitch that the kid in blue jeans had just thrown would place him in the top ten percent of professional pitchers. Jack would know. He had been there.

The two boys were positioned along the third-base line when Jack approached. The catcher was closer so Jack walked to a spot next to him. He smiled at the boy and let his gaze roll toward the young pitcher. Jack knew that people liked him when he smiled. Plus, a fan stopping to observe a little baseball was as natural as watching a sunset. Jack was casually standing close to the young catcher as he waited for another pitch from the blue jean boy.

He gave the boy a nonchalant nod and a "Hey, there." The kid nodded back and the ancient ritual of baseball kinship was underway. Jack noticed the name 'Harold' on the back of the uniform and saw his opening.

"Great name for a catcher. First or last?"

The boy looked at Jack and grimaced.

"First. It's kind of a team joke. Long story."

Jack was instantly aware.

"I get it. It's a guy thing. So, they call you...."

The kid gave Jack a gap-toothed grin.

"Skip. Makes no sense, I know," he said. "You been on a team?"

Jack returned the grin with a nod.

Skip called to the pitcher.

"Just one more, Dunc. I'm gonna need this hand later."

Jack's fine-timed eye noted that the next throw was appreciably slower than the last. The boy started walking toward Skip and Jack. He did not seem concerned that a stranger had popped into the moment. Jack was aware of the comfort level and sent another "Hey, there," his way. The boy nodded and joined Jack and Skip.

"I'm Jack Ridley. Is 'Dunc' a name you got for dunking batters?"

The boy shook his head.

"My mom named me Duncan after something she was reading," he said. "It means 'Warrior,' is what she told me."

"I'm betting it fits into the batter-dunking part, based on your throwing," Jack said. "You aren't playing for this team?"

Duncan appeared a bit wistful when he answered.

"I did last year. Graduated and I'm done. I just came by to see this loser."

He gave Skip an elbow in the ribs which is the international guy signal that the two were buddies. Jack liked both of the boys immediately. They were exactly what he had been ten or so years ago - high school kids bonded over the same game that had given Jack many happy moments. He saw that the catcher's mitt Skip was using was a ragged mess.

"I bet you could use a better mitt, especially if you're catching this guy. I've got an extra one over at the Crusher field. How 'bout you come to the game tonight and it's yours?"

Both boys pondered the idea of a stranger *giving away* a catcher's mitt. A good one could go for as high as a couple of hundred dollars, or more. Duncan spoke first.

"You want to *give* him a catcher's mitt?"

Jack was nonchalant.

"I've got a few. It's used, but not as used as this one," indicating Skip's battered mitt. "It's no big deal. I get them at cost. Part of a sporting goods store I'm in with."

Jack didn't need to get into particulars about his situation. He was aware that such a gift to a stranger was slightly out of the ordinary.

"Really, no big deal. Show up tonight and I'll have it for you."

The boys let that soak in for a moment. Then Duncan spoke to Skip.

"I was just heading back home from the co-op. Can't stay for the game 'cause I gotta get some chores done. Try and hit the ball today, okay?"

Skip spit some sunflower seeds in Duncan's general direction and looked at Jack.

"Nice talking to you. I like the idea of the mitt."

Jack was quick to respond.

"See you tonight. Six or so would be good."

Skip gave another grin, nodded, and headed toward the dugout to start the game. Duncan and Jack were about to part ways, but Jack delayed the moment with a question. Although he was keenly interested in the boy's throwing ability, he kept it below the radar.

"Any chance you're going by the Zone bar? I've got a car there and could use a lift."

The fact that this was all occurring in a small town, and was part of a baseball introduction, made it easy for Duncan to agree to giving a total stranger a ride.

"Sure, it's on my way home if you don't mind a raggedy old truck."

Jack followed Duncan's lead, past the right field fence, toward the parking lot. Conversation was easy enough.

"So, what last name fits with Duncan?"

"It's James," Duncan replied.

Jack's response fit his nature, as he had an eye and ear for the symmetry of things.

"That has a nice ring to it. 'Duncan James.' Sounds good for a baseball player. Plus, the girls can call you D.J."

Jack threw in the last part just for laughs, and he chuckled at his lame humor. Duncan smirked.

"Hasn't happened yet."

They arrived at a beat-up old Ford pickup, which clearly saw use as a work truck. The doors were unlocked, standard for a small town. Duncan climbed in the driver's seat and Jack found his spot on the torn bench seat.

"Reminds me of a truck my dad had. Just like home."

Duncan headed toward the access road, past the game which had started. Jack thought he detected a small sadness in Duncan's glance at the players. His observation was gentle.

"Looks like you miss playing with the guys."

"Sure do."

Jack waited to see if Duncan had any more thoughts on the subject, and the wait paid off.

"I played four years of high school there."

"So, you pitched for that team?"

"Nope," Duncan answered. "Played third and shortstop. My dad wouldn't let me pitch 'cause he said the high school coaches would screw up my arm."

Jack waited for a follow-up to explain what happened next, but Duncan was silent.

"After graduation?"

"My dad died right before then. Wasn't much sense in playing baseball after that."

Jack surmised that Duncan would have laconic answers to questions in this area. But the youngster began to elaborate.

"I'd thought about trying to play in college. My dad had been talking about picking a school, but that all stopped. Plus, mom needs my help on our little farm. Shoot, even my sister came back home to help."

Jack knew that plans go off-track pretty easily. He wanted to say something about the future bringing other chances, but thought better of offering advice to a kid he barely knew.

"I'm real sorry to hear about your dad," was all he could manage.

Duncan glanced in Jack's direction and gave a nod, signaling thanks for the condolence. They were pulling up to the Zone bar and Jack pointed to his Mustang.

"Pretty sharp ride," Duncan noted.

"It used to be, but it's getting kinda used."

"How'd you leave it here?"

"I was here for about five minutes and a fight started. Got popped in the head and somebody drove me out of here."

Jack avoided the part about who did the driving, to her apartment. Too much information. He returned to a thought that was blossoming in his head.

"You guys be sure to come to the game tonight. I appreciate the ride."

Jack reached into his car and retrieved two passes.

"They give me two of these for each game, and they're yours."

"Thanks, man. See you tonight," Duncan said, and pulled the truck into gear.

The old pickup rumbled away from the bar and Jack turned to his car. There was plenty of time to get something to eat, and he always liked a long nap before a game. Jack eased his car down the street towards the Happy Motel he'd checked into yesterday.

What he'd seen today gave him plenty of food for thought. Maybe his mother was right. She always said that things happen for a reason. If he'd gone somewhere else besides the Zone last night, he wouldn't have ended up getting clonked in the head and then seeing some kid with a rocket arm.

Jack remembered the various pitchers he'd played with and against. They'd been the best in the game. After he got some food and a shower, he settled down to sleep. Jack drifted off thinking of those pitchers and if there was a crazy chance that this young kid could be one of them.

4

THE PAST IS CLOSE BEHIND

The announcer's voice rumbled through the ballpark.

'Now batting, number nine, Jack Ridley.'

Some of the tech-savvy fans used their cell phone apps to get details about the new player. Jack approached the batter's box and smiled at the opposing catcher, as well as the umpire. It was an 'another day at the office' sort of smile.

The radio play-by-play man was doing his job.

"Since being called up last month, this Ridley kid has been lighting up some pitchers. He's appeared in twelve games and, although it's not enough at-bats for a reliable statistic at this point, you can say he's batting just under .350. That includes last night's walk-off homer against these same Braves. I can't remember a rookie getting off to such a good start."

Jack took his usual practice swings and readied himself for the pitch. He had seen this pitcher on television but hadn't faced him before. What Jack had learned was the guy had a big-league fastball and a more than decent curve. He hadn't seemed to be a finesse pitcher and Jack figured the first pitch would be an attempt to blow one by him.

He was right, as the pitcher launched a fastball that was heading outside the plate. Jack checked his short swing, and saw the ball go outside the black. The umpire surprised him and called it a strike. Looking back at the ump to complain about the bad call would be useless. Jack resisted the urge and just stared at his bat. That was protest enough. He knew that rookies got the short end of these things.

So he dug in and waited for the next pitch. The ball started out looking like a tight curve but it didn't break. It was heading toward Jack's head and he dropped to the ground. He didn't get there in time and the ball smacked him in the helmet. Jack lay there in the dirt and tried to shake the fog from his head. Then he heard a ringing and his name being called.

5

LET'S MAKE A DEAL

A voice cut through the haze. "Jack? Mr. Ridley? Jack? It's your four o'clock wake up, Mr. Ridley. Time to head to the ball park."

Jack rolled out of bed and headed to the bathroom. His head still ached from last night's meeting with a bottle. He took two aspirins and washed them down with a scoop of water in his hand, right out of the faucet. No need to clean up, as he'd be sliding in the dirt soon enough.

Glancing in the bathroom mirror told Jack that the start of a beard would fit into tonight's action. After all, those Hooters clowns had started a bar fight. They probably figured to resume things before, during, or after the game. The rough stuff was a good way to get hurt. Besides, Jack worked out his aggression by playing hard-nosed baseball. Leave the goon play to the guys who needed it.

There had been a few ballgame scrapes in his past. Enjoying life in the ballpark was Jack's mission, and he always hoped any melee would be over before it came to involving the pitchers. They were always the last ones to get to a scuffle, because the bullpen was usually located behind the outfield wall. There was no need to sprint into trouble. Jack's main concern as a catcher was looking after the pitchers. All of them.

His selfless play showcased an aspect of Jack's game that made it easy for both teams to like him. Jack wasn't interested in getting his hands or any other body parts banged up in a fight. If he was catching that day, he made sure that his pitcher on the mound was safe. Then he looked after the others.

If the whole bullpen started streaming out onto the field, Jack would usually find an opposing player he knew. Then he'd just hang out on the periphery of the entangled players. Once, during a set-to, he made arrangements to meet for drinks after the game. It was another example that proved the rule: Most folks left a Jack Ridley moment with a smile on their face.

He wondered if his car would choose today to act up. He figured that the old adage was true. Things tend to go bad at the worst moment. But the car fired right up and Jack grinned in the mirror.

"I guess this ain't the worst moment," he said to himself.

Then he started chuckling, remembering his mother's comments on situations like this.

"Everybody says it's Murphy's Law that things will go wrong. But the real saying is 'you should *prepare* for when things go wrong.' Think about it."

Jack laughed again. His mother had such a neat perspective.

"You could look it up," she always said.

"Mom is always right," Jack murmured.

He made a mental note to stop at a garage before bad things really started happening to his car. The short ride to the Crusher ballpark was uneventful, including rolling down the little main street in Jason. Catching a glimpse of a familiar face would be a bonus, but none appeared right away. Jack had been coming through these small towns for a few years now, to play a bit of baseball, and he enjoyed seeing a friendly face. His ready smile seemed to give folks a calm feeling.

Some of them wondered why a fellow hitting his mid-twenties

would be knocking around the semi-pro leagues, but small town people don't incline toward prying. A man's business was his own, as long as he didn't swerve into their path too often.

Jack liked to ease through places he visited to see what faces he would recognize. It was not uncommon for local folks to see him and say things like "Put your long johns away; Jack's back in town." Or maybe they'd say "Mildred, the Almanac was wrong this year. Jack's a bit early."

These little goofball moments were exactly what Jack needed. It helped mitigate the realization that he was close to the end of his idyllic pastime. There was always a small jab in his memory to remind him that he'd had different plans all along.

The children were Jack's favorite. Kids were invariably ready to laugh at any silly stunt he'd pull. And for children, there was almost nothing Jack wouldn't do to amuse them. He'd crawl in a sandbox and pretend he was a 'monster' or a giant worm, and the kids would squeal with feigned fright. Or he'd prance around like a dancing pony and the children would beg for a ride. The mothers on hand would laugh and tell Jack to never grow up. There were times he wanted to fulfill their wish.

Swinging by the park brought some luck, because that's where Jack saw one of his favorite kids. He'd met her and her folks in the same place last season, and her dad was a baseball fan. Jack didn't remember the last name, something Italian, but the little girl's first name was Suzy. Jack was happy to talk sports with Suzy's dad. Her mother once said that one of these days her cousin Mary Kate would come to town, and she'd make an introduction.

Lately, Jack was thinking that might not be such a bad idea. All his old friends were getting married and they looked pretty happy about it. He didn't plan to stop and tease the child this trip, because he needed to get to the park and meet Skip and Duncan. But he did lean out his window and yell.

"Wake up, Little Suzy!"

The little girl and both her parents laughed. Jack had told Suzy the Everly Brothers song from 1956 was written just for her.

As luck would have it, Jack was parking his car just as Duncan rolled up in his battered pickup. Skip was lolling in the passenger seat with some sort of ice bag on his head. Jack had been ready to chide him about playing a lousy game, because that's how guys compliment each other. But now, with an injury to contend with, Skip didn't need any jokes about his condition and Jack knew it.

"Looks like they tried to score on the wrong guy." Translation: 'I'm sure you took a shot but you played a fine game anyway.' Skip gave a small grimace.

"Some guy tried to kill me at home plate but he didn't get it done."

With that, the hellos were complete and Jack got down to business. He reached into his trunk and pulled out the best catcher's mitt he had.

"Hold this over your face the next time," he said to Skip.

The mitt was basically new and had never seen a game. Skip was surprised.

"Man, I thought you were talking about something you'd been playing with. This is great!"

Duncan was also suitably impressed.

"You're gonna *give* this dweeb a new glove?"

"Well, doggone it," Jack drawled. "He's gonna need it if he spends any more time catching you."

Both of the boys were looking at Jack as if he had just climbed out of some spaceship.

"C'mon, it's no big deal," Jack protested. "I told you I've got a thing going with a sporting goods store. It'll help your game, Skip."

He smiled at both boys and the deal was done. Duncan and Skip had Christmas morning looks on their faces, and that was enough for Jack.

"Go grab your seats and I'll get to warming up the pitcher," Jack said. "This should be a good night. Randy's brought in an ex-college guy doing a little rehab. Gonna be fun."

Duncan motioned toward the stands with a head-jerk.

"C'mon, Harold," he directed at Skip.

Duncan grinned at Jack and Skip pretended he was going to take a swing at his buddy. Jack had a feeling there weren't too many people who got away with using Skip's real name. The boys headed to the seats, examining the new mitt, and Jack made it to the locker room. He was already thinking about a way to get a once-over for Duncan with this baseball team. Any baseball team, in Jack's opinion, should be interested if things panned out the way he envisioned they could.

Jack went directly to Randy's little office in the cinder block building adjoining the dugout. The 'office' was really a wide spot in the hallway. In truth, it was downright depressing, if you considered some of the palatial environs the big leagues had for their players. Jack pushed aside this mental detour into his past life and came right to the point.

"Randy, you remember saying you'd like me to play a few more games?"

"Heck, yes," Randy replied.

"Well, I've got a deal for you."

Jack paused a moment to put this idea into the best light.

"How about I play a game or two next weekend, same money, and I bring along a kid to throw an inning? Or part of an inning?"

Randy had a quizzical look on his face. The prospect of Jack Ridley playing an unexpected game or two for his team was as welcome as a track owner being told that the spirit of Secretariat was coming to race. But Randy had never heard of a player proposing to bring someone to pitch in a game. He stalled to get a minute to think.

"Don't you have a deal for next week in Braxton?"

Jack had anticipated the thought and had his white lie bluff ready.

"Already talked to them. They'll take the following weekend and I wasn't booked then, anyway."

This was partly true. Jack didn't have definite plans in two weeks.

He had already started easing out of games he would have surely been in a few years ago. Lately he'd been thinking it was time to be a grown-up businessman and his summer hiatus baseball days were ending.

'Baseball ending,' Jack thought to himself, with a large dose of sadness. His final out was closing in. You get extra innings for only so long. The last out always comes.

Ending is part of the game, as sure as rain in springtime. *Everybody* gives up playing, sooner or later. For a lucky few, it's as late as forty, or even later. Some never get past eighteen. For all of them, it's somewhere in-between. But everybody stops, and everybody knows it. It's the part about coming to terms with the concept that doesn't come easy.

It was pure luck that Jack had left a hole in his game schedule. In truth, he hadn't had any conversation with the Braxton coach about swapping weekends. That wouldn't be a problem, Jack was positive. The man knew that Jack wouldn't be coming around much longer, and his game was always welcome.

A future game with Jack Ridley, or two, was enough to make any coach happy. If there were any issues, Jack was willing to add another game. He was beyond confident that the switch would work. Even if he never played in Braxton again, the coach would acquiesce. Jack had won numerous games for him in the past.

On the ride to the ballpark, he'd gone over this scenario in his mind before mentioning it to Randy. Even if Randy did the inconceivable, and didn't let Jack bring Duncan along, there were other teams that would be interested. Jack could see that Randy was leaning his way, so he decided to go all-in.

"Look, if he gives up a run on the first batter or two, I'll take him out myself and get the run back for you at the plate. You've got nothing to lose."

Jack knew he had him, but Randy needed certitude.

"So, you play next weekend and I let you have somebody throw?"

Jack had a follow-up.

"You pick the inning, but you tell me the inning before. That way I can ease him in. He's young, but good," was all Jack would admit at this point.

"Okay, then, it's a deal."

Randy breathed a sigh of relief. He'd been expecting a weak lineup next week and this was a real break. Even if the kid gave up a home run to the first batter, Jack had promised to remove him from the game and get the run back. Randy knew Jack could manage that, and more, with relative ease.

How did he get this lucky?

6

TAKE ME OUT TO A SMALL GAME

Warm-ups were over, and as the home team, the Crushers took the field. Jack headed to home plate and lobbed some good-natured kidding at the umpire. "Make me look good, Blue."

That was the generic name for all umps, unless there was a real conflict going on. Jack had heard some astoundingly colorful names thrown at umpires, usually right before or directly after the offending party was thrown out of the game. This guy was one Jack had seen before, but didn't know personally.

With some umpires, you had to maintain a constant distance. Depending on the individual, that suited Jack just fine. Some were staying on the field for love of the game. Others were trying to develop their skills and climb higher in the athletic world. It was all a crapshoot, and you had to be in the right place at the right time.

In Jack's opinion, the best umps were barely noticeable. They didn't behave as if the game revolved around them. Calling balls and strikes, covering the bases for put-outs, and maintaining general order is all that's necessary. It was that straightforward, and Jack respected the process.

Even if a call was questionable, Jack was reluctant to get too invigorated about it. For starters, it did absolutely no good. More importantly, as a catcher, he couldn't afford to cultivate grudges. These people would be making close decisions about the outcome of his game. They started the game with "Play Ball!" Jack always felt the part about 'playing' deserved his focus.

Jack's trip to the batter's box was interrupted by Duncan and Skip yelling his name. They were behind the visitor's bench and Jack noticed they were not alone. In the brief moment he saw them, it appeared they were with dates. Jack was mildly surprised. It hadn't occurred to him that these awkward teenagers were capable of getting attention from the ladies.

"Well, I'll be," Jack muttered. "They probably impressed some locals with a new catcher's mitt."

Right now, Jack's thoughts were on his pitcher, a youngster named Tim George. Helping Tim rehab his game was the main project for the night. He had an innocent choirboy face that disguised his intense approach to pitching. Avoiding 'overthrowing' was an issue, so Jack stressed that Tim hone his mechanics. The kid had reasonable command of his pitches and he would not be facing any menacing hitters tonight.

Jack figured Tim would be fine with medium work – maybe letting it loose with an occasional 85 mile per hour fastball. That would be on the sluggish side for the big leagues, but was at the top end of what these batters could handle. But speed was only part of the equation. Another facet of pitching was always in play. It was embodied in the baseball adage that Jack's father had preached.

"Pitching and real estate are based on the same thing, Jackie-boy. It's about location!" Sometimes he would repeat the word three times, just for comic effect.

Like most things a parent tells a child, it made more sense as Jack got older. The world was full of big, strong kids who naturally threw harder and faster than boys their own age. Their eager fathers would promptly label them a 'pitcher' and shove them toward the local high school or American Legion team.

Early on, the plan would work, based on pure biometrics. When a kid is bigger and stronger than everyone, short-term physical success follows. But these kids never learned to pitch. They were throwers, and if a batter has enough time to get used to a thrower's speed, he'll get hits. What makes the difference is the ability to put a ball where the batter has trouble. Every batter has spots in the strike zone that cause problems. An innate ability to help pitchers find those spots had given Jack a ride to the top of the game. He was slowly letting go of the ride, because he had no choice.

Jack believed in the mental process. A pitcher has to believe in his pitches. The worst batter in the major leagues has the ability to take any pitcher over the wall, if the pitcher puts the ball in a bad spot. And that spot changes, for the same batter, with every pitch. It depends on the situation. Any pitcher will tell you it's a different proposition if they have an 0-2 count on a batter, compared to a 3-0 count. That applies with the *same* batter, and it changes with the *same* batter's different at-bats. The combinations are unlimited.

Young pitchers inevitably contemplate such possibilities as they develop. Some figure that power-pitching is the best way out of a jam. During 'pitching philosophy' discussions, Jack taught that they should consider alternatives. He would bring Greg Maddux into the picture.

"This was a guy who barely threw a ninety mile an hour fastball. But he was a Hall of Fame pitcher because he could put the ball, depending on the situation, where the batter couldn't hit it."

Jack also preached the Maddux adage: 'It's not your arm that makes you a great pitcher. It's that thing between your ears.' He made sure to credit the source.

"That's a direct quote, boys."

Such counter-intuitive thinking doesn't sink in right away. Pitchers get in a fix and they naturally lean toward throwing harder.

Jack reminded them that Maddux actually said that he was successful 'because he learned to throw *slower*' when he got in trouble.

With some of the grandfathers of wanna-be pitchers, Jack could rely on a pitcher from their own youth.

"You ever hear of Tom Seaver?"

That usually got the doubters' attention. Everybody knows about 'Tom Terrific,' the mainstay of the 'Miracle Mets.'

"He was a guy who laid it out perfectly. 'Pitching is three things: velocity, placement, and movement. The least important of them is velocity.' Hall of Famers set all those records with this method, so you ought to try it."

He'd helped numerous pitchers start on that very path. All of these concepts were on Jack's mind, even when he wasn't thinking about them. But come game time everything crystallized.

When Mr. Blue yelled "Play Ball!" Jack would snap to reality, and begin another chapter in the game that had always called to his soul. There would be soaring hits and double plays and fine-tuned pitches. All the things that make baseball a great and satisfying subscript of the American psyche would arrive. There would be bedeviled batters and there would be a win for his team. But tonight, there would be no stolen bases at second. Jack was sure of it.

Predictability ruled the first inning. Tim kept the ball low in the strike zone, where Jack directed. Ground balls were neatly delivered to first base. Jack and Tim eased back to the dugout together and Jack gave him an 'attaboy' slap on the back.

"Right on target," Jack said.

He decided that if Tim had no injuries, he would get his shot with some professional club. With any luck, he might get as high as Triple A.

Jack was in the lineup as the fifth batter, and wasn't counting on getting to the plate during the first inning. His premonition proved accurate as the Crushers also went down in order. The Hooters pitcher had respectable stuff, at least for this level. He'd pitched for a mid-level college, but declined to accept a major league team's offer to languish in Single A ball. Jack respected that decision, for life at that level was brutal. Poverty wages and a small chance to advance were the rule.

Another issue was bubbling under the radar tonight. The fellow that incited the fracas that got Jack smacked with a bottle would appear soon. He would merit special attention. The guy's name was on the tip of his tongue, but Jack couldn't quite pull it up. The Hooter's fourth batter was a quick strike-out, and the fifth batter grounded to short. Sure enough, their next batter was the charmer Jack was seeking.

Giving the guy something to think about was easy. Jack called for time and went to the pitcher's mound without looking back. On the way, he remembered the clown's name was Jerry.

"Don't say anything, this is for his benefit," Jack said, jerking his thumb back toward Jerry. "All pitches down and away, right?"

As Tim nodded, Jack motioned with his hands downward, suggesting that a 'settle down' moment was needed. He then backed toward home plate while animatedly pointing. With luck, it appeared to be an admonishment. Jerry needed to think the pitcher was out of control. Jack arrived at the plate and spoke to the umpire, knowing Jerry could hear him.

"He's all pissed off. Says some guys from the Hooters team dumped beer on his sister and roughed her up last night. He blames this guy," Jack said, jerking his thumb in Jerry's direction.

"Been talking all day about knocking him in the head. I can't stop it. He's nuts."

Jack noticed Jerry almost imperceptibly edge away from the plate. The psych job was working. Jerry leaned away from the first pitch, a fastball low on the outside corner.

"Strike one!" the umpire loudly called.

The plan to mess with Jerry was off and running.

"Jeez, he can't even get it inside when he's trying!"

Jack signaled for the same pitch.

"Blue, if he beans this guy, run him out of here. He's a jerk."

The same thing happened for strike two. Jack was almost smiling inside his catcher's mask. During the next wind-up, he sprung the trap.

"This is it. He's gonna do it."

Jerry was stepping away from the plate as the ball was released. His weak swing wasn't even close. Jack was heading back to the dugout before the umpire had "Strike Three!" out of his mouth.

The second inning was all the Crushers needed. The batter before Jack beat out a throw from third and was happily on first base when Jack poked a curve ball over the left-field fence. He didn't watch the ball as it traveled, in order to be polite, and jogged around the bases. As he crossed home he saw Duncan and Skip high-fiving each other. Strangely, their dates seemed uninvolved in the moment.

The rest of the game went pretty smoothly. Jack got a double with nobody on and the Hooters were content to walk him his next two trips to the plate. His pitcher went seven innings and was never in trouble. Nobody stole second. Jack knew it was a good night for everyone, except for the beer-dumping Hooters.

After the final out in the top of the ninth, Jack headed back to the dugout. Duncan and Skip were waiting with huge smiles as a welcome. Their dates were there too, slightly behind them. When Jack got closer he realized that the 'dates' were roughly 25 and 50 years of age, respectively. They were looking at Jack with slightly bewildered faces.

7

PLEASE ALLOW ME TO INTRODUCE MYSELF

Jack approached the group, slightly discomforted by the turn of events. He had subconsciously decided that the boys would be telling him how they had enjoyed the game, and then introducing their dates. An 'aw-shucks' delivery was ready in case the boys brought up the catcher's mitt. But the presence of one woman slightly older than the boys, and another decidedly older, made the moment almost awkward. Duncan spoke first.

"Great game, dude!"

Jack managed a smile. Skip was hanging on to the catcher's mitt like it was the Holy Grail. But the two women were tentative and still looking at Jack. The pause in the conversation seemed much longer than it was, until Duncan spoke again.

"Jack, this is my mom. And my sister."

Normally, Jack would have figured out this connection much sooner, but things just hadn't added up. He rebounded by being mannerly.

"It's a real pleasure to meet you, Mrs. James."

He gave Duncan a sideways glance.

"I bet your sister has a name, right?" Duncan displayed his eighteen-year-old younger brother side.

"I call her 'Dumb-Yell' but it's really Danielle."

Jack caught a hint of exasperation from Mrs. James, but she didn't say anything about her son's comment. Jack looked at the girl for the first time. She had an attractive but wary air about her.

"My pleasure, Danielle. I'm Jack Ridley."

Both of the ladies gave him a perfunctory smile and returned his greeting, but they weren't as warm as the boys'. That made sense. There was no telling what they had been told about this stranger who was giving gifts to teenagers. What was completely understandable within the confines of baseball could easily be taken the wrong way by an outsider. So, Jack figured he had better get things on firm ground. He naturally took his case to Duncan's mother.

"It was great meeting your son at the high school game, Mrs. James. I think he has potential."

She was reserved. Bordering on wary, like her daughter. She wasn't quite sure why this man was taking an interest in her son. It occurred to Jack that this was probably the reason she had come to the game in the first place. Duncan had probably babbled about this ballplayer he'd met, an older man, who invited him to a game. And the stranger gave a gift to Skip. He had to have an ulterior motive, maybe even a sinister one.

If Jack had a deficiency in his makeup, he was slow to realize that not everybody operated from decency and kindness. Every so often, Jack had his feelings bruised when someone mistook took his meaning. He wanted it to be clear that his interest was this boy's baseball future.

"Well, Mr. Ridley," said Duncan's mother. "You certainly made a nice gift to Skip. And Duncan tells me you think he should play baseball."

"Please, I'm Jack. I'm not old enough to be a 'mister' just yet."

Jack hoped a small bit of humor would help the flow of conversation. Danielle still hadn't said anything, beyond her minimally polite smile. Jack thought he detected a hint of disapproval in her aspect, so he tiptoed.

"I just think Duncan might be able to play a little baseball if he wants to. *If* it suits you."

Duncan's mother seemed to take this in with a hint of disapproval. But she eased toward friendliness.

"Call me Sally."

Then she shifted things back to neutral.

"I'm not sure if Duncan should play anymore. We have the farm that needs attention."

The remark hung in the air and it seemed to be a topic that the group had already covered. Jack decided to move into familiar territory.

"My dad's mother was named Sally. It always seemed sweet and friendly to me."

He was giving the moment his best smile but couldn't tell which way his effort was taking things. Danielle was still silent and she appeared to be sizing Jack up. Jack felt compelled to at least attempt to make her an ally if he was going to have a chance to let Duncan play. The boys had somehow edged away from the 'older folks' and were examining the mitt for some reason. Jack had to say something to the ladies, Danielle in particular.

"I'm sorry to say Duncan didn't mention having a sister," he ventured. "Of course, we've just met."

As far as Jack could sense, Danielle was slightly perplexed by this whole affair. She looked at Jack with what he took to be a thoughtful air.

"What you did for Skip was nice. Please don't think I don't appreciate it."

Then she paused to put a finer point on things.

"I just can't figure why an older guy is interested in these kids."

The implication wasn't lost on Jack. His natural kindness had been misinterpreted before. He waited a moment and hoped he didn't come across as a well-intentioned oddball.

"I'm just a guy who likes baseball," seemed innocent enough. "I've seen Duncan throw and I think he has potential."

By now, the boys had drifted back to the conversation and were listening in. Jack took a hopeful breath.

"I can't say how far he might go, because there are lots of variables. But I've seen pitchers who are the very best and I've got a feeling he could be one of them."

At this point, Jack thought he might be saying too much. After all, these ladies didn't know if his opinion amounted to warm spit. Almost on cue, Duncan chimed in. He had caught a subtle implication in Jack's speech, even if the ladies hadn't.

"How far did you go in baseball, Jack?"

Inwardly, Jack flinched at his inadvertent revelation. His baseball past raised questions on many levels, and he couldn't rationalize its entirety, even to himself. It would be impossible to make sense of it, on the fly, at this moment.

"Pretty far," was all he thought he should say at this point. "Things didn't work out for me," he added, attempting to shore up his position.

People tend to equate self-reporting with honesty, so admitting he had at least a small issue might help gain some credibility. Jack was relieved that no one pursued it, at least for the time being. Sally and Danielle James seemed to be waiting for a larger explanation, so he played the only card he had.

"I was thinking we could get a chance for Duncan to throw a bit for the Crushers. I think the coach would go for it."

He refrained from mentioning that he'd already set it up. It would look like he was meddling in family business. These folks didn't know his heart was in the right place.

"A few pitches would give Duncan a feel for some better competition, and the coach would get to see a little bit of what he can do."

Jack hoped his little proposal made sense, or at least wouldn't be rejected outright. It seemed clear that both ladies would have to incline toward the idea, if it was going to get any traction. Jack didn't have much experience as a negotiator, but he felt that the next comment on the subject shouldn't be from him. Luckily, it was Duncan who chimed in.

"Mom, it can't hurt to throw a little, if Jack says so."

Skip had seemed a happy but clueless sidekick, up to this point. He chose this moment to reveal a bit of wisdom, by not saying anything. He just looked at Duncan's mother and sister and gave what appeared to be a wise nod. The ladies took the same tack, and were silent. They appeared to be thinking it over.

"We can talk about it tomorrow," said Duncan's mother.

Danielle didn't convey any thoughts one way or the other, but she was looking at Jack. He was in protection mode, and let his easy smile do its work.

"About time we should be heading home," Danielle said. "We'll drop you off, Skip."

"That's good," was Skip's only comment of the evening.

Duncan added, "Mom, how 'bout Jack comes out tomorrow and we can talk about all this?"

His mother didn't seem negative about the idea, but she wasn't bubbling with enthusiasm, either.

"That's fine," she said. "You know the way, Jack?"

Duncan jumped in.

"I'll map it out, Mom." He aimed a high-five at Jack. "It's about six or seven miles out of town, on the main highway."

Jack wondered if he'd driven by it on his way in. His mind flashed away, just for a second, to a random thought. He might have, in the past, driven past dozens of farms that had a baseball project just waiting to be discovered.

The idea made him smile again and it gave him a benevolent appearance. The 'good-nights' were passed around and the James family, plus Skip, headed off to a small SUV. Duncan called back to Jack.

"You'll see the barn after the closed Mini-Mart. That's us. If you get lost, anybody can guide you."

They all disappeared into the night and Jack walked to the locker room. He decided to grab his equipment and shower at his little motel. Randy had already left. Jack could easily meet with him during the week to set up Duncan's try-out. It could even wait until the game. Jack drove back to his room and made a mental note to let the clerk know he'd be staying on for a while.

Showering off the game's grime made him feel better. He headed to bed and didn't need to set an alarm. Revisiting the day's events edged Jack toward drifting off to sleep. Life is such a strange combination of haphazard events. You could go left on a particular street on a particular day and your life could go toward a wholly unexpected destination.

Conversely, a right turn might take you in a vastly different direction. Lives and families and destinations were determined by mere chance. If Jack hadn't gone to the Zone after yesterday's game, he wouldn't have ended up in an apartment next to a high school baseball game. He'd have no idea that Duncan and Skip and Sally and Danielle existed. The randomness of the whole thing was just amazing.

'Random,' he thought. That word sent him dozing.

8

A SERIES OF RANDOM EVENTS

The *Superior Sports Talk Show* host was enjoying her visit with rookie phenom Jack Ridley. The kid had just turned 20 years old and had been the highlight reel of several Reds games. He had been called up to Major League baseball after playing only parts of two seasons in the minors.

Viewers would know the host was a serious journalist, because she was dressed in one of her glitzy outfits. Her megawatt smile was the perfect accessory.

"Tell us, Jack," she beamed. "What's it like to be baseball's overnight sensation?"

Privately, she had decided that Jack was the cutest ballplayer she'd ever interviewed. Jack was new to this side of baseball. He had garnered some attention while playing in high school and American Legion ball, more than most. But the chats with local reporters and writers were more of a neighborhood visit. This encounter was under hot lights and surrounded by studio assistants and camera operators.

There had even been make-up in what the 'production manager' called a 'green room.' Jack was a bit off-balance as he tried to give the TV reporter a good answer. Still, he looked professional.

"I guess it seems that it was overnight when you look at me only being with the team for a few weeks," he said. *The eager reporter saw her opening.*

"But what a few weeks it's been! Your on-base percentage is at the top of the league, even though it's a short span."

Even at this young age, Jack came across as a level-headed player.

"It's been a nice start," he admitted. *"But this is the first time the pitchers are getting a look at me. I think things will even out after they've seen me a few times."*

"You're just being modest," she smiled. *She turned to the camera.*

"This could be the new face of baseball, folks. Jack Ridley, future star for the Reds, is humble about his success."

There was the hint of a blush on his face when Jack responded. The reporter hoped the camera angle caught the slight flush. It made Jack seem that much more appealing and down-to-earth.

"You're being too kind. I've had only part of two seasons in the organization to get started. The guys are being so helpful and I'm just hoping to stick with the team."

The reporter asked about Jack's background and playing history. His modest background and relatively quick ascent to the big leagues made a fine story, and his general good nature and affable attitude were clearly evident. She knew that Jack's likability was coming through loud and clear. Her viewers were going to love it. It was time for a human interest question.

"So, what's it like being the new kid on the block? Are the other boys being nice to you?"

Jack grinned at the reference to fitting in at a new school.

"Everybody in the organization has been great. They're making me feel right at home. It's a random sort of thing, really. There're lots of guys who could be here."

"Random?" *The reporter's honest reaction was obvious.*

"Let's look at some tape and see if it's random."

Her face said volumes. This guy was not random.

9

MEANWHILE BACK AT THE FARM

Sleeping in was part of Jack's plan. He was in no hurry to drive to the James farm. Appearing too eager to get this try-out going might sour Duncan's mother on the whole idea. Jack knew that Duncan absolutely needed her approval to make this attempt. Duncan was going to need every aspect of his support system to get through the long-term process Jack knew was waiting.

Fate could someday see this kid facing the league's best hitters. That required supreme confidence. Conversely, it could come to nothing, and Duncan's talent would never see the light of day. He absolutely needed his mother, his sister, and perhaps even his goofy pal Skip behind him. Steering him into a conflict without their backing would doom any chance for success.

Jack had time to ease his way through a shower and shave. After a leisurely breakfast at the little diner on the town's main street, he took a moment to appreciate the surroundings. The stores around the diner had a rustic appeal that tended to lift his spirits. That, and the friendly people who ran them, had a way of bolstering his basic good-hearted nature. When he came to a crisis in his sports world, he had come to places like this to find strength.

There were baseball organizations in the small towns, and Jack played with various teams without any expectations. It was as if he were a gifted horse trainer who couldn't work his magic - because he didn't have any racers. To soothe his soul, the trainer visited carnivals or county fairs where he could see, and even interact with horses.

Jack had thought about such a comparison. He saw the similarities in his life, cut off from his benevolent obsession, and the life of a downtrodden trainer who found redemption in a beleaguered horse named Seabiscuit. The horse had been mistreated and devalued through the best years of his life. It was only when the two lost souls, man and horse, found each other that they achieved greatness.

When Jack's original baseball dreams had been sidetracked, he accepted the inevitable as gracefully as he could. There was one lucky aspect that helped him adjust. He had invested his baseball money and was a part owner of an equipment store in his home town. It had every indication that he could expect success and security.

There were even other businessmen who were encouraging him to open other locations. They figured to capitalize on the sports mania that had gripped the country. People would need equipment for a huge variety of athletic programs that were burgeoning everywhere. Jack saw the wisdom in their advice and knew a time would come when he should pursue life as a business mogul. Still, he yearned for just one or two more trips to the fair, where he might see a nice horse.

His Seabiscuit analogy was on his mind as he drove toward the James farm. Duncan had a real talent for throwing a baseball. Jack was sure of it. Still, the boy would need training and support and even a bit of luck to climb the baseball mountain. The path was fraught with huge pitfalls. But Jack believed he might, with a few breaks in the right places, steer the kid to the top.

Lurking under the surface was something from his past. He knew a few people who just might be able to throw one or two of those needed breaks Duncan's way. Jack's natural inclination to try to help people was in full swing now. He hoped that he could convince Duncan's family to make the attempt. Maybe Duncan had a bit of Seabiscuit in him and would dominate the game when he got his chance.

The closed-down Mini Mart was just where Duncan had said it would be, and the barn appeared right on cue. The farmhouse and surrounding fields had a Norman Rockwell look to them. Jack gently pulled into the gravel drive toward the house. He was amused when a sheepdog of one sort or another quietly approached his car. The bucolic setting was complete. Duncan was alerted somehow, and he came bounding out of the house and loped toward Jack's car.

For some reason, the dog didn't bark. He advanced to the exact spot Jack would have to step when he exited. Duncan arrived as Jack cautiously opened the door.

"Elvis might lick you to death," Duncan laughed. "He's just glad you're here. Me, too,"

"Such a cool name for a dog," Jack countered. "Never knew one named 'Elvis' before. How'd that come about?"

Duncan was hugging the dog and smiling.

"He was born on January 8th, just like 'the King,' so my dad said he had no choice but to give him the same name."

Jack thought it was a beautiful parallel.

"It's perfect! Elvis had such a great voice." He scratched the happy dog's ears. "I bet you're a great singer, too."

Elvis gave a shake and headed off toward the barn. Both boys watched him disappear inside and Jack turned to business.

"Everybody here?"

Duncan shook his head.

"Danielle's over at Cori Klee's. Dodging the issue by hanging with her friend. Probably not back 'til dark."

Pausing ever so slightly, Duncan glanced at Jack. He spoke, with a slight grimace.

"She was betting you wouldn't show."

Jack was privately relieved. He'd surmised that Danielle was cool toward him. The fact that she opted to avoid seeing him during this visit confirmed Jack's thinking. It was fine with him. There'd be less pressure when he was talking things over with Duncan's mother.

'Sally,' he corrected himself, as he walked with Duncan toward the porch steps.

The place looked just as he had pictured it, with a wrap-around porch on a wooden two-story farmhouse. There was even a tree with a tire swing on a rope.

As they reached the steps, Sally James came through the door drying her hands on a dish towel. The family had just finished lunch, which Jack took for good timing. There'd be no awkward 'have a bite with us' moments. Sally did have a friendly look on her face. Apparently Duncan had been talking Jack up prior to his arrival.

Jack was immediately struck by the onset of years that showed on her face. In the daylight he could see that she had clear blue eyes and her nose crinkled up in a winsome way when she smiled. She had fine cheekbones and sandy hair that framed her face very attractively. Clearly, she had been a beauty in her youth. However, years of farm work and the recent loss of her husband had taken a toll on her appearance. Her greeting was warm enough.

"It's good to have you here, Jack."

"I'm glad to be here, too, Mrs. J... Sally," Jack responded. "I told you it would take me awhile. It's just the way my parents always wanted it. Even when their friends wanted me to call them by their first names, my folks wouldn't have it."

Sally nodded her agreement.

"They were probably right in teaching you to lean toward polite. Good manners can never hurt."

Jack made a mental note that Sally James appreciated manners and that fit right in with his basic inclinations. He was raised to say 'Yes, ma'am' and 'No, Sir,' and he did it without thinking. Jack would not have to feign anything for Duncan's mother to know his heart was in the right place.

He decided to dive right in after she'd asked him inside. They were soon seated in the farmhouse kitchen. There was a relaxed atmosphere that helped alleviate Jack's concerns. Sally and Duncan sat on one side of the rectangular oak table, facing Jack.

"I suppose you're probably wondering what some stranger is doing showing an interest in your son," he said.

Sally merely raised her eyebrows slightly and nodded, which Jack took as his cue to continue.

"I just happened to see Duncan throw a few pitches before Skip's game. I think he has quite an arm. At least, the potential to have one."

"Duncan has it in his head that you've played some baseball and know about these things," Sally responded. "Is that correct?"

This question went right to the heart of Jack's situation. The completely honest answer covered a spectrum that was so broad that, sometimes, even Jack had trouble believing it. He vacillated between wanting to forget that the events that brought him here ever happened, and needing to relive them time and time again.

He took a deep breath, and with a steady gaze at Sally James, began to recount his baseball existence for the ten-thousandth time.

10

HE JESTS AT SCARS THAT NEVER FELT A WOUND

J ack Ridley was an all-American kid who was born to play baseball. The game became his alter ego. Even as a child, Jack loved the feel of the stitching on the leather ball he could barely hold in his little hand. He lived for the moments when his father called 'Let's throw a few' and Jack would race to the backyard to commune with the baseball angels. Giving his heart and soul to the game came easily to him, and he eventually ascended to the pinnacle of the baseball world.

Advancement through youth baseball, Little League, high school, and American Legion ball was the same for Jack as it was for every other player who ever existed. He outdid them all. His talent was more than physical. Of course, he possessed the ability to hit and throw a baseball at a high level. Grasping the finer points of a situation, and understanding the game's psychology, was his gift.

The catcher's role suited him perfectly, because he could play a chess-like game of strategy with each opposing player. If a batter showed a tendency to swing at a particular pitch, Jack noticed it immediately. He remembered what type of pitch worked previously, and how the batter adjusted. The information was filed away and used to Jack's advantage, *during the next encounter. It helped in matching a pitcher's strengths against a batter's weaknesses.*

The analysis included details beyond batter traits. A good catcher always had to know the score, the inning, and how many outs his team had. Strategizing had to include knowing who was batting next and who was due up after that. All these factors go into deciding what pitch should be called at any given moment. Once a batter got on base, Jack's analysis of the subtleties of the moment only intensified. If a runner displayed any quirks or mannerisms that foretold his intentions, they were obvious to Jack.

Some runners would behave differently, once they formulated an intention to steal second base. They actually appeared to change before Jack's keen eyes, before and after they decided to make the attempt. That change betrayed them. Some would stand on first base, and when they got the sign, they would wipe their hands on their uniform. Others might step off the bag backwards or readjust their cap. Everyone has a telltale sign and Jack was good at observing all of them.

He was like a poker player, always watching his opponent to see if there was a 'tell.' If a player did anything out of his regular routine, Jack could surmise how it fit into the man's game plan. Consequently, he was prepared to throw to second, and his put-out ratio was higher than most. People assumed the young catcher had a superior arm. Jack knew it was mostly because he had a miniscule jump on the situation.

His basic instinct for the finer points of the game, coupled with the requisite physical skills, gave Jack a slight edge. And that was the difference. Elite athletic performances are measured in minute detail. In races, whether track, swimming or bicycling, the winner is determined by hundredths of a second. Olympic medals are won by razor-thin point totals. Baseball was no different. A player who could give himself an advantage, however small, would find himself on the winning side, over the course of a game, or a season. It was not an isolated occurrence.

Jack had read that basketball great Larry Bird had the ability to predict the outcome of a play. He would put the ball where a teammate was going to be, or where the opponent wasn't. Hockey superstar Wayne Gretsky excelled, in his own words, by 'skating to where the puck was going to be, not where it had been.' Jack loved that concept, and knew exactly how it applied to his game. If you can base your decisions on what your opponent is going to do, you have a jump on everyone.

The idea that there might be some kind of future in baseball began to grow when Jack's father struck up a friendship through the American Legion. John Ridley had attended college on an R.O.T.C scholarship, and after serving in the Army, he joined the local post. There he met Ralph Cooper, who coached the team. Pictures of previous Legion players on the wall caught John's eye. He saw a young Mickey Mantle and Johnny Bench in their Legion uniforms. Ralph realized a new member was interested in the players, so he introduced himself.

"I see you noticed the Legion players. My name's Cooper, by the way. I coach the team here."

John was happy that he'd met a friendly face on his first visit to the Legion. He admitted he knew little about the system.

"Never knew that much about Legion baseball," John said. "Now I see these famous ballplayers played when they were young."

"Lots of big names played Legion ball," Ralph smiled. "Guys like Ted Williams, Roger Maris, Reggie Jackson and Roger Clemens. Lots of 'em. It's fun, and kids from different schools get to play together in the summer after the high school season ends. It gives them more time to develop skills, and helps with teamwork and leadership."

Ralph saw that the newcomer appreciated the idea and continued his discussion.

"What's really cool is when you have kids who played together on a Legion team meet up later on, when they're playing in high school or college. They play hard against each other, but they're respectful and show what competition is all about."

John asked what ages were eligible.

"Thirteen to nineteen is the national requirement. Our team is high school kids."

Ralph noticed the wheels turning in John's head.

"When my boy is old enough, we'll see if you can use him," John said.

And with that, Jack's introduction to American Legion baseball was predetermined. He played continuously, with his high school team, and then Legion ball, and his prodigious baseball skill became well-known.

It almost seemed preordained that Jack had been able to advance, relatively quickly, to be counted among the best players. There was a little luck included. His high school coach had been affiliated with the Reds organization, and it wasn't a huge leap for him to let his friends know he had a prodigy on his hands. The Reds had a devotee before the other teams knew Jack existed. It happened that baseball scouts, high school, college and professional, coveted Jack as a player, but fate intervened and the Reds won out.

Originally, Jack made college plans, which were derailed when his fifty-year old father suffered a stroke. After high school graduation, collegiate baseball would have required Jack to be away from home. He opted to remain at home and help his mom, knowing he could postpone baseball. As his father became more and more feeble, Jack realized that he would not be leaving for school in the foreseeable future.

The Reds were still interested and offered a three-year contract. They were in need of a catcher who could augment their pitching corps, and Jack fit the bill. Both the major and minor-league teams were situated close to home. It would allow Jack to earn an income, and still be available for his father. The season was half over when Jack signed to play professional baseball.

Due to his late signing, initially Jack saw only sporadic play. Through the winter, along with his mother and sister, he watched his father's sad debilitation. John Ridley finally slipped away the next spring, and Jack was in a fog when he reported for his second season. He took refuge in the game and used the ballpark as his safe harbor.

Despite his grief, Jack played well enough to be called up to the major league team mid-season. He was a pleasant surprise to the coaches, and was projected to be an integral part of the team's future.

Rookie players are a strange commodity in professional sports. They are a vital cog in the team's future, but can be a harbinger of an established player's eventual departure. It is a never-ending cycle. Today's nobody will someday be the face of the franchise, and the pattern repeats itself. The relationship between the current players and a newcomer is complex. There can be instant kinship or downright hostility. The scenario is played out in rookie hazing episodes.

Some teams are benevolent. Rookies might get easy duty: They are required to stand on chairs at dinnertime and sing their college fight song. Or they are conscripted to perform valet service for the veterans. Many a first-year player has heard 'Rookie, go get me a pizza,' or the like. On the other end of the spectrum, some exchanges are downright abusive.

Jack was in a unique situation. He arrived with the team long after spring training, which is where most of the rookie rituals take place. He wasn't an unknown entity, so he didn't receive the hazing applied to an anonymous group of newbies. It turned out that a certain veteran pitcher took a shine to Jack, which was the general reaction of the players and team management, anyway. The pitcher simply designated Jack as his unofficial bodyguard and chauffer. This shielded Jack from spontaneous hijinks that other veterans might concoct, and it also allowed quality time between a knowledgeable veteran and a willing beginner.

The fellow's name was Mike Franz. He was approaching the end of a workmanlike career, and he had volumes of experience that Jack absorbed. They discussed all aspects of pitching and batter tendencies. For Jack, it was akin to a graduate course in baseball psychology. He relished it all, and didn't mind the fact that Mike decided that Jack would drive him on his social outings. Jack was not a fan of alcohol, so he was the perfect foil for the Mike Franz drinking escapades. Mike and a teammate or two would have a night on the town, and Jack would drive them safely home or to the hotel when the team was traveling.

Mike wasn't the only member of the establishment who liked Jack. The team owner, Mr. Hutchens, came under Jack's good-natured spell almost from the start. The charming rookie fit easily into the owner's world. On one of Jack's visits to the Hutchens' home, with Mike and his friends, Jack met Mr. Hutchens' daughter. Olivia was a beginning college student and had worked in the team office. She was Mr. Hutchens' only child, and he showered her with attention, affection and material items.

Most people expected the owner's daughter to be a pampered debutante waiting to inflict herself on the country club world. She was entirely the opposite. Somehow, Olivia avoided becoming a high-maintenance, spoiled nightmare and was a down-to-earth polite girl and a humble delight. In fact, she was very much like Jack, in that she also was a talented and high-spirited individual. The phrase 'she had her mother's good looks and her daddy's money' fit her perfectly.

It was inevitable that the two youngsters were drawn to each other. Mr. Hutchens had no problem with his daughter keeping company with Jack. He was a polite and decent kid, and Mike Franz was an informal chaperone. Olivia would occasionally tag along with Mike's crowd, and she and Jack would marvel at the veterans' ability to occasionally abuse their bodies with alcohol and still play baseball at the highest level.

Even after Jack's partial season, he maintained contact with Mike and the Hutchens family. 'Mr. Hutch,' as the players called him, had a Thanksgiving gathering and anyone affiliated with the team was welcome. The players who lived in the area attended, along with most of the front office folks, coaches, and clubhouse workers. It was a loud, happy and raucous celebration. Every culinary selection known to man was there. The holiday cheer flowed freely. Mike and his friends wasted no time in indulging in Mr. Hutch's bar and its wide array of all manner of alcohol. Everyone was in high spirits and Mike drank more than his usual amount. Jack was true to form and stayed with soft drinks; another reason Mr. Hutchens was happy to have him around his daughter.

At the end of the evening, Mike bellowed at Jack.

"C'mon, rookie, you're driving me home."

Jack had expected the task, and led Mike, who was slightly stumbling and weaving, into the car.

He was pleasantly surprised when Olivia joined him.

"I'll help you get him home," she said.

She was great company and Jack liked having her around. They eased Mike into the back seat and Olivia happily jumped into the front with Jack. A light snow was falling and there were already Christmas lights on the streets. It gave the world a holiday glow that both Jack and Olivia enjoyed.

ALEX MURPHY

Their passenger was gently snoring so there was no limit on their conversation. Jack had told her about his family, about his father's illness, and trying to cope with his loss. She was a sensitive and understanding person, and easily allowed Jack to dispel his grief. It occurred to Jack that he had never met a young woman like Olivia. The possibility that they might develop a deeper relationship was dawning on him. Olivia had met Jack's mother and younger sister and liked them both. She had not traveled the short distance to visit his family, but she and Jack had discussed it.

Suddenly she blurted, "We've talked about visiting your mother and Ashley, so why don't you get them to come to our family Christmas dinner?"

Jack thought that would be a great idea and said so. Olivia grabbed her phone.

"I'm calling Daddy right now to set it up."

"It's pretty late, will they still be up?"

"Heck, yes," she said. "People will be there half the night. He won't mind at all if I call him."

The ensuing happy and impromptu father/daughter exchange gave Jack a warm, glowing feeling. Her caring relationship with her father and mother was a reprieve from his own family loss. Olivia's sympathetic nature complimented her sweet and well-grounded outlook. Jack was starting to think that this kind-hearted young lady might someday be a part of his life.

Olivia had punched the number and Jack could hear her father answer. The night was quiet and tranquil and Mr. Hutchens' voice was warm and clear.

"Hi, Button. Are you all right?"

"Just fine, Daddy," she gushed. "I have a great idea. How about we have Jack and his mom and Ashley come to our family Christmas dinner? It would be great if they were there."

His answer was easy and welcoming.

"I think that would be fine, sweetie. I'll tell your mother and you tell Mrs. Ridley we'd be so happy to have them join us."

Olivia was palpably joyful.

"Perfect! We're close to Mike's house and we'll be right home."

Jack was driving through an intersection, with a green light in his favor, and no oncoming traffic. His eyes were on the road but his ears were listening to Olivia's words. At that moment, he caught a glimpse of a car blasting into the intersection from the right, running the red light. Olivia had turned in her seat, and her eyes were on Jack as she talked to her father. She was finishing the call. A positively beatific smile wreathed her face as she received the good news from her father.

Olivia ended the conversation.

"I love you, Daddy."

Those were her last words. Mercifully, she didn't see the oncoming car as it exploded into the passenger seat.

11

THE BABY NAMED CAKE

J ack told his story to Sally and Duncan without interruption. When he reached the part about the crash, he paused and wiped his eyes. He would never get over the memory of the devastation. The waste and unfairness of it all was perpetually heartbreaking. Olivia had been his age and would never get any older.

Sally tried to ease the moment and gently intervened.

"I take it Olivia did not survive the crash?"

She hoped Jack did not see her question as an intrusion. He was grateful for the interruption because he could only shake his head at this point.

"So awful," Sally said.

Reaching across the table to pat Jack on the arm felt inadequate, but it was all she had. Both Sally and Duncan were overwhelmed by the sad finality of Olivia's story. They had expected an uncomplicated baseball saga about hopeful competition and failed dreams. Instead, they were handed a narrative that began with youthful exuberance, and ended with bitter heartbreak that could never be remedied. Their collective memory would retain the mournful tale forever.

It was like any tragic story that they heard about some unfortunate but unknown stranger. They were, of course, saddened and distressed over anyone's loss, but it was an abstract event. Abstract, that is, until it applied to someone they knew. Then it became personal and identifiable. It was no longer something they had heard about some anonymous person. It had happened to someone in their lives, and that made it inextricably bound to their own being.

There was much more Jack was unable to tell. He had hidden the details of his rise to the major leagues, and his all-too-soon failure, in some remote recess of his being. Five years had elapsed, and he was no closer to reconciling the sad events than when he began. Thoughts of Olivia and her senseless loss came to him at unpredictable moments, and he was desolate once again. The cruel memory, coupled with his father's passing, became the nadir of his existence. Intertwining with his departure from major league baseball, the grief-stricken events put him in a dark place that nearly swallowed him completely.

Occasionally, he could reignite the purity of the game and its place in his heart. This small reprieve enabled him to hang on. He had hoped that the depths of the downward bouts would decrease with time. That had not yet been the case.

These thoughts darkened his face, so Sally refrained from saying anything. Jack was hoping that he had answered her question about his basis for judging baseball talent. He could not, at the moment, go into further details about the end of his professional career. Duncan continued to sit silently, asking no questions, and Jack was grateful for the pause.

Mercifully, Sally didn't appear to want to pursue details about the ball club. She keyed on teammates and competitors.

"So you got to work with top notch players?"

Jack was still composing himself and only nodded. After a long moment, he was able to speak.

"I guess it sounds hard to believe, but I did see the best players in baseball. I think Duncan is capable of getting to their level."

Sally let it all soak in for a minute.

"How would you go about finding out if you're right?"

Jack's quick answer demonstrated his confidence.

"Give him a chance to pitch to a few good hitters. Nothing fancy. I could get him a shot with the Crushers."

Sally seemed to be giving the idea sincere consideration, so Jack decided to add what he thought was the logical capstone to his proposal.

"I'm not sure yet how Duncan will handle the better hitters who will eventually come his way," he said. "But I have no doubt that he can shine against any team the Crushers will play. It's a start."

He saw Sally was looking closely at his face, probing for any insight. Jack softly repeated himself.

"I have no doubt."

Sally was still on the fence.

"So he just shows up next weekend and pitches?"

Jack gave his best understanding look.

"Not exactly. I'd work with him this week and make a plan on how to face a few batters. I'll be looking at who might be playing and pick a few guys I think he can handle."

Duncan was looking hopefully at his mother and he finally had the courage to join the discussion.

"Mom, if Jack thinks I can do this, I believe him."

Sally was contemplating some place far away from the kitchen where the three of them were sitting. Then she turned her gaze on Duncan. She had a look on her face that Jack couldn't interpret. It was as if she was viewing her son in a new and different way. She seemed to be seeing him as a person, somehow changed from the kid he was when the day started.

Her affect was also wistful when she turned to Jack and spoke again.

"My husband David, Duncan's father, wanted Duncan to be able to play baseball. When he died, I guess things just got sidetracked."

Again, she had that slightly removed and sad look. Duncan

appeared ready to add a comment to his mother's thinking, but at the mention of his dad he held back. To Jack, it was a signal that he wasn't making a youthful, headlong rush to respond. Instead, he was taking a more measured approach to the matter. Jack was gratified to see this side of him appear.

Remaining calm and under control is required for a pitcher. Jack made a mental note to focus on that aspect of Duncan's nature. It could be a weapon in head-to-head battles to come.

Sally was still mulling the question over, and maternal instincts intertwined in the decision. She turned to Duncan to make an important point.

"Cake, if what Jack is suggesting works out, it would be fine. But have you thought about what happens if it doesn't?"

Jack was feeling better, and he risked interrupting Sally's train of thought. He couldn't resist getting sidetracked by the nickname Sally had just used.

"What does 'Cake' come from?"

Sally gave Jack a subtle smile. It seemed to momentarily lift some sort of cloud that had been over her during the conversation.

"From Duncan's father," she said. "He read everything he could get his hands on. So, he knew a lot of words and he liked to wrap ideas around them."

She paused and seemed to be drawing on a memory that she was gently pulling into the present.

"He was a world-class nicknamer. When I wanted to name the baby 'Duncan' he liked it well enough. But he teased me and said we should use a middle name of 'Hines' so we could always have a cake around. It sort of stuck."

Jack was taken by the familial sweetness of the nickname. It was a glimpse into the finer points of a family dynamic that existed only in this household. All families have nuances in their relationships that are specific to only them. Jack was a natural observer of human nature, and his talent wasn't limited to baseball. He could easily grasp the meaning of just that one word.

When Duncan's father or mother called him 'Cake' it was an instant shorthand way of saying 'I love you and you'll always be my little boy.' The thought made Jack smile and Sally seemed to understand what he was thinking. The faraway look in her eyes was there again when she spoke.

"I always liked it when David called him 'Cake.' I didn't use it very much before, but now I use it a lot. It takes me back to a happier time."

Jack knew he was being included in an affectionate moment with this family and it made him feel special. Sally had posed an important question and Jack thought he might steer it to Duncan via another angle.

"She's right, buddy. You're going to get hit sometimes. You think you can handle it?"

Again, Jack was impressed by this young man's sanguine outlook.

"Everybody gets hit sooner or later. You just shake it off and focus on the next batter," Duncan answered.

He paused for a moment, and looked directly into Jack's eyes.

"What you're asking is what I will do if it goes badly and you tell me it didn't work."

Jack held his gaze and waited for more. Duncan didn't hesitate.

"I'll keep doing what I'm doing. Helping my mom keep this farm afloat – glad that I got a shot that I never thought would come my way."

Jack could not have said it better. All ballplayers have a shelf life. Some handle it better than others when their time is up. What Duncan was saying was that he understood this basic reality: His shelf life may have already expired, but he was willing to face a definite, final and brutal answer.

Men twice Duncan's age hadn't been able to face that moment. Jack had seen it. He briefly reflected that his baseball hiatus during the past few years was basically his way of dealing with that very same question.

So the issue was firmly before them, and Jack knew the next

comment should come from Sally. She had one final question and she once again looked directly at Jack.

"Why are you doing this?"

For Jack, the answer touched on the basic reason his life had been so intertwined with baseball. He hoped his answer didn't appear obtuse, but he could tell from Sally's response that she understood completely.

"Do you like music?" he said. "Or art? Or the way little things like a sunset or a waterfall sort of grab you and make you glad to be alive? Because they're pretty and they add to just being human?"

He was being bold enough to look squarely into her eyes and he felt his words were making some kind of a connection.

"That's baseball. It's perfect. The game, the strategy, everything about it, and more than I can explain. I think your son has a place in that. And if I can help a little bit to get him in that direction, I should do it. Just because."

His little speech was an encapsulation of his Theory of Baseball and he hoped he got it right. Somehow, he needed to see this kid succeed. He held Sally's gaze and she seemed to shift into a benevolent mode. She made her decision.

"I guess we'll be seeing you here this week to get Duncan ready for next weekend."

Jack smiled and Duncan jumped up to hug his mother.

"That's another bet Dumbo lost!" he exclaimed.

Jack got the import of the remark. He grinned at the prospect that he might have two-thirds of the family on his side. He stood to leave.

"Well, I should get going so I get a fresh start on this. I'm okay with anytime. Tomorrow, if it's good for you?"

Duncan was eager and Sally was agreeable.

"That'd be fine," she said. "We're here all day. Just show up whenever you're ready."

Sally smiled at Jack and they all walked to the door.

"This is going to be fun," Jack said.

The moment seemed nearly cathartic. Jack took a chance and

gave Sally a little pat on the shoulder after high-fiving Duncan. It was her pleasant demeanor that allowed him to go one step further into being his human, hopeful self. Jack looked at Sally one last time.

"I really like the idea of your husband calling Duncan 'Cake' for a nickname. When I get to know you better I'll ask you if he had any names for you."

Sally didn't say anything as she closed the door. But at that moment Jack saw a hint of a smile. Then her nose started to crinkle. The faraway look in her eyes was unmistakable.

12

WHEN ACCIDENTS HAPPENED WAY
BACK WHEN

J ack parked in the players' lot and approached the clubhouse. He used the tunnel that was a direct link from the parking area inside the stadium. It was an easy way to avoid fans when you weren't up to the ordeal of autograph seekers. They loved their major league heroes and the players loved them, but they occasionally disrupted game preparation.

As a rookie, Jack was new to the adulation that is heaped upon professional athletes. Sports encounters could be challenging. Interacting with devotees was less of a chore for Jack than for some of the other players, but it was a grind. Flat-out exhaustion from never-ending travel can erode anyone's best intentions.

The clubhouse required some adjustment. It was always a 'locker room' in high school, because there were actual lockers. None existed in the clubhouse. It was a large room with cubicles lining each wall. Each player had an area for personal items and street clothes, with a chair in front. The only locked portion was a small safe-like box where valuables could be stored.

Jack saw the clubhouse manager as he passed through the door. The players called him 'Clubbie,' but his name was Rick Ross. He had always been friendly toward Jack, especially during the early days when Jack was unsure of his place with the team.

Rick was also close to Mike Franz and had been included in some of the escapades with their rookie chauffeur. There had been a time or two when Rick needed Jack's help getting in and out of the car after one of Mike's more eventful jaunts. So, Jack was comfortable with Rick and considered him a friend.

Jack had come to the clubhouse to get some equipment repaired, and to pick up a few items he had left at the end of the season. He hadn't been there since they'd played their final game. Spring training would begin soon. It had been a few months since the sad and tragic Thanksgiving. Christmas had been a dark, ominous non-event. There was certainly no celebration to be had after Olivia's loss.

Jack walked toward Rick and gave him a quiet greeting. It was way too soon for any exuberance connected with the team. Jack had expected a subdued response from Rick, but he was surprised when he received only a tight-lipped, curt nod. There was a worried look on Rick's face that Jack had never seen.

Walking further toward his cubicle, Jack saw a few clubhouse employees and a couple of other players. No one spoke to him. One person actually turned away and avoided eye contact, which was an entirely different reaction from the norm. Jack had enjoyed success in his short months in the majors, and people with the team had always shown positive feelings toward him. Things had suddenly changed and it was as if the fire-hose of warmth and acceptance from the team was shut off.

Jack was taken aback by this new turn of events. There was no one close to his cubicle and teammates in the vicinity were drifting away. By the time Jack turned to leave, the area was deserted. He saw no one as he departed.

Only Mike might have an explanation. Jack left the clubhouse and drove straight to Mike's house. They had spoken briefly after the accident, but it had seemed better not to visit during the aftermath. As devastating as the accident was, Mike was not injured. The impact was centered on Olivia, while Mike was passed out in the back seat. He barely awakened.

Jack received multiple bruises and a severe concussion from being banged into the door and dashboard. Still, he had been able to walk away from the destroyed vehicle. The concussion disoriented him, and it took some time for him to recapture his senses. He had no idea where he was or who he was. Arriving at the scene, Mr. Hutchens saw the worst of it all. The team owner had heard the explosive accident over the telephone and frantically called the police. He had then raced to the general area Olivia had mentioned on the phone call.

The accident wasn't hard to find. The two cars were in pieces in the intersection. The other driver was beyond intoxicated. He had been drinking straight from a whisky bottle when he rammed Mike's car. He was unconscious and the odor of whisky was everywhere. Mr. Hutchens preceded the police by two minutes, and saw Jack, alone and wandering in the street. He bolted to him and grabbed his shirt.

"Where's Olivia?" he screamed.

Jack was exhibiting the characteristics of a head injury. He couldn't understand what Mr. Hutchens was saying, or why he would be talking to him. Jack was in a fog from the blow to his head and didn't know who Mr. Hutchens was. Alcohol permeated the scene, and Mr. Hutchens assumed the worst. By that time, the police had arrived and they swarmed the smashed car. Mr. Hutchens was frantic.

"Is my daughter there?"

The police mercifully tried to keep him from seeing the carnage in the front passenger seat. When he realized what had happened to his only daughter, he went into shock. The combination of trauma, the gruesome scene, Jack's incoherence, and Mr. Hutchens' misunderstanding of what had happened settled into a white-hot anger that he could not control.

None of this was apparent to Jack after the accident. It was a couple of days before he remembered driving with Mike and Olivia. When he was told she had died, he was inconsolable. He could not speak to anyone at the funeral, which further compounded the issue with Olivia's parents. Jack had seen no one connected to the ball club until spring training preparations were underway.

All of these convoluted events were tumbling in Jack's mind when he arrived at Mike's house. Mike's wife appeared drawn and troubled when she let Jack in, with barely a hello. Jack had visited Mike after the crash to see that he was alright, but they hadn't discussed the details. Mike was uncharacteristically subdued when he spoke.

"This is a bad thing, Jack. There's been some stuff going on with the team since the funeral. Some bad stuff."

Once again, Jack was struck by his own slow awareness when people acted on unkind intentions. He sucked in a breath and tried to face the issue.

"It's about the accident?"

Mike looked sad and helpless when he answered.

"I know it wasn't your fault, but there're people who don't see it that way."

Mike haltingly continued.

"You're in the third year of a three-year rookie contract. They have to pay you for this year, but they don't have to play you. They don't intend to re-sign you."

Jack was dumbfounded. He had seen none of this coming. Swallowing hard, he asked a question that he could barely formulate. Mike was the only one who would give him a straight answer. It was quick and final.

"Is this coming from Mr. Hutchens?" Jack stammered.

Mike looked at Jack with complete resignation. There was nothing he could do to protect his young friend. He nodded and choked out a barely audible answer.

"Yeah."

The word hit Jack like a sledgehammer to the gut. He was being told that his time with his baseball team was over, before it had barely started.

13

PAINTING THERAPY

Jack rolled out of bed with an aura of expectation that he hadn't experienced for a long time. During the past five years, he had been operating in some sort of emotional dead zone. Not in terms of his kindness in interacting with others, but more like a ship without a rudder or a preacher who had lost his religion.

Lost motivation is a show-stopper. The ship could still be a pleasant place to be, but rudderless, it wouldn't go anywhere. The preacher could be as kind as a summer breeze, but if he wasn't motivated to do pastoral work, he wasn't of much service to the congregation.

This dawning opportunity to help launch the career of a young man like Duncan appealed to Jack's innate sense of fairness. His deep appreciation of baseball and its healing potential were perfect motivations. A long-dormant blossom was peeking out of the snow.

Walt Whitman, who had reportedly said 'Baseball will repair our losses' gave Jack a method to assess the events. Whitman's idea seemed to apply to the inchoate plan for a kid Jack barely knew. He felt invigorated about working with Duncan and getting him ready to throw. This weekend, the youngster would face grown men as batters. Granted, they weren't high-level professionals, but they had played the game and they could hit a baseball thrown by an average pitcher.

Pulling into the driveway, Jack saw Sally and Duncan walking from the barn to the house. He felt a little foolish when he reflected on his comment to Sally about nicknames with her husband. In the cold light of day, it leaned toward prying into her private world. After all, she had been widowed for a relatively short time. Jack hoped that she would see it as a gesture based in kindness, and not a clumsy remark.

'Cheerful enough' Jack thought to himself, as he saw the smiles on their faces. Maybe he was wrong in thinking that Sally might consider his comment as odd. You never know how people take things. Telling one person that you liked his or her coat should be flattering. Some were happy that you noticed them. Then again, others might feel you were intruding. It was getting to the point that it was best you didn't interact with anyone. Some folks look for reasons to be offended.

Today, however, it looked like things were getting off to a good start. Jack looked for neutral ground.

"Where's that dog with the great name?"

"He roams the fields, on and off," Duncan answered. "He'll come back, now that somebody new is here. We were wondering when you'd show up."

"I didn't want to be too early," Jack said. "I know that farm folks are known for sleeping in pretty late."

Both Duncan and Sally grinned, because it was such a reverse metaphor. Sally even flashed to a phrase her husband would have used to describe it: 'It was an antithetical remark.' She realized this was the first time she was prompted to think of her husband, since his passing, without sadness. She welcomed this cheerful thought and considered it ironic. Baseball had completely dropped off the family radar. Any happy moment, even one springing from this sports revival idea, was welcome.

Duncan continued the joke.

"It was great, sleeping while somebody else got the tractor fixed."

"Well, there you go," Jack countered. "Danielle must have gotten up early to pay off the bet she lost."

"Shoot," Duncan snorted. "She wouldn't even talk to me when I told her that last night. And no, she's not working here today. She has a teaching job at the high school. But school's about done for the summer."

This was news to Jack. He'd somehow gotten it in his head that she'd returned home to work the farm when her father took sick.

"A teacher? That's great. My mom is a teacher. Let me guess. Your sister teaches chemistry or some other smart subject."

Duncan snorted again.

"Ha! She teaches English. She likes poetry and stuff like that."

He was in sibling rivalry mode.

"When she starts spouting poetry, I call her 'Dumbo' and that backs her up."

The remark earned Duncan a sideways glance from his mother. Jack sensed that Sally was using her 'mom telepathy' to discourage her young man from bashing his sister. Jack took a chance and intervened on Sally's side.

"Easy, fella. Dumbo's kinda rough." Jack raised his hands in a sort of surrender gesture. "My mother teaches English, too. It's where I got interested in all those big words. Like 'placate.' Almost rhymes with 'cake'!"

Jack looked at Sally with his own sideways gaze to see if she might be amused. He also hoped that his joking would ease her slight displeasure at Duncan's hacking on his sister. Hence, he used the word 'placate'.

Sally got it. She was thinking that there was more to this baseball-playing fellow than met the eye. Most jock types, to her knowledge, didn't use words like 'placate' and it intrigued her. In a strange way, it seemed like a manner of talking that suited her husband's memory.

"I thought there was some connection there," she said. "You have a way of phrasing things that tells me you've read a book or two."

Jack grinned at the thought.

"Mom was always reading to me when I was a kid. She liked Edgar Allan Poe, at least his sweeter stuff. I remember 'Annabel Lee,' and everybody knows 'The Raven,' I suppose."

He noticed that Sally tuned in on the Poe reference.

"Poe is a favorite of mine. Maybe we'll read some of his poetry."

Jack wanted to believe that Sally had been distracted from being miffed at Duncan's comment.

"Well, if you'd like, I could recite some for you. My mom read his poems to me so many times they sort of seeped in."

"Really! That's pretty nice. I read a lot to both my kids. Not sure if it had any positive effect on this one," and Sally sent another glance at Duncan.

Jack figured she hadn't completely bypassed Duncan's wisecrack. He knew it was sibling code for loyalty, and he surmised that deep down, Sally knew it, too.

Getting to like this family was easy. Jack welcomed the change in attitude. Despite his outward convivial nature, he hadn't really liked anything for some time. A poetry segue into the baseball plan fit the moment.

"It was many and many a year ago," he quoted, "in a kingdom by the sea, two guys started playing baseball, and that was you and me."

He gestured at Duncan and himself for a clumsy ending for Poe's words.

Sally laughed out loud and clapped her hands.

"Perfect!" she giggled. "How do you get this pitching thing started?"

"Well, we've got all week to throw a bit and get our strategy worked out," Jack said. "How about I hang around and help out here, as well?"

Duncan leapt at the chance to have some company.

"Great! We can talk while I paint the barn. That's next on the agenda."

Jack seamlessly recognized a path to get to know Duncan.

"You are in luck. I'm pretty good with a paint brush."

All three of them were smiling as the boys peeled off to the barn and Sally headed back to the house. Duncan found some old barn clothes for Jack, so he wouldn't get paint on what he was wearing.

"Here's a shirt my Dad wore around the barn. It oughta fit you."

The boys were happy in their youthful exuberance, and the quiet satisfaction that comes from doing a good job for the sake of the job itself. Sally welcomed the attenuated warm feeling that was creeping over her, brought on by the resurgence of happy memories about her husband. The sadness she felt when he was brought to mind was slightly abated, somehow. She began to reflect on what was happening, now that a stranger named Jack Ridley had appeared.

Like so many men and women who have farm work in their blood, Sally James was a level-headed methodical person. It was her habit to endure life's disappointments as stoically as she knew how. In truth, she used basic routine as a mechanism to help her deal with her husband's passing. She masked her pain and hid her fragile moments in layers of workday distraction. The mind tries to protect the bereaved soul by clinging to the familiar, and subtly avoiding the disruption imposed by loss.

Jack's unexpected arrival highlighted Duncan's talent, which was an area that had been unintentionally neglected. Sally's husband had been Duncan's baseball guardian, and she was ruefully aware that she was ill-equipped to complement his effort. It would take a leap of faith to believe that an unknown guest might be the answer, and Sally dared to hope that fate had kindly intervened. She resolved to prudently monitor the situation to see if this newcomer might be a blessing. For now, trusting in the kindness of a stranger did not seem perilous.

This baseball-playing outsider seemed good-hearted, in a way that Sally could not immediately define. Returning to the safety of her own chores, she smiled at the thought that her David would be amused at this random outcome. Due to a timely twist of fate, she now had two Tom Sawyers painting the barn. It was close enough to whitewashing a fence that the analogy was sweetly complete.

14

NAME THAT TUNE

Jack and Duncan dove right into the painting job. Like any project, it wasn't really work if you didn't have to do it very often. Asking a painter to pitch in on a family barn-painting would be a painful moment. It would be like asking a music performer to drop over to your house, and 'play a few songs' for the crowd. Such things just aren't done.

But an ebullient soul such as Jack's embraced the 'Zen' approach. A little painting while meditating on life's mysteries was a pleasant diversion, because he didn't do it regularly. He had pleasant memories of painting now and again for his mom. She was downright joyful with new colors in the house, and what kid doesn't like making his mother smile?

Duncan had started spreading paint on the barn the week before. Having a little help and conversation was a blessing, and they took right up where he'd stopped. They scooted along faster than Duncan imagined possible. By now, Duncan was aware that Jack had been some type of real professional athlete, and it was intriguing that Jack would dirty his hands. He was surprisingly meticulous, while

Duncan had expected that a ballplayer would be indifferent to a mundane chore.

"You're really getting into this."

"No use doing a lousy job," Jack countered. "Just gotta do it over sooner or later. Plus, it looks crappy afterwards and people would know you're the one who did it."

Duncan was considering the workaday wisdom of this observation when Jack started laughing.

"It reminds me of the story about a guy whose dad was telling him how to get along with girls. The father said, 'Just lay it on thick! There's plenty to go around.' I was just a kid when I heard that joke and I thought it was about painting!"

Jack shook his head and was still laughing as he spoke again.

"I think of that when I'm painting and I lay it on thick. Whatcha think of that," he grinned at Duncan.

The youngster was unimpressed.

"Whatever rocks your world, I guess. I just try to get through these jobs as quickly as I can."

Jack understood the tentative response.

"That's the way it is with chores, especially family stuff. I used to resent it when my dad had jobs for me. Now I wish I had been more helpful."

Duncan shifted the topic.

"My mom was really into your story about playing big league ball. I remember hearing about Mike Franz years ago, but not much after that. I think he's retired now."

Jack was reticent about discussing details from his past.

"I heard he wasn't playing but has some kind of coaching job."

Duncan was interested in the usual fan data.

"What kind of guy is he?"

"He's a great guy," Jack answered. "I learned a lot from him in a very short time."

"You ever hear from him?"

Jack shook his head. He wanted to focus on the baseball task at hand, but also wanted to be polite. A brusque comment would interfere with the trust he wanted to build. He gave the question a moment's reflection and then answered.

"Nah. I lost touch with the whole organization."

There was much more to the story of Jack's departure, but that needed to be told at a later date. He was relieved that Duncan seemed content with a short answer. Jack took a few more swipes with his brush.

"No use wearing ourselves out," he said. "We need a water break and then we come back."

Duncan readily agreed and they walked over to the water pump. At first glance Jack thought it was an actual pump but it was a spigot that worked when you lifted the handle. At any rate, it was great well water and Jack dunked his head under the stream.

"A perfect 'down on the farm moment' if you ask me," he said to Duncan. Elvis took that moment to arrive and he stood at the pump next to Jack. He watched the process as if the boys were in the yard every day.

Duncan took a gulp of water and left the handle cracked open slightly. Elvis managed a drink from the little stream and then plopped down in the shade. It was the perfect observation post for monitoring the baseball lesson. Jack sat on a little bench by the pump and turned the conversation toward the main topic.

"Okay, I'm going to have to know a thing or two about you to be able to get this pitching thing ironed out."

He paused to get the question framed properly.

"Are you a thinker or a doer?"

Duncan looked at him blankly, so Jack explained his reasoning.

"What I mean is, would you be better trying to think your way out of a pitching jam or would you try to just blast your way past a batter?"

Duncan understood his point, and responded truthfully.

"I don't rightly know. Like I said, in high school my dad wouldn't let me pitch. I could always just throw hard. But my dad did start talking about what you're saying, and then we ran out of time."

The 'throwing hard' remark opened an area Jack wanted to address.

"Would you pretty much rely on fastballs or could you use a curve, or what?"

Duncan searched his memory for the right answer.

"When I did throw in practice, I just put the ball over the plate to see if they could hit it. I can throw a curve, but my dad said throwing a curve too soon would hurt my arm."

Jack agreed immediately.

"He was exactly right. You probably avoided an injury and we don't have bad habits there to worry about."

It was time for Jack to look at Duncan's fundamental mechanics, but he remembered their alternate mission.

"First, we'll get a big chunk of this barn done to make your mom happy," he said. "We're getting a lot more done than you would alone, so she'll like that."

Duncan took it one step further.

"It's a lot more than I would get done in twice the time we've worked. It's funny how that happens. Two can get more done in the same time as one person working twice that time."

"That's your first lesson in teamwork!" Jack grinned. "Not bad for a farm kid."

They took a last gulp at the water 'pump' and headed back to the barn.

"One of my secrets is to always paint in the shade," Jack said. "It's cooler and allows the paint to dry more slowly. I've read that's good for it."

"Can't hurt," added Duncan, "and it makes the work easier. I vote we go until the sun takes over, and then we get some lunch."

Jack was on board with the plan.

"Sounds great. We've got all week and we can go easy on this job and get in a little pitching, too."

They continued swabbing on the paint for another hour, and managed to stay off baseball. Instead, they talked about girls and music. Discovering they liked both, Duncan was smart enough to avoid saying much about either. He admitted that he really didn't have any girlfriends in high school, but hung around in groups with various kids.

"There's a movie theater open on weekends that we'd all go to, or the ice cream shop in town."

"Pretty much the same for me as a kid, too," Jack added. "Most small town guys don't find someone to settle down with until they get past college or move to a job."

Duncan seemed glum at the prospect.

"Don't get bummed about it," Jack said. "You might not be in college or heading off to a job right now, but things will change, kiddo. Faster than you think."

The easy conversation allowed Duncan to shift to a personal topic.

"No real girlfriend for you, Jack?"

Jack shook his head and tried to look nonchalant. The hard truth was the only time he'd found himself thinking about a possible relationship was when he started to get to know Olivia. He had a rough time admitting that to himself, and he certainly was in no shape to talk about it.

"No, not really," he gently deflected.

There was no reason for Duncan to have read anything into the details he'd heard last night about Olivia. Jack was relieved that the youngster didn't take any wild guess in that direction. Locker-room talk about women certainly wasn't going to be part of his dealings with this young man. Jack wasn't the type.

Duncan shifted to his next topic.

"What about music? Myself, I like country and mom's old rock. Lots of stuff, except rap."

Jack had to laugh, because Duncan had his own playlist pretty much covered. Except for one thing.

"I was exactly the same at your age," he said. "But I've listened to a little opera once or twice. Plus, I play a little guitar."

"You're kidding!" Duncan exclaimed. "Opera's a bunch of screeching, if you ask me."

Jack was amused at Duncan's reaction. He'd felt the same, on the way up.

"Well, Dunc," he said. "Mind if I call you 'Dunc'?"

Duncan gave him a dismissive wave and Jack continued.

"Shoot, if I'm gonna drag you through the baseball world, I'll probably call you a lot worse." He was rewarded with a lop-sided grin.

"If you get to know the story line, there's some pretty intense stuff going on in opera. But the best thing is, opera singers are amazing, from a physical standpoint. They're like power-lifters. Those people belt out songs like a cannon. And it's none of that amplified auto-tuned crap you hear on the radio. It's the real deal."

Duncan seemed unconvinced, so Jack upped the ante.

"I'll let you hear some in my car sometime."

Duncan seemed unimpressed.

"If you say so."

Jack remained in his mentoring mode.

"It's okay if you don't like it. It isn't for everybody, and if it doesn't grab you at first, give it time. It can grow on you."

At this stage of the conversation, they found a stopping point.

"Let's get these brushes cleaned out," Jack said. "Here's another trick I use. If I'm coming right back the next day I just leave the brushes in soapy water overnight, and I'm good to go in the morning."

Duncan grunted his approval and they washed up for lunch. They ambled to the farmhouse and found Sally on the porch.

"I was thinking it was about time for you to stop," she said. "How's the painting coming?"

Duncan was enthused.

"We got quite a lot done, Mom."

"Good for you," Sally said, as she turned to lead them into the kitchen. "I made some sandwiches. And there's fruit and milk and soda pop."

They gathered around the table and tore into lunch.

"You need fruit and protein and veggies if you want to take care of your body," Jack told Duncan. "The teenage junk food has to stop, if you haven't already."

Sally was pleased. She directed a subtle gaze at her son.

"Maybe he'll listen to you, Jack. Are you listening to this smart man?"

Inwardly, she chalked up another good mark for Jack in the progress report. They chatted over lunch and Jack was looking around the kitchen. In the corner he saw an acoustic guitar, and from a distance it appeared to be a nice one. Sally followed his line of sight and halfway expected his question.

"Don't tell me you know something about guitars?"

"A little," Jack said. "My dad played pretty well. He used to get my mom all misty-eyed playing Gordon Lightfoot songs for her."

He looked a bit closer at the guitar and stood up and took a step or two in its direction.

"Holy cow, is that a Martin?" he breathed. Sally was impressed at evidence of his knowledge in an area unrelated to baseball.

"It's David's old D-18. 1970, or thereabouts. He was a Lightfoot fan and got the guitar so he could learn some of those songs."

Jack was barely listening as he approached the guitar.

"Can I touch it?" he said, reverently. He knew that this guitar was a treasure.

"Now you're going to tell me you can play Lightfoot tunes," Sally laughed. "What a coincidence."

Jack was still waiting for permission.

"Oh, sure, I didn't mean to keep you waiting."

Jack picked up the guitar, gently, because it was in pristine condition.

"This is just beautiful," he said.

He strummed once, to find the guitar out of tune.

"I can try to tune it but these old strings might break. But, I can get new ones at the shop in town."

He started to gently adjust the tuning pegs and Sally was impressed.

"You can tune that thing by ear?"

"Not perfect, but the strings can be tuned relative to each other. Here, I'll show you how you use the frets to get the sound for the next string."

Sally had thought that tuning was done only by very good musicians. When the guitar was tuned, Jack motioned to Duncan to see if he wanted to play. Duncan shook his head, which Jack took as a signal to try it out. Tuning the guitar was, to Sally, a considerable feat, but she was positively mesmerized when Jack began to play. Since she had mentioned Lightfoot tunes, Jack softly eased into 'Early Morning Rain.'

"Jack, that was David's favorite song! This is too much!"

"I know a few of those. Dylan, too," Jack said as he put the guitar back in the corner. "I told you my mom was into poetry. She said those guys were great poets, and she was right."

Sally was grinning widely at this revelation, and Duncan was pleased that his mother was enjoying herself. The truth was that she'd been moping around the house regularly since losing her husband. Duncan had tried to be cheerful, but there are limits on how helpful folks can be when they are sharing the same loss. Duncan decided that Jack's arrival was somehow just the thing that was making his mom smile again.

Jack could see that both Sally and Duncan were having private thoughts, and he figured this might be a good time to leave. There was no telling when Danielle would arrive, and he thought he should pick another time to answer any questions she might have about this little baseball plan.

"Thank you so much for the lunch and letting me play that great guitar," he said. "How 'bout I head back to town and go see Randy

Powers on some details about this weekend's game? I have to figure out if it's Saturday or Sunday."

Enjoying the unexpected music revelations, Sally smiled agreeably.

"That would be fine. Whatever suits you."

"I'll come back tomorrow and we'll get back to painting. Don't start without me," Jack told Duncan. "I'm going to be sure it's right!"

It was clear he was joking. Duncan grinned and sent Jack out the door with another high-five.

"Take my number so you can call or text," Jack added.

He had enjoyed himself today, and was smiling all the way to his car. He waved at both Sally and Duncan, who were standing on the porch. Jack headed down the driveway, happy with the progress.

Sally reflected on the day's events. Her thoughts returned to the night before, when Jack told about the Hutchens family and the accident. She had been listening intently to the heartbreaking story. Mental math told her that Jack had lost his father not too long before Olivia died. That meant that Jack and Duncan had been about the same age when their fathers passed away.

Jack had embarked on a career effort at roughly the same age Duncan was now, Sally calculated. She easily grasped how difficult it would be for her son, in view of his current age and maturity level, to start his own journey. To complicate matters, Jack had faced his troubles relatively alone. And now he was at her kitchen table, willing to assist Duncan in an attempt to grasp whatever might be available from his own fraying dream.

All these thoughts had gently coalesced into her decision to let Jack try to help, and today's events had been encouraging. Some might consider her choice hasty or ill-advised, but she wasn't having second thoughts.

Sally was a delicate blend of pragmatist and dreamer. Everything she had heard and seen served to solidify in her mind that she was on the right track. Duncan's hopes might not be attainable, but it wouldn't be because his mother could not dare to dream.

15

YOU GOTTA TRUST THE PITCH

On the drive back toward town, Jack was feeling invigorated about the visit to the James farm. He'd been right about his thoughts when the day started. Getting Duncan a chance to show his stuff was going well, even though they hadn't touched a baseball. Yet.

For now, the actual mechanical act of throwing was the least of Jack's concerns. He had seen enough at the high school game, if only briefly. His highly developed skill level told him there was no question Duncan could throw, in terms of velocity. But the kid had to show he had other pitches, or the ability to develop them. The final question would be whether he possessed the psyche that major league pitchers must own.

It's a paradox: The *least* important aspect of pitching is speed, but there's a caveat. You have to be able to 'bring the heat,' as it's called, when required. Duncan would need a mix of pitches, starting with the fastball, a breaking ball, and a change-up.

A top-notch pitcher possesses variations of these types of pitches, determined by changing the grip on the ball during the delivery. Jack would show Duncan that there were different versions of a fastball, intended to add movement in the ball's travel to the plate. How the pitcher holds the ball is critical.

Some baseball fans think throwing a fastball is simple: The pitcher blasts the ball to the plate in a feat of strength. If that were the case, the strongest weightlifters would be Hall of Fame pitchers. Pitching dynamics are more refined. Two and four-seam or split finger fastballs are a pitcher's foundation. Subtle changes in the grip convert a fastball to a cutter, or a sinker. Curves and change-ups provide off-speed pitches.

That was the hidden beauty of pitching, to Jack's thinking. The subtle possibilities combined to allow a fascinating spectrum of outcomes. Jack needed to parcel out information to Duncan in small doses. It was similar to learning math. If you were weak in the basics, you would never advance to a meaningful level.

Jack began preparing a mental list of the items he would bring to Duncan. The basics would come without much fanfare. They would start by working on a fastball. Beginners sometimes thought they had to show what an impressive arm they had, and they'd throw all-out. That was a great way to get an injury real fast. Jack liked the analogy he'd heard about auto racing. The saying went 'You can't win the race on the first lap, but you sure can lose it.'

The same precept applied to baseball. A pitcher couldn't win the game in the first inning, but he sure could overpitch, get injured, and be out of the game, or even a career, at the very start. Jack resolved to start with Duncan's fastball, which is basically thrown straight and hard. Then, they would address various fastball grips, which enhance ball movement.

There would be plenty of time, during this week and more, to develop Duncan's pitching repertoire. They'd refine his fastball into a cutter, which breaks toward the pitcher's glove side as it reaches the batter. For breaking balls, they would work on a slider, which slides sideways and downward through the strike zone. It is thrown faster than a curveball, but slower than a fastball, with a shorter break than a curveball.

All these pitch variations spring from manipulating the grip on the ball at the point of release. There are even variations in arm angle during delivery. These combinations affect the path the ball travels. The entirety of pitches could be baffling, but Jack found it fascinating. As is always the case, people flourish in areas they like. They improve, because detail work becomes easier. Jack had certainly put in the hours learning his craft as a catcher.

Sorting through these thoughts, Jack was mildly startled to realize his passion for the game was being rekindled. All those feelings had been shoved deep into his subconscious mind for years. It felt good to re-connect with the game that had given him peace and rectitude. Maybe this effort with Duncan would allow him to recapture a small part of a happier time in his old life.

That contented thought was in his head as he arrived at the wood veneer plant where Randy Powers worked. Jack intended to discuss ways he could insert Duncan into a game this weekend, and make sure Randy approved. Jack entered the front office and saw a young lady at a desk.

"Excuse me, Ma'am, I'm looking for Randy Powers."

What he heard next gave him a mild start.

"You're Jack Ridley, right?"

"Yes, Ma'am," he answered, wondering how this girl knew him.

His mind sprang to the little bar fracas a few nights back. He hadn't done anything wrong, but there were probably versions of the event that claimed he had. Luckily, his concern was misplaced.

"My neighbors are Phil and Betty Venturi," the receptionist said.

The name drew a blank, and Jack was searching for the connection.

"Suzy Venturi's parents? They talk about you all the time. They say you kid around with Suzy?"

Jack flashed on the name and grinned.

"Oh, yeah! What a great kid. She's going to be an Everly Brothers fan!"

"That's what Phil says."

"Quick, tell me your name," Jack said, "so I can tell Suzy when I see her."

"It's Samantha. I babysit Suzy sometimes. She thinks you're some kind of rock star!"

Jack chuckled at the image.

"Maybe to a three-year-old. That's why kids are such fun. They'll believe anything."

"Well, she's seen you at baseball games and that's enough for her. You playing this weekend?"

"That's why I'm here," Jack answered. "I came to talk to Randy."

Samantha pointed down the hall.

"First door on the right. See you at the game, okay?"

"You bet. Let me know if Suzy comes. I'll get her a ball, if she wants."

Samantha grinned at Jack and he left her desk. The first door was open and Jack rapped on the wall. Randy was at his desk writing on some papers. He looked up and saw Jack.

"Hey, man, what're you doing here?"

Jack motioned to a chair in front of the desk and Randy nodded. Jack took a seat and began his proposal.

"It's about putting my guy to good use in a game this weekend. We talked about a few batters and I just wanted to see how it would work best for you."

Randy shrugged and seemed unconcerned.

"I'm counting on you to make it work. Like you said, if he gives up a run, you'll pull him and we're pitching someone else."

Jack was fine with the approach.

"I figure we'd be up a couple of runs first. I don't want to put him in if we're down and the other guys can just tee off."

"Sounds like a plan," Randy said. "I trust your ideas. What are you up to? You got ideas for the kid?"

Jack shrugged. He wasn't evading the question; he really didn't know what his steps might be.

"I just want to see how he does against some okay hitters, and take it from there."

"So, if he does good you're thinking you might get him signed somewhere?"

Randy was showing polite interest. Jack answered slowly.

"Could be. I'm not sure where to go right now."

Randy didn't know all the details of the story with Jack's past, but he knew there had been a connection with the Reds.

"I know you did pretty well with Mike Franz," he said. "I hear he's with them in player development. Might be an idea."

He left the thought hanging and Jack mulled it over.

"Maybe we'll go there. Just don't know. It really depends on what Duncan can do."

"Duncan? James? I know him," Randy said. "I remember he played in high school. He was pretty good, but I didn't know he pitched. Don't know what happened after his dad died."

Jack was circumspect in his response.

"I guess that's what we're going to find out."

He stood to leave and added a final thought.

"I'll have him warmed up and on the bench, and we'll see if he should go in. Thanks a bunch."

Randy walked Jack to the building's main entrance and smacked him on the back.

"No problem. Remember, I've got nothing to lose. If he costs me a run, you're on the hook to get it back."

"You're right," Jack laughed. "I'll have to buckle down. See you Saturday."

He waved at Samantha and headed out the door. He was ready to go back to the motel and think about whether he'd missed anything. Randy's comments about Mike Franz were worth some thought. If there was a way to get Duncan in front of the Reds, it sure would speed things up. There was just one problem: Contact with the team would require fortitude that was in short supply.

Jack checked his rear-view mirror as he backed out of the parking lot. He glanced at the face staring back at him. He wondered whether he had it in him to go back and face the same people who had broken his heart.

16

DOWN ON THE FARM

The next morning Jack was glad that he'd slept in late. There hadn't had any dreams about his past. His dreams ranged from parts of the crash that killed Olivia, to bits of his baseball days. He always found himself starting an at-bat and never seeing the result. Or worse, he dreamed of the moment right before the drunk hit the car, and was always trying to avoid the impact.

He never could. Jack would wake up agitated, and sometimes it would take him several moments to realize what was happening. Usually the dream was so real it seemed like he was reliving the event, devastated once again.

The thought occurred to him that there might be a connection between no bad dreams and a happy chapter from the Duncan Project. That's what he was calling it: the Project. It was like a job remodeling a house, he thought. Some design changes could make everything better, but whether he was the right fixer-upper was the question. Improvements were long overdue. A possibility that the Project would work for Duncan and for himself began to stir in his hopeful mind.

All these notions swirled in his head as he headed to the James farm once again. After breakfast at the diner, he drove in a round-about direction. Instead of the straight run to the house, he took the opposite direction, so he would arrive at the farm from the other side. The drive would be good for clearing his head and thinking about how he would get started with Duncan's pitching program. Plus, he reminded himself, there would be a bit of barn-painting included in the day.

He ended up driving a route that surrounded the farm. It was a good-sized property, and was planted with corn and what Jack thought were soybeans. It seemed to be an operation that would be bigger than Sally and Duncan could manage. He told himself he might ask about those details, if it wouldn't be too close to prying.

When Jack arrived, the morning was half-spent. No one was in sight so he went to the porch and knocked on the door. Sally appeared from the kitchen, wiping her hands on a dish towel. Her greeting was pleasant.

"Hello, Jack, come on in. Duncan is off on the tractor doing a little late planting."

Jack admitted he knew very little about farming.

"Is it a timing thing for when you plant stuff?"

Sally didn't mind a rookie question.

"We plant in stages. It's called succession planting. Some crops do better in different conditions, like temperature, daylight and weather. So, you strategize what gets planted, and when."

Jack was impressed with the answer. Basic, but complex.

"I always thought farmers planted in the spring and harvested in the fall."

Sally gave a small shrug.

"We do. With cycles in between. You don't want everything needing harvesting at the same time."

Jack was hoping that Sally wouldn't decide he was totally uninformed.

"I don't guess the three of you manage everything around here?"

"We get some help from local guys when we need it."

"I don't know the basics, but that explains how you're hanging on to a place this size," Jack observed. "I figure that it's a lot of never-ending work."

"That's true," Sally admitted. "You kind of have to have farming in your blood. But, you're right. We are just hanging on, for now. I'd hate to have to start selling off pieces of the farm, but that's what happens to family operations, anymore."

She paused, and Jack couldn't help but see a slight shade of melancholy pass over her face.

"It would kill me to have to leave here. It's something about the land. I grew up on a farm. Then I met David while I was in high school, at an FFA event at the State Fair."

Jack was feeling ignorant, but he had to ask.

"FFA...?"

"Future Farmers of America. It's an educational group for kids interested in agriculture and leadership and service."

"So kids get together and learn about...." Jack left the question open so Sally could fill in the blanks.

"Science and technology in the food and agriculture industry. Kids learn about all aspects of farming, and farm marketing. It's a great way to learn how farming is a business that impacts all of us."

"Sounds interesting."

Jack was happy to learn. Sally was happy to teach.

"Very. The kids are hard-working and they learn how to make a difference in their communities. You'd like the idea, Jack. Part of the creed says 'I believe in being happy myself and playing square with those whose happiness depends upon me.' It's for work, and home, and everything."

Sally gave Jack a thoughtful look as she considered her words about the FFA.

"I'm thinking that applies to what you're doing with Duncan. You're playing square."

Jack liked the comparison. He had to admit that he was feeling better, somehow, about life in general since he'd happened upon this 'Project.' And it made him feel good knowing that Sally was noticing.

"So, it's like a sports team. The FFA kids are on a team trying to win the farming game," he said. Sally was on the same wavelength.

"I'd say so. It was great for me. I met David, who was sweet and kind. And kind of cute! It also got me a partial scholarship to college, which helped tremendously. So, here I am."

Jack was thinking that this was another example of how random events shaped your life. If Sally had gone to band camp, she'd have found a whole different set of experiences. Amazing, but as natural as breathing.

Sally shifted gears.

"What about you, Jack? You grew up wanting to be a baseball player, or what?"

Jack laughed at the memory.

"When I was a kid, at least a little kid, I thought I was going to be some kind of ninja warrior! You know, the stuff on Saturday morning television. But when I starting playing baseball, I was hooked. I loved playing catch with my dad, to start, and then it was Pee-Wee ball. Then you go to Little League and travel teams, high school, and Legion ball. It's all I did."

Sally was just listening, letting Jack set the pace.

"In high school, things started happening," he continued. "The coach was a good guy. He played in the Reds' organization. He knew guys who scouted games to see if anybody had potential. I didn't know it at the time, but some college scouts came to games and talked to my dad. There was talk about some big schools that really got me pumped up. Stanford. Notre Dame."

He paused and had a sad look on his face that told Sally this part of the memory was difficult.

"Is this when your dad had the stroke?"

Jack nodded. When memories of his father bubbled to the surface, tears were not far away. He felt strange that this woman, whom he'd barely met, could tap into those feelings. Usually, when someone edged into conversation about his father, he would steer things away into safer territory.

"When he died, I didn't want to go far from my mother and little sister. Ashley was only 13 or so. I got out of high school but baseball was on hold without my dad. I figured I should stay close to home. Working construction was a diversion, something different to do. The summer was almost over when I was able to think of playing again. The Reds had offered a contract during high school, and I asked the coach if they were still interested. Their minor league team was close enough, so I wouldn't be too far from home, for too long. When they agreed to put me on the team, I signed."

"So you went from there to the big team?" Sally asked.

"Not right away. I was only with the minor league club for six weeks or so at the end of the season. I started with them the next spring and got called up about halfway through that season. That's when I met Mike and then it happened. I'd barely been on the team and then it was over."

Sally wasn't sure how the difficulty with one team could impact other teams.

"Was the team owner able to turn the other teams against you? I mean, can an owner be that powerful that the other owners wouldn't touch you?"

Sally had gone, inadvertently or not, to the heart of the matter. If Jack was as good as he seemed to have been, other teams would want him, wouldn't they? Jack breathed a sigh, because the answer had impacted a huge part of his life, and not in a good way.

"I know it sounds weird," he allowed. "First of all, I was just a kid and didn't know how to handle things. Everybody was in shock after Olivia died. I didn't realize that I was being blamed, by a few people, but especially Mr. Hutchens. It hit me pretty hard. I had no friends in the clubhouse after that. It was impossible."

Jack tried to explain it another way.

"Have you ever been crazy-mad in love with someone, and they tell you they're done with you? Or worse, they get ugly about it and throw you aside? I mean, someone that meant so much to you basically threw you away as if you didn't matter at all? It smacks you down so hard that you can't figure out who you are. Or if you matter. At all. Just like when someone gets dumped by a girlfriend. They can't start over with someone else."

Jack paused to gather his thoughts and pull back from the emotion of the memory. This was the most he'd ever talked about it, and he was wondering why he was telling Sally so much.

"It was like that. When I got dumped by the team, I was so messed up I couldn't even think about playing ball."

His story was bordering on the bizarre, Jack knew. Sally might think less of him and he angled toward a better explanation.

"I know this is weird. I just had to get away. Mr. Hutchens was a friend, at least I thought so, and it just screwed me up when he turned on me. I had put the money I'd made into the sports store, so that's where I went. It was crazy. I was like a guy running a dating service, who wasn't able to go on dates. I'd sell baseball stuff but didn't want to be around baseball. Other teams called, but I was so messed up. It was like going to a family reunion after you'd been thrown out of the family."

Sally had been listening to the entire story. The sympathy she felt for this young man, a kid, really, welled up in her. She wished she could say something to help it all make sense, but it was like hearing about an accident after it happens. You want to help, but it's too late.

"So how did you find yourself playing again? I mean, you met Duncan because you played with the Crushers the night before, right?"

Jack could see the conflict in the scenario he'd offered.

"That's another strange part of it. It's sort of like when guys take a vacation and ride their motorcycles around, for a few weeks. They just go places to see what's there. There're guys who spend their days behind some desk in a bank, and then for a few weeks they escape. They grow their hair and don't shave and ride a Harley. You know? Sort of like those 'Wild Hogs' guys."

Sally laughed out loud at the image the movie created. A few straight-laced guys went out on a motorcycle vacation and ended up getting beat up by a motorcycle gang. One of them even met a girl, Sally remembered.

"So you went out and burned down some gang clubhouse?"

Jack grinned at the thought.

"Not quite. In the summer I would drive on little trips and I saw small teams playing. After a while, I met some guys playing pick-up games. The first time they just needed a sub. Nobody knew about my past, so I sort of eased into playing again. So here I am."

Jack paused to reflect that this was the first time he had put the past sequence of events into some coherent order. Somehow, it all fit into the scenario that was developing in this town, on this farm, in this kitchen.

"It's strange," he started in again. "I was just getting to the point where I was going to be done with my 'motorcycle trips.' I was okay with that. Focusing on running the store was my plan. There're some bankers who want to expand into a few stores, and I was thinking that would be a good thing. They're saying there could be franchise opportunities, and I'd do better than I ever would have playing baseball."

"It's not strange," Sally noted. "You're a smart kid and you're making things work for yourself. I'm just glad you're including Duncan for a little while."

She smiled at Jack and gave him a cheerful pat on the arm. Just then they heard the sound of an engine approaching.

"That's Duncan, driving the tractor back in. We're sitting here gabbing and now it's time for lunch. But this was talking we needed."

Duncan had seen Jack's car and came bounding in like a happy puppy.

"Back to it, buddy!" he exclaimed.

"We can eat lunch first," Sally said. "I have to keep my boys going strong!"

And with that jovial comment, the three of them sat down to a cheerful lunch before painting. They were sprucing up a barn, and sprucing up their own perspectives, all with the same strokes.

17

PITCHING IS UPSETTING TIMING

Painting the barn was in full swing, but pitching was quiescent. It occurred to Duncan that he and Jack hadn't started what was supposed to be the reason they were together. Still, a relaxed relationship had begun, despite their age difference.

To a nineteen-year-old, someone who has attained the advanced age of twenty-five appears to be a wise elder. To a forty-year-old, a twenty-five-year-old has just begun living and has no life experience worth discussing. And so it goes.

Jack had an easy way about him that made Duncan feel accepted and comfortable. What Duncan didn't realize was that baseball had very nearly been excised from Jack's life. Simply by Duncan being himself, he was playing a part in reviving Jack's baseball yin and yang. It was as if Jack had been a young physician who had lost a patient through no fault of his own. Consequently, he believed the failure dictated he was through as a healer. When forced to treat and save an emergency patient, he cautiously began to consider there might be a chance to return to medicine.

Reducing these terms to such clarity hadn't occurred to Jack, just yet. He was just behaving naturally, and the result was therapeutic. Painting was a convenient diversion, but Duncan was the first to invoke their primary purpose.

"So, are we gonna start throwing, or what?"

They were a couple of hours into the second painting session. They'd covered nearly one whole side of the barn and Duncan was pleased with their progress.

"Sure," Jack allowed. "We've got enough done, for starters, so your mom won't think I'm a total bum. Plus, we're losing the shade."

"I don't think she believes you're a bum," Duncan philosophized. "She says you're a complex guy. I think it was that guitar stuff. Women are suckers for guitar players."

Jack laughed at Duncan's humor.

"Well, if I were any kind of a guitar player, I'd let you know. I'm just a hacker. Someday I'll show you guys who can really play."

Duncan was putting the brushes into the soap pail.

"How about we head for the trees? We can throw in the shade."

"Perfect," Jack replied. "I've got my glove and pads in the car."

They retrieved the necessary equipment and walked toward the group of trees next to the barn. Jack could see the worn spots in the grass.

"I guess you threw here with your dad?"

Duncan nodded.

"It was a good place to talk things over. It's funny how you can get to things that aren't so easy, when you're playing catch."

Jack understood exactly what he meant.

"I did the same thing. When you're eighteen, you can get a little sideways with your folks. I suppose it's part of becoming your own person. What was it Mark Twain said? 'When I was eighteen I couldn't believe how stupid my father was. When I was twenty-one, I couldn't believe how much he had learned in three short years.' That's so right."

Jack paused to reflect.

"The only problem is, my dad was gone, and at about the time I was supposed to be learning how smart he was. Yours, too. Life gets pretty unfair, sometimes."

Duncan was silent. Once again, Jack found himself voicing feelings that he hadn't been able to formulate, until now.

"I hope I'm not saying too much, Dunc. I think I would have liked your dad a lot."

Processing Jack's words and the thoughts they brought to mind occupied Duncan for a moment. He, too, had been unable to talk about the loss of his father with anyone outside his family. It was strange that this newcomer was able to broach the subject, and it didn't agitate him. Instead, it caused a calmness to come over him that he welcomed.

"I'm realizing what a great guy he was," Duncan said. "He built this place up and took care of my mom and me and Danny. I always felt safe because of him."

Jack paused and let that warm thought sink in for a while. Having a safe place as a kid made all the difference. He felt sorry for the kids in the world who didn't have that feeling in their lives. Starting to think about another sad topic would distract him, so Jack eased back toward more familiar ground.

"That's a new name you're using. I've heard 'Danielle' and 'Dumbyell' and now it's 'Danny.' Do you have your dad's nicknaming ability?"

Duncan gave him a sheepish grin.

"There's more. When mom's not around, I call her 'Dumbo.' That really sets her off. Sometime I just use 'Bo" for short. It still gets her going."

Jack had to chuckle.

"Sibling rivalry. It's because you're so close in age. What is she, twenty-one?"

"Nah, she's twenty-four," Duncan corrected.

"Oh," Jack said, "I thought she was just out of college getting a teaching job."

"No, she had a job up where she had been student teaching. She wanted to try the big city life. But she came back here when dad got sick. Truth is, it was a big thing she did. She gave up something she wanted, to help mom. And me."

"Well, dude," Jack offered, "I'm sure you let her know that you appreciate it, one way or the other."

Duncan let that thought percolate.

"I suppose. Maybe I shouldn't say 'Dumb' and just use 'Bo'. Maybe that'll do it."

"Maybe," Jack laughed. "In the meantime, show me how you grip the ball. Did your dad talk to you about different pitches?"

"A little. Mostly, it was two fingers on the laces, like this."

He demonstrated how he placed his fingers, and Jack began the lesson.

"That's a start. We'll cover a lot of that. But let's go with a basic idea I want you to keep in your head. How many pitches do you need?"

When Duncan started to answer, Jack stopped him.

"It's a trick question! Let me ask you this: Have you heard of Warren Spahn? One of the greatest left-handed pitchers, ever. Won more games than any lefty. He had an interesting perspective that will help you: 'Hitting is timing, and pitching is upsetting timing.' Make sense?"

Jack looked to see if Duncan was getting the point and took it one step further, via Mr. Spahn. 'A pitcher needs two pitches - one they're looking for and one to cross them up.'

"That's where you'll win," Jack added. "Upsetting their timing." He had one more gem. "Three or even two great pitches are better than five average pitches. So, we will make sure the basics are strong before getting too spread out, okay?"

"You're the boss," said Duncan, matter-of-factly. "I was about to ask you what was your favorite pitch, but I think I know the answer."

"Go on," Jack invited.

"It's the one that gets the batter out. And you'll probably say it changes with each batter and each pitch count."

Jack jabbed a fist at Duncan.

"Perfect! Good job. Nobody could say it better. Learn to do it and you can pay off the farm and let your mother retire. Maybe your sister, too! Really."

That happy thought got Duncan grinning. Jack motioned that they back away from each other until they were about fifteen yards apart. He had to step over Elvis and the dog scooted over to the side. He seemed to enjoy watching the show.

"That's plenty, for now." Jack said. "I just want to get loose and look at form. Don't throw hard. You always want to warm up this way."

Duncan began throwing the ball, using a soft overhand motion. Jack continued the easy chat.

"Fine, Dunc, just toss it easy. What's the easiest pitch for you to throw?"

Duncan hesitated just a second, because he thought Jack might be posing another trick question. Jack was waiting for an answer.

"I guess the fastball is the most straightforward. You just wind up and let 'er rip."

Jack agreed.

"Probably right. It's the least dynamic pitch, in terms of air affecting what the ball does. But what do we know from Mr. Spahn and Mr. Seaver and Mr. Maddux?"

"Ball movement." Duncan made it a statement, not a question.

"Exactly! But it starts with the ability to put a fastball over the plate at least seven out of ten times. No joke. If you don't have consistent strikes, everybody is going to stand there and wait for a walk. In about three starts, that pitcher is looking for another job."

Jack wasn't trying to sound tough. It's just reality.

"Have you ever seen a pitcher walk a guy on four straight pitches? Most times, when the fourth pitch was coming, that batter wasn't swinging. He was able to just *stand* there and accomplish two things: If it's ball four, he gets on base and he adds four pitches to the guy's pitch count. That pitcher is four pitches closer to tiring out and hasn't accomplished a thing. That's why they keep an eye on 'first strike' stats. When you get started with a 0-1 count, you're miles ahead."

Duncan knew this, from a philosophical standpoint, but he hadn't reduced it to analytical terms yet.

"Don't forget," Jack continued. "In the show, anybody can hit fastballs, if they don't have to worry about other pitches. Henry Aaron, one of the greatest hitters ever, said that 'hitting is about good guessing.' He said he was able to guess, with reasonable accuracy, what type of pitch was coming. When you know that, you're a hitter."

Duncan agreed with the logic.

"That's what they're talking about when they say 'that pitch fooled him' and the batter misses?"

"Attaboy," Jack said. "But I don't agree with calling it guessing. What Aaron was doing was 'predicting' the next pitch, based on the pitch count, what a specific pitcher usually did in a given situation. On the other side of the equation, there are guys with great hands and reflexes. Those types caused another old saying: 'It was a great pitch for fifty feet or so, but then the guy hit it!' Great stuff, huh?"

Duncan agreed with the truth in that maxim. Sometimes hitters did guess right.

They had continued lightly throwing the ball throughout the conversation, so Jack switched to mechanics. He explained, in minimalistic terms, how a pitch starts with legs and proceeds through rotating the body while 'cocking' the release. It is much more complicated than that, but Jack believed that slower now would aid in speed later.

He had Duncan demonstrate his fastball grip. Jack decided to use a four-seam grip, for starters. This provides the straightest throw with the least movement, and usually the highest velocity.

The four-seamer is a staple in a pitcher's arsenal. Jack showed Duncan where to place his fingers on the laces and emphasized that the grip should remain relaxed.

"This is all we need today," he said. So, they began in earnest.

"Same grip, same speed. We need to know what the ball is doing with each pitch."

After a dozen or so medium-speed throws, Jack stopped.

"Tell me how your arm is feeling? Any soreness, tightness, or anything?"

"It feels good," Duncan replied. "I can't feel any problems." Jack decided to step it up one slight notch.

"Okay, we're going to add maybe ten percent velocity. I mean you should be at about seventy percent of your top speed. I'll be mad if you try to smoke it today, got it?"

Duncan nodded his assent, all business.

"One final thing," Jack said. The goal here is for the pitch to be in a spot about as big as a softball. Every time. Control is the issue. If you can't put it over the plate, it doesn't matter if you can throw two hundred miles an hour. Imagine I've got a softball here in a square box. That would be about a five inch square target, right?"

Duncan nodded, and returned to his former location. The boys didn't know that Sally had heard the first smack of the ball in the catcher's mitt. That sound was well-known, but she hadn't heard it since her husband had died. She had sensed that Duncan did not want to share the memory - the memory of playing with his father - so soon. She had left it at that.

It was not an unkind position from Duncan. Sally compared it to someone keeping his or her diary private, until they were ready to involve someone else. It was understandable that there were elements that Duncan enjoyed with his dad that she could not replace.

On this day, the sounds that she had associated with 'her boys' playing catch resonated in the backyard. She felt happy and unburdened, just for a moment. Perhaps Duncan would be able, she hoped, to recapture a part - any part would do - of what he had with his father. She walked, quietly so as not to disturb, over to where she could see and hear the instruction.

The calm and quiet way Jack spoke to Duncan was impressive.

His easy flow of baseball knowledge was remarkable. Duncan was hanging on every word, and Sally saw that her son achieved a new level of maturity. Somehow, this stranger had tapped into a level of communication with Duncan that was as intense as any she had seen. She realized that if anyone was capable of teaching her son how to pitch a baseball, it had to be Jack Ridley.

The boys were not aware that Sally had approached. She feared, momentarily, that there might be some 'guy talk' between them, because they considered themselves to be alone. It was gratifying that neither of them, especially Jack, used any profanity. Jack achieved emphasis by using simple, direct language. What was most pleasing was that Jack was ultimately concerned with Duncan's well-being. He was solicitous to a fault.

When Duncan first came home talking about this stranger, all her battered antennae had gone up. Now, after a few short days, she was convinced that Jack had her son's best interests at heart. Sally felt vindicated that her quick decision about Jack Ridley had been the right one. Interestingly, she could believe that Jack's intentions for Duncan extended to her family as well.

For the first half-dozen throws, Jack didn't say anything. He just caught each pitch in what seemed to Sally to be the same location.

"You need to use the exact same arm position every time," he told Duncan. "You're dropping your shoulder a bit."

Sally couldn't see the difference, but Jack nodded after two more throws.

"That's the way. Remember, the fast ball delivery has to look the same when it becomes a change-up. That's the Warren Spahn 'mix 'em up' pitch. And it's not a softer throw, like some people think. It's a different grip, with the *exact* same motion. We'll get to that, but for now, we get this arm motion burned into your head. Sound okay?"

"Right," Duncan said. "I just need to be thinking about exactly what I'm doing for every pitch."

"Exactly right. The good news is, after about 100,000 repetitions, it becomes muscle memory. It's like a genius piano player. They perform intricate parts he or she isn't even thinking about. That will be you," Jack grinned.

It was time to fine-tune the lesson.

"Tell you what. I've seen what I need. You're doing a good job keeping it at low speed. Now that I know you're coachable, we can walk up to the edge. Your arm feeling okay?"

Duncan nodded, waiting for the next gem to fall his way.

"Okay," Jack cautioned. "We're going to combine three strikes with slightly increasing speed. That is, if you maintain control and each pitch is in the box. You can step back a bit if you want."

Duncan retreated a few steps and prepared to throw.

"Remember, same grip, same motion, same location. If anything changes, we stop and regroup tomorrow. Don't forget about *slight* speed increase."

Duncan locked in his four-seam grip. He completed his wind-up, duplicated the proper arm motion, and followed through. The ball smacked into Jack's catcher's mitt, straight and true, right in the middle of the plate.

Jack only nodded, threw the ball back to Duncan, with a thumbs-up. Duncan readied the second pitch, and it was exactly as before, only slightly faster. Jack made the same return throw and grinned. The third pitch was the same once again, straight down the middle, and faster still. Jack held the mitt straight out and let the ball blister squarely into the leather.

It gave a resounding crack and Jack yelled.

"Strike Three!"

Duncan leaped as if he'd just struck out the side, and Jack had his reward ready.

"That's how you end the game, pal. Three straight strikes!"

Jack gave Duncan a swat on the back and they turned to walk to the farmhouse. Both of them saw Sally at the same moment. Duncan was enthusiastic.

"Mom, did you see that? It was perfect!"

Sally beamed at both of them.

"I sure did, kiddo. You were great."

She turned to Jack and enhanced the compliment.

"Not bad yourself, Mister."

Jack shyly bobbed his head. He hadn't realized Sally had been standing there, nor for how long. Jack didn't believe there had been anything improper said, but you never can tell. He really wanted to make this work, and having Sally's approval was part of it. If she ever came to doubt him, Duncan wouldn't be far behind. But Sally was grinning and came over to clap them both on the back.

"You guys look great together," she exulted.

They turned and headed toward the house and Jack saw another car enter the drive.

"Hey, it's Dum... Danielle," Duncan said, after a quick glance at Jack.

The exchange didn't go unnoticed by Sally. Now she was wondering what she was hearing. Was Jack was going to coach this kid *and* get him to quit calling his sister a name that set her teeth on edge? That would be some trick, she thought. She couldn't say which one would be more important to her, if she had to choose. For now, she decided to pray for both.

Duncan skipped over to Danielle's car. Jack realized he and Duncan had painted and thrown for the better part of the afternoon. The time to sell Duncan's sister on the project was coming, but Jack wasn't sure what it would take, or if he was ready. He had planned on being gone when Danielle arrived. It was best to wait next to Sally as the siblings approached. Jack smiled as best he could, and then Duncan spoke.

"You should've see us throwing, Danny. Jack says I'm doing good!"

"I do, too," Sally added. "I saw most of it, and Jack's got him off to a good start! And barn painting, too!"

Danielle observed her mother and brother's enthusiasm, and didn't know what to think. She had been suspicious from the start. For two nights now, since Jack's first visit to the farm, she had heard them speak about this unknown 'Jack.'

A few ballplayers in high school and college had crossed her path. For the most part, she found them boorish braggarts who were free and easy with girls' feelings. So, with her, Jack was starting with a called first strike.

"Is that right?" she said, and looked coolly at Jack.

Jack kept the smile on his face.

"Doing the best I can. I think Duncan really has potential. And we're going to find out this weekend what he can do with the Crushers."

"Really?" Danielle said with feigned confusion. "I heard something about what the Crushers can do in a bar. I hope that's not where Duncan is heading."

She maintained her gaze at Jack and he knew she was waiting to see how he'd react. He decided now was not the time to parse words with her. It would only get in the way.

"We're just working on pitching," he countered. "If he handles a couple of batters okay, we'll see what's next."

Sally tried to bring the conversation back to friendly ground.

"I need to get supper going. Maybe you'd like to stay, Jack?"

Jack could see that he would have to walk on eggs with Danielle throughout the evening. He angled for a graceful exit.

"C'mon Sally. The lunch was great and I appreciate it. I can see you folks need to spend some family time together. I'll come back tomorrow."

He turned toward his car and tossed the catcher's mitt into the back seat. After starting the engine, he eased out of the driveway. Reaching through the window, he waved goodbye.

"See you tomorrow," he called.

Danielle watched him drive away and then turned to look at her mother. She wasn't angry, but her comment could have been called contentious.

"Sally? Lunch *and* dinner? Who is this guy?"

Duncan answered her question and Sally was impressed by his calm but pointed response.

"He's the guy that got you out of helping me paint the barn. And he's the guy who told me to quit calling you 'Dumb-yell'. I'm beginning to think he was wrong both times."

Sally managed not to smile as Duncan took her by the arm, and they both marched into the house. She didn't care for the nickname Duncan had reverted to, but a small voice in her head told her that Danielle had it coming. Supper was quiet that night.

18

HEARD IT IN A LOVE SONG

Jack drove away from the James farm as gently as he could. There wouldn't be any spinning tires or flying gravel. He wasn't that stupid. Why let her know she had torqued him with a few words? Danielle was baiting him, obviously, and he had a pretty good idea why.

It wasn't the first time people had questioned his motives. He felt he tried to treat people fairly. He also knew some folks had a different angle. They operated out of self-interest, and Danielle probably figured he was the same.

It was discouraging. If this had been anyone else giving him a hard time, he would be walking away right now. But Jack wasn't going to run out on Duncan. He was a good kid and Jack had made a deal. He didn't know how it got started, but he made a commitment and was going to see it through. If Danielle didn't appreciate the effort, she'd just have to watch her brother do it. Duncan would be able to take better care of their mother than Danielle ever could, *if* Jack pulled it off. That would serve her right.

Of course, Jack's hopes that Duncan would get a major-league contract were probably unrealistic. But stranger things had happened, and Jack consoled himself with the thought that Duncan and Sally believed in him.

He headed back to town and decided he'd go to the Zone bar, where the little dust-up had occurred. He just wanted a sandwich and a beer. There was a nice bed and a TV waiting for him at the motel. While walking inside he noticed that a little band was rehearsing. A good song always interested him, so he walked to where they were set up.

"Mind if I listen a bit?" he asked the drummer.

He approached the drummer because in his experience they were usually ignored and liked any attention that came their way. Jack had fiddled with a garage band in high school, and had met a drummer or two.

"Fine with me," the fellow said. "People are always here when we rehearse."

"Cool," Jack said, looking at the equipment. There was a Telecaster on a stand next to the drums, a Fender bass and an organ. If he had to guess, the Telecaster would lean him toward thinking they were a country band. But, you never can be sure. Springsteen played a Telly all the time, and he wasn't considered a country player, by any stretch.

"What kind of stuff do you guys play? Maybe country?"

The drummer noticed that Jack was inspecting the guitar.

"We do a couple of country tunes, but classic rock is most of it. You play? I saw you checking out Buddy's axe."

"Not so you'd notice," Jack admitted. "I was in a three chord rock band in high school. We played old stuff because our lead guitar guy's dad was a 60's fan, and that's all he knew. He sort of let me chop along playing rhythm. My name's Jack, by the way."

The drummer stuck out a hand.

"I'm Tom. Over there's Buddy." He looked at Buddy and said, "This here's Jack. He's probably better than most of the guys that sit in with us."

"Why do you let people sit in?" Jack asked. "They usually screw up the song."

"I told you he knew what he was doing," Tom laughed at Buddy. "Sign him up!"

Then he spoke to Jack.

"The owner likes to have his drunk buddies play a song or two with us. It makes them happy and that makes him happy. He writes the check, so we're kind of stuck."

Jack tried to sympathize.

"That's gotta be rough. I'm gonna get a sandwich and a beer and come back. You're the happening thing in town tonight."

Tom had that nonchalant air that lots of drummers carried.

"If you want to pick out a song or two, it's fine with us. Come back and talk it over."

Jack went to the bar and asked for breaded tenderloin. The one they made in this place was about as big as a dinner plate. That and a beer would wash down great, and he'd enjoy just crashing tonight. About that time, a bass player showed up. The boys noodled with their sound mix long enough for the food to arrive. Jack eased back toward the band with his supper, and the band swung into a pretty good version of 'Proud Mary.'

'That has to be a tune that every bar band in the world plays,' Jack thought to himself. The sandwich was half-finished and he decided to keep the rest for later. Single guys are always into leftovers. Expecting the next song to be another Fogerty tune, Jack was tickled when the band started playing 'Mustang Sally.'

Buddy saw Jack perk up and leaned over to speak.

"You know this one?

"We played that one in high school! You must have seen the car I'm driving," Jack grinned.

"Well, hell," Buddy said. "If you play the guitar, I could do that cool organ part. Want to try?"

Normally Jack wouldn't hang himself out like that, but these guys were pretty friendly. Plus, he had heard them play the song and was pretty sure he could handle the Wilson Pickett tune. The bass player had sung the song with a sultry voice and Jack was intrigued. There was nobody around that he could see, except a few guys drinking beer at the bar.

"Why not," he said. "Can't hurt."

Buddy handed over his Telecaster. Jack hit a chord and it sounded great.

"Nice action on this one. Let's do it. You were playing in 'D', right?"

"That's it," said the bass man. "I'm Bobby. Do you play the intro with the same couple of notes like the original?"

"Sure do," and Jack started playing.

The others exchanged approving glances and quickly joined in. Jack had assumed the organ playing would be pretty basic but he realized that Buddy was playing the original from the recording. He was also interspersing the horn parts from the same arrangement.

The band was much more sophisticated than Jack had imagined. Over-all, the song sounded great, and Jack felt confident enough to join in on the background chorus parts. They finished the tune with a flourish and high-fived all around. Tom was nearly exultant.

"That was perfect, man!"

"You have to come do that one with us," Buddy added.

"Thanks, fellas, I'm booked Saturday night, and don't know what I'm doing Friday," Jack said. "But you guys sure play it great."

Buddy wasn't giving up.

"Look, we have to put up with a half dozen drunks the owner shoves on us. You might be the only cool dude who comes along. So we're gonna save that tune for you. We're here Saturday, if your plans change. If you're free on Friday, we're playing at the American Legion."

"Can I get in there? I played Legion ball and my dad was a veteran."

"That'll do, but they have dinner open for everybody on Fridays," Buddy said. They call it 'Bring Anybody Friday,' so if you can come by, you're on!"

Jack was pleased at their friendliness. It helped dissipate the edge he felt when he thought about the curve balls Danielle was throwing at him.

"Tom; Buddy; Bobby. I got it. See you if I can."

He thanked them again and headed toward the front. While skirting the bar he walked by some booths close to the exit, and heard a familiar voice.

"Baseball *and* guitar. I don't think I can stand it."

Jack recognized the voice after a moment's reflection.

"Patty," he said. "Who saved me here last week."

She was sitting with three others in a booth, and Jack felt slightly disadvantaged by the numbers. He forged ahead.

"You really helped me out and I owe you a dinner or something. I realized too late I didn't have your number."

Jack hoped she wasn't going to berate him for hustling out of her apartment. Better yet, he hoped she wasn't going to mention that he was ever *in* her apartment. But she was a good sport, and started introducing him to her companions.

"This is Jenny, and Misty and Tammy," she said. "College friends." Inclining her head toward Jenny and Misty, she continued. "These two work at Culver's and Tammy works in the same office with me."

Jack rolled through the names in his head, trying to remember them and be polite. The one named Tammy spoke up.

"I know," she giggled. "Four girls whose names all end in 'eeee'. Pretty weird, right?"

Jack was smiling, mostly because Patty hadn't made him look silly.

"Not at all. They're nice names. Is Culver's the restaurant by the highway? I think I saw it on the way in."

The ladies didn't realize that Jack was avoiding the issue that was bound to bubble to the surface. Somebody was going to ask how he met Patty.

"That's it," Jenny said. "It's a nice place with great food. Come by and you'll get the family discount."

Her friendly comment and demeanor prompted Jack to address the topic head-on. There might have been some talk about the past weekend, and he'd best get out in front of it. For one brief moment, he flashed on the sobering thought that maybe Danielle's remark about the 'Crushers and the bar' included him ending up in Patty's apartment. Maybe Danielle was thinking he was some kind of player. Now was the time to start setting the record straight, if it needed straightening.

"Did Patty tell you about how she saved me when some guy whacked me with a bottle? She knew I'd had my head scrambled, so she took care of me and didn't let me go wandering off alone. I probably would have walked out of here right in front of a car or something, if not for her."

Jack hoped that this straightforward and truthful rendition would head off any rumors to the contrary. He didn't notice any of the girls exchanging knowing glances. Maybe this one time, with luck, the truth just might win out. After all, he really had nothing to do with going to her apartment. She took him there, and everything that happened indicated that she was just being an angel of mercy.

"So this is the guy?" asked the one named Misty. "Patty said she met a baseball player who got clobbered, but didn't mention anything about a rescue. You're some kind of hero," she directed at Patty.

"I think so, too," Jack said.

Relief poured over him. Apparently the details about the visit hadn't been mentioned. It never occurred to him that by being silent, Patty might have been avoiding loose talk and innuendo about herself. He decided she was an upright nice girl and he would speak kindly about her, starting now.

"I meant what I said about a dinner," he added. "Tomorrow night, if you want. I hear Culver's is the perfect place."

He winked at Jenny, for effect, and was rewarded with her giggle. Patty knew that Jack wasn't a permanent fixture in this town, and there was no reason to get any ideas.

"You don't have to buy me dinner, Jack," she said. "You can hang out with us anytime you want. And let us know when you're back in town for a game. We'll all show up."

"Well, there you go," Jack said. "I do owe you a good turn, and I'm going to be here Saturday and Sunday. Shall I get four tickets for all of you?"

The girls looked at one another and smiled. Finally, the one named Jenny spoke up.

"I think it would be great, so let's go!"

Jack clapped his hands like a magician.

"It's a done deal. Which night?"

Patty spoke for all of them as she looked at the group for approval.

"Saturday's good for me," and all the others nodded.

"Okay," Jack said. "Come to the ticket booth and there will be four tickets in Patty's name. I hope you have a great time. And Patty, thank you again."

Jack headed out the door and didn't hear the teasing Patty endured.

"Ooh, he's cute," Misty said. "And you just want to hang out? Better drink some more, girlfriend."

Before long Jack was back in his room and happy to lie down. He'd put a lot into painting and throwing with Duncan. Danielle hadn't done him any favors and that bothered him. But Jack was painfully aware that he couldn't make everyone happy. If it turned out that he had only Sally and Duncan's approval, he would have to be happy with two out of three. That would be a good day at the plate, in anybody's scorebook.

Still, he hoped Danielle's attitude wouldn't mess things up. If that happened, it would be too bad, because he liked Duncan and Sally.

He always preferred to just get along with people, but that girl seemed to be looking for trouble.

Conceding that Danielle might be good-looking didn't require that he let her add to his problems. Her support would be nice, but not essential. She could 'eat her lunch all by herself,' as the man said in the Eagles song. That happy thought took Jack to bed and a working man's sleep.

19

THE BEST-LAID PLANS OFTEN AIN'T

Elizabeth Ridley always tried to arrange her schedule so that either she or his father would be at Jack's ball games. It wasn't always possible if the high school team had to travel. But for local games, Jack was pretty sure to see one of them, or both, in the stands. He knew they weren't there for cheerleading. His father was an avid student of the game, and his mother just wanted to be there for her son.

John Ridley wasn't like some other dads. He never yelled during a game. Jack had seen a teammate's father berate an umpire, or coach, or even his son. It was always embarrassing and usually compromised the kid's play even more. If Mr. Ridley had something to say about a particular play, it waited until the ride home. Sometimes, the thought was important enough that the conversation would continue after supper. But his dad's calm and analytical approach to the game helped Jack develop a quiet and competent demeanor that translated into confidence. Especially with the pitchers.

For after-school games, Ashley was old enough and didn't need supervision at home. They weren't so close in age that they competed for space, and not so far apart that they didn't know each other. With his baby sister, Jack was a calm and steadfast protector.

Ashley looked up to her older brother. He wasn't always attentive, but *he certainly was kind. By the time she was past toddler stage, Jack was involved in his own world of Little League. But if they were home together, Ashley could coax him into having a tea party, or watching a Disney movie.*

They grew up in a pleasant situation, and Jack didn't mind the fact that he had the occasional role of caretaker. Their mother was eminently good-hearted but also a pragmatic down-to-earth individual. She didn't get excited about run-of-the mill bumps and scrapes, so when it came to childhood drama, Ashley went to her brother for sympathy. It was another example of Jack's considerate nature that everyone liked.

By the time Jack was in high school, Ashley had grown into a sharp and independent little girl. Invariably, she came to Jack for help with homework and emotional support. When trouble arrived and Mrs. Ridley needed to explain matters to her children, she naturally wanted Jack with his little sister.

She waited until Jack came home and she sat her children down in the front room. Her demeanor was peculiar, Jack could see. It was clear they had been called together for a crucial issue.

"I've got some hard news, kids," she said somberly. "Your dad got sick today and had to go to the hospital."

The truth was that he'd suffered a debilitating stroke, and was not likely to recover. He was not yet fifty years old, and his robust nature had given no hint of poor health.

"When he gets better, he will come home and I'll take care of him here."

She did not voice what she expected. All indications were that he would suffer a steady decline and would not live out the year. Ashley had been sitting with her brother while this bad news was delivered. She didn't understand all that her mom was saying; instinctively, she knew the worst day of her life had arrived.

When the frightened tears began, Ashley clung to Jack throughout the evening. They were inseparable. Her brother put her to bed, speaking softly and soothingly until she eased into merciful sleep. By morning, Jack had made a decision. Any plans to go away to college would have to be postponed indefinitely.

"Mom, I don't need to start anything right away. I can go to school later when things get settled."

His mother feared the disruption would derail his schooling completely. Jack assured her that he did not plan to forego college permanently. He joined with his mother in home care when his dad was released from the hospital. Jack discovered very quickly that it was actually a home hospice arrangement, and that his father was slowly drifting away.

John Ridley's speech and thought patterns had deteriorated to the point that he could not speak clearly enough to be understood. It was a painful process, and Jack did his best to explain to Ashley what was happening. He also took pains to shield her from the more disturbing aspects of his father's condition. After nine months, their father finally slipped away, and Jack was Ashley's support and refuge.

Mr. Ridley died the summer after Jack graduated from high school. The college semester loomed, but Jack's first instinct was to stay home so he could help his mother and sister. That arrangement precluded any of the big school programs that had recruited him. As the summer waned, Jack hit on an idea that would keep him close to home.

"The Reds are still interested in me," he told his mother. "They have a minor league team close by, and they want me to play. I'd make better money than working construction, and still be close enough to help here."

His mother was troubled but eventually allowed that Jack would know what was best.

So Jack joined the minor league toward the end of the season, after signing a three-year rookie contract. His signing bonus went right into the bank. It wasn't long before some local businessmen got him invested in a new sporting goods store. They proved to be prescient in their business acumen. Jack became an absentee owner in a business that allowed him to play professional baseball.

Some players find the transition to life after baseball to be difficult. For Jack, that goal had already been met. He had a successful partial season, and returned to business during the offseason. His growing celebrity and hope of a fruitful major league career combined to push sales upward.

Jack was ready to play at the beginning of the next season. He took up *where he left off with the minor league team, and became the heir apparent to the big club's catching position. His hitting averages were in the upper echelon and he advanced to The Show late in the season. Sportswriters projected him as a starter for the coming year, as Jack played in numerous games for the remainder of the schedule.*

It appeared that his contract had been timed perfectly. If he had a breakout season in the final year of his contract, he would be in a position to demand and receive top dollar from the club. Maybe he'd become a free agent and let the rest of the league compete for his services.

Whatever the result of contract negotiations, it was a foregone conclusion that Jack Ridley was going to be a wildly successful and wealthy baseball player. Everyone in the organization told him so. It was all they talked about at the owner's Thanksgiving party for the team and club employees.

As Jack left the party with Mr. Hutch's daughter, all agreed that he had become the Golden Boy. Some even said he might become the owner's son-in-law, and could be one step away from becoming their boss. That was fine with them. From the moment he had arrived, the young catcher had treated the entire Reds family kindly. Be it team members, office management, or cleaning staff - all met with courtesy and decency from Jack. Everyone looked forward to the bright days ahead, with Jack Ridley as the face of the franchise. Nothing was going to interfere with such a promising future. Absolutely nothing could.

20

OPERA MEETS BASEBALL

T he roundabout route to the farm had been a pleasant deviation, so Jack headed that way again. He bypassed stopping for breakfast, opting to eat the other half of the huge sandwich from last night. Water from the pump would do to wash it down.

Looking back on last night's events was refreshing. Music with the band at the bar had been an unexpected diversion. You never know when you are going to run into a good player. Jack had been in similar bars when patrons sit in with the band, and last night could have been a musical ordeal. That was usually the case. But sometimes a random librarian-looking guy rips off amazing guitar runs or astounding keyboard technique. Talent appears everywhere and in surprising places.

The high school knock-around bands in Jack's youth hadn't been terribly inventive. They were just a few guys banging on guitars and drums. At times, they made sounds that weren't eviction grade. Some of the kids liked them and had them play at parties. It was a great way to meet people, especially ladies. A guitar was a great ice-breaker.

Exposure to 'cover songs' was a side benefit. That's how Jack knew a few of the tunes the band in the Zone had been rehearsing. If he happened to be at hand when they were playing sometime, Jack wouldn't object to joining in on a tune or two. They had seemed sincere about inviting him to play, so why not?

The thought of musical talent appealed to him right now, as the morning sun made everything look new and fresh. He glanced at his song list and chose one that always brought him to thoughts of beauty and grace. He had meant what he said to Duncan about classic rock and country and opera. While he had not been raised in an opera-loving home, he had periodically heard some of the more notable singers.

Then, in his senior year, an interesting thing happened. The music teacher at the school, Mr. Zishka, was also a baseball fan. It was easy to notice Jack working his way up the team ladder, and the two of them became friends. Inevitably, Jack's inquisitive nature caused him to delve into areas beyond baseball, and the music teacher's insight crept into their wide-ranging debates.

Once, they were discussing exercise and training as essential for game preparation. Mr. Zishka compared the process to voice training. Like most folks, Jack had assumed that singing talent was a naturally occurring gift. He was intrigued when Mr. Zishka explained that pitching and high level singing were comparable, to the extent that both required mastery of physical mechanics.

Fascinated, Jack wanted to know more. He discovered that producing operatic sound depended on a delicate relationship between the larynx, diaphragm, abdominal and even back muscles. The skill of world-class opera singers impressed Jack immensely. He learned that they filled huge opera houses, not with amplification, but with sheer physical power.

"They are like athletes," Jack noted.

Mr. Zishka told him that one singer had written that opera singers 'were the power lifters of the singing world.'

That thought captured Jack completely. Imagine: power lifting as a concept relating to mere singing. He wanted to know who had originated such an idea. Mr. Zishka did an interesting thing when Jack asked his question. The teacher did not give an outright answer.

"Opera is about all kinds of things in life," he said. Then he suggested a strategy for Jack to find the answer himself.

"You come up with something that you would be interested in, coming from an opera song. Let me know, and I'll find a piece that will have more meaning for you."

Jack thought it over for a day or two. He knew opera could be about battles, death, intrigue, betrayal, and love. When he had formulated an idea, he approached Mr. Zishka.

"I'd like to hear one about a girl who loves a boy. It'd be a switch from the usual 'boy chasing girl' idea."

"Well, there's plenty in that direction," was Mr. Zishka's quick response. "I've got one in mind where the girl is telling her father about a boy she loves. How's that sound?"

"Great," Jack countered. "What is it?"

"It's a piece about one hundred years old, but it's powerful and current. I hope you like Italian!"

This was Jack's introduction to Puccini's 'O mio babbino caro' which Mr. Zishka said was sort of the 'Twist and Shout' of opera. Jack was hooked. The music teacher explained the song's premise.

"This one is the story of a girl telling her father about a boy she loves. If the father doesn't accept him, she intends to jump into a river."

"Okay, that's for real," Jack said. "Who sings it?"

Mr. Zishka was running through some famous names in his head. Numerous opera singers have graced that particular song.

"There's plenty, and you get to pick your favorite," he said. "But I'm going out on a limb and tell you mine. It's the same person who made the 'power lifting' comment that I like."

And so came the moment Jack heard music as more than cute lyrics and catchy pop tunes. Mr. Zishka gave him a CD from soprano artist Renée Fleming.

"Her singing takes you to a place of beauty and warmth," he said.

"It's powerful and direct. The emotional depth is hard to describe, but you know when it grabs you. At least, that's it for me."

Jack understood completely.

"I get it. I know it's not the same thing, but baseball can do that for you. It can be just beautiful, and perfect, and makes you feel you're connected to something larger than yourself."

"Exactly!" Mr. Zishka agreed. "And it's interesting how people take meaning from different sources. It doesn't have to be only one thing. You want to guess if there've been ballplayers singing opera on the way to the ballpark?"

Jack thought combining the two seemingly different areas sounded cool.

"That makes sense. How can a jock not like a singer who sees weightlifting in her art?"

He played the song about a girl who desperately wanted her father to accept her love - so desperately that she threatened to harm herself, if he decided otherwise. Like many folks who are captured by the beauty and majesty of opera, Jack was changed forever. Fleming's singing was graceful and powerful and it reached him on a visceral level.

Heading back to the farm, Jack included music's spiritual uplift in the journey. He was giving it his best, trying to help Duncan find his way into baseball - the world of beauty and grace and athletic excellence. But despite his best effort, Danielle was hacking on him, and he couldn't understand why.

Clearly, his spirts and outlook needed a boost. And 'Babbino Caro' did not fail. By the time Jack pulled into the driveway, the People's Diva, as her fans called Fleming, had brought his flagging psyche back to game form.

Welcoming shade provided the location where Duncan was setting up paint cans on the other side of the barn.

"Hey, Jack," he called. "I thought you'd be here later. Going out on the tractor was my plan, but painting can start now. Your help means a lot. I thought I'd be on this barn for the whole summer. We're gonna get it done a lot quicker."

Jack was in a much better mood than the one he'd left in last night.

"I originally wanted to make your mom happy so she wouldn't think I was useless. Now I want to make sure it's a good job. Can't say I'll be here for the whole thing, but at least your mom seems to like the effort."

Duncan was enthused.

"You bet she does. She's a big fan of yours."

Jack went ahead and faced the issue.

"But there's somebody who's not?"

"Danny's working on it," Duncan said with a grimace. "She got her attitude adjusted after you left last night. Hasn't figured it out yet. She thinks jocks are a problem. She sees you show up and hears you're going to be a 'baseball help' for no reason. So, she's not sure what's going on."

Jack listened, knowing that an interruption would probably get in the way of Duncan working through the issue.

"Could be partly my fault," Duncan admitted. "I let them get used to the idea that I was done with baseball. I guess I was. Then you appear, out of the blue. With your baseball idea, and all. She was just surprised, I suppose."

Jack was philosophical about the issue.

"It's not required that she approves, but it'd be nice if everybody is pulling in the same direction."

"Trust me, she had a 'come to Jesus' moment with mom last night," Duncan said. "Mom likes what you're doing and knows you're coming from a good place. She told Danny to give you a chance."

That made Jack feel better. He wasn't looking for a prom date; he just wanted to be appreciated.

With that happy thought, the boys grabbed their brushes and dove in. They had a rhythm going now, and were putting paint on the wall with surprising speed.

"Have you done a lot of painting?" Duncan asked. "You're pretty good."

Jack didn't mind discussing his work philosophy.

"As I said, when I was young, my dad had jobs for me that I didn't like. I realize now that I spent more time complaining and avoiding the work than it probably took to do it. For this job, it isn't so bad because we're only doing it once. Plus, I learned from my uncle 'if a job is worth doing, it's worth doing well.' He had a song about it. Every time I start to hear it, the darn thing slips away. I'm gonna remember it someday."

Pausing to search his memory, Jack could only recall a short phrase.

"It says 'breathe a spell' and 'any work that's worthwhile doing is worth doing well' or something like that." Jack ended the moment with a sheepish grin.

Duncan was humoring Jack's lyrical diversion. If his new-found mentor wanted to spout a weird song, there was no harm in it. They began talking about today's topic: taking the fastball and making it continue to look like a fastball while it was really an off-speed change-up.

Jack was silently grateful that Sally and Duncan were sending Danielle a change-up of their own. The painting continued without interruption for a couple of hours. Jack re-emphasized the importance of being able to deliver a pitch that put the batter off-balance. And the change-up was the way to do it.

When it was approaching noon, they were mildly jolted when Sally appeared and told them she'd been working on a lunch surprise. She complimented them on the large amount of work they had been able to accomplish.

"Two sets of hands are really better than one," she laughed.

Jack was struck by how friendly and vivacious she appeared when she was amused. 'She sure must have had the boys lined up when she was young,' he thought to himself. In spite of himself, he noticed similarities between Sally and her daughter. He was immediately embarrassed that his mind went in that direction. Berating himself for the images, he must have had a troubled look on his face. Sally noticed.

"What's wrong, Jack?"

"He's just hopped-up because Danny's treating him so lousy," Duncan chimed in. "I didn't tell him about our little discussion last night."

Sally sighed and turned toward the house.

"Put the brushes away and come in for lunch," she said. "Let me tell you a thing or two about my daughter."

————

The boys headed to the outside water pump to hose off and wash their hands. Then, the three of them sat down for a dining experience that Jack would never associate with a farm lunch. Sally had been working hard; while the boys were painting, she was preparing food that a fine chef would envy. Jack would be a poor contestant on a cooking show, so the entire experience was a revelation.

Sally started them off with what she called a Harvest salad. It had spinach and walnuts, with dried cranberries and blue cheese. She sprinkled in chopped tomatoes and some avocado, with a hint of red onions, topped with raspberry jam, red wine vinegar and walnut oil. Jack was so impressed that he started writing down the ingredients.

"Are you going to get into cooking, Jack?" Sally asked.

"No, I'm going to show my mom that I'm meeting people who *can* cook," he laughed. "She's always saying that I'm a 'TV dinner single guy mess' and I just might show her different!"

Sally shifted into high gear when she presented them with an entrée designed to shame mere sandwiches. She had actually prepared homemade crêpes to accompany smoked ham with salted butter. Fresh from the oven, provolone cheese melted on the ham in a glorious landslide. Jack was entranced with the whole experience.

"I've ever had anything like this," he exclaimed. "It's so darn good. Plus, I don't think I've ever had crêpes. How did you make them?"

Sally looked slightly peeved, for a brisk moment. Then she explained her exasperation.

"To do it right, you need to make them the night before. And to tell the truth, I was upset with you-know-who. I decided to work off the snit by making something special. So, crêpes are the logical 'night before' item."

Jack was intrigued by the effort.

"So you make some kind of batter, or what?"

"You are getting into this, aren't you?" Sally said. "Duncan, pay attention. It's called 'culinary arts' and you might learn something."

"Well, golly," Jack countered. "Some of the best chefs in the world are men. Everybody knows that! I just need to spend some time on it. My mom said if I learned to cook, ladies would notice."

"She's exactly right," Sally said. "Tell her you've learned the secret to making crêpes is to make the batter the night before. You let the batter stay chilled overnight, and then you cook them individually in a skillet. I'll show you the recipe."

"Well, it's all just amazing and tastes great. For someone like me who gets by on restaurants or fast food, this is an eye-opener. I really would like to make this for my mother. And my sister. They don't believe I can do anything useful!"

Duncan had been viewing this exchange with silent amusement. His mother and his baseball expert buddy sounded like a couple of Martha Stewart wannabees. The word 'culinary' made him laugh outright. He decided it was time to steer the conversation toward a less happy topic.

"Back to last night's little talk. For once, you got on somebody besides me."

Sally grimaced slightly at an inward thought. Jack steeled himself just a bit for whatever revelation might be forthcoming. She began tentatively.

"When your kids are young, you try to keep close watch on their behavior and language. It's basically that children are just learning, so if they say or do something stupid, you owe it to them to jump in and set them straight."

She paused to mull this over.

"When they are supposed to be adults you need to back off a bit to allow them to be their own person."

Jack tried to be helpful.

"That makes sense, because I've read that brains don't fully develop until the mid-twenties anyway." He injected humor by adding self-deprecation. "I'm waiting for it to happen to me."

Duncan grinned and Sally raised an eyebrow to let Jack know she appreciated his point.

"I read it too, in anatomy class. It's called 'pre-frontal cortex' and you're right."

Jack was thinking that there was a world of knowledge that he could learn from this woman. He certainly hadn't started the day anticipating cooking and anatomy. Sally returned to her topic.

"Last night, we were enjoying a great moment. You two had just knocked out a big chunk of the barn painting job. I have to say, when you said you'd help, I thought it might be for a couple of hours. Just for show, sort of. But you've got Duncan doing more than I ever thought would get done. It won't be long, at this rate, the whole thing will be finished. I've wanted that, for a long time."

She paused to sip the lemonade she'd prepared to top off the lunch.

"In addition to the barn painting, I've watched you start working on pitching with Duncan. I had thought that was going to be some quick deal as well. But you've really put your heart into that, I can see. Duncan has been paying attention to what you are saying, like never before. I know he is learning from you. You know things about baseball that nobody here could teach him. This hare-brained idea he brought home scared me at first."

Sally stopped to look directly at Jack.

"But you showed me you mean business," she said. "You've given Duncan a bounce in his step that hasn't been there since David died."

Jack held himself perfectly still. Sally was discussing personal aspects of her life, and Duncan's life. Jack wanted to be respectful. It occurred to him that she probably hadn't broached her husband's passing at all. It was too fresh. What she was doing isn't easy.

Most folks aren't very good at introspection. Looking at details of your own life requires objectivity, and Sally's attempt was honest. Jack was making his own bid at renewal, helping Duncan fulfill a potential that few people possessed. There are only a hundred or so people on the planet who can perform at the level Jack envisioned for Duncan. And his mother was talking about coming to believe that it was possible. Belief would be essential, for any hope that this kid could succeed. Now that Jack knew more about Sally, he wanted it for her, too. Sally must have been on the same wavelength. She began to speak about having the same feeling.

"All of this was combining to let me think that your plan for Duncan just might work. Maybe he *could* pitch a little with the Crushers, to see what he can do. And it's something that I can't do at all for him. I don't know anything about helping with baseball. With his dad gone, I never would. And I was afraid that meant Duncan never would get a chance. Then you arrive, and are really trying to make it work. I started to allow myself to be happy about it."

She sniffed a bit because she was emotional about the words she had been saying. Moreover, she was slightly angry about what she was going to say.

"So, we were finishing the day. These nice things were going on, and Danielle came home. I wanted her to be supportive about what you were doing for her brother. She should see that things were developing that were making him happy. We haven't really been able to just be joyful about anything since..." and she paused, with memories of the past year flowing back to her. "And instead of saying something nice about it, Danielle just popped the whole balloon."

Sally was getting a bit worked up over the topic, Jack thought. But he didn't speak. She needed to have her say.

"After you left, she basically said it wasn't right for you to be getting involved, and I just wanted to slap her! Can you imagine that?"

She grimaced at the thought.

"I can't believe I was thinking that! I've never touched these kids, ever. But it wasn't right, and I told her so. I told her how hard you've been trying with Duncan, and she should respect that. I told her a lot more and she wasn't too happy about how I was handling it."

Duncan had been silent the whole time. When his mother paused, he patted her arm to show support.

"It isn't that bad, Mom," he said. "She's as tough as you are, and just as stubborn. But she knows you're right. And she thinks she should have been a little nicer to Jack, too. I told her about the way you're helping," he directed at Jack.

Sally brightened at that.

"She said that to you?"

"Not exactly. I get the feeling that's how she's thinking. I talked to her this morning before she went to work, and she's not mad about it."

Sally collected herself and continued.

"She's not a bad person. She's really sweet and loving. It's just that she has some misgivings about athlete types. Danny was never that into sports, but she didn't put down Duncan's playing baseball. Then, in college, she met this boy that played basketball. That's a pretty serious sport at the school she attended."

Jack nodded, aware of the syndrome.

"She wasn't too sure about dating a ballplayer, but it did become pretty serious by her senior year. I know they had talked about making plans. She told him about wanting a family, the whole thing. So, it wasn't just casual. Her father and I figured the boy was going to be the one."

Jack could imagine what happened next.

"It didn't work out and she's wary of ball players?"

Sally nodded once.

"It's way worse than 'didn't work out.' She thought they were serious. No ring yet, but then she found out he was pulling the same thing with another girl."

Jack assumed the worst.

"There was an ugly break-up?"

"Not at all," Sally answered. "No talking. You don't do that girl wrong and expect to discuss it! No, siree."

Thinking about the event made Sally shake her head.

"Danny just walked away from him and never looked back. He tried to tell her it was a mistake; he was sorry; they should get back together. It was the whole self-recrimination thing. She wouldn't have any part of it."

Sally paused with a wry grin at the memory.

"I was kind of proud of her, in a way. She made it clear she wasn't going to put up with that sort of stuff, and that was that. She stuck to her guns, too. He spent six months trying to remake his act. Nope. Nothing doing! Mess with that girl and you don't get away with it."

Jack was impressed.

"Good for her! It's the same thing I tell Ashley. The college boys are after her, too. What's that saying? 'People tell you all the time who they are. You just need to listen to them.' That's the hard part, 'cause you don't want to believe they're capable of messing you over."

Sally came back to her point.

"That's all true, but she shouldn't be rude to you because of the baggage she's got. She should look at what you're doing for her brother, me, and maybe our family, and be happy about it."

Jack decided it was time to be his encouraging self.

"Well, let's give her some space." Then he grinned at Duncan and winked at Sally. "If I can get this knuckle-head on track, there might be something for her to be happy about, after all. Maybe. *If* I'm lucky."

Duncan showed he had a wise-crack of his own.

"Don't worry, Jack," he said. "She does think you're cute."

21

IT FEELS DIFFERENT UNTIL IT DOESN'T

Pitching class was back in session. Jack profusely thanked Sally for the lunch. As the boys walked to their positions, Duncan complimented his mother.

"She put a lot into that, for sure. I don't know if it was because she was jacked up about Danny giving you a hard time, or because she wants to be nice to you for helping out. Probably a bit of both."

Jack was glad for the encouragement.

"Either way, she's some kind of a food artist. Did she do a lot of that fancy cooking when you were growing up?"

"Not really," Duncan said. "She'd pour it on for something special, like a birthday or Christmas. I'm thinking she just has this part of her lurking in the background, and she rolls it out on occasion."

The idea of hidden talent struck Jack as being applicable to what they were attempting here.

"If you think about it, we're working on bringing out a talent you have. And believe me, Mr. Cake, it's a talent. Not everybody can throw a baseball into little three-inch squares sixty feet away. And remember, those little squares move every time."

Duncan was in a teasing mood.

"I've heard it's sixty feet and six inches, but who's counting?"

Jack took a playful swing at Duncan.

"Good idea - jerking me around. Remember, your mom likes me."

The jousting continued as Duncan gave Jack a shove.

"I'd rough you up but an old guy like you probably has a heart condition."

They both were laughing as they arrived at their throwing site.

"You get my point, right?" Jack asked. "There's your mom, out of the clear blue, throwing down a cooking exhibition that any TV food show would love to have. Some folks just amaze you. People walk up to a microphone, just nobodies, and belt out a song that makes you never forget their voice. You see some guy on the street painting portraits of people he's never seen before. And they look perfect, like something out of a museum. You just have to sit back and be ready to appreciate what they can do."

Jack paused for effect.

"Then there's you. Some jackass who can throw a ball. If he plays his cards right, he might get to throw to the big boys. Another thing of beauty."

Duncan responded in a somber tone.

"Only one problem with your analysis."

Jack waited for the answer.

"I'm not the jackass. I'm the Dunc-an. You're the Jack-ass."

"Okay, that did it. Now, I'm throwing at your head."

Jack took the ball from Duncan and repeated the demonstration of the grip they were using the day before.

"We were throwing a fastball using this four-seam grip. It gets to the plate relatively straight, so most guys like it when they need to throw a strike. Make sense?"

Duncan agreed.

"Sure. Your curve might not be in the strike zone as often as a straight pitch."

"Exactly. Here's the kicker. You have to be able to throw it by them, a fastball, that is, but if they are expecting it, they'll take you out. That's where off-speed stuff comes in. So we're going to build on the same grip, using the same throwing motion."

Duncan nodded his understanding.

"So, if they're expecting one pitch, you try to give them something else, right?"

"It's that easy," Jack said. "And it's that complicated."

Jack mimicked a baseball windup.

"Your goal is that the batter gets accustomed to a regular delivery, each one indistinguishable from any other. When different pitches come from the same look, the batter is at a disadvantage, in the half second, or less, they have to make up their mind."

He motioned for Duncan to hand over his glove, and put his own hand inside.

"You get used to adjusting your grip for each pitch so you never look at the ball. Your hand, and the grip you're using, is always concealed from the batter. It's all inside the glove. He can't see your hand, and the ball, until the ball is being released."

Jack returned the glove.

"So you've got a guy expecting a fastball. Could be for a lot of reasons. Maybe you're behind in the count and he knows he's looking at the pitcher's default mode: Throw the fastball because that's the most guaranteed strike."

Duncan was listening intently and Jack took his slight nod to signify understanding.

"But, if you've got the guts to change it up on him, and you can throw a strike, an off-speed pitch will have him swinging so far out in front of the pitch he'll never hit it. Because, when the change is thrown to look like a fastball, it's moving about ten percent slower. The human eye can't see the difference. And that's enough."

Duncan hadn't heard this analysis before.

"What do you mean, the human eye can't see?"

Jack was in full instruction mode.

"It's not that the eye can't see. It's physics. You have less than one half of a second to decide what you're going to do with a ninety mile-an-hour fastball. The eye has to see the ball and decipher speed and trajectory during the first two-thirds of the distance to the plate. And in that short period of time, if the change is thrown right, it looks like a fastball. The decision to swing is made too soon. Bingo, you get a swing and a miss. They say the ability to pick up on a thrown ball and hit it is the hardest thing to do in athletics."

Jack paused for effect. He had one more point for emphasis.

"Hitting a ball thrown by a major league pitcher is so difficult that one of the greatest athletes ever still had trouble."

Duncan was all-in, and waited for the answer.

"Ever hear of Michael Jordan? He tried baseball as a second career. Only hit .200 at double A. It ain't easy, kid."

Jack let that soak in and Duncan mulled it over.

So much information was rolling around that Jack wondered if Duncan could handle it all. If a pitcher could master the basics to 'trip up' a batter's timing, he would be equipped to outduel the best hitters baseball had to offer. But Duncan seemed comfortable enough so far, so Jack emphasized the mechanics of the change-up.

"The trick is having the batter see the same arm speed for *both* the heater and the change. That's critical. A fastball is thrown with an aggressive power move. You have to show the batter the same motion, so he thinks it's a fastball in the half-second he has to analyze what's going on."

Jack held the ball with the four-seam grip.

"Do you see how the ball is separated from your palm? Basically, held there by your first two fingers? That gets the ball out of your hand, faster, with less resistance from your hand."

Duncan quickly saw the mechanics.

"So, if you put the ball farther back in your hand, it gets released slower?"

Jack was pleased at his student's grasp of the concept.

"Right, plus you increase the 'hand friction' by having all your fingers on the ball. That extra contact slows the ball just slightly as it leaves your hand, and there's your pitch."

Jack took it one more step.

"Some pitchers have trouble at first with a change, because they don't feel they have the same control they do with a fastball. Well, you don't! So, you de-focus on throwing the ball to a spot, and just throw to the plate in general. You let the speed do the work. I used to tell the guys, 'It's like when you were starting out. You weren't thinking about pinpoint control, you were just trying to get it across the plate!' Do that, and the ball does the rest."

Duncan was adjusting his grip on the ball, and Jack showed him a thumb placement underneath the ball.

"They call this the 'claw' grip, because when your thumb is down low, like this, your four fingers form a claw on the top of the ball. Plus, the ball is shoved back in your hand. More friction. Slower release. Slower pitch. Changed timing."

They started tossing the ball from their original distance. Jack reminded Duncan that they were starting at half speed, to get loose. After about ten minutes, Jack decided they were ready.

"Go ahead and start with the four-seam fastball. Give me six or seven to get the feel of the release again."

Duncan went into his motion and delivered the ball right down the middle of the plate.

"Good speed, good placement," Jack said. "Keep 'em coming."

The next half dozen throws were well-placed, and Duncan maintained the same speed. It was time to change velocity.

"Now add ten percent so we get closer to a real time motion," Jack advised.

Duncan pumped up the speed for a few pitches and Jack was happy. This kid seemed so coachable.

"Okay, let's revise the grip and ease into the changeup. Don't worry where the ball is going; your grip and arm motion are what matter."

Duncan adjusted his four-seam grip into the four-finger claw grip. It felt clumsy and he said so.

"Feels really weird."

"It should. You've never done it before. After a few thousand repetitions, you won't think about it. You can modify where you place your thumb, where it feels more comfortable. The point is the ball is deep in your hand. You get a little drop on the ball when you bring your thumb up closer to your index finger. Sort of a circle. That's called a 'circle change' and some use it. Others don't."

Duncan nodded and settled in. His first pitch sputtered out of his hand and bounced.

"It feels like it's gonna fall out of my hand."

"Different, right?" Jack countered. "It feels different, until it doesn't. Just focus on the same delivery as the fastball, and we'll be fine."

They continued practicing the same throw, again and again. Duncan was getting the ball more consistently to the strike zone. When he started to sweat a bit, Jack called a halt.

"Looks to me like it's settling in. Your arm position looks good. I'd say you're just a bit off in the motion. The batter has to see the same 'explosive' move to the plate, but you're getting there. Feeling any arm trouble?"

Duncan shook his head and wiped his eyes with his sleeve.

Jack thought it would be a good time to sit and rest, and let the idea of the slower pitch soak in.

"The thing about the change is, it's just a hair behind the fastball, in terms of arrival at the plate. If you could see the two pitches simultaneously, the fastball is just past the plate while the change is at the front of the plate. It's that close, but it works because of the timing the batter has to have, to get wood on the ball. His same swing, because the pitches look the same, means he's barely behind the fastball and barely in front of the change."

At the risk of overdoing things, Jack threw in another teaching point.

"You know, there's something else just as important as your arm."

Duncan was ready with an answer.

"What Maddux said? That thing between your ears?"

Jack smiled, gratified that the kid had been paying attention.

"Yes, but I was thinking of legs. Lower body strength is just as important as arm strength for throwing. If you want to prove it, compare your normal throw to what you get sitting down and trying to throw. Most folks don't know that big league pitchers spend more time on strength training than they spend actually throwing. But we'll get to that later. For this weekend, we'll be looking at three batters, max. You won't have much of a strength issue."

Again, Duncan seemed to be absorbing all the information. Jack felt comfortable with the kid's progress so far. He decided to call a halt with a bit of levity.

"So far, so good, Mr. Cake?"

The nickname seemed to amuse Duncan.

"Okay if I call you J.A.? How 'bout Mr. J.A.?"

They both laughed and high-fived. Today's lesson was a lot to handle, and Jack decided they should give it a break.

"We've had a big day. How about you just keep practicing the grip, getting your hand used to the feel? You need to be able to pop into different grips for different pitches without really thinking about it. When you're pitching, these basics aren't on your mind; you'll be thinking about placement and batter tendencies. But we'll get there soon enough."

They turned and headed back to the house. Elvis had been watching them and he got up to join them. Jack gave the dog a pat and sent a joke his way.

"You getting all of this, buddy?"

Elvis looked like he was thinking it over, and Duncan laughed all the way to the house. Getting out of there before Duncan's sister got home seemed like a good idea to Jack. He wasn't sure how he would handle talking with her after last night's little visit. Both boys were surprised to see her standing off to the side, observing their approach.

She was positioned where her mother had been, the day before. When the boys were throwing, a person stationed beside the barn was just out of their sight line.

Duncan spoke first.

"You're home early."

It was more of a question than a statement. Jack just waited, not knowing what to say. Danielle seemed thoughtful when she responded.

"Today is the last day of school, Duncan. The kids were finished right before noon. I finished a few reports, and here I am."

Her demeanor didn't seem quite the same as the last time, to Jack's thinking.

Duncan jumped in.

"You told me that. Sorry, Danny, I've been wrapped up in other stuff. How did it go?"

Danielle was ambivalent.

"It's been okay, for a first year. The kids are different from the first job I had. They just seem less inclined to do their schoolwork. I used to hear the older teachers talk about how the kids behave these days, and I thought they were just complaining. Now, I'm not so sure."

Duncan was conciliatory with his response.

"Well, I hope things get better for you, if you stay there."

She had a thoughtful expression on her face when she responded.

"Thanks, Cake. Or should I call you Mr. Cake?"

The look softened slightly when she said 'Mr. Cake' and Jack could see she was teasing them both. Then he wondered how much of their prior conversations she had overheard.

"I see you've been hard at it," she continued. "How's it working out?"

Duncan took up the slack.

"Pretty well. Jack knows his stuff."

"I can see that," Danielle said. "I'll be looking forward to the result."

The three of them had started back to the house, and Duncan broke the silence.

"Jack, are you hanging around, or what?"

Before Jack could answer, Danielle intervened.

"How about you go in and let mom know I'm home? I want to have a little talk with Jack."

Duncan peeled off without any comment. He did give Jack a sideways glance as he left. Jack was left standing there, sweaty and disheveled. He wondered if he was going to have a nice talk, or if he was headed to the woodshed.

Danielle motioned toward the fence that ran from the barn toward the first rows of corn, and spoke directly to Jack.

"Let's take a walk past the fence down to the creek."

Jack didn't see any woodshed on the way, but he still wasn't betting that a nice chat was coming.

22

SORRY SEEMS TO BE THE HARDEST WORD

"Can I say something first?" Jack asked.

He hoped to start things on a friendly note. Danielle didn't answer right away, and his nervousness caused Jack to speak hurriedly.

"Oops, with an English teacher, I should say, 'May I say something,' right?"

Danielle gave him a rueful smile.

"I'm off duty. So, I guess my mother was giving you my life story?"

Jack was quick to try to set her mind at ease.

"Not really. The topic of teaching came up, and I said my mom was an English teacher. One of them said you were, too. Or, maybe it happened in reverse order."

He gave a little shrug, hoping it appeared disarming.

"It's okay," Danielle said.

She paused for what seemed a long time, and she looked across the fields, and back toward Jack, and then back to the fields. Then she took a deep breath.

"I need to apologize to you. I spoke to you disrespectfully, and I was out of line."

Jack tried to smooth things over.

"It's no big deal."

She was not to be denied.

"My dad used to say, 'When you're wrong, act wrong.' So, here I am. It's just that I wasn't sure what was going on. You showed up, and both my mother and Duncan were saying what a wonder you were. And there's my mom, telling you we call him 'Cake.' I've never heard her tell anyone that."

Jack started to speak, and she held up her hand in an unofficial stop sign.

"Please, let me get through this. I've thought a lot about it. The three of us have been banded together, dealing with losing my dad. Everybody says they know how you're feeling, but they don't. The only ones who know are us. And I was thinking we were slowly getting it together, and then you come into the picture. It's complicated. I didn't know what your motivation was. I didn't know how your involvement would affect our handling of the situation. And worst of all, I didn't know if you would change things with Duncan. I know we jerk each other around a little bit, but deep down, I'm still his big sister and I look out for him."

Jack listened to it all with a bit of wonderment. Danielle had shown him a breadth of self-awareness that revealed a lot about her. It is not easy to be so forthcoming about your mistakes, especially with someone you barely know. Jack admired her show of character, and wanted to say so. He took his own deep breath, and tried a gentle question.

"May I talk now?"

Danielle shrugged and tried not to look embarrassed.

"I know this is an oddball situation," Jack said. "If I hadn't seen Duncan throw a great pitch, I wouldn't be here. I felt weird even approaching him and Skip."

"I heard about that catcher's mitt. People just don't give things to total strangers."

Jack spoke quietly.

"Some do. You can get this, can't you?"

He paused for a moment, because he needed to get his next words perfect.

"Life can be just too sad sometimes. You know that. When you lose someone, you realize how stupidly some people treat others. Maybe they've never had anything go wrong in their lives. What was it Shakespeare said? 'He jests at scars that never felt a wound.' Well, I've felt 'em. So have you. I'm just tired of all the meanness that goes on, so I deal with it by trying to be nice to folks."

Jack paused for a breath, and he realized that Danielle was intently observing him. He stumbled ahead.

"I know. People tell me I'm weird, trying to be a good guy, but I don't want to live the way they do. And you'd be surprised. Sometimes, people are nice right back."

Danielle realized that Jack's behavior should have spoken for itself, but she'd missed it.

"The nice people would be my mom and Duncan, while I was being stupid," she confessed.

Jack tried once again to put her mind at ease, permanently.

"Let me answer your questions, okay? Here's my motivation: Your brother has a lightning bolt for an arm, and it would be a sin to waste it. I think I can help avoid that, so my plan is to give him a chance to develop as a pitcher. Next, I was hoping the effort would be good for Duncan. Seemed like he was all alone, baseball-wise. Then I met your mother, and she is a neat person. I started hoping my involvement would be good for her, too. Finally, it never occurred to me that I would change things between you and Duncan. I don't think that's possible. I know he calls you goofy names, but deep down, he looks up to you and relies on you. Nobody could change that."

He stopped for another breath after his speech, and hoped it made some kind of sense.

Danielle thought that Jack had put it all in a nice perspective. A sort of calm came over her, as she realized she had an ally in looking after her kid brother.

She offered Jack an olive branch.

"I appreciate that. I like what you're doing for Duncan. Watching you work with him, I could tell that you're doing the right thing. And I felt like a fool for what I said. This is me, acting like I'm wrong. I'm sorry, Jack."

Jack gave her his best grin.

"Apology accepted. Call me J.A."

Danielle laughed out loud.

"You're too much. I can see you're going to grow on us. So you get to call him 'Cake,' I guess. That's fine with me."

Her smile was a little less tentative, now.

"It wasn't all your fault," Jack said. "Your mom explained to me that you had reason to wonder if a ballplayer was worth a damn."

Danielle returned to looking exasperated.

"She did, did she? Well, I guess I had that coming."

Jack had to defend Sally.

"Don't be rough on her. I think she had it in mind that I might be backing out, and things had been going pretty well. Don't worry, I made a promise. I am a man of my word. I'm going to see this through, as best I can. And if it doesn't work, I did my best. Mom always said 'All prayers are answered; sometimes the answer is no.' So, let's say our prayers for Duncan and see what happens."

Danielle liked this turn of events. She knew now that Jack was truly going to help her brother. Including Jack in her general classification about jocks from the past was unfair.

"I guess my mom figures I judge all men by the way the one she talked about behaved. And maybe I do, to some extent."

"No need to go into that," Jack said. "The past is over, right?"

Danielle thought she owed Jack a bit more.

"I met a guy in college, and didn't know he was some kind of sports hot shot. He was a charmer, and before I knew it, I was in a relationship. There were warning signs, and I blew right past them. I don't know why. Girls think 'it's going to be different' with them. *Dumb.* We were making plans, I guess. I even told him I wanted kids, like my mom. My mistake was thinking it would be like my parents' relationship. My dad would never do anything to hurt my mother, and that's what I wanted."

Danielle had to stop for moment as the memories of her father's kindness washed over her. She wondered if she would ever find such unbridled affection in a relationship. Reflecting on the possibility she might not succeed triggered self-doubt every time. Her voice revealed her misgivings.

"God, I was *dumb*. I caught him with one of my roommates when I came back to school from a trip home. And that was that. No more boyfriend."

Jack was sympathetic.

"Sounds pretty rough. You deserve to be treated nice, I know from Duncan and your mom."

They had looped around the fence and were heading back to the house. Jack was so immersed in the conversation he didn't notice that they didn't make it to the creek.

"You saying that means a lot," Danielle said. "I've been kicking myself for two years for getting sucked in by a charmer. Then you showed up, being a charmer. That's my excuse and I'm sticking to it."

Jack laughed at the reference to the song that used the same line.

"Are you going to break into a country song, or what?"

"You don't want to hear me sing. But mom did say you could show me a thing or two on my dad's guitar."

"Maybe one or two. But don't get carried away. I only know three chords. Or so."

They were nearing the porch. Jack wanted to say something nice, while they were still alone. He owed it to her, seeing as how Danielle had made the effort to patch things up.

"You know, you and Duncan have a great relationship for siblings. I could see that when he was trying to tell me you had a reason for not liking me. I like that, standing up for his sister. And I think it's kind of cute when he calls you 'Bo.' Very endearing."

Danielle gave him a sideways glance, as they climbed the porch steps.

"Easy, J.A. Don't go charming on me."

Jack was chuckling when they walked through the door. Sally liked what she saw.

"Looks like you two are doing fine."

Danielle directed a cool gaze at Duncan.

"We found out we have a common enemy. *You!*"

Even Duncan joined in the group laughter.

"I told you, Dunc, it's all about timing," Jack added. "And that one was pretty well-timed. When I really start working you, you *might* think I'm the enemy."

Everyone was grinning and Sally had food on her mind.

"Are we putting dinner together?"

All three were looking at Jack.

"You're asking me? I don't live here. But dinner sounds great."

"Okay, that's settled," Sally said. "I'm starting chicken. Danny and Jack, you start the salad. Cake, you get some biscuits going and set the table. Everybody, march."

Dinner was another happy experience. Jack enjoyed the family atmosphere and Sally was thinking their little group was healing, bit by bit. They hadn't laughed much since David James had passed away.

Jack regaled them with a story or two about baseball; Danielle recounted details of the kids' antics at school; Duncan let them in on his new-found pitching knowledge; Sally did her best to embarrass her kids about their childhood.

Nobody has the goods on a kid like their parents. Sally set the bar high. Both of her children were covering their eyes at her recollections. Their chagrined reactions made Jack laugh uproariously. He hadn't felt this good in years. While they were doing the dishes, Jack remembered he had bought an item for Sally.

"Hey, I left something out in my car."

He went out and brought back a package marked 'Andrews Music.'

"Know what they sell at the music store?"

Jack reached in the bag and pulled out new guitar strings.

"Thank God," Danielle breathed. "I thought it was going to be some 'self-help' book. Hard telling what you jock types are into."

"Nice," Jack smirked at her. "You realize your mother is on my side. I can probably get pictures of you with braces. Or worse."

He looked at Sally for support.

"Any of her 'powder the baby' shots lying around?"

Danielle hid her eyes. And so it went, until the dishes were put away.

Jack started re-stringing the guitar. An old Martin with new strings is a delight, and Jack strummed some chords.

"Can you play some techno stuff on that?" Duncan asked.

Jack was appalled.

"On a Martin? Do I look like a techno rebel? Good Lord."

To Sally, he continued the ribbing.

"What kind of music freak did you raise?"

Danielle jumped in.

"I believe mom deserves those acoustic love songs dad used to sing to her. Right?"

Sally nodded her faraway look and Jack was happy to play a Lightfoot tune for her. He figured 'Song For A Winter's Night' was love song enough. Sally even sang along on the harmony at the end.

"There's nothing like acoustic music and hanging around singing songs," Jack said, as he finished the tune. "Unless it's poking one over the wall," he lobbed toward Duncan.

The evening continued, and Jack realized it was the first enjoyable gathering he'd had in years. He had left his mother's home at a young age to join the baseball team. The athletic comradery lasted only a few months before he lost his place. Returning home to run the sporting goods store gave him a diversion, but he was operating in a fog.

His father's passing and the departure from the team had placed Jack in emotional gridlock. The summer travel he hoped would jog him into some sort of revival hadn't worked. He would return to the store in the same personal freefall. Even easing into occasional baseball games, to soothe his psyche, had not restored him. But now, by the grace of happenstance, he felt his spirts being revived.

The night ended with happy words from everyone. As he said goodnight to the James family, Jack reflected that these strangers were helping him reboot his personal outlook. Helping to build Duncan's future was, at a minimum, edging toward salvaging his own. That pleasant thought got Jack safely back to the motel and sent him toward dreamless sleep. That hadn't happened in quite some time.

23

THE LAWMAN COMETH

Morning arrived with a text alert on Jack's phone. Unlike so many of his generation, he didn't like the gadget. He avoided social media because he'd seen false and unflattering stories about him after he left the team. In addition, there had been salacious items about Olivia, which were completely untrue.

There could be no basis for such stories. Jack was angry that someone could fabricate such deceit, and then had the temerity to spread their evil fiction. It insulted Olivia's memory and reputation, and disrupted her family's ability to deal with her loss.

As the years passed and Jack's thinking about the sad circumstances became clearer, it occurred to him that Mr. Hutchens' anger could have been fueled by such lies. He wanted to tell the team owner that those aspersions were just that - baseless lies. But he had tried to reach him and was stonewalled.

Momentarily, Jack had to concentrate to realize what the alert was. They were so rare. He rolled over and saw the message. 'Can you come see me at work? Questions about weekend. Randy.'

Jack had no idea what the meaning could be. His sense of

impending misfortune was alerted. Nothing had gone right for him for so long. He began to think his hopes for progress with Duncan were about to be dashed. Reproachful thoughts dominated a quick shower and shave.

'Here we go again,' Jack said to himself. He had dared to think that something good might come from this Duncan project. Enjoying family moments with Sally and her kids might have been too much to ask. Now fate was rising up to remind him that he was destined to arrive at the 'Happiness Party' just as the door was being closed. He had flown too close to the sun, once again.

Hunger wasn't a motivator on most mornings, and today was no different. On the drive to Randy's veneer plant, Jack couldn't help but think that his life had somehow unfolded into a Greek tragedy. His mother's love of literature had shown him how writers told a classic story: Man could try to be happy, but life would soon slap him down. The Icarus story reverberated – how the boy and his father were imprisoned and made wings to fly away from their torment. The boy was told not to fly too high, or the sun would melt his wings. Of course, the boy disobeyed, and soon his wings were useless. He fell into the sea and his helpless father couldn't save him.

Perhaps he was destined to live out the 'Annabel Lee' poem; the things he loved were bound to be taken from him. Jack could make a list of what he had lost: his father, baseball, even Olivia. And now, possibly, his chance of getting Duncan started was about to be added to the disappointment parade.

A gloomy cloud was closing in on him, and Jack tried to shake it off. He tried to focus on something his mom had said about moments like this. 'Worry is a payment you make to misfortune before it is due.' But his usual good nature was wearing thin. He was tired of having to bounce back. Still, he put a smile on his face when he walked into the plant office and saw Samantha once again.

"Hi there," he said. "I'm back again looking for Randy."

She seemed less exuberant this time, and the cheery smile was gone.

"He's in his office," she answered, and gave a sideways motion with her head.

Jack walked to the door and noticed that Randy was not alone. There was a man in a sheriff's uniform sitting across from Randy's desk. They were in a discussion about a document in the man's hand. The man didn't see Jack standing in the doorway, but Randy looked up.

"Mr. Ridley is here now."

Jack stepped into the office.

"Mr. Ridley, I'm Derek Schroeder, with the Marren County Sheriff's office," the man said. "There's been an investigation initiated that involves you."

He waited for Jack to say something out of surprise, or guilt, or general chattiness. It was a standard police tactic that sometimes got results. But Jack just waited. He looked at Randy to see if he had anything to add, but he was also silent. Mr. Schroeder put the document on the desk.

"There's been a complaint filed regarding an incident last weekend at the Zone Bar here in town."

A second pause gained no additional information. Jack had learned long ago that just because someone said something to or about you didn't mean that you were obligated to say something back. Mr. Schroeder waded in again.

"It seems there was some kind of fight at the bar and the complaint says you were involved."

Jack looked at Randy and the meaning was clear. 'Why am I here?' was written on Jack's face. Randy took his cue.

"Who is behind this?"

Schroeder was in full investigation mode.

"That's confidential."

Randy didn't know this Schroeder fellow. The guy might be a cowboy with a badge, ready to arrest someone. It was time to find out if any of this impacted Jack or his ability to play for the Crushers. Randy came to the point.

"So, why are you bringing this confidential information to me and Jack?"

Schroeder figured events were proceeding according to the playbook.

"It seems your team and this fellow were responsible for a little fracas that caused quite a lot of damage. Some property got damaged and a few faces got busted up."

Randy had heard about the event, but from an entirely different perspective.

"What sort of investigation have you conducted, or are you just reading from what Jerry Schaefer is stirring up?"

That approach seemed to change gears for Schroeder.

"So, you know Jerry."

Randy stifled a laugh.

"Everybody knows Jerry. Doesn't matter if they want to or not. He runs around telling everybody how important he is, because his daddy owns some businesses. One of them is a restaurant, that Hooters place. They have to let him play on their team because his daddy says so."

Both Jack and Randy noticed Schroeder blink and readjust his tactics.

"It's true that Jerry is a material witness."

Shuffling his papers allowed Schroeder to stall.

"Figures," Randy said. "Let me guess. He ran to his daddy after starting trouble at the Zone. Told his daddy his story but left out the part about him causing the whole thing. Am I getting warm?"

Schroeder was getting a new impression. His effort to please old man Schaefer, and reap the reward of a job as his company security chief might be slipping away. He tried to regroup.

"I have other witnesses to interview."

He turned to Jack.

"I have one question. Were you there with anyone?"

Jack had serenely observed the whole exchange. His initial concern abated. Small town justice might not go against him, after all. Speaking to his store lawyer wasn't necessary and a few answers wouldn't hurt.

"That's two questions. Yes, I was there and others were present."

Schroeder felt the need to reassert his position as law enforcement guru.

"Don't need the attitude, Mr. Ridley. Just tell me who was there."

Jack looked at Randy.

"You will have to ask Mr. Powers the names of the fellows on his team who were there. I don't know them. The only person I know is a young lady I was talking to at the bar."

Schroeder had his pen ready, in officious mode.

"And does this young lady have a name?"

"Patty Patterson," Jack said, and waited to see if that mattered.

Schroeder had a visible reaction, as he stopped writing to look at both Jack and Randy. He swallowed once, and Jack watched his Adam's apple take an elevator trip.

"The mayor's daughter was there?"

Inwardly, Jack was thinking that the town was getting smaller by the minute.

"I don't know anything about a mayor's daughter. A young lady named Patty Patterson helped me out of the place. That was after one of your boys cold-cocked me with a beer bottle. Beyond that, I won't be much of a witness."

Schroeder was readjusting his assessment of the whole scenario. He didn't clue in to the fact that Jack was suggesting that the guilty parties were connected to him. If he had, Jack was one step ahead. He was prepared to say he had meant the guy who had blindsided him was a local actor. Whoever he was, using the bottle as a weapon would be hard to explain.

Randy took the initiative.

"So, if we've got some guy attacking Jack with a bottle, you'll be charging him with some type of battery?"

Schroeder hadn't seen that coming and just looked blankly at

Randy. The whole landscape of how he had planned this visit had just turned 180 degrees. Randy advanced his argument.

"I mean, if the damn bottle broke and Jack is injured and probably needs stitches, isn't that some kind of crime?"

The investigator was still silent, so Randy stood up to indicate that the meeting was drawing to a close.

"Tell you what, Mr. Schroeder. You go back to your office and ask the sheriff if it's okay if you go see Mr. Schafer. Ask Mr. Schafer if it's okay if you investigate the real trouble-makers here. Let's see if the bar has videos and all that modern high tech stuff. That way, you'll know what really happened. Maybe do a for-real investigation. Sound like a plan?"

Schroeder was at the door and couldn't think of a way to recover whatever stature he'd lost in coming here. He already knew that he'd been handed a line of bull, which got him running off half-cocked. He should have known that the Jerry Schafer kid was a manipulative jerk, just like his father. Jerry had sounded pretty convincing when he came to the sheriff's office, saying that Jack and some others had jumped him.

Holy crap, Schroeder started thinking. The kid was major stupid for thinking his story would hold up. Schroeder shifted to another reality. For his part, he was double major stupid for coming straight to Randy with the complaint. He ruefully admitted to himself he should have gone to the bar first, and talked to the manager. Or the bartender. Or the winos in the parking lot.

Now he was going to look ridiculous with the sheriff, and worse with Mr. Schafer. He was nuts to have thought he could curry favor with that windbag. There probably never was a lucrative security job, even though the old man had hinted pretty strongly at it.

What had begun as career day was rapidly losing steam. And now he had to worry about the mayor after his daughter weighed in. This ship had just hit an iceberg. Schroeder looked at Randy and tried to salvage his own deflated ego.

"I'll let you know if I need a follow-up."

He headed down the hallway and was passing an embarrassed Samantha when Randy called after him.

"That's fine. And I'll let you know when I get the team behind the guy running against your boss."

Jack appreciated the rejoinder. He didn't know if Randy was standing up for him, or for his players. Or both. Either way, Jack liked what he had seen. His notion of fundamental fairness objected to what Schroeder had attempted, but maybe the end of the guy's shenanigans was in sight.

"You handled that pretty well," Jack said to Randy. "Remind me to keep you on my side."

Randy just shrugged.

"He called and said he was coming by with something concerning the team. Claimed it involved you and you might not be playing this weekend. All a load of crap. When he got to his story, it just honked me off, what he was pulling. So, I just gave it back to him."

Jack shook his head.

"Go figure. One more story to tell, I guess. But I'm glad I'm here."

He shifted to reporting his game plan progress.

"I've been working with Duncan and I think he's going to do fine. He'll have a real good fastball and I'm dialing in a change-up. Haven't got to a curve yet, but I'll let you know. Should be okay with what he'll see here."

"Sounds fine," Randy said. "You know what you're doing. See you Saturday night."

"Right," Jack added. "I also need four tickets for Patty Patterson and her friends."

Randy had no problem with the request.

"I'll let the ticket folks know. You know what to do when you get there."

Then he had a question.

"What's up with her? You seeing her?"

Jack smiled and shook his head.

"No, sir. I just figure it's good policy to be nice to someone who helps you make the sheriff go away."

———

Stopping to talk to Samantha was necessary. She looked a bit wide-eyed at having law enforcement roll past her desk, and Jack wanted to smooth things out.

"I take it you heard most of that?"

She nodded, not knowing what to say.

"Well, it just gives you a clue as to what kind of guy you shouldn't hang around with."

Jack smiled and headed out the door. He had skipped breakfast so he stopped for a drive-thru bite. Then he took the direct route to the farm. Any trepidation he once had about the place and Duncan's family was gone.

Duncan had been friendly from the start; Sally had warmed up pretty quickly, and now she treated him like an honored guest; last night Danielle had proved to be considerate and good-hearted. Plus, she had a wicked sense of humor.

When Jack pulled into the drive, Duncan was mowing grass on the tractor. He looped back toward the house and shut down the machine.

"Hey, Jack, you're ahead of schedule. I got some hay mowed this morning and thought I'd get some of this grass cut. Was planning to get done before you arrived."

He must have spent some time in the field, because he was covered with dust and hay. Jack was looking around and didn't see the others. Duncan noticed the search.

"They're gone to set up at the farmer's market. It's on Thursday morning, down by the courthouse."

Jack smiled at the reference.

"I thought for a minute this morning I was going to the court-house my own darn self."

Duncan looked surprised.

"What the heck happened?"

Jack was in no hurry to tell the story, so he stalled.

"It's a long story. How about I tell it when everybody is here?"

"They should be back any second," Duncan agreed. "I'll get hosed off and we'll get started?"

Jack had an idea to get two birds at once.

"Hey, you show me how to drive this thing and I'll get the last of the grass cut. You can get cleaned up, grab a drink, and get your glove."

Duncan was agreeable once more, and showed Jack how to start the tractor, use the clutch on the mower, and locate the gas and brakes.

"You just drive in circles and then you're done. Don't fall off, and here's the kill switch if you screw up."

He stepped back, tossed his straw hat to Jack, and watched him start the engine. Easing the machine forward was elementary enough, and Jack got a thumbs-up from Duncan. Jack shifted his attention to the mowing as Duncan headed to the water pump.

It wasn't very difficult, just a larger version of a riding mower. Jack was thinking that this was the same way the painting started: It isn't work if you don't have to do it all the time. He made a few circuits, and was cutting a final swath back toward the house. He'd been at it long enough for Duncan to get the dust washed off and changed into a fresh shirt.

Duncan was standing by the tree where they had started throwing. As Jack approached, he saw that Duncan was pointing toward the road. Jack looked in that direction as he came to a stop and killed the engine. Danielle was bringing her car to a stop and Sally was in the passenger seat. They both got out; Sally was smiling and Danielle was laughing out loud.

"Jeez, Cake, you've got him doing your chores! Painting and mowing, while you're goofing off!"

Duncan had a 'Who? Me?' look on his face.

"He wanted to drive the tractor, so I let him."

Sally shook her head.

"Lordy, Jack, you've got the farmer look down perfect."

Jack sat on the tractor in his best farmer pose.

"I just need me some overalls and I'm all set."

Duncan had his glove ready, so Jack jumped off the tractor and got his mitt from his car.

"I've got an idea," he said to the group. "We're doing okay on the throwing, and if you are all okay with your jobs, how about we go into town? We just need a few pitches today."

He shifted to Sally.

"You've been cooking here enough; how about I take everyone to that little diner, and then we catch the afternoon movie at that oldie place? They've got 'The Godfather' showing."

He waited to see if the three of them were interested.

"C'mon, it's only a buck and we're due."

Duncan jumped at the chance.

"I'm in, let's go."

Sally was next.

"Why not? We're sorta caught up."

Danielle smiled her acceptance.

"Okay," Jack said. "We throw a little and then we go."

The boys turned to their task and the ladies went into the house. They were continuing whatever conversation that brought them home, and they had a good laugh going. Jack was thinking that his idea about a little group diversion was playing out pretty well. Once again, he reflected how life takes unexpected turns, if you let it.

Around this time last week, he was figuring to play another weekend of games - games that were increasingly losing any appeal to him. By now, he would have been back at the store, shoving papers back and forth, with the same empty feeling that had settled in upon him for too long. But today, he was having a great time, in moments that he could have never imagined. He grinned at the thought that this was a scene right out of reruns of the old 'Green

Acres' TV show. He even heard the song in his head: 'Farm living is the life for me.'

Duncan didn't need to rehash their warm-up routine. They started tossing the ball as if they'd done it for years. They repeated the tight-zone medium pitches. When Jack was satisfied that Duncan was secure in the mechanics they had discussed, he called a halt.

"Okay, we're doing great with the plan for a basic fastball and a change. I'd like to see what kind of curve we can work in, and those three should get us by any batters we face this weekend."

Jack paused to consider his next words.

"The most common pitch in baseball is the fastball. It's thrown about 70 % of the time. And I've got confidence you will be strong here. I saw it with Skip."

Duncan gave what he thought was a wise nod and waited for Jack to continue.

"What will sell this idea, initially, is your fastball. That's because they haven't seen you yet. But, if that were all you had, you'd be done pretty quickly. That's why the off-speed stuff is important."

Jack looked closely at Duncan to make sure this was all soaking in. Duncan was locked in and Jack knew to proceed delicately. Keeping everything light and easy was paramount. Avoiding making the youngster nervous was job one. The variable in the equation, Jack started thinking, was himself. Duncan had the right stuff; it would be on Jack if Duncan couldn't showcase his talent. If Duncan clued into just how small the window of opportunity was, it might reduce him to fragile nerves and guaranteed failure. So, Jack was gratified when Duncan spoke his mind.

"I'm not worried about being able to burn it when I need to. We're not even close to throwing hard, yet."

"Confidence is great," Jack smiled. "Let's be sure to bring along a few more tools. What kind of curve did you learn in high school?"

"It was pretty basic," Duncan answered. "I was just twisting my wrist and trying to get an arc on the ball."

"That's a start, but poor technique can get you injured. Twisting puts a lot of stress on your arm, so we need to start with the right grip and alter the arm motion a bit."

Jack held the ball and demonstrated.

"What a fastball is doing is spinning from bottom to top, or maybe you'd call it in reverse. That helps it remain straighter, in terms of gravity. With less change in direction, it's faster."

Duncan nodded, signaling his understanding. Jack continued the lecture on spin dynamics.

"The curve spins the other way, from top to bottom, or forward like a rolling ball, if that helps you visualize it. That way, the leverage comes from the air in front of the ball. It causes a greater change in the ball's motion."

Jack demonstrated the difference in the spin. It starts with hand placement on the ball.

"Getting this?"

Duncan grunted and Jack continued.

"You grip with the middle finger on the right side of the 'horse-shoe stitch,' bottom to top, and your index finger is next to it. You can begin with leaving the pointer finger off the ball and actually 'point-ing' at the plate. Long term, that's a bad idea because sharp-eyed batters can see the grip and know what's coming. The next step is putting your thumb on the other side, basically in the opposite horse-shoe, on the opposite stitch."

Getting the grip adjusted was easier said than done. Jack grinned at Duncan's earnest effort.

"Don't worry, it sounds more complicated than it is. And it becomes second nature, real fast. When you release the ball, the middle finger goes down, while the thumb comes up. There's the necessary hand motion. Like opening a door handle."

Duncan mimed the twisting action and Jack approved.

"Now we're talking about the throw. With the fastball delivery, your hand goes more straight to the plate, ending up low. No higher than your opposite knee. That's the most efficient place for your hand to go, because of the power behind the throw. But the curve motion ends up a little higher, close to your opposite waist. That imparts more spin on the ball."

Nodding once again, Duncan thought he was getting the picture. Jack was ready to demonstrate the lesson's coup de grâce.

"Remember I told you there are differences in arm position that result in changes in the ball's delivery? This is a great example. The arm motion, coupled with the different hand release, puts the spin on the ball that makes it come in at an arc. That lessens the time the bat can connect."

Duncan was thoughtful with his response.

"Because the different air pressure makes the ball behave differently."

Jack was pleased at the analysis.

"Perfect! Some guys get real freaky about air pressure by throwing a knuckleball."

Duncan laughed nervously at the thought.

"Jeez, I hope not. A knuckleball can go *anywhere*."

Jack returned to confidence-building.

"Relax, that's not our plan. You've got plenty of arm to throw it by them when you need to. We'll have enough off-speed to mess up their timing to get strikeouts. Or balls the infield can handle. Don't forget, an out at first is still an out."

Jack grinned his support.

"You get twenty-seven of them, strikeouts, fly outs, or ground balls, and you win the game."

They returned to their throwing distance.

"Give me the same three fastball strikes first," Jack said.

Duncan bought them home; 1 – 2 – 3.

Then Jack changed the format.

"Switch to the curve grip, and give me one at half speed. Remember the hand motion and the arm position."

Duncan's throw was respectable, although high.

"Don't worry about placement, just work on the mechanics."

The next few pitches looked good and had a nice, predictable arc.

"The thing is, when you're using more speed, the air effect is greater and the snap at the end is greater," Jack said. "It all adds up to a pretty confusing pitch."

He had imparted all the instruction Duncan needed for one day.

"Let's just ease through a dozen or so of these. No need to stress anything, and we've got time before Saturday to map it out."

Duncan continued throwing the curve with good results. Jack signaled a finish and they headed toward the house.

"That's more about a curve than I've ever been told," Duncan said. "Good job, dude."

Jack gave him a congratulatory whack on the back.

"Stick with me, kid, you might learn something."

They arrived at the porch and met the ladies on the way out. Sally was bubbly and Danielle was smiling.

Sally said, "All set for this grand adventure?"

"All set. But my car is a bit tight for four people," Jack allowed.

"My little SUV will work," Danielle replied, so Duncan escorted Sally to the front passenger seat. He and Jack climbed in the back.

"Take us downtown," Jack grinned at Danielle.

24

THE CONFESSION AND THE GODFATHER

On the drive into town, Duncan wasted no time in mentioning their prior conversation.

"Jack, you said something about almost going to the courthouse. What was that about?"

Sally half-turned in her seat to look at Jack. He could see Danielle watching him in the rear-view mirror. Jack took a deep breath, and began the story.

"When I woke up this morning I had a text message from Randy. He wanted to talk about this weekend, and I thought something had screwed up the plan for Cakeman here to play."

By using a joking version of the family nickname for Duncan, Jack hoped to defuse any concern about the matter. He saw his effort had fallen short. All three of his companions were listening intently. It made him collect his thoughts. They didn't need any of the worry, albeit misplaced, that he had felt this morning.

"Don't worry," he was quick to add. "There's no problem. Randy got a call from the sheriff."

Danielle was the first to jump in.

"The sheriff! What the Sam Hill did you do?"

Jack involuntarily snickered at her phrasing. He hadn't heard that one for years.

"Relax," he smiled. "As you know, there was a ruckus at the Zone Bar after the game last weekend. It was the night before I met Duncan at the high school game. I hadn't been there too long when that Jerry fellow showed up."

"He's a peach of a guy," Duncan chimed in.

Jack concurred.

"Yeah, I got that impression that night, and then again this morning from Randy. Anyway, I was talking to this girl."

Danielle's eyes were visible in the rear view mirror, and Jack noticed her eyebrows arch slightly. He couldn't tell if she was reacting to the 'girl comment' or the observations about the charming Mr. Jerry.

"This guy came over and started giving her a hard time. She told him off and he grabbed me. I shoved him away, and somebody whacked me with a bottle. That's when the lights went out."

There was silence in the car and then Danielle spoke.

"The Zone is two or three miles away from where the high school game was. How'd you end up over there?"

Jack couldn't tell if there was the slightest bit of derision in her tone. She had glanced at him in the mirror when she posed the question, and Sally had given her a sideways glance. Jack wondered if this had all been related to her earlier comment about the Crushers at the Zone. He decided to plow straight ahead, as he had nothing to hide in this discussion.

"It turns out that same person I was talking to took pity on me. I was stumbling around, dazed from getting clobbered by that bottle. She didn't know where to take me, so she took me to her apartment, which is right next to the high school diamond."

They had arrived in the little town square and Danielle parked in front of the diner. No one moved to get out of the car, and they remained silent. Duncan was looking over at Jack as if he'd just started speaking French. Jack knew what Duncan wanted to ask, but it wasn't going to happen in front of his mother and sister. If the front passengers had a reaction, Jack couldn't see it.

"No, it wasn't like that," he hurried to add. "I was out on my feet, and she said she was able to walk me along. I woke up in the morning and that was all."

Jack realized the situation appeared a bit dicey, but he didn't want to be painted as a roving playboy.

"You can go see her and ask, if you want."

Sally opened the door.

"Fine by me, Jack," she said. "You don't have to convince me you're doing the right thing. And she probably did you a favor. You might have gotten hit by a car or something."

They all were trooping into the diner and Duncan punched Jack on the arm. He didn't say a word, but he had a devilish look in his eyes. Jack shook his head and just held the door for all of them. They settled in a booth in the back. Jack was grateful for the privacy because there was more to the story. Before he could begin, Duncan had to pipe up.

"Who was this mystery girl?"

Jack didn't hesitate.

"Her name is Patty Patterson and she's a nice person."

Sally and Duncan looked surprised. Danielle looked at the menu. Duncan yelped.

"Patty Patterson! The mayor's daughter? Man, she is hot!"

Sally gave Duncan her 'mother-in-charge' look, and Danielle hid behind the menu. She seemed mildly amused by the situation. Jack started again.

"All I know is she helped me out and that was all. She's in college. I saw her and her friends at the Zone the other night when I went there to get a sandwich. She seems like a good kid."

Jack felt helpless and realized he was repeating himself. Sally came to his rescue.

"This started with something about Randy and the sheriff."

Relieved to return to safer ground, Jack got back to the timeline.

"When I got to Randy's office this sheriff guy was there. He started asking questions about what happened at the Zone. Seems this Jerry guy had filed a complaint saying I had started a fight. The guy hadn't done any investigation; he just came to Randy to screw with me."

The exasperation in his voice was apparent.

"Lucky for me, Randy sort of took him on and told him what he could do with his investigation. Randy also knew this Jerry guy is some kind of rich problem child."

Danielle finally contributed to the conversation.

"He's got that part right."

Jack was glad to see there was some agreement at the table.

"So you know this guy?"

"He was a couple of years ahead of me in high school," Danielle responded. "He was a spoiled jerk then. Looks like he's still got the touch."

Jack agreed with her assessment.

"I don't know why he went to the sheriff with this lame story. Unless he figured he was in hot water over causing damages at the bar. Plus, the guy doing the investigation didn't check with anybody on the scene to see what happened. Some guy named Schroeder. He just believed Jerry right off."

Duncan jumped in.

"I know that Schroeder guy. He was a security guard at school before he got a job with the sheriff. He's a real Barney Fife."

Jack shook his head and defended the Mayberry Deputy.

"Barney tried to do the right thing. He just bumbled a little. Schroeder ran off half-cocked because he's trying to get some kind of job with Jerry's father. Not the same thing here."

Sally tried to return to a useful area.

"So, is anything going to happen with this?"

"I doubt it," Jack continued. "Not after he talks to any of the witnesses. Schroeder made it sound like he'd come to arrest me.

That's why I said I thought I was headed to the courthouse. He was really just blowing a lot of smoke. I don't think anything will come of it, and neither does Randy. In fact, Randy thinks having the mayor's daughter involved helps out."

Sally and Danielle were taking all of this in and Duncan enjoyed watching Jack squirm a bit. The lady from the diner arrived to take their lunch orders, and everyone was happy with Cokes and cheese-burgers. Conversation shifted to the farmers' market scheduled for the next day. Sally explained that they usually sold a few dozen bushels of sweet corn.

"It's not a money-maker. More a networking thing. All the growers get together to compare notes. Plus, we get the low-down on what's happening around town."

Lunch arrived and they made short work of it.

Jack was tempted by dessert, but the ladies declined. He didn't want to be rude, so he told Duncan they would indulge another time. He couldn't resist joking with Sally and Danielle about their healthy decision.

"You know what the lady said on the Titanic, don't you?"

When they said no, he supplied the answer.

"I could have had the cheesecake!"

The laughter subsided and Duncan made a point.

"There's that 'Cake' thing again," and the joke was complete. They finished their lunch and Jack asked for the check.

"Not for you!" he said as Sally reached for her purse. "I told you, you've been making the dinners at home. Today is my turn."

They left the diner and walked across the street to the movie theater. They all had seen 'The Godfather' before, but who can resist such a classic, especially with one dollar admission?

As luck would have it, they all preferred to sit toward the back of the theater. It was one of those old venues that had seen all manner of entertainment and performing arts; live shows, comedy acts, plays, movies, social and civic events. It was usually on the brink of closing, which is common for small towns. Like a lot of the old theaters, it had a small balcony and viewing boxes on each side. There were relief design walls and the ceiling had arches with joining rosettes and intricate scroll work.

Jack always marveled at the workmanship and dedication it took to build such a thing. He preferred seeing movies in these theaters, as opposed to the modern mall experience with its bland bare-wall boxes. Before the show would begin, he liked to just look at the architecture and color schemes. He'd imagine the workers, now long gone, as they toiled away on the marvelous aspects of the building's design.

They had trooped into the next-to-last row with Sally in the lead. Duncan peeled off to the concession stand and Danielle was next. Jack fell in behind her, realizing it had been years since he had sat next to a girl in a movie. The thought was rolling in his head when Danielle piped up.

"I like to get a feel for the surroundings before deciding on Cokes and popcorn."

Sally agreed.

"Me, too."

Both of them looked at Jack and waited for him to take the hint.

"I was only waiting to see who wanted diet and who wanted regular," he smiled. "It's too dangerous to ask a lady, y'know."

Sally completed the circle.

"Diet is fine, Jack," and Danielle smirked.

"Same for me, J.A."

While Sally was giving Danielle a puzzled look over what 'J.A.' might mean, Jack headed back to the entrance.

"Three diets and one of those popcorn tubs, please."

The young lady at the counter took his twenty-dollar bill and started to make change.

"Keep it," Jack said. "It's worth it just seeing this neat place."

She smiled right back at Jack.

"You can pour on hot butter over there." She indicated the counter with condiments and a melted butter dispenser.

Jack gambled that his 'dates' wouldn't mind that he doused the popcorn with 'liquid fat.' He headed back to the seats and saw that Duncan had joined them from the other side. Jack was next to Danielle, once again.

The movie was starting with the great scene where the undertaker was speaking to the Godfather. Some boys had abused his daughter and he was asking for revenge. It allowed Jack to silently pass the drinks down the line, and he handed the popcorn tub to Danielle. She served as the center point for sharing, and both Sally and Jack grabbed a handful. It didn't take long before Danielle gave a loud whisper.

"You forgot the napkins, J.A."

There was just enough light from the movie screen for Jack to see both Sally and Danielle giggling as he got up to go back to the concession stand. He returned with a handful of napkins for each of them. When he passed the bunch to Danielle, he couldn't resist a bit of pestering.

"Don't make too much of a mess."

She kept her eyes straight ahead but Jack could see a hint of a smile in the movie darkness. Then came a part of the movie Jack had forgotten. The Sonny character started up the stairs with the maid of honor during the wedding reception. Jack remembered that a torrid love scene was about to happen.

Jack must have shifted in his chair or changed his breathing. Maybe Danielle was some kind of lie detector savant. Perhaps she could tell when the blood pressure of the guy next to her spiked. Jack's discomfort caught her attention, and he could feel her gaze on him. He searched for some other place to look, besides her or the screen. She leaned over, and whispered loud enough for Sally to hear.

"Better cover your eyes, Jack. It's about to get steamy up there."

Blood rushed to his face, and Jack could hear Sally and Danielle snickering in the dark. He actually did put his hand up over his eyes, which made them laugh harder.

And so it went. The movie was captivating, as usual. For the four of them, just being together was entertaining. Jack realized that he hadn't had such a good time in years. The jokes and the family warmth sent a gentle peaceful feeling over him. Just for a small moment, the hurt and confusion in his life went to a place far away.

25

SITTING ON A PITCH

The movie ended with Michael Corleone becoming the new Don. As usual, when Jack emerged from a daytime movie, returning to real life in broad daylight was a transition.

"Makes you want the movie to go on forever, so you don't have to return to reality."

Sally joined in.

"I get the same feeling, Jack. That's why we're dreamers who like poetry."

Duncan piped up.

"Okay, you dreamers, where to now?"

Jack thought it might be a good idea to swing by Randy's office. Maybe there had been further developments with the sheriff.

"Let's go see if Mr. Schroeder has any new bright ideas. It would be a good time to introduce you to Mr. Powers," he directed at Duncan.

"Fine by me, if you two don't mind." Duncan nodded at his mom and Danielle.

They agreed and headed to the veneer plant. Samantha was glad to see them at the office and she greeted Duncan with a smile.

"Duncan! I haven't seen you since school. What've you been up to?"

"I'm working the farm with my mom and sister. Mom, you remember Sam? She was the lead in the play I did when I was a sophomore. She can sing great."

Sally gave Samantha a happy smile.

"I remember that show! You were fantastic. Does Randy know what a great actor he has here?"

"He ought to. It takes great acting to put up with some of the nubs who come through here."

Samantha winked at all of them. They decided she was hilarious. When Randy came out of his office to investigate the commotion, they were still laughing.

Jack led off.

"Randy, I've brought Duncan to meet you before the game this weekend. Also, here's his mom and sister."

Jack was about to get into names when Randy recognized Danielle.

"Ms. James, I remember you from parent-teacher night. You had my daughter Tricia in class last semester."

Danielle paused a beat to search her memory bank.

"My step-daughter, actually," Randy said. "You wouldn't connect her to me. Her mother is Mandy Towne."

Danielle locked in immediately.

"Tricia Towne, I remember. She graduated early, right?"

"That's right. She's started college and is working at the school placement bureau. She says she wants to go into teaching, just like you."

"She was a great kid," Danielle recalled. "Tell her I'm pulling for her. When she's ready to student teach, I'm the one to talk to."

"This town has everybody knowing somebody," Jack noted. "If one person doesn't know the next guy, there's somebody around the corner who does."

Randy was eyeing Sally and said, "I've seen you in town before. You're Ms. James' mother?"

"That's right," Sally said. "I'm Sally James and this is my son Duncan."

Randy gave Jack a sideways look.

"I know Duncan, too. This is getting to be a family affair."

He paused while looking at Duncan.

"I remember you playing in high school. You didn't go to play in college?"

Duncan gave a short answer.

"No, sir. We had some things come up."

Randy wasn't deterred.

"No worries. If Jack says you're ready, then you're ready." He turned to Jack. "Great visit we had this morning, eh?"

Jack was wondering about any follow-up from the sheriff's office.

"You learn anything else?"

"Not from my end," said Randy. "Mr. Sherlock Holmes went to the Zone and got some answers. I checked with the owner and she said he'd already been there by lunchtime. We won't see any more on that."

Jack was relieved at the news.

"Glad to hear it. Don't need any more complications in my life." After a pause, he returned to business. "So we show up Saturday night and get warmed up. We can decide what to do then, okay? Thanks again, buddy."

Randy gave a thumbs-up, and 'nice to see you again' was exchanged all around. Jack herded his group out the door and back to Danielle's car.

"That's a relief. No telling where that kind of story-telling ends up. Especially when someone thinks they can make hay out of it for themselves."

Jack added the details of what Randy had said about the investigator's motivation for pursuing the bogus report. They were nearly back to the farm when he got through the story. It was time to shift the conversation to a pitching concept that he wanted the women to understand, as well as Duncan.

"If you ladies don't mind, I'd like to run some ideas past Mr. Cake here. He can think them over, away from throwing. Plus, it'll give you guys an idea about what he's doing. You can keep an eye on his performance."

They were agreeable. Sally had told Danielle about Jack's teaching method, and she welcomed a close-up view. Jack began with a summation of their progress.

"I know there's a lot of information we've been going through. The truth is, the best pitchers are always working on their mechanics, even after all the basics are committed to muscle memory. Remember what I've already told you - getting the right grip for different pitches will become automatic. What I'm talking about now is avoiding any behavior that might tip off a really good hitter about what you're going to throw."

Duncan, as usual, was listening intently to what Jack was saying. But this time, he wasn't sure of the meaning.

"You mean things like holding your glove differently while you're changing the grip?"

Jack was pleased that Duncan was cluing in, but it was just a start.

"Yes, sir, but it's *lots* more. Some guys stand differently on the rubber. Others look different in their windup. Some start showing a longer time between certain pitches and it's a perfect tip-off. If a guy pauses for a second or two to ready himself for his fastball, or vice-versa for his curve, the other team will notice. It's called 'tipping your pitches,' and it can kill you."

Duncan nodded slowly, taking it in carefully. Jack wanted to emphasize his next point.

"Do you remember the 'Love of the Game' baseball movie, where the guy says 'They keep track of everything?' He was talking about stats, like first pitch ground balls, or first pitch swings, or walks, or bunt tendencies. The list is never-ending. *Everything* gets tracked.

We're talking about intangibles that don't go onto a stat sheet, but they get noticed."

Jack was gratified that the ladies were fixated on the topic almost as tightly as Duncan.

"For instance, if you start showing a delay before throwing your fast ball, compared to other pitches, guys will know what's coming. They will sit on that pitch and knock it into next week. I guarantee it. So you have to develop an automatic delivery which is *exactly* the same, every time, for every pitch. I'm talking timing, delivery, positioning, and whatever gum you're chewing. Ladies, you watch him when I'm not there, so he doesn't get off-track."

Both Sally and Danielle were impressed with this high-speed instruction. These details of the game had never occurred to them. Danielle posed a question.

"What does 'sit on a pitch' mean?"

Her participation was encouraging. It meant she was taking the training seriously, and would be part of Duncan's development.

"It means a batter has a particular pitch in mind that he is looking to hit. He 'sits' there until that pitch comes. Maybe he knows a particular pitcher throws a first pitch fastball eighty per cent of the time he faces a new batter. That means, statistically, that a batter can bet the odds that he'll see a fastball and be ready for it. He's 'sitting' on that pitch."

Jack paused to switch the analysis to the other side of the equation.

"From a pitching standpoint, it works the other way, too. Some batters are first pitch hitters. So you avoid getting the first pitch to them where it's hittable. You keep that pitch close to the edge of the strike zone. Maybe even slightly out of the zone. You might get the guy to 'go fishing' and there's strike one for free."

Jack thought it might make sense from another perspective.

"You'll see batters not even swing at a pitch that was a strike all the way. Maybe that wasn't the pitch they were expecting. Could be they were 'sitting' on another pitch. Maybe they were sure an off-speed pitch was coming, and the fastball was on them, before they could react. Or they plan to take pitches until they're convinced the pitcher can get three strikes across the plate."

Jack checked to see if his students were getting the idea.

"If a batter is ahead in the count, three balls and no strikes, the manager will probably signal for him to take the fourth pitch. On the other hand, there's a strong possibility it's going to be a fastball, because that's the best pitch to get a strike. So, if the batter is a solid fastball hitter, the manager might 'green light' him to go ahead and swing. He's sitting on a fastball for that pitch. There are so many things going into the decision that no one gets it right all the time. Remember, the best hitters in baseball are successful only about 25-30% of their at-bats."

This massive amount of information was impressive. Both Sally and Danielle always considered baseball a rudimentary game. Until now, it was 'someone throws a ball and someone hits it.' As in all families, when one family member is performing a function that requires high-level performance, the others are intrigued. They are slightly amused that one of their own can do it. Danielle voiced the thought.

"Golly, Cake, I can't believe that you can put all this together. But you're still a dweeb."

They had arrived home and were getting out of the car. She made the mistake of making that remark as Duncan was walking up behind her. He gave her a hip-check into the car's fender, and bolted away before she could whack him for his trouble. It made Jack laugh to see these two working on each other. He noticed Sally's semi-exasperated look and knew she wasn't really upset with her kids. This was just an oblique way of expressing affection, and Jack had a nice homey feeling being able to observe it. When Duncan circled back toward the other three, Jack played along.

"I'm going to get out of here before she hurts you. How 'bout we get together tomorrow and run through our three pitches? Then we work on speed and delivery."

"What time are you thinking?" Duncan asked. "I was hoping to get done with chores and stuff and be able to swing by the high school game. They still have a few on the schedule."

Jack was willing.

"What time do they play?"

"Starts at four."

"Okay," Jack said. "If you want to paint, we'll do that early and then get some throwing in before the game. I'd be happy to go see it. If you've got tractor work, I'm off the hook until we throw. Your call."

Duncan mulled it over.

"You take the morning off. I'll be on the tractor until lunch. We throw an hour or so after that, and then it's game time. Sound good?"

"Fine by me," Jack said. He turned to the ladies.

"I'll see you after we throw, if you're here."

"There's always lunch if you want, Jack," Sally said. "One more hungry man can't hurt."

Jack smiled at the thought. Both Sally and Danielle were standing there gazing at him, and he gazed right back. The angle of the sun and their adjacent posture made him think they looked similar, once again. Then Danielle edged toward friendly.

"Show up, Jack. Maybe I'll make a cake."

Uncertain whether she was joking about Duncan's nickname or actually planning to bake something, Jack could only nod his acceptance. He noticed that both Sally and Danielle had that crinkle-nose look right before they started to laugh.

26

BACK WHEN I WAS A PLAYER

Jack drove to the motel with glowing thoughts about his moments with Sally, Duncan and Danielle. He couldn't remember when he'd been so relaxed and content, just sharing company. The tinges of humor and acceptance with this new family were inviting. Feeling invigorated, Jack decided it was time to call the sports store manager. Progress reports were overdue. When he got back to his room and could relax, he'd find out if he had missed anything in the retail world.

During the drive, he reverted to his inspiring music, namely opera. He knew he was selling himself short with such a wide array of vocalists to choose from, but he was a loyal listener. It didn't take long to dial up 'the Marriage of Figaro.' It was his favorite piece. Rather, it contained his favorite.

'Figaro' came to Jack via the movie 'Amadeus.' It revealed Mozart's life and compositions, which Jack found astounding. The man had talent of towering proportions. He infused music with artistry and emotion that reached Jack on an indescribable level. Jack agreed with the actor who played Mozart's competitor: The music expressed such longing and complete benediction that it had to be the voice of God. Who wouldn't admire a composer who had inspired Beethoven?

Intrigue, human foibles and confused identities provide a humorous 'Figaro' plot. The Countess ultimately forgives her husband for his intentions with another woman, but not before planning to expose him. A graceful duet with her servant delivers the ruse.

When Jack needed inspiration, he chose the duet. Of course, he preferred the People's Diva. Her soaring soprano revived his spirits. Plus, he liked the theme: A cheater deserves to be busted. That's why there are rules, Jack figured. He reflected that he had been busted for some reason, but had not cheated. Whether the ledger would be balanced, he waited to discover.

He drove by the park and saw moms and dads with their children. There were babies on swing sets and there were merry-go-rounds launching kids into bumpy landings in the sand. On the periphery, fathers threw baseballs. It reminded Jack of playing catch with his dad. No matter how tired his dad might be when he got home, there was always time to toss a ball back and forth.

Jack loved the feel of the stitching on a dirty leather ball and it gave him peace. Somehow, a banged-up ball opened doors with his father. They talked about Jack's day at school, or other times they would say nothing at all. If Jack had a problem, he found that he could discuss anything while a baseball was sailing back and forth. Jack missed the simple rhythm of those moments, just as he missed his dad. Arriving at the motel brought Jack back to reality. It was time to call the store manager.

"Hey, Jon, are you keeping us in business?"

Jon Richter managed the details of running the sporting goods store. Richter and the bank manager had assembled the area businessmen who started the store when Jack signed his first contract.

"We're holding on," Richter said. "I thought you were going to be back here this week."

Jack kept details to a minimum.

"There was a bit of other business here in Jason. I expect to be back there next week if that suits you. By then, there could be some other irons in the fire."

Richter needed to attend to store expansion.

"Make sure we see you next week. We've got some folks interested in other stores."

"That'll work," Jack answered. "I'll be there and you can work your magic."

With that out of the way, Jack figured he'd find some supper and call it a night. There was a Chinese place a few blocks from the motel. He decided to phone in an order and enjoy a short walk to the restaurant. Sweet and sour chicken is always a safe bet. Jack made the call and headed out to pick up the food. The night was pleasant and he didn't see anyone on the way to or from the pick-up.

He had left the TV on during his absence from the room. It gave the impression someone was about, in case anyone saw him leaving and wanted to get curious. When he got back to the room, a Braves and Mets game was already in progress. Ordinarily, he wasn't interested in watching television, but baseball was an exception. He dug into the chicken and washed it down with a diet Coke.

Not surprisingly, he heard some familiar names in the game. In particular, a player named Duane Baxter was advancing to the batter's box. Jack had played against him in the old days and hadn't found him to be a pleasant individual. The announcer was describing Baxter's plate appearance.

"Baxter has had an increase in his on-base percentage every year since his rookie year with Chicago."

Jack interrupted a swig.

"It was St. Louis."

The color commentator corrected his broadcast partner.

"He began with the Cardinals, Charlie, but you're right, he was traded early to the Cubs."

'Chalk one up for J.A.,' Jack thought to himself, and grinned at the private joke. Using 'J.A.' made him think of Danielle. He had to admit, she had her own version of a wicked curve. Calling him 'J.A.' was artful. She was witty and entertaining. Maybe there would be similar moments in the future.

Jack finished the chicken and dumped the containers in the trash. He stripped down and took a quick shower before bed. The game continued during the shower, and while he brushed his teeth. He had been counting the names of players he knew and he had gotten up to six by bedtime. Play had reached the eighth inning, and the game was still tied at two-all. Jack decided to stretch out with the TV on to watch the finish, or nod off, whichever came first.

The drone of the game gave Jack a pleasant drowsiness. It brought the relaxed feeling that came when he didn't need to set an alarm. He always felt great when he woke up when his body decided it was time, not the clock. Listening to the play-by-play with his eyes half closed, he was nearly asleep when he heard the announcer.

"Duane Baxter will likely be making his final plate appearance of the night; he's had three so far with zero hits."

Jack drowsily added, "Serves you right, you idiot," as the announcer continued.

"He's made contact with the ball tonight, but right at third twice and once to short."

Jack kept up his own commentary.

"They keep the ball low for a reason, Duane. 'Cause you can't hit a slider."

The pitcher was a guy named Nalley, whom Jack didn't know. Nalley ran the count to one ball and two strikes. Jack was thinking ahead: 'Baxter will be looking for something off-speed; he'll think Nalley is okay with a two-two count.'

What he meant was exactly what he'd been teaching Duncan. The batter would predict that the pitcher wouldn't go to his fastball, a more likely strike, when he could risk wasting a pitch. He'd try an off-speed pitch that might entice Baxter to swing, for strike three. The color commentator came in almost on cue.

"Nalley is ahead in the count. He can afford to work the edge or try something off-speed to see if Baxter gets nervous."

That was exactly Baxter's thinking. He had a moment more to prepare if a fastball wasn't coming. So, when Nalley threw a curve, Baxter was ready. The ball didn't break as well as Nalley hoped, and Baxter lashed it to right center.

The center fielder raced over to try to make the catch, and realized he could not get there in time. He tried to grab the ball on the first bounce, but it caromed off the side of his glove. It was the worst thing that could happen for an outfielder. The ball had just bounced past him and he was alone in right-centerfield. The right fielder was sprinting to help, but he would never get there in time.

Jack knew the outcome and breathed, 'Oh, Lord' to himself. The announcer neatly joined him in the sentiment.

"This could be trouble!"

Baxter was already half-way to second base.

"He's on his way to a stand-up triple," the color man added.

The centerfielder was still chasing the ball and Baxter got greedy.

"He might go for the insider," the announcer yelled, meaning an inside-the-park home run. Jack thought the same thing, and he immediately remembered a similar play, with the same Baxter.

The center fielder was deep in the outfield when he retrieved the ball. Baxter was rounding third and was going to try to score. Any play at the plate would require an extraordinary throw from center field. Jack spoke to the centerfielder via telepathy.

'Rip it, kid!'

Duane Baxter was a six-foot-four, two-hundred-forty pound first baseman. By big-league standards, he was an average hitter, fielder and thrower. However, aggressive play was his strength. He had been the bigger and stronger kid all of his life. On an infield play, he liked to go into second and see if he could break up the double play by taking out the second baseman. If a run-of-the-mill tag would do, Baxter liked to spice things up with a hard put-out, preferably to an opponent's face. Jack remembered his own moment with Duane

Baxter during his brief stay with the Reds. And it had happened on an inside-the-park attempt.

Outfielders can throw a ball from the deepest parts of the outfield and make a play on an advancing runner. A notable few can get the ball all the way to home plate. Baseball fans can cite their favorite, perhaps Jose Guillen or Paul O'Neil. A youngster named Kevin Logan was playing centerfield tonight, and this one play would place him in that rarefied group. His throw would be on highlight shows for years.

Logan scooped up the ball, and in one motion, fired the ball home. It screamed toward the cut-off man, straight and true, well over three hundred feet. It did not bounce. Baxter was well past third when the ball was thrown, but the ball beat him by five feet. He was preparing to blast the catcher, ball or no ball. In a split second, the ball and then the runner arrived at the plate. Baxter wasn't going to slide. He was going to find out if the catcher could survive a vicious collision.

Jack saw it all unfolding and knew what was coming. The catcher snagged the ball, perfectly positioned to make the tag. His right hand instantly covered the ball, so it would not be dislodged. Baxter lowered his shoulder and delivered an NFL hit on the smaller man's chest.

Both bodies slammed backward and the catcher tagged Baxter. They landed on the plate in a crumpled heap. The umpire was right on top of them. The crowd erupted as the umpire shouted an emphatic "Out!" and signaled the call with a closed fist.

Jack watched it all and remembered his first meeting with the charming Mr. Baxter. There was a smile on his face as he drifted off to dreamland.

27

WHEN PUSH COMES TO SCORE

T he crowd was healthy for a late-season game. Given that neither team had any hopes for the playoffs, attendance was a sign of good things to come. Talk of some of the younger talent in the Reds' farm system invigorated the faithful. A number of players had been called up late in the season, including a young catcher. Commentators were already calling him the next Johnny Bench. The comparison was based not only on his catching and batting skills, but also on the fact that he very nearly came to the majors straight out of high school.

Big league ballplayers attract attention, and Jack Ridley was not yet used to it all. There were sportswriters who wanted to interview him on his thoughts about the game, and there were female fans who wanted to discuss his theories of dating. Jack gave it his best and tried to be polite. Some of the established players wanted to see how tough he was. Pitchers would throw high and tight to disrupt his batting. One or two players were not above hard tags and rough play at home plate, attempting to rattle his game. Jack took it all in stride. After all, these guys had won their place in professional sports the hard way, as well.

The Cardinals were in town for three games and the Reds manager decided to play some of the younger boys. It would give the veterans a rest *and allow the team to evaluate the new talent. Jack caught the whole game and had one hit in three at-bats, including a walk. He felt that he was having a good game and began to think that he might stick in the league. In the top of the seventh inning, the rough customer on the St. Louis roster came to bat.*

Duane Baxter relished the role of bruiser. While most players come to the batter's box with some type of greeting, on his first trip to the plate Baxter ignored Jack's friendly grin. The rookie catcher kept his distance after that. This was Baxter's third at-bat. With two outs and the bases empty, the Reds were enjoying a three to nothing lead. Jack didn't feel this to be a critical at-bat; even a hit wouldn't hurt the team too much.

The scouting report on Baxter was that he had trouble low in the strike zone. He was a big fellow and his preferred pitch was waist high and above. If you got careless with a pitch up in the zone, this strongman could make you pay. The pitcher got ahead early with two fastballs that hugged Baxter's knees. The first was a called strike; the second was a swing and a miss. Jack decided to try to take advantage of the big guy's aggressiveness with a curveball.

Unfortunately, the pitch didn't curve enough. It hung up in the zone and Baxter crushed it to centerfield. For a big man, Baxter had better than expected speed. The ball was clearly not going to be caught. Baxter rounded first base without hesitation and headed for second.

The centerfielder was also a newcomer, named Willie O'Banion. His teammates called him 'O.B.' as in 'Oh, be there to catch it.' He usually was, but not this time. What should have been a stand-up double became a triple when O.B. misjudged the bounce. The ball skewed past him, deeper into center field. Baxter was closing in on second, and had a head-on view of the error. This enabled him to not break stride and head for third base.

As Baxter continued to run, O.B. had his back to the plate still chasing the ball. The third-base coach misjudged the time it would take O.B. to retrieve the ball, and he signaled Baxter to try for home. The runner made the turn at the same time O.B. reached the ball. It was too late to stop; the runner was committed.

Observing all this from his home plate position, Jack hoped the throw would be in time for a play at the plate. No one in the stadium had any idea that O.B. was concealing a cannon under his jersey, disguised as his right arm. If the third-base coach had a better idea of how quickly O.B. would recover, he would never have sent Baxter home. Even an average outfielder might have made it close. As it was, the league was about to be introduced to an arm that would discourage greedy base runners for years to come.

O.B. fired the ball to Jack, on a laser line, straight to home. It didn't deviate from its straight course. It didn't bounce and seemed to pick up speed. Jack didn't have to move at all. He was positioned to make the tag, and he caught the ball when Baxter was a full ten feet away from the plate. Instead of letting up and admitting that he was out, due to a highlight reel throw, Baxter bore down on Jack. He was going to see if an unconscious catcher could tag him out.

Baxter had been the biggest kid on every team. He had been able to bully his way through encounters on and off the field, with what seemed to him to be great success. His calculus gave him several instant conclusions: Home plate was being guarded by a rookie who had been stupid enough to be friendly. That proved he was a pansy and deserved to be abused. This catcher was road kill waiting to happen.

The idiot had caught the miracle throw and was crouched at home, ready to try to make the tag. So Baxter blasted into Jack like a moose crashing through a windshield on a mountain road. The kid would be dazed, if not injured; enough to drop the ball.

Jack had seen all of this unfolding as Baxter rounded the bases. He wasn't sure of the outcome until he saw O.B. whip his monster throw to home. Jack knew instantly, from the ball's trajectory and speed, that the runner would be out. He also immediately processed Baxter's intention.

The impending collision did not concern him. Jack wanted to accomplish two things. First, he was going to make sure that he hung on to the ball. Protected in his mitt, covered by his throwing hand, the ball was in a vise. It was going to take an act of God to loosen his grip. Second, he was determined to tag the runner like he'd never been tagged before. The man was bigger and stronger, and he clearly intended injury. Jack felt justified in retaliating in kind.

When Baxter came barreling in, Jack was in position in front of the plate. Baxter lowered his shoulder to try to maximize the damage he could cause. Jack was already rolling his body backward, to absorb and dissipate the body blow. He also had the mitt and protected ball cocked to his right side to give him optimal leverage. Merely tagging the runner was not going to be enough, not for this dirty player. Jack was going to deliver a hit, equivalent to the one Baxter was trying to inflict.

As the two players collided, they fell backward. The tag had not yet been made. They were in mid-air, and the runner reached to touch the plate. Jack timed his action to coincide with the moment Baxter's body was extended, and his arms were outstretched. It left his face unprotected.

Jack swung the glove as he would a baseball bat, with all the strength he could muster. He was in mid-air, but it was a two-handed blow. In addition, he was already twisting his body to add additional torque to the swing. The result was that Jack hit Baxter squarely in the face, as solidly as if he had swung a brick into his head.

The padding in the catcher's mitt is on the palm side, not the backhand side. So, Baxter received slightly less than a two-fisted punch. They landed in a heap on home plate and the umpire screamed "Out!" The twisting motion that Jack had initiated, before the tag, caused the players to land relatively side-by-side. Jack was able to spring up immediately.

Baxter was not so lucky. The blow to his face temporarily stunned him, but not enough to render him unconscious. Unfortunately for him, his unprotected face snapped down into the plate, not soft dirt. Centrifugal force accomplished the rest. The Mighty Baxter was out cold.

The Cardinal trainer was on the scene almost before Baxter's head stopped bouncing, followed by both teams. The benches had erupted. The Reds were incensed because of Baxter's blatant unsportsmanlike conduct; the Cardinals had to answer the bell or lose face. Jack stayed out of the melee. He wanted to be close by when Baxter revived. Jack's competitive fighting spirit had been completely aroused. When Baxter was in a sitting position, and about to be helped to his feet, Jack squeezed in close for just one moment. He stuck his hand in Baxter's face, with one finger raised.

"How many fingers?"

Baxter had no trouble seeing which one it was. He had passed Jack's concussion protocol.

28

ICE CREAM SOLVES EVERYTHING

Thursday dawned crisp and clear about 9 a.m. Jack was looking forward to the high school game with the James Gang. He wasn't particularly amped up about another ball game, but he was enjoying spending time with this family. Another prodigy to nurture probably wouldn't appear, which suited Jack just fine. Marching this one down the aisle was proving to be a challenge.

This morning, he was in no hurry. He remembered that Duncan had told him to arrive at lunch, after the tractor work was complete. Jack decided a slow lazy shower wouldn't hurt. He'd be getting sweaty at the farm, painting and pitching, so he planned to come back to the motel and clean up again before going to the game with the family.

The shower is a great place for thinking and singing. As for thinking, Jack figured that 'the Project' was coming along pretty well. He had been able to articulate what he knew about pitching, in a manner that seemed to work for Duncan. *If* the kid could put the knowledge to work, along with the arm he possessed, Jack felt that the next step wouldn't be far away.

In order to get the plan on track, Jack knew he would be stepping back into the baseball world that had wronged him. His pride would take a beating, again, in merely facing any of that crowd. Who wants to go back to a party after they've been shoved out the door? Worse than that, he'd been basically shoved out the door and told to never come back.

For the sake of the Project, Jack was prepared to swallow his pride. He had to be bigger than that. Settling his thoughts by water therapy in the shower always helped. Today's shower thinking led Jack to an anecdote about Steve Jobs. A biographer reported that the guy could be mean-spirited, but you had to admit that he was a thinker.

Jobs had said, "We don't know where it will lead. We just know there's something bigger than any of us here."

That was top-level thinking! Project-wise, Jack wasn't *sure* where any of this was leading. He knew where he hoped it would lead, but he couldn't guarantee success.

As to the 'bigger' part, that was easy. To Jack, baseball was 'bigger.' It always brought enhanced levels of serenity, beauty and security. Whitman was right again: 'Baseball will repair our losses.' Jack was all in. Baseball was bigger than any of us. And Jack was all for helping Duncan become part of 'Bigger.'

For the singing part, Jack was on less solid ground. He knew that singing can lift the spirits and take you to a place that is inaccessible by any other means. His singing diva had proved that. By the same token, Jack also knew that he wasn't the vehicle for taking anybody anywhere on a singing trip. And he was fine with that. You don't have to own a painting to appreciate its beauty.

So, Jack let the good feelings that had been coming to him - the Project, Sally's kindness, and even Danielle's improving attitude - coax him into singing. He belted out 'We Are The Champions' because he had heard it so many times at the ballpark. It seemed to apply to recent events, just a little.

After his Freddy Mercury imitation, Jack brushed his teeth and leisurely got dressed. He was still in no hurry. A stop at the diner for a bagel and coffee would do for now. There would be lunch at the farm. So, he moseyed toward town and saw remnants of some fruit-type stands by the courthouse. He had forgotten that today was farmer's market day. Sally and Danielle would have been there, he remembered.

They would have started early, on a farmer's schedule. Both were working while he was lazing about. He'd keep that to himself. He strolled around the small town square, and recognized a few faces. Over by the little grocery store there was a familiar pair; little Suzy and her mother were approaching.

Jack remembered that the girl at the front desk at Randy's office had told him their last name.

'What name did Samantha use?' ran through his head.

He was searching his memory bank, trying to remember, before their paths met. The name, he recalled, had something to do with an old carburetor. He'd used the pneumonic trick - associating a name with an item that would jog his memory. Connecting the name to old automobile engines had made sense, somehow. His father had tinkered with cars, and they used parts that no longer existed in modern autos. The carburetor was one of them.

Jack was in trouble. They were walking his way. What did their name have to do with a car part that fed gas to an engine? The gas came through a fuel pump; was the name 'Pumper' or 'Plumlee?' They were almost there. Jack's mind was racing. The gas flowed from the pump through a valve called the: He had it!

"Suzy Venturi, you little trouble-maker!"

The little girl giggled and ran the remaining steps to give him a hug. Her mother was right behind.

"What a memory you have, Jack!"

He mentally congratulated himself for the save.

"Who can forget such a fine Italian name? Are you doing some family shopping?"

"We came to the farmer's market and now we're just looking around. Summer vacation is here and we're taking a few days off to get reacquainted."

Betty glanced at Suzy.

"You got it right; she's my little trouble-maker."

"She's such a fun kid," Jack said.

"And she's learning your Everly Brothers tune. When she gets up in the morning, we say, 'Wake Up, Little Suzy.' Then she says, 'We gotta go home,' and laughs like crazy."

Mrs. Venturi began giggling, mid-story.

"You ought to see it. It's hysterical."

Suzy realized they were next to the ice cream shop.

"Mama, can I get some ice cream?"

It was the same place Jack had visited last week. He had just seen the owner, Willie Quinn, working behind the counter. Jack expected Betty's approval, but she looked troubled.

"Oh, sweetie, we've got to get milk at the grocery and we're already late getting to Grandma's."

Suzy's little face looked so disappointed; Jack couldn't help himself.

"How 'bout I get a cone while you take care of the grocery run? I bet she's been good all day!"

Suzy was instantly ready to plead her case.

"Mama, pleeeeze?"

The sun was shining, the birds were singing, Jack was smiling, and things had been happy all morning. Betty gave a 'well, okay' motion with her hands.

"Okay, Suzy, you've been so good today. You stay here with Mr. Jack and I'll be right back."

She started to give Jack money for the cone and he waved her off. Suzy didn't wait for her mother to leave for the grocery. The little girl bolted into the ice cream store and vaulted onto one of the counter stools. Jack looked at her five-year-old face, beaming at Mr. Quinn. Norman Rockwell couldn't have painted a happier scene.

"We need two cones, Mr. Quinn," Jack said. Looking at Suzy, he added "chocolate or....?"

"Chocolate!" she bellowed.

The deal was done. Jack had the money on the counter and Mr. Quinn handed over two cones.

"Thanks, pal," Jack said, and grabbed some napkins.

He knew from experience that kids and cones always needed clean-up.

"How 'bout we go outside, sweetie? That way, your mama can see us when she comes out of the grocery."

Suzy smiled, nodded happily, and headed toward the door. Jack pulled it open and motioned outside.

"Now, stay close here, away from the street, okay?"

"Okay," the little girl answered, and stepped outside.

She had the cone in her hands and fierce determination on her face. It was time to lick up the ice cream before any of it dripped. Jack saw a blur approaching from the side and realized it was a kid on a bike.

'Get off the sidewalk' and 'Watch out, Suzy!' blasted through his mind simultaneously. He was able to grab Suzy's shirt and pull her back in time. The kid swerved straight into the trash can on the sidewalk. He'd missed Suzy, but his bike clanged into the metal container. It reverberated with a hollow 'twang' that was audible in all directions. The next sound Jack heard was a wail from Suzy. Her cone was smashed on the sidewalk and tears were already forming. Jack had his napkin on her face in a flash.

"Don't worry, baby girl. We've got plenty of ice cream."

Mr. Quinn had heard the commotion and was at the door immediately. He saw that Jack had things under control and Suzy was safe. Jack caught his eye and looked at the cone on the sidewalk. His raised eyebrow got silent approval and Mr. Quinn went inside for a replacement.

By this time Betty Venturi had rushed out of the grocery and saw the bike, the trash can, and Jack tending to Suzy.

"Are you alright?" she called to her daughter.

Suzy gave short, jerky nods, while Jack tended to mop-up duty. It was obvious to Betty what had happened. The kid with the bike was picking it and himself up from the sidewalk. Jack got to him before the frightened mother could.

"You okay, buddy?"

Betty had caught her breath and jumped in.

"Gerry Hyde, you could have hurt Suzy! You keep your bike on the street or I'm telling your mother!"

The kid looked terrified and didn't speak at all. By this time, Mr. Quinn was back with a new cone. He handed it to Jack, who was kneeling down, at eye level with Suzy. He smoothed her hair and put the cone in her hands.

"All better, Suzy. You're fine, now. Don't cry."

Suzy had started the post-crying staccato breathing that comes after an upset. Jack gave her a final hug and steered her back to her mother. Betty had also recovered.

"Jack, thank you so much. That could have been bad."

"Everybody's fine. Glad nobody's hurt. You two get along to Grandma's now."

Betty and Suzy collected themselves and headed to their car. Jack turned to young Gerry.

"That was close."

Gerry was unsure what was going to happen.

"Gosh, mister, I'm sorry."

"Nobody got hurt," Jack repeated. "But let's ease up on the sidewalk, okay?"

The kid nodded and Jack helped him get situated on the bike, in the street. The boy shakily pedaled away while Mr. Quinn and Jack headed back into the store. Jack grinned at the aftermath.

"Quick reaction with the ice cream, dude. Now I need to sit down and start over."

He had the remnants of his own cone in his hand.

Mr. Quinn laughed at Jack's messy sight.

"They're on me, buddy. You done good!"

———

Neither one of them noticed the women, across the street, observing the events.

Sally and Danielle had packed up from the farmer's market and had gone to get a bite at the diner. Content that they sold all their sweet corn, the morning was theirs to enjoy. After coffee and croissants, they went to the dress shop to look at materials and gab with Mrs. Rogers.

Danielle had known Elaine Rogers since childhood. As children, they had shared sleepovers; as high school classmates, they attended all the games and parties. They had plenty to talk about, new and old. Danielle was interested in Elaine's progress in graduate school. Elaine had been the class whiz in chemistry and was close to completing her pharmacy doctorate. Sally and Danielle were pleased to hear that Elaine would be home soon. They would soon have another 'girl-fest' and catch up.

The ladies decided it was time to head home and they all went outside for a lengthy goodbye. They were standing on the sidewalk, under the awning that advertised the shop. The awning and the few trees in front of the store kept them shaded and partially obscured. Still, they could see the surrounding area clearly. The few shops across the street were in plain view, especially Mr. Quinn's ice cream store.

They heard, more than saw, the commotion that erupted when the boy and his bike crashed into the trash can. Turning to the sound, they immediately saw a little girl being tended to by a male figure. Sally thought the man looked a lot like Jack Ridley. She started to say something, but in doing so, she peeked at Danielle. Her daughter was already alerted to the scene. Sally glanced at Mrs. Rogers, and then at Danielle, and then back across the street at Jack. The three women watched together. Danielle was riveted.

They could hear Jack talking soothingly to the little girl.

"Don't worry, baby girl."

"Why, that's Betty Venturi's daughter," Mrs. Rogers half-whispered.

Sally and Mrs. Rogers exchanged a small smile. Danielle's gaze did not waiver. They watched Jack tend to the little girl's tears, and saw him direct that a new ice cream cone be delivered. When Betty Venturi came blasting out of the grocery, they half expected a noisy scene to erupt. But Jack had everything under control.

He was giving the little girl a new cone. Then he spoke calmly to the boy with the bike, and all was well. Betty Venturi left with Suzy, and Jack and Mr. Quinn went back inside the ice cream store. Sally and Mrs. Rogers felt as if they had just witnessed a dramatic scene from some award-winning movie. Sally explained who the helpful man was.

"That's Jack. Pretty nice, huh?"

"You know that guy?"

Only Sally answered.

"We both do," and Sally turned to include Danielle in the conversation.

But Danielle wasn't available. She wasn't paying attention to Sally or Mrs. Rogers. She was still looking across the street, at the now empty sidewalk, and gazing at the door of the ice cream store. It had just closed and the two men were visible through the glass window.

Danielle had her hand up to her face, partially covering her mouth.

"Oh, my," she said.

She lowered her hand to her heart.

"Oh, my."

29

I ALWAYS WANTED A NEIGHBOR
LIKE YOU

Mr. Quinn and Jack took a breather after the sidewalk rescue. The entire town knew Mr. Quinn, and he knew most of them. It was no surprise that he and Jack would catch up on what had transpired since Jack's last visit. Mr. Quinn knew that Jack had played with the Crushers last weekend, but he hadn't been aware that Jack was still in town. Jack gave him an update on his plans.

"I'm staying through the weekend. Going to play two games."

Mr. Quinn was pleasantly surprised.

"Well, that will give me a chance to bring Maureen. It's neat to see the kids who were little just last year, it seems, and now they're grown."

The years had rolled by like secret whispers. Like billions of folks before him, he had the same reaction.

"Lord, where has the time gone?"

Jack was smart enough to know, as a twenty-five year old, he had a limited perspective on the topic. But his old soul devised an observation.

"Every one of the kids that came through here will go where life takes them. But they will return to this very spot with the best memories. Because of you. Little Suzy will come back and talk about this morning, for years."

Mr. Quinn gave a nostalgic smile and returned to more solid ground.

"What kept you here longer, this time?"

Jack grinned.

"It was the ice cream."

After another wry smile from Mr. Quinn, Jack told the story.

"It's pretty interesting. I ran across a kid that I think can throw. I'm spending some practice time with him, and if you come to the game Saturday, you might get to see him a bit."

Mr. Quinn was interested.

"A kid from here? Who's that?"

"Duncan James. You know him?"

Mr. Quinn's face brightened and he nodded.

"Oh, sure. Since he was a baby. Mo and Duncan's mother were in the ladies' group at church. I knew his father from when they first came to town. He was such a fine man. Would help anybody."

Mr. Quinn paused, and shook his head admiringly.

"Dave could fix anything. If you needed a light on your back porch, he knew how to run the wire out there. If you had a banged-up wall, he could patch and sand it and you'd never know the hole was there. Everybody knew he would help them. You had to be careful about shooting your mouth off about needing something, because David James would show up to handle it."

His face darkened just a little.

"After he died, people should have been running to Sally to help her. But I guess they forgot who fixed their tire, or got their car started, or worked on their house."

He gave Jack a thoughtful look.

"You would have really liked him. Lord, I miss that guy."

Jack was pleased to hear good things about Duncan's father.

"I sure like his family. I told you what's up with Duncan. Sally's a gem, the way she's keeping the place going. Danielle seems like a nice person, too."

Mr. Quinn had a mischievous smile on his face.

"Nice person? That girl is a peach! She's a perfect mix of her parents. She's got her dad's super heart and straight shooter attitude, and her mom's smarts and personality. Gonna be some lucky guy who ends up with her."

Mr. Quinn left the topic open but he noticed that there was no comment. Jack just looked pensive and then changed the subject.

"Well, I sure hope I can get Duncan on the right track."

"He's a great kid, too," Mr. Quinn said. "I remember his dad said he was going to be quite a player. But, things sorta stopped when Dave passed away. The family was probably in shock, and I guess baseball fell by the wayside."

Jack tried to bring the conversation full circle.

"Well, I hope I can help."

Mr. Quinn smiled, noting that Jack had avoided any talk about Danielle.

"You sure picked the right bunch."

He gave Jack a pat on the back as his visitor headed out the door.

It was time to visit the farm. There had been plenty of excitement for one day, Jack figured. He retraced his steps to his car and fired up the engine. Funny, he thought, the car had been running fine lately. Maybe he'd gotten some water in the gas tank. He hoped his good luck with the car continued. The longer route to the farm was the best way to enjoy the morning's peace and tranquility.

He was on an opposite path from Sally and Danielle, so they did not see each other as they traveled. The women had lingered at Mrs. Rogers' shop for a moment or two after the 'ice cream' escapade. Sally and Mrs. Rogers had noted Danielle's reaction to the incident. Their intuition told them there was more to the story. Mrs. Rogers took the oblique path.

"So, you know that fellow? He's not from here, I don't think."

She left the thought hanging in the air, to see what it might catch. Sally fielded the question.

"He's the guy who's been working on baseball with Duncan. Doesn't live here."

Mrs. Rogers was intrigued.

"Really? He sure helped out with Suzy."

Then she lobbed an underhand pitch to Danielle.

"Pretty nice, right?"

Danielle's answer was delayed while she sorted through a whole spectrum of emotions. She had originally felt that Jack was an intrusion in their family rehab mode. Acceptance dawned, with her mother's help. Maybe the newcomer might be good for Duncan. Everybody deals with loss in different ways. It could be that dabbling with his old pastime would help her brother regroup.

The evidence inclined Danielle toward seeing Jack as a positive influence via baseball. That gave her a perspective on this visitor she had not anticipated. Jack's personality and kindness, to her family, were pleasing attributes. And today, she saw Jack's sweet nature with a child. That told her that he possessed another level of attractiveness. It was a lot to process. So, she opted for simplicity for Mrs. Rogers' question.

"Yes, he's pretty nice."

Sally observed it all with a twinge of irony. She could see what was happening and she certainly knew her daughter. Obviously, Danielle had her own issues. Returning home to help her mother had to be a challenge. Sally wasn't sure how deeply Danielle had been impacted by the boyfriend event, but it couldn't have been easy. Now, in the midst of the upheaval in her life, this stranger appeared. There had been initial doubt, if not a bit of animosity.

Sally was certain that Danielle had revised her initial view of Jack Ridley. She felt serene in that knowledge. Clearly, Jack was an honorable and decent person. His dealings with her children would not be influenced by self-interest. Sally was content to bide her time, and see what fate had in store for all of them.

"I guess we better get back home," Sally said.

It was a move to divert their attention from what Mrs. Rogers had surmised. Danielle was happy to seize the opportunity.

"Please make sure Elaine calls me when she gets home. We can catch up."

After mutual goodbyes, the James ladies climbed in the pickup truck. Sally was not inclined to pry, but she couldn't resist a thought about the events in town.

"That was sweet, Jack and Suzy."

Danielle kept her eyes on the road.

"Uh-huh."

The minimal response gave Sally something else to contemplate. She knew her daughter. The less Danielle said, the more she was thinking. When they arrived at home, Jack was there with Duncan. They were preparing to throw a bit and Elvis was observing. The dog usually gave his humans initial recognition, and then stayed on the sidelines. Duncan had completed tractor duty and was brushing off the dust.

"Okay, how about I hose off before we start?"

He headed inside while Jack greeted Sally and Danielle.

"I saw the farmer's market stands in town, but I was telling Duncan that I missed it. Things go okay?"

Sally answered for the both of them.

"We did fine. Sold all the corn. Might have sold more. I have to figure out how to get more there the next time."

Jack looked at Danielle and joked.

"Danielle, I like your 'Farmer Jane' look."

She blushed, realizing she had the morning's grime on her face and clothes. Again, Sally noticed that Danielle stayed silent. More thinking going on, it seemed.

"Don't worry, Jack," Sally said. "We'll get gussied up before you have to be seen in public with us at the game."

Jack was momentarily surprised.

"Great. I thought it was just me and Duncan, but it'd be nice for all of us to go."

"Duncan said you were going, and asked if we wanted to come along," Sally volunteered. "I hope that's okay."

Jack was emphatic.

"Well, sure. It'd be fun."

He was still waiting for Danielle to join in, and looked in her direction. She might have taken his prior statement the wrong way.

"I didn't mean you look bad. I meant you've been working and doing good."

Having to backtrack and explain yourself is always awkward. Jack felt even more inept. Danielle was still just looking at him, and he figured his explanation was failing. He raised his hands, palms up, and completed the clumsy moment.

"Sorry, Danielle."

She smirked at him, ever so slightly, and gently shook her head. Duncan returned after his brief clean-up, and Danielle finally spoke. She shifted her attention to her brother.

"Cake, what time do we leave to see your old team? Maybe afterwards we can spend some of the market money on a bite."

She glanced at Jack, for effect, and jerked her thumb toward him.

"J.A. says I worked pretty hard. Maybe I deserve a night out?"

An interesting thought fired through Sally's mind. A few days ago, the remark might have had a bite to it. Today, it was playful and evocative. She had an insight into how her thoughtful daughter was processing the earlier events.

Duncan had no basis for cluing in. He went right to timing for the game.

"They start about four o'clock. There's plenty of time for supper afterwards. If we leave here at three-thirty or thereabouts, it should be fine."

Sally took them back to some kind of schedule.

"Okay, kids. I've got lunch meat before you boys get started."

"Fine by me," Jack said. "We won't be throwing too much today. None tomorrow, if Dunc is going to do any pitching Saturday."

They trooped into the kitchen and started making sandwiches. Sally was ready to discuss logistics.

"How do you plan to work this thing with Duncan?"

Jack thought it was a good time to have some perspective on what might be accomplished. He'd made a mental list, and ran through it for all three of them to consider.

"First, the deal with Randy is we're gonna be ahead in the game. That's for two reasons: The team can't be asked to take a loss if things go bad, which they won't."

He added that last part with a glance toward Duncan, for emphasis. Sowing any seeds of doubt in this kid's head was not part of the program.

"Second," he continued, "I want to have a feel for the batters coming up when Duncan goes in. If they've got somebody hitting well, it wouldn't be fair for his first chance."

He paused, and made the next statement as definite as he could.

"I am very confident this will work. But, there might be a guy or two that gets some wood on the ball. That's not a deal-breaker."

He looked once more at Duncan, who was hanging on his words.

"You need to know if we give up a run, I've promised Randy we stop right there. Again, I don't think that will happen. But if it does, I walk out to the mound with Randy. You hand the ball to him, with respect, and go to the bench. No issues."

There was a thoughtful silence at the table. To Jack's surprise, Danielle spoke first.

"Cake, I think you can do this. And Jack knows what he's doing. If he says this is going to work, I'm a believer."

She patted her brother on the arm and got up to get milk on the table. Sally sat there with a contented look on her face. Whatever happened with this weekend game, she felt that she and her children had turned a corner. The kids were exhibiting a better dynamic between them, and she couldn't remember when she felt more upbeat.

————

The boys headed out to decide which was first, painting or pitching. Duncan put in his vote.

"If it's all the same to you, I was up at dawn on the tractor. I'd like to throw a bit and since we're not throwing tomorrow, I could get to painting then."

Jack agreed that it was a better use of their training time.

Duncan had a caveat.

"You can't tell mom and Danny that I wimped out on painting."

Jack was in on the scam.

"I'll take the heat. I'll tell them I'm the one who needs to slow down! Which ain't far from the truth, bud."

Jack checked the time.

"Look, it's already about two. We'll get in an hour or so and get ready to go see your buddies."

Their warm-up process began smoothly. Before long, they quickly got down to business.

Jack laid out the plan.

"Give me about ten medium-speed fastballs. Then we'll switch to change-ups. We finish with curves. All slow, okay?"

Duncan nodded.

"We'll just use high-school signals this weekend," Jack said. "One finger, fastball. Two is curve. Three for change-up. That's usually for a slider, but we're not there yet."

Jack got into position and gave the fastball signal. He wanted his pitcher accustomed to seeing the sign and reacting without thinking. Duncan read the signal and fired the first pitch. Jack noted that the throws were in the 'little box' they had discussed. He nodded approvingly, and ten more medium heaters arrived. Continuing to give the fastball sign, Jack decided to try and trick his student.

Without any change in behavior, Jack showed three fingers; a curveball. He was pleased that Duncan made no outward indication, beyond his usual quick nod that he had the sign. And here it came: An arcing curve that traveled exactly where it should. Jack had to stand up and congratulate the kid.

"Great! Here I was trying to screw you up, and you just zoomed right through it!"

Duncan merely gave him a small grin and readied himself for the next sign. What was significant in Jack's little deception was that in practice they had gone from fastballs to change-ups. Duncan demonstrated, in throwing the curve, that he was alert and adjusting to changing conditions. Jack was delighted at this little victory.

To celebrate, he switched the next sign to a change-up. Same result. Duncan nodded, and the change came floating in. Jack was pleased once again, but he had an adjustment.

"Remember to keep the same motion. You *explode* toward the plate, and let the deeper grip do the work."

Secretly, Jack was ecstatic. At this half-speed effort, Duncan wasn't able to do much exploding. As they increased velocity, his mechanics would only get better. They continued through the pitches, at a dozen or so repetitions each. Jack called a halt.

"You know, that many pitches equates to about a third of a complete game. And I don't see you that tired. How are you feeling?"

Duncan was in his element. He was feeling strong and accurate, and felt like he could continue throwing for hours. But he downplayed his condition.

"Pretty good. You need a break, old man?"

Jack laughed. He could build on this kid's gutsiness and decided on one further test. Duncan's development was on target and Jack was brimming with confidence. He wanted to see if what he glimpsed last week was truly there, or if the whack on the head at the Zone had disrupted his fine vision skills.

"How about we try just a bit of velocity?"

Duncan was ready.

"I thought you'd never ask!"

Jack was quick to rein him in.

"We're not going nutso here. Under control, with slow increments, for a half-dozen pitches. Maybe more. I want you to keep it in the box at all times. Start with our last velocity, and dial it up a small amount each time. Part of my plan is to see what control you have over velocity itself. Another part is seeing what happens to your control as you speed up. And the last part is finding out what your top end is. Got it?"

Duncan nodded and readied himself once again. To Jack, he seemed to be deliberate and unexcited. Exactly what he needed to be.

Jack cautioned, once again. This was important. He wanted the kid pitching within himself.

"We don't need an arm blown out!"

Dropping into his crouch, he signaled for a fastball, and waited to see if his grand experiment had promise. The first pitch was just where they'd left off - medium speed, in the box. Jack returned the ball without comment. Another fastball signal. The pitch came in, slightly faster. Same location. Another signal. Same result. Jack was pleased with the progress.

Each pitch was on target, and the increase in speed was consistent each time. Jack estimated that they were in the eighty-five mile per hour range, and he knew Duncan had plenty more to give. Jack let the final pitch smack into the glove with a resounding crack and stood up. He wagged a finger at Duncan, to say 'you're on track,' and motioned toward the house.

"We're gonna be just fine," was all Jack said.

Supportive, but not too enthusiastic was the strategy. A pitcher needs to maintain an even keel during the ebbs and flows that will come in a game. Still, Jack was feeling good about the coming test. He gave Duncan a grin.

"Tell me, Mr. Cake. Are you topping out in speed?"

Duncan returned a lopsided smile and shook his head.

"Not even close, Boss," he said evenly. "Not even close."

Jack mulled over the comment. He could see that the Project was considering the possibilities.

"How much velocity you think we need?"

Duncan's question confirmed Jack's thinking. Jack wasn't going to address that thought at this point of the development, so he dodged the issue.

"In the show, rookie, we say 'velo.' You'll get it, someday."

Then he went inside to let the ladies know that practice was over. Duncan delayed, visiting Elvis. Sally was in the kitchen and Danielle was out of sight.

"We're wrapped up," Jack said. "How about we head on in to see the 'Skip' show?"

Sally was agreeable.

"Do you need any clean-up?"

"I'm just gonna use the water pump," Jack said. "Didn't work that hard."

Duncan arrived, and Jack continued.

"I didn't work up much of a sweat, and who cares what a teenager smells like?"

At that moment, Danielle entered the room.

"Good Lord, don't make it worse than it is."

Her hack on Duncan produced smiles.

Jack thought it was interesting that he was having this type of conversation with a brand-new family.

"You'll be outside, Cake," Sally added. "Nobody will notice!"

"Don't bother me. If we're done picking on Duncan, let's go!"

Jack was out the door and headed to the pump for a quick douse. He didn't care if his hair was a little wet; it would dry soon enough.

Duncan took a turn at planning.

"Jack, you want to drive or come back for your car?"

Jack realized he'd need to at least drive one way, and Danielle would take her car.

"How about I drive now and don't have to come back late?"

"We'll take Danny's car," Sally said. "One of you want to keep Jack company?"

Duncan volunteered his sister.

"Danny, you go. I've spent enough time with him."

Danielle paused, just a beat.

"Why not? I've been wanting to hear this opera chick Cake says you're talking about."

Jack feigned shock.

"Calling La Diva an 'opera chick' might get you fined or something."

That didn't get any laughs, so he went for an easy exit.

"Okay, let's go."

They paired off toward the vehicles. Danielle smiled as Jack opened her door. He fired up the car and dialed in the Figaro aria.

"Just listen," he said. "The first time you hear this music, she will grab you for good."

Danielle complied and waited. The graceful duet started as they got on the road to town. Danielle listened intently and she knew she had heard it before.

"That's the thing from Shawshank! You know, where the guy plays it over the prison loudspeaker."

Jack agreed with her memory.

"That's right. It's so cool they chose this piece for the movie. It gives people a chance to hear opera that they wouldn't otherwise."

Danielle was enthusiastic.

"Do you remember where the guy said 'I have no idea what those two Italian ladies were singing' but it was about something so beautiful it can't be expressed in words?"

Jack was pleased that she knew the story.

"You just figured out what opera can do! Some of the vocals are too beautiful to describe. Fleming's, anyway."

Danielle had to tease him.

"Does she know about your crush?"

Jack gave her an evil look.

"You don't have to own a painting to appreciate its beauty," he replied.

"Heard that one before, Jack. You're pretty deep, for a baseball player," Danielle said.

"No," Jack answered, "it's just getting deep in here."

They had arrived at the high school diamond with Sally and Duncan right behind them. As they parked, Danielle remained on the opera theme.

"Do you know what it's about?"

"Sure. The one woman's husband is trying to fool around on her. She's telling her buddy about her plan to smoke him out. Or close to that."

Danielle got out of the car and stood next to her mother. She pretended to glare at Jack.

"Figures. Another guy who can't behave. Men!"

She gathered her mom and Duncan, and headed to the bleachers. Jack lagged behind. He knew he was in a losing battle.

"Hey, it wasn't me, you know!"

She continued to huff along, acting miffed. Sally was amused and Duncan was baffled.

"What the heck was that?"

"She likes opera, I think," Jack said, loud enough for Danielle to hear.

They grabbed seats on the first base side bleachers. Skip was close by, warming up the pitcher. Duncan happily started in on his pal.

"Don't get the mitt dirty, you loser!"

Danielle looked at Jack and repeated her earlier remark, slightly revised.

"Boys!"

Jack figured the best defense was no defense at all. The game mercifully started and they enjoyed watching the high school kids in action. Skip had a respectable game and the good guys won, three to one. One of the boys came bouncing toward the dugout, yelling something Jack had never heard.

"Butterburger baseball!"

Welcoming the chance for someone else to provide answers, Jack gave Danielle an inquisitive look.

"It means they go to Culver's to celebrate," she said. "The restaurant sponsors the team, and the manager gives the boys half off when they win."

Jack thought it was another beautiful example of small-town living. Skip was approaching and he introduced Jack to the coach, Steve Corey.

"Here's the mystery man with the catcher's mitt, coach."

"Well, thank you, young man," Coach Corey said. "That's a big help to Skip."

Jack knew what to say.

"My pleasure, Coach. Glad you like it."

Skip chimed in.

"Mr. Ridley has been coaching Duncan. He's throwing with the Crushers this weekend."

"That so, Duncan?" Coach Corey was genuinely interested. "You learning anything?"

Duncan was emphatic.

"Jack knows a lot about pitching, Coach."

Steve Corey had been playing and coaching baseball for forty-five years. It took about three seconds for him to put the names 'Jack' and 'Ridley' together. He looked at Jack and a light bulb went off.

"The Reds?"

Jack knew that Coach Corey had heard his story. How much of it was another question. Jack nodded and waited to see if this would go well. Corey's eyes widened, and he included Sally and Danielle in his smile.

"That's great you're helping Duncan!" the coach enthused. "He has some kind of arm."

For privacy, he leaned Jack to one side.

"When his dad died, Duncan just backed away and was done. If you can get him back into the game, that'd be perfect!"

Jack was relieved that the focus was on someone else.

"That's the plan, Coach. Come by the Crushers game Saturday and see if he gets in."

Skip had been talking to his teammates and came back to the group.

"Mr. Ridley, I've got an idea. I've told the guys how you're helping Dunc. We all know you're painting the barn. How 'bout you give us some pointers in practice, and the guys show up and paint?"

Skip completed what was a lengthy speech for him, with a glance at the team.

"All of us."

Jack looked to the Coach for guidance.

"Fine by me," Corey said. "You're at practice for a couple of hours. They help Duncan for a couple of hours. Everybody wins."

Jack shrugged and agreed.

"Practice tomorrow?"

"Ten!" the team responded as one.

"Then we go to Duncan's," Skip said. "You're about half done already, and we all can wrap it up."

Jack looked to Sally.

"If it's okay with you, I'm good."

The plan was set. Jack and the James Gang headed off to supper at the regular diner. They let the kids go to Culver's on their own for some 'team-time.' After a nice meal with the usual Danielle-to-Duncan-to-Jack ribbing, they split up. Jack headed to his car and the others got into the SUV. The Mustang had just started when Danielle appeared.

"My purse is on the floor."

"What secrets would I have found in there?"

She didn't respond to the joke, so Jack held the purse out the window. Danielle paused for a brief moment, and gave him a careful look.

"I had a good time, Jack. Thanks for the ride and the music lesson."

Jack smiled.

"I told you she would get to you. See you tomorrow after the practice?"

Danielle nodded and headed back to her car. Jack waved at the others and pulled away. It occurred to him that he had not been in a car with a young woman since Olivia. The thought gave him a strange mixture of sad and glad that he would have to think about for a while.

30

AND RIDLEY SHALL LEAD THEM

J ack fell asleep with visions of extra help on the barn project dancing in his head. Getting the painting done ahead of schedule would be a tremendous boost for Sally. The deal with the high school team meant great timing, as well. Jack was free until ten, so he slept late. He awoke with a curious enthusiasm about the day's prospects. About nine he stopped for a small breakfast and then headed to the high school practice. Coach Corey was there getting things started. Jack approached and went to work.

"Put me where you want, Coach."

"I was thinking we would run through individual drills, instead of a scrimmage," Corey said. "You could jump in at any point, maybe batting or fielding, with any points you have. That way, all the players hear everything. Later on, they can work together as a group on what they learned."

The plan sounded great to Jack. He figured the Coach would know the way his kids learned best. So, they started with hitting. Coach Corey gathered the team so Jack could demonstrate his swing.

"It starts with balance," Jack began. "If your balance is wrong, how can you maintain a level swing? So, feet about shoulder width apart. Some guys stay back in their stance, as part of their 'loading' for the pitch. That comes down to personal preference. Some major leaguers start with an open stance and close when the ball is thrown. Either way, you want to allow your head to be level during the swing. Your 'eye on the ball' is shot if your head is bobbing around. I like to be far enough off the plate so an inside pitch doesn't 'handcuff' me, but not so far I can't get to an outside pitch. The goal is getting the barrel of the bat to the ball. I reach over to make sure I can touch the outside of the plate with the bat."

Jack demonstrated the stance.

"Next, we 'load' body weight to your back foot, to prepare to transfer weight to the front. That initiates your power move toward the ball. This all occurs before your hands start to move. As the pitch is released, you have 'loaded' your swing and you're stepping toward the pitcher. You can't wait until the ball is released to 'load and step.' You'll never get the bat around. Don't start to extend your hands away from your body, as that costs power. It's an 'inside-out' move. Your hands start back and swing through until they're fully extended."

A couple of the boys were rolling their hands through a swinging motion.

"Both hands on the bat for better strength," Jack continued. "And your head is relatively still. If you swing right-handed, your chin starts on your left shoulder and your body pivots during the swing. Your chin ends up on the right. The 'body turn' and the arm swing add to your power."

Jack looked around at the players to include everyone.

"All good?"

Twenty heads nodded solemnly.

"There's plenty more to the swing, but keep the basics in mind. You need to go through the motion about 10,000 times, until you do it without thinking."

Jack switched his approach.

"I think of the pitch, at least a level fastball, like it's a ball rolling toward you on a table. Your chances of making contact are greater if you swing on the same plane as the ball. It's like sweeping crumbs off the table."

He demonstrated with his hand, in a flat motion.

"You wouldn't do as well if it were a golf swing. That requires the arc of the 'contact point' to be exactly where the ball is."

Jack motioned again, with his hand making a U-shaped dip.

"Which of these has a longer time, during the swing, to make contact?"

Jack observed a few of the boys duplicating his motions.

"That's good; if you visualize the flow of the bat, it helps your muscle memory maintain the action. I try to put it all together in a 1-2-3-4 motion. One is loading, or gathering strength; two is stepping toward the pitch and transferring power; three is seeing the ball, because you watch the ball throughout the swing, all the way to contact; and four is hitting the darn thing!"

Affecting a rhythmic cadence, Jack announced the steps.

"Load, step, see, hit."

He realized the four-beat repetition equaled a song meter. Some of the boys were playfully acting out their swing with a slight dance effect. Jack got the joke.

"Load, step, see, hit," he said, rhythmically, and paused for emphasis.

"That, boys, is the *only* rap you'll ever get out of me!"

The entire team laughed at the image.

"Coach Corey knows all this stuff," Jack graciously added. "He'll be walking you through your repetitions. Like they say: 'If you want to do it the best, you just gotta do it the most.' I like what Coach Knight used to say: 'It's not the will to win that matters. It's the will to *prepare* to win.' You prepare your swing, boys, so it works when it's show time."

Thoughtful nods bloomed everywhere. Jack looked to Coach Corey and realized that he had his cell phone out, taping the instruction. Jack asked for guidance on the next step.

"Should we do run-throughs, or switch to fielding?"

Jack wanted the boys to be reminded that their Coach was in charge, as their ongoing mentor. It was another aspect of his 'team mentality' that always endeared him to coaches and teammates.

"Let's maximize our time with Coach Ridley, boys," Coach Corey said. "We can do reps on our own. How 'bout we switch to fielding?"

Jack was happy to oblige.

"I've spent most of my time behind the plate, but I've learned from some great infielders. The first rule: Stay low on the ball. If it gets past your glove and your body knocks it down, you've still got a chance. You can always come up to the ball; if you wait to get down to a hit ball, it's too late. Approaching the ball, not waiting for it, is the important thing."

Jack demonstrated the fielding position.

"Usually, big-leaguers want to come *to* the ball. Waiting can cost you. Dealing with a fast runner requires that kind of positioning. It cuts down the distance for your throw to first, and allows you to time the bounce. You know, taking the ball on the short or long-hop."

Several of the boys were going through an imaginary fielding motion.

"Looks great!" Jack said. "You need short, choppy steps getting to the ball. That's best for adjusting and changing direction. You stay in front of the ball and gather it in to your chest. This maintains balance and controls your center of gravity. It also helps a controlled throw to first."

Jack paused to seal the deal.

"Here's the point, guys: You need speed, but you can't rush it. If you are late to first, you have a runner on first. Not good, but if you blow the throw, you have a runner in scoring position. Nothing jerks your pitcher more than having to deal with a guy ready to score, when he shouldn't be there at all."

Again, Jack saw nods, as the boys took it all in.

"Coach, would you like me to go with pitchers and catchers?"

Jack figured that would give the Coach the chance to reinforce the drills on his terms. The catchers and pitchers would get Jack's closer attention.

"Great idea," Coach Corey assented.

Motioning toward the sidelines, Corey divided the team.

"Pitchers and catchers with Coach Ridley over there. The rest stay with me to run though what we've seen."

He gave Jack a thumbs-up and started the drills.

Jack took the four pitchers and two catchers over to the bench. He ran through an abbreviated version of what he had been teaching Duncan all week. Before he knew it, Coach Corey returned with the rest of the team.

"Coach, I can already see improvement in these guys. This has been a big help."

Jack returned the compliment.

"Your pitchers and catchers will have some new ideas as well, Coach. I hope to hear good things about their progress."

The mood was positive and upbeat. Skip jumped in.

"Hey, we're due at Duncan's for a painting lesson."

Coach Corey added some helpful advice.

"Boys, you'll need junk clothes, and it wouldn't hurt if you bring a paintbrush. I doubt Mrs. James has a box of them."

The players went home prior to gathering at Duncan's. Jack headed to the farm wondering how many of the team would follow through. They were kids, after all. He arrived and explained the morning's practice to Sally and Danielle. It wasn't long after that the boys started to trickle in. They had enthusiastic greetings for Duncan and a 'how-do-you-do' for the ladies. Coach Corey wasn't far behind. He walked up to Jack and smacked him on the back.

"That was the best practice ever. You have great teaching skills."

Jack thanked him and told him that the boys' help on the barn was a fine trade. Coach Corey wasn't through.

"I've been thinking about that, too. This is a great team-building project. I'm going to get something like this going every year. It won't hurt these boys to see what it means to help out in their community."

Sally smiled at the idea and reflected that Jack's positive influence extended to more than baseball. Coach Corey quietly took Jack aside.

"You know, they all showed up. That says a bunch."

The boys attacked the barn with their brushes. Jack had his hands full, moving ladders, and keeping the help supplied with paint. Jack halfway expected that Elvis would be animated by the activity, but he calmly observed the action. Within a few hours, the team completed the job. Sally and Danielle happily watched the effort and admired the finished product.

"Thank you boys, this is great," Sally said.

One of the guys approached.

"Mrs. James, Duncan's dad was always good to us. He helped my dad build the deck at our house. We should have been here sooner."

Sally hugged the boy and smiled.

"Frank Dorsey, you are a sweetheart. Please tell your parents I said so!"

Coach Corey was spearheading the clean-up detail, and the boys said their goodbyes. All of them came to Jack and told him how helpful his talk had been. It was an all-round 'barn and baseball' lovefest. Before long, the crew left and everything was quiet again. Sally and Jack walked around the barn, admiring the work. The fresh paint was gleaming in the early evening sun. Sally's blithe smile revealed her serenity.

"Those boys went to town, didn't they?"

Jack was introspective.

"Almost all of them told me stories about your husband and the kind things he did for them. I think this whole day came from him."

Sally didn't respond. She thoughtfully linked her arm in Jack's and headed back to the house. Danielle and Duncan were on the porch watching them approach. Duncan was elated, mostly because his summer drudgery had been removed from his shoulders.

"Time to celebrate!" he said. "What do you say, Danny? Jack said there's a band at the Legion tonight. Let's go and I'll show you my dance moves!"

Danielle nodded, looking at Jack and her mother. Sally's happy mood completed the benevolent day.

"Sounds good, Cake," Danielle smirked. "We should celebrate Jack's getting your job done in just one week."

It was obvious she was glad that the work was complete. Looking at Jack, she wisecracked her appreciation.

"The barn is done *and* we get a night on the town! I'm gonna celebrate and brush *all* my teeth!"

This girl's humor was insane. Jack burst out laughing.

"Okay, gang, the Legion for supper at six? It's 'Bring Anybody' Friday. Then it's oldies with the band!"

Jack was looking forward to the evening with the family. Sally renewed her hold on his arm.

"We'll do it. And thank you, Jack, for making this happen. All of this."

Duncan and Danielle had turned to go inside to get ready. Sally hung on to Jack's arm for a second longer. She released her grip and looked at Jack with a thoughtful expression on her face. He was about to say something along the lines of 'it was my pleasure' or something equally trite. Then Sally patted his cheek.

"You know, Danielle's been calling Duncan 'Cake' all week. That's new for her. And he hasn't called her 'Dumyell' or 'Dumbo' since right after you showed up. That's a pretty good trick, Jack."

Then she gave him a sweet smile and headed back into the house. Jack realized that a gentle wave of contented acceptance was rolling over him. He couldn't decide if it was because he felt good about helping Sally get her barn painted, or because Sally was being kind and affectionate. Then he realized that he didn't care where the feeling came from. He just liked it. He liked it a lot.

31

DO YOU KNOW MUSTANG, SALLY?

Jack waited to see if he should drive alone, so he used the time for a water pump visit. Scrubbing up was easy, because the team did the dirty work on the barn. Before long, his three companions returned, dressed and ready for dinner.

"Mom and Duncan are going to drive together," Danielle said. "How 'bout an opera ride?"

Sally and Duncan stepped off the porch and headed toward Danielle's car. Duncan nudged his mother in the ribs.

"Opera," he whispered. "That's what she's thinking."

Sally smiled and climbed in her daughter's car. Danielle walked to Jack's car and eased into the front seat. Her driver was waiting, and turned the key.

"Okay, you ready for more musical heartache?"

She wiggled her hand, palm down, for the international 'so-so' signal.

"I'm more of a Sara Bareilles fan, but what've you got?"

"Sara's great!" Jack answered. "Just different. For opera, this is my all-time favorite."

He explained the drama of 'O mio babbino caro' and let the vocal do the rest.

Danielle was impressed, but hid behind gentle banter.

"I like it, but we gotta call this girl and let her know she'll never be happy without you."

Jack rose to the challenge.

"Jealousy is such an ugly emotion."

They both grinned and enjoyed the late afternoon drive. Jack decided to take a chance, and ask a question that had been bubbling up for a few days.

"Tell me something, if you would."

Danielle didn't say anything; she just turned a bit to look at Jack. He chose some careful words.

"Don't get me wrong, but when we met you weren't too friendly. And now you're saying nice things."

Danielle paused and looked at her hands, as if the answer were written there. She exhaled slowly. For a second, she looked like an athlete making a record attempt in an Olympic event.

"I'm not real proud of how this started. Do you remember the stupid thing I said about the Crushers at the Zone?"

Jack gave her his best surprised look.

"It was only one stupid thing?"

She shot him a menacing glance; he chuckled and said, "Okay, I'll shut up."

Danielle began again.

"Cake came home talking about this great guy he'd met. Some guy who was going to help him play baseball. How he'd taken him to the Zone to get his car. Something about a fight there, which I'd heard about. I put two and two together, not in your favor, because of how I'd heard the story. Then, I hear how you're making a great impression on my mother."

Continuing to examine her palms, she glanced at Jack.

"I'd been in 'family survival' mode since my dad died. You know, 'us against the world' sort of thing. I didn't want someone else being part of that. And then I see you painting with Duncan. I was supposed to be helping on that job. And you were wearing a shirt that was my dad's. Can you believe that?"

She looked incredulous.

"I was mad that somebody was getting me out of a lousy paint job! Because you had on a ratty old shirt that was hanging in the barn for years! Just crazy. So, I smarted off to you. I felt like a jerk when I did it. And then I caught it from mom and Duncan. Do you know how hard it is to be told you're wrong, when you already know it?"

Jack thought he'd slip in a conciliatory word when she paused for a breath.

"It wasn't a big deal, and I thought your apology took guts."

She didn't say anything, and Jack eased back to the topic.

"How'd you hear about the fight? You know, the version that did me in."

Danielle paused, and covered her face in embarrassment.

"Jerry Schaefer," she mumbled.

Jack laughed out loud.

"Just perfect. How did you run into that charmer?"

Danielle still had her eyes covered.

"I saw him at the store the next morning, black eye and all. I thought it was polite to ask what happened. He told me this whopper about a guy who played for the Crushers and sucker-punched him at the bar. Said it was a guy named Jack Ridley, and there you are."

They had arrived at the Legion hall, and Jack shut off the engine. He wanted to hear the end of this, and was shaking his head in amazement.

'Here I go again,' he thought to himself. Once more, somebody made up a story, and this time only luck kept it from biting him on his stupid behind.

"Well, I was lucky you didn't hold it against me."

Danielle wasn't through.

"I wasn't convinced, even after mom and Cake sat me down that first night. I did a little more investigation."

Intrigue inched into Jack's mind.

"So, there's more?"

Danielle nodded.

"Jerry threw some names around, and one of them was somebody I know. At least, I know who she is."

Jack should have seen it coming, but he was in a state of mild amazement. His antenna was in sleep mode, and he asked a dumb question.

"Who was that?"

Danielle gave him a sideways glance.

"Patty Patterson."

For the second time that evening, Jack felt his stomach lurch. There was no hope that a rendition of him ending up at Patty's apartment could end well. He dared to turn his head to look at Danielle, and waited for her to lower the boom. Surprisingly, a crinkly look on her nose began.

"Don't worry, I got the whole story. She told me you were just talking to her and being nice. How Jerry started trouble. That you only pushed him away when he grabbed you, and that one of his buddies clobbered you in the head. How you were out on your feet and she didn't want to leave you there 'cause you might get hurt."

Danielle was starting to enjoy the distressed look on Jack's face.

"She said she took you to her place because if she took you to the hospital there'd be a police report. You didn't deserve that, because you hadn't done anything."

Then she paused. She reached over and patted Jack's hand, hanging on the gearshift.

"Patty made it clear that you were a perfect gentleman. She thinks you are the sweetest guy around."

Jack marveled that he'd dodged a dilemma.

"Wow. For a minute there, I was afraid she was going to tell the truth."

They both burst out laughing and headed inside. They were still laughing when they found Sally and Duncan seated at a booth.

"Jeez, I thought you were lost," Duncan directed at them.

Sally ignored his joke.

"Brenda's working tonight. She'll be right back with diet Cokes for all of us."

She winked at Jack.

"See, I learned at the movie."

The four of them ordered dinner and regaled each other with the barn painting saga. Sally was especially pleased.

"Duncan, now you're free for other jobs this summer."

Duncan thought Danielle should get her fair share of the attention.

"You know, Danny got cheated. She was looking forward to sharing the painting fun. We should give her a project of her own. Like maybe, putting on a new roof."

The kidding continued and dinner progressed as planned. Jack proposed dessert.

"This celebration should go all the way, with ice cream or something."

The group was looking at the dessert menu when a fellow with a guitar case walked by their table. He noticed Jack.

"Hey man, we're ready to go. You gonna play with us?"

Danielle gave Jack a look that was simultaneously amused and inquisitive.

"You know this band?"

Jack downplayed it all.

"Just some guys I met over at the Zone. We played a couple of tunes the other day."

Sally was enthused.

"Jack, play a song with the band!"

Even Duncan joined in.

"My buddy, the rock star."

Jack could only shake his head. The band started playing, and a few people in the bar were dancing. Sally was on a roll. She knew she could throw curves at Jack, and get away with it.

"Are you going to be dancing, Jack? C'mon, I bet you are a dancing fool!"

Danielle and Duncan thought that was hilarious. Their mother was teasing Jack, and somehow it seemed to fit. The family fabric had always included good-natured ribbing. And now, Jack was part of the dynamic. He became the rookie, and was about to be required to sing his school song.

The idea of playing with the band was intimidating. Jack would be okay, strumming along, but he didn't want anything to go wrong and make him look foolish. The idea that Sally thought he was making progress with 'the Project' appealed to him. He didn't want her to decide he was a flop at anything. This guitar idea just might do it. Duncan probably wouldn't lose faith in him as a baseball player if he clanked a few chords, but Danielle probably would. He was beginning to want her to appreciate him, too.

In the beginning, she came across as critical. He had thought he'd be lucky if she merely tolerated him, as he tried to help Duncan. Then she gravitated toward acceptance. Recently, she was behaving as if she actually liked him. Jack welcomed that. He hadn't realized it, but the damage of that long-ago Thanksgiving night extended beyond baseball. He had not spoken to a woman, with more than social niceties, for years. Somehow, Danielle was bridging that gap.

Suddenly, the band was finishing a song and the bass player was waving at Jack.

"We've got a friend here to help! Let's get him up here."

The entire James family starting hooting and shoved Jack toward the stage. The other guests were vaguely amused, until a few of them realized that the 'friend' was there with someone they knew. In a small town, if you wander anywhere in public, you are going to run into one or two familiar faces.

The entire room was soon in on the act. Duncan actually had them chanting "Jack, Jack!" Any initial thoughts about anonymously playing a tune evaporated, and Jack's confidence eroded. He had played baseball in front of forty thousand fans, but twenty-five dinner patrons made him think twice.

A half-dozen steps got him to the band. The guitar player named Buddy handed Jack the Telecaster, and moved to the keyboards. Jack took one of the picks in the holder on the mike stand, and struck a chord. These guys knew what they were doing. The stage mix was low, and he could hear the other players. Tom, the drummer, leaned forward and looked at Jack.

"Mustang Sally, right?"

Jack nodded, and played the intro riff. The singer leaned into the microphone.

"We've got a tune about Sally and her Mustang!"

Jack suddenly honed in on the song's name. He hadn't made the connection to Sally James. He hoped the coincidence didn't appear too goofy, and it was too late to play something else.

Concentrating on playing his part as best he could, Jack didn't see Sally's reaction. When she realized what song was being played, she bolted from her seat. 'Mustang Sally, you better slow your Mustang down' began, and the show was on. Danielle and Duncan were looking at their mother, amazed that she started dancing along with the tune. When she pulled them to the dance floor, first Danielle, and then Duncan, they were dumbfounded. They knew their mother *could* be more free-spirited than most, but this was new territory.

She had both of her kids dancing with her, and locals who knew her were joining in. Pretty soon, there was a raucous crowd dancing and singing along. There's nothing like spontaneous joy to get folks to shed their inhibitions. People in town hadn't seen Sally enjoying herself for a long time. They were happy to be part of the celebration, whatever it was.

The song ended and Jack handed the guitar back to its owner, amid a proper ovation. The band didn't badger him for another song. His polite smile and friendly demeanor told them he'd had enough. The Legion crowd was a different story. They realized that he was part of Sally's moment, and called for more. Jack just smiled and Bobby came to his rescue.

"We'll give him a rest, and get him back later, folks."

There was a stream of people stopping at the table to say hello to Sally, and tell Jack they liked his playing. Sally was all smiles, as there were well-wishers she hadn't seen for some time. Jack gave his best 'aw-shucks' thanks to everyone; Danielle and Duncan were amused by the ruckus.

The band played out their set and took a break. They came to speak to the group and give Jack their approval.

"That was great!" Bobby said. "We get stuck with some owner's drunk cousin too often, but you can play with us anytime!"

Jack told them how much fun he'd had and he hoped to do it again soon. They were able to sneak out before the band started again.

Sally was still buzzed when they got out to the parking lot.

"Jack, how did you pick out that song? David used to play it and we'd dance our butts off!"

Her children were feeling the amazement of watching their mom's free-spirited display. Danielle was still laughing.

"Who are you and what have you done with my mother?"

All of life's cares had momentarily disappeared, for all of them. Jack had to admit the truth.

"The song was an accident. When I met those guys earlier this week, they started playing it, and it's one I know. It never occurred to me that it had your name. Pretty weird, huh?"

Sally was bubbling.

"Loved it! Made me feel like a kid again."

Jack was thinking that sooner or later in life, you realize that your parents were young once. They probably did the same things you did, years before. You thought you were a pioneer in life experiences, when your folks had already been there and had the t-shirt. The same thing occurred to Duncan.

"Mom, you're acting like a kid. It's great!"

Jack was happy to see it; to be a part of it. They divided up at the cars and Jack had some parting guidance.

"Okay, Cake, time to get some rest. We don't show up until 4:30 or so to get loose for a 7 p.m. game."

Duncan nodded. Sally was with the program.

"He's going right to bed and there's no chores tomorrow."

"Good deal," Jack said. "Have something to eat around two or so, and keep the water coming. Some tonight, too." He stepped Duncan over to the side and said, "You need enough water so you need to pee. By the time you're thirsty, it's too late, okay?"

Duncan nodded again and headed back to Danielle's car. She was already behind the wheel, and Sally was in the front passenger seat. Jack issued his parting guidance as Duncan climbed into the back seat.

"I'll get the other guys warmed up and ready to go. Then I can take care of you. Sound good?"

After Duncan's thumbs-up, Jack stood by his car, ready to see them off. He was preparing to wave good-bye when Sally got out of the car. She walked toward Jack, and he thought she might have forgotten something. She approached and spoke softly.

"Hold still."

She reached up and hugged Jack. She just stood there, for what seemed to Jack to be a long moment, and just held on. Then she smiled, patted him on the cheek, and walked back to Danielle's car. The car pulled away and Jack was alone in the parking lot.

The neon signs gave an eerie glow to the surroundings and Jack remained there, bathed in the multi-hued colors. The subtle lights seemed to penetrate his consciousness with the evening's emotions, and left him awash in peaceful cognition. Coming to this town, and the week he had spent with people he barely knew, had led to an unexpected but happy outcome. Life's random turns could be heart-breaking or heartwarming. The past week belonged in the latter column, and Jack was feeling better than he had felt in almost forever. Random was good this week.

32

HOPE SPRINGS ETERNAL

No dreams. No headaches. Jack wished he could always wake up like this. Even before he realized what day it was, and remembered what was to happen that night, Jack rolled out of bed in a euphoric mood. Last night had given him a new kind of peace. Although many elements were in play, he felt an odd calmness. Tonight's game might serve as an entrée for a new way of life for Duncan. Even better, it might allow Jack to shed his baseball demons.

Conversely, he knew that he might never fully escape the past. He might ultimately be a sports store maven who once played baseball, but didn't quite measure up. In the face of totally disparate outcomes, he was somehow reconciled to both.

A verse from Paul Simon bubbled up: 'I was in crazy motion 'til you calmed me down.' It brought the moment into focus. Jack sorted through the past week's events to pinpoint what brought him to this perspective. One week ago, to the day, he expected to play another game to stave off the inevitable. His 'crazy motion' would eventually grind down the memory of what might have been. The benign addiction would erode, and he would take his place in the real world. He was about to throw his last coin into the wishing well. Fate diverted him - to place a bet on a kid throwing a baseball.

Jack had read about people who achieved success after years of effort. They had been ready to give up, and they tried 'just one more time.' Maybe there were instances where people were about to overcome whatever barrier had been in their way, but they stopped knocking on the door - right before it opened. Was this past week telling him to knock one more time? And finally, was he being called to knock for someone else? Jack felt that his 'crazy motion' had been calmed by an inadvertent but lucky meeting with Duncan and his family. Each one of them had resonated in a particular aspect of his being.

He decided to extend the peaceful easy feeling for as long as he could. The luxury of doing nothing afforded a late lunch and rest before the evening game. A power bar, water, and TV would allow him to doze until it was time to leave. A 'Back to the Future' marathon was playing. Jack traveled back in time with Marty and Doc Brown, and contemplated the future. Those guys had managed to wrangle a happy ending in spite of multiple pitfalls. There was even a girl in it for Doc. And she was a teacher who lived in a farmhouse.

Jack awoke to knocking on the door. He checked the peephole and was surprised to see Randy Powers. Jack opened the door and welcomed the Crushers' coach inside.

"Sorry that I don't have anything to drink," Jack said. "I was going to get a late breakfast if you want to come along."

Randy pointed to the rickety chair next to the bed.

"Mind if I sit?"

Jack motioned him over. He had the same foreboding he felt when he read Randy's text. That turned out to be the sheriff's visit to Powers' office. Maybe Jack's luck was running out and the odds were against getting Duncan his chance. Or maybe, Jack wasn't the guy to help him get there.

Randy got right to the point.

"I wanted to run something by you about our deal. Do you remember Gordon Bowen?"

Jack blinked back several dozen pages in his memory.

"Gordie? With the Reds?"

Randy nodded.

"Right. He's still there. We keep in touch in the off-season. He lives in Jonesville."

Jack was tentative, not knowing where this was leading.

"So, he's around once in a while."

Randy looked confused about what he needed to say.

"He keeps in touch about baseball and what we're doing here. There hasn't been anything useful, baseball-wise, but we still talk."

He paused and looked at Jack.

"You probably don't know that his folks are doing poorly. So when the team travels, he stays home to go look in on them. You know, home health care and all that."

Jack had met Gordie's parents and liked them.

"I'm sorry to hear that Gary and Grace are ailing," he said. "I hope they get better soon."

Randy was not surprised that Jack remembered Gordie's parents, and knew their names. It was another example of what was so likeable about Jack.

"It's more of an age thing, buddy. Gordie's doing a great job taking care of them. But that's not why I'm here."

Jack waited for what was coming. This is what people with a checkered past must go through, he thought. They never know when some aspect of their former life might jump up and disrupt or destroy what they had been rebuilding.

Once again, Jack sagged under the unfairness of it all. He had done nothing wrong. There was no checkered past. But he had to rebuild; a rebuilding effort based on elements that he didn't understand. Was Randy here to tell him that some inexplicable combination of circumstances would disrupt the Project? Had Gordon

Bowen's acquaintance with Randy Powers somehow conspired to prevent Jack from getting a chance for Duncan?

What would he tell Sally? And Danielle? They would decide that he was the most inept jerk who ever lived. Jack was very nearly holding his breath when Randy continued.

"Jack, I'm just gonna come out and say this. You've come up in conversation. There're guys who thought the way it turned out was just wrong. Gordie's one of them. I'm one of them."

The old familiar kick in Jack's gut returned. He had maintained life at a healthy distance from pro baseball, since the sad events of Thanksgiving five years ago. As to dealing with any particulars of his involvement, and the questions that came with those particulars, he kept that door tightly closed. And now that door was being pried open. Randy had more.

"When you showed up for last week's games, I was glad to see you. Didn't think anything about it. And when you said you'd be interested in another weekend, that was cool, too. Your deal with the James boy is fine with me. I was glad we got that little item with that sheriff settled."

Jack tried to help him along.

"So, what's the thing?"

Randy plunged ahead.

"It so happens that Gordie was driving through here yesterday, going back after visiting his folks. He stopped to see me. I told him you'd been here, and would be here this weekend. I let him in on your plan for the James boy."

He paused, and Jack was trying to sort out how this would end badly for him. Randy screwed up his face and continued.

"I hope it's not an issue for you, but Gordie is going to be here Sunday to see how you do with this kid."

Jack almost laughed out loud.

"That's it? I've been hoping for a chance to show people what Duncan can do, and you say there's a big league scout who is dropping by to see him?"

Jack shook his head and wondered if he heard things right.

"Holy cow, if you think that's bad news, let me know when you have good news. I'll rent a place for your 'tell-all' party."

Randy was optimistic, but still guarded. He decided he'd gloss over the crux of what he had said to Jack: The scout wanted to 'see how *you* do.'

"I wasn't sure he's ready, and maybe it'd be too much pressure," Randy added.

Jack was so relieved that he nearly chortled his answer.

"Shoot, he might not get in the game, if we're behind. Remember the deal? Plus, he ain't gonna know Gordie is there."

He paused to give Randy a closer look.

"We're not going to tell anybody, are we?"

Randy shook his head, relieved that Jack had no issues so far. He didn't think it was time to tell Jack about the other questions Gordie was asking. Jack was back to game planning.

"So, we get up a run, or two, or three, in the late innings. I pick a spot where Duncan isn't facing any heavy hitters, if they have any. Then he throws what I figure to be about ten pitches."

Randy was impressed.

"So, you've got him where he can throw it by these guys?"

"I feel pretty good, at least at this level," Jack said. "It's not like I'm throwing him to the dogs at Wrigley or anything. I'm thinking he'll get a ground out and maybe a strike out or two. If we're in the seventh or eighth inning when he comes in, we'll see about him finishing the game."

This satisfied Randy.

"You'll put it together. If Gordie likes what he sees with this kid, I'm sure he'll talk to him."

Randy changed the subject.

"I've got some uniforms in my trunk. How 'bout I head out to the James farm and get Duncan set up?"

"Great," Jack answered. "That'll save me a trip."

Jack was interested in getting something to eat.

"Let's get some lunch and I can get back here to stretch out for a couple of hours before it's time to go to the ballpark."

Randy suggested a sandwich shop Jack hadn't visited, and they enjoyed an uneventful lunch.

While they ate, Jack was able to ask a few questions about the team they were facing that night. Generally, these industrial league or company club teams had one or two ex-college players who were playing for love of the game. They had occasional talent, but not enough to sustain them in the minor league grind. Or, they simply had better things to do. Some went to grad school. Others had jobs with a future. That was the case with tonight's team from Sandusky. Randy knew two of the players had been good college hitters.

"If you want my guess, those two might give your boy some trouble. But we'll see them a couple of times before you plan to bring him in, so we'll know more by then."

Jack felt he knew as much as was possible at this point, and headed back to his room for the usual pre-game nap. Randy went to the farm to deliver uniforms, thinking that tonight's game might be very revealing.

After setting the clock app for 4 p.m., Jack crashed at 1:30. That would give him plenty of time to get to the ballpark, get loose, and warm up the two pitchers Randy had planned. Right before he closed his eyes, Jack reminded himself that he would need to explain his plan to the guys. One was hoping to extend his playing time past his college days; the other was an affable sort Jack had played with before. The second one might be happy not throwing at all.

The good thing about this level of play, and what Jack was counting on, was that no one treated these games as any serious encounter. Batting and hitting statistics weren't that important. Most of the guys were happy to play and weren't concerned about winning or losing. The ones that were reliving their 'glory days' could be difficult. Jack was good at staying away from them.

The alarm did its job right on time, and Jack took a hot shower to loosen up his muscles. As always, a shower led Jack's mind to wander.

He had a lingering intuition about tonight's game. Yogi Berra's 'fork in the road' was upon him. Berra was famous for his malapropisms. Jack's favorite was well-known: 'It's *déjà vu* all over again.' Yogi's observations of life were all the more incisive to a ballplayer, because he had been a Hall of Famer. A catcher, even.

Tonight's fork in the road led to two distinct paths. Jack had come to this town, this summer, to ease out of his baseball reverie. But for a chance meeting with a young player, retail obscurity loomed. Now, with Duncan's potential in the balance, this game presented a decision point for Jack.

The hot water pounded on, and an analogy from the Seabiscuit movie popped into Jack's head. The horse got a late-career chance to race against an odds-on favorite, named War Admiral. The formidable opponent appeared unbeatable, and Seabiscuit's trainer made an observation about appearance, compared to performance.

"'Maybe he's the kinda horse that just looks good in a paddock."

It meant that looking good in practice didn't always equate to playing well. Duncan definitely *looked* like a thoroughbred. Jack knew he had talent - talent that could propel him to the top of the game. But there are promising performers who wilt under the bright lights, on all types of stages. All the potential in the world amounted to nothing if, for whatever reason, a player reverted to average when it was show time.

Another baseball truism rippled through the steam in the shower: 'Don't leave your game in the locker room.' You have to be able to 'bring it' during the game. You can't allow nerves, or itinerant disappointment, or whatever distraction confronted you that day, to control game performance. The fork in the road to be chosen tonight would be determined by how the thoroughbred named Duncan emerged from the paddock, and raced on the track.

It was going to be simple, and simultaneously complex. The outcome tonight would impact the arc of several lives. Duncan would succeed, or he would not. He would progress as a ballplayer, or not. Jack would surrender to the business world, or not. Sally's faith in

Jack would pay dividends, or not. Jack would be able to pursue what he realized was a budding interest in Danielle, or he would not. These thoughts swirled, as Jack toweled off and dressed to leave for the game.

There are times in life when you look back, with the perfect clarity of 20/20 hindsight, and see what events transpired to cause certain paths in your life to occur. Jack wondered how many times people walked into an experience, and knew up-front that what happened in the next few hours would define years to come? He hoped that whatever role he was going to play would, for once in his life, contribute to something positive. The negative world had been beating on him long enough.

33

PUT DUNCAN IN, COACH

A few Crushers teammates were already at the ball park when Jack arrived. Some were loosening up, tossing a ball back and forth. Others were doing a little light jogging in the outfield. The opposing team from Sandusky had not arrived. Their town was only an hour or so away. They belonged to the same industrial league as the Crushers.

The Sandusky team was named 'Storm.' Jack figured they were associated with some manufacturing outfit, or another business. It really didn't matter. More than likely, the team was comprised of local players who were enjoying playing a few years after their college or high school days. If they had a ringer, someone who was a standout, he would find out soon enough. A couple of players from last week greeted Jack.

"Glad to see you're still here, man," one of the guys said. "You sure made a difference."

Jack was in a good mood.

"I couldn't stay away. Too much fun around here."

He looked around to see if Randy Powers was in the dugout. Jack silently thanked his new-found luck that Gordie wouldn't arrive until tomorrow. Duncan might need a little time to get his bearings. A player pointed out the college kid who was rehabbing his shoulder, and Jack went over to get things started. He introduced himself, and found out the guy's name was Charlie Kotarski. Jack opted to smooth the moment with a little humor. He rolled out one of his standard lines, a friendly remark about an obvious heritage.

"Kotarski. That's a fine Irish name."

The lame joke helped determine what kind of person he was meeting. There weren't too many names that were more obviously Polish than 'Kotarski.' Misstating the heritage was a way of assessing personality.

Some people just aren't the humorous type. They would state the obvious, saying 'it's Polish'; or German, or whatever. They weren't into kidding, and responded poorly to joking. The worst of this type of personality assumed that all persons inclined to humor were deficient thinkers. In their world, you can't have humor and serious thoughts in the same body. This response told Jack two things: This person needed neutral, middle-of-the-road contact. Second, they weren't much fun and were best avoided. Some of them actually got ugly if somebody joked with them. Kotarski responded perfectly. He affected an Irish brogue.

"Kiss me, I'm Irish."

Jack laughed out loud. Humor would make this guy easy to work with. So, Jack returned the joke and did his best Irish accent.

"Sure, and your friends wouldn't be calling ye 'Ski', laddie?"

There's no better introduction to a man than getting a laugh three seconds into meeting. Jack asked about Ski's throwing experience.

"I had a slight labrum strain at the end of college ball. No surgery, but slow rehab. I've been working back to throwing. It feels pretty good."

Jack didn't say what was on his mind. Labrum injuries require time. Sometimes there is no recovery. He hoped this Ski fellow was ready for the effort. Jack looked him in the eye and gave an honest comment.

"Let me give it to you straight. I've done this for a while, and I think I'll know if you've had enough. Will you listen to me when we get there?"

There was something in Jack's delivery that made Ski believe him.

"Sure. I'm not here for a setback."

The rest was easy. They agreed on the signs to use in the game and got down to warm-ups. Ski had a decent fastball and an acceptable curve. Jack's quick assessment was that Ski would be fine tonight; finding his way to a pro team might require a bit more work.

Jack waited until the back-up pitcher arrived to explain his plans. The good news was that the second guy, Joe Renihan, was unconcerned about pitching time. Tonight, he was needed in the outfield. Only an emergency would bring him to the mound in this game. There weren't too many emergencies in this league.

Jack had both throwers ready to go in twenty minutes. He had encouraging words for Ski.

"You'll be fine. We've got Renihan, and maybe Duncan to help win this thing."

Duncan had arrived and was trying to stay on the periphery. It was like showing up at a party where you don't know anyone, and the person who invited you hasn't appeared yet. Jack corralled him and eased through a gentle warm-up. It would be some time before he saw action, if at all.

"Just stay loose," he told Duncan. "Your job tonight is to learn what you can."

Duncan's naturally laid-back personality would serve him well. Jack would be able to concentrate on the other team's hitters, and how and if Duncan should be used. Randy Powers had shown up. Jack let him know that Ski and Joe were ready and they agreed with the plan.

A few spectators were starting to arrive. Jack remembered to make sure there were tickets for Patty and her friends. Game time wasn't far off. The teams were collecting in their respective dug-outs. The old familiar vibe was underway.

As the home team, the Crushers took the field, and the first Storm batter approached the plate. Jack had already exchanged pleasantries with the umpire. Umps were like everybody else. Some wanted to enjoy the moment and joke around; others were into a more serious approach.

For the batters, Jack's first interaction was always casual, even brief. A nod or quick smile would do for starters. This was the time to observe and learn. Where did the guy place himself in the batter's box? Was he a nervous swing-at-the-first-pitch kind of guy, or was he a laid back wait-and-see hitter? What did his warm-up swings reveal? Did he have a balanced power swing, or was he a chopper, just trying to get the ball in play? Maybe he was a speed merchant, ready to lay down a bunt, and try to beat it out to first base.

There were many assessments to be made in a very short period of time. Jack Ridley was comfortable with all of them. This aspect of the game was one of his strengths.

Jack decided that this fellow was inclined to assess the situation a bit more than most. He would probably wait to see what kind of stuff a pitcher had. This would be a good time for Ski to groove one and see what happened. So, Jack called for a fastball, dead center, and waited. The pitch was on the money and the guy was taking all the way. The game was on. Jack worked his way through the first three batters. Ski got a strikeout and two infield ground-outs.

On his way back to the bench, Jack saw Sally and Danielle in the stands. He gave them a nod, nothing exuberant, and they did the same. There would be no crazy cheering tonight. Jack sat next to Duncan, and they discussed the opposing pitcher's technique and strategy. Duncan was developing the ability to analyze the game. The Crushers went down in order. Jack could see that the Storm pitcher had reasonable stuff, at least for this level. Holding up during later innings was another matter. Jack headed out for the top of the second inning, with guidance for Duncan.

"Keep your head in the game. I'm guessing you'll get in tonight."

Ski was on the money for the first batter he faced in the second inning. He got him swinging on a solid fastball after Jack had called for two successive curves. The next batter made it to a 2-2 count and topped a ball to the second baseman. The throw to first made the second out routine.

Jack used the next batter to work on Ski's confidence. That meant pitches on the edge. Ski threw to alternating sides and each one was close. But the umpire had a different opinion, and the count ran to 3-2. Jack wasn't going to back down; he called for another on the outside corner. It split the black, just above the batter's knees, so in Jack's opinion, it had to catch the strike zone.

The umpire called ball four. Jack thought the batter celebrated a little too much for a ball that was too close to let pass. That merited Jack's close attention at first base. The guy was one of those dancers, hopping on and off the bag in an attempt to distract and rattle the pitcher. Jack knew from this frenetic behavior the runner would be trying to steal, and it wouldn't take long. The third base coach was popping out signals and the count went to 1-1.

Coaches give many signals, and it's impossible to know which one is real. The steal sign could be any of them. But when the runner got a sign and started clapping his hands, something told Jack that now was the time. He signaled for Ski to throw a pitchout, the hard and outside throw that a catcher can receive in an aggressive move toward second. It gives him a split-second advantage.

Jack had guessed right and got the jump. The runner bolted, but a laser throw beat him to second base. The inning was over, and the Crushers came rolling to the bench with joyful shouts and high-fives.

The crowd was having fun too. Jack saw Patty and her friends doing a four-person wave and it made him laugh. There were a number of Duncan's old teammates there as well, Skip included. Jack waved at all of them on the way back to the bench. Baseball was supposed to be fun.

The Crushers were batting in the bottom of the second, and Jack was batting fifth. The guy ahead of him was named Greg Graves, who had the interesting nickname of G.G. He reached first on a blooper over third. Jack had been schooling himself on the Storm pitcher's tendencies. Generally, he tried to burn the first pitch. He'd be a little juiced up because of a fluke hit, Jack figured. A fastball was probably on its way, and that's what Jack was sitting on. He laced it past third.

The Storm third baseman was too far off the bag to make the play, and the ball was headed to left field, just inside the foul line. G.G. was halfway to third and had a clear view of the left fielder heading to the fence to retrieve the ball. G.G. decided to put on the gas and try to score. He was 'rounding third and heading for home; a brown-eyed handsome man' as the Fogerty song says. The throw was nowhere near in time, and Jack cruised into second base, standing up.

Jack hoped his chance to score would not be wasted. A two-run lead might hold up until the late innings. That would get Duncan in the game. Any kind of hit would bring Jack home, if he got a jump on it. He knew the batter behind him from last week. His name was Ed Stites. He was a solid kid and had a respectable college career. A degree in business administration landed him a bank job as a manager trainee. Stites had spent a little time in the Orioles organization, but only long enough to have a cup of coffee.

During last week's game, Stites and Jack had a lively discussion about capitalization costs. The sporting goods store advisors wanted to expand into more markets, and Jack was interested in all the angles. Ed was a smart cookie, at least smart enough to know that banking had a better future than knocking around in single 'A' ball. He shelved any thoughts of professional baseball to pursue banking. Chasing flies in the outfield for the Crushers was a fun diversion.

Jack was in full cheerleader mode. He yelled from second base as loudly as he could.

"Bring me home, Big Money!"

The encouragement must have worked, because Ed looped one over the second baseman's head. Jack knew it was a hit when it came off the bat. He was instantly headed to home, swooping around third like a vengeful homing pigeon. Two runs in is a good inning in anybody's book.

The Sandusky pitcher could have been rattled by having two runs scored with only one well-hit ball, but the remainder of the Crushers' lineup wasn't that strong. The next three hitters flied out, and Ed was stranded on first base. The Crushers took the field for the top of the third inning. Jack went back to work behind the plate. Ski was having a better than average night; his control was good and Jack had him working the edges of the plate. His occasional curveball got him several swinging third strikes.

Overall, Jack thought Ski was doing well at this level. He had good enough stuff for a minor league club, maybe even 'AA' ball, but Jack's honest assessment was that he wouldn't advance further. There were hundreds of pitching prospects with the same ability. Ski was also dealing with labrum issues. Jack didn't think his arm would hold up, long term, to the rigors of professional baseball.

It was too bad, because he was a likeable guy. But the day was coming when he would be told baseball was done for him. The thought reminded Jack of a moment from his past life. As a young catcher, he had met a minor league manager named Greg Puntarelli. Jack wanted to learn about every aspect of the game. He asked what a manager's greatest challenge in professional baseball was. Greg's answer gave Jack a sobering moment.

"I hate having to watch dreams die. Especially when it happens to poor kids who have no other way out."

Jack had expected 'finding the right talent' or 'dealing with agents.' Maybe even 'having to work through players' injuries.' Something predictable. Not a remark that grabbed his soul. The honest response reduced the proposition to the bare essentials. Baseball is a beautiful thing, but at its basic level, it's a business. There's always inventory to replace.

These thoughts ran through Jack's head, as he watched his team bat in the bottom of the sixth inning. He shook them out of his mind because he would be third up. His catcher's equipment was already off. On his second at-bat, Jack had taken the Sandusky pitcher deep. The ball sailed toward the left-center fence, and Jack thought it was gone. Only a spectacular leaping catch by the athletic center fielder saved a run.

When the catch was made, Jack was nearly at second base. He stopped on the bag and stood and applauded. The center fielder returned the respect by tipping his cap and waving. Jack always showed esteem for solid play. Now he waited to see if the competition had another great moment in store.

The great catch resulted in no additional scoring since the first two runs. Jack brought Randy over for a little discussion with Ski.

"Buddy, you've thrown really great. I think you've gotten in some quality innings and I don't want you to risk any setback."

Jack turned to Randy.

"My job is to help this team and this pitcher. You've seen what you came to see. His arm has had enough."

Ski wasn't inclined to argue with Jack. Clearly, he was a capable and experienced player. His opinion carried extra weight, and Randy shrugged his agreement.

"What's your plan?"

Jack grinned at both of them as he motioned Duncan over.

"I think Duncan can give us a couple of innings. Joe can close for us, if we need him. Or, bring Joe in now and Duncan closes."

Randy was mulling the whole thing over. The second Crushers batter had just struck out. Jack was due up. Randy and Ski and Joe and Duncan were all standing together, in a sort of baseball huddle. Jack had an idea as he grabbed a bat.

"Tell you what. I get us an insurance run, and Duncan comes in. If I'm out, Joe takes us to the last inning and then Duncan goes to work. Deal?"

Joe and Randy and Ski were all chuckling at Jack's audacity. Duncan looked like he'd just swallowed a bug. Randy shook his head and laughed.

"Sure, Jack, bust one outta here."

Jack turned to Duncan.

"Throw a few easy ones and be ready."

Duncan grabbed his glove and went to the sideline bullpen. Jack headed to the plate, ready to engage in psychological warfare. He smiled once again at the umpire and directed his first salvo at the Sandusky catcher.

"That last crappy fastball almost didn't come down. He ain't throwing that again."

Jack's intention was to challenge the pitcher. He knew his opponent didn't have an unhittable fastball. Whatever he threw on the first pitch, Jack was going to be slow, swinging or not. The pitcher would think Jack couldn't keep up with him.

The plan worked. The pitcher tried to blow one by him, and Jack let him think he succeeded. Jack barely got his bat in motion and took the called strike. The catcher got a second psychological volley.

"Dang!" Jack said. "That was fast."

Jack knew that if the pitcher tried a second fastball, he'd have him. And that's what happened. The next pitch was headed right down the middle. The guy had no movement on the ball at all. Jack delayed his swing and slashed at the empty air. This time, Jack didn't say anything. He stepped out of the batter's box and stared at his bat, with the best harried look he could manage. He knew the catcher was watching him and was fooled by the worried display. Jack would have bet his car the catcher believed another fastball would get strike three.

He would have won another car. The fastball came cruising in, right in the middle of the plate. But it wasn't fast enough. To Jack, it was more like batting practice with a big league pitcher. He timed it perfectly, and let loose with his silky-smooth swing. Picture-perfect body rotation and wrist action delivered incredible power. The ball rocketed off the bat and went straight over the center field wall.

It appeared to be climbing all the way. Jack had crushed it, farther than anyone had ever seen a ball travel in this park. He didn't gloat; he just dropped the bat and headed to first. The ball was disappearing in the distance as he approached the bag, and both teams watched it go. The third baseman even gave Jack a swat as he trotted past. All of the Crushers greeted Jack at the bench, but there was no boisterous celebration. They were awed by what they had seen.

After he put his equipment back on, Jack headed out to where Duncan had been throwing. They had a few moments while the Sandusky team regrouped and got the final out of the inning.

"Alright, Cake. You're gonna do your thing. These guys can't hit you, I'm sure of it."

Duncan looked a bit nervous, but nothing serious. He nodded and didn't say anything.

"Same 1-2-3," Jack said. "rolled out of bed Fast, curve, and change. I'll give you location with the glove. Are you loose enough to throw hard?"

Again, Duncan just nodded.

"Great. Let's start by keeping it on the corners. I'll give you which side to throw to. When I call for a fastball, don't go all out at first. The time will come to throw hard, and I'll give you this."

Jack waggled his fingers.

"That means you burn it, okay?"

Duncan nodded one last time.

"Got it."

He was all business and had a look of determination on his face that Jack liked immensely. Big league top competitors had the same look when they pitched. Just then, 'strike three!' reverberated from the plate. The inning was over and it was time for Duncan to show his stuff. He headed for the pitcher's mound like he'd been doing it all his life. Jack walked to the plate.

'This is going to be fun,' he thought, and everything else melted into the background. It was just Jack and Duncan, doing what baseball players are born to do.

––––––––

There was no public address system at the little ballpark where the Crushers played. But when Duncan walked to the mound, he was accompanied by wild cheering, led by Skip and the high school contingent. After the warm-up pitches, Jack fired the ball to second base and the ball went 'round the horn. Duncan paced the infield grass, and his teammates chattered their encouragement. His pitcher seemed tentative, so Jack intervened.

"Time, Blue!" he called, with a glance toward the umpire. He jogged to the pitcher's mound.

"You got this, Cake. Alright?"

Duncan gave him short, jerky nods, and Jack could see a few butterflies had arrived.

"This is just like back at the barn," Jack said. "These guys can't touch you. They might as well not even be here."

Duncan allowed a short grin, and Jack figured all was under control.

"Let's fool 'em with a curve, and then we'll see if they can catch up to fastballs."

Jack turned to head to home plate, and looked back over his shoulder at the Project.

"This is gonna be cooler than the other side of the pillow!"

That got a grin and Jack knew that there would be no hits this inning.

The Sandusky batter had watched the exchange on the mound and his curiosity drew him into Jack's plan.

"What's so funny out there?" he asked.

It was just a passing remark, not mean or aggressive, so Jack gave a friendly response.

"I had to explain a joke to the kid."

Jack gave the curveball sign and kept talking. Some batters don't know what to do when they're hearing mindless gab.

"So, this set of jumper cables walks into a bar."

The batter glanced back at Jack to see if he was actually telling a joke. He neglected to step out of the batter's box, and the ball was on its way when he looked back toward the mound. Duncan's curve came floating in for a called strike.

"Nice," the batter said. This time, he kept his eyes on Duncan.

Jack acted surprised.

"Hey, he fooled me, too. I'll have him send you another easy one, and we'll call it even."

He signaled for a low fastball, just as he told Duncan when he visited the mound. As Duncan went into his windup, Jack interrupted the flow.

"Hey! Doncha want to hear the rest of the joke?"

The batter's eyes imperceptibly drifted away from the pitch, for half a heartbeat. The ball was on its way as he readjusted, and he barely got the bat moving. Down in the count with two strikes, the kid was so far behind he should have quit then. Jack kept up the chatter.

"The bartender looks at the jumper cables and says 'Don't you start nothin!' Get it?"

Jack could hear the umpire snickering. Baseball is so much fun. Jack stood up and smiled at the batter.

"Remember this game," he said. "Someday you'll tell your grandkids where you were tonight, and who was pitching against you."

The poor batter was completely confused. He had no idea what to expect.

Jack returned to his crouch and signaled for a fastball on the outside of the plate. This guy would never get around in time. Duncan smoked it right on the corner; the batter waved at it for strike three. Jack knew the worst was over. He fired the ball to third for the 'go-round' and jogged out for a quick assessment.

"You feeling okay?"

Duncan nodded, resolutely. He was feeling the rush of the moment. Jack had been paying attention to the Sandusky line-up, so he knew which batters were next.

"These next guys aren't any better than the last guy. We can get by them with good placement. So, if you're feeling good...."

Jack paused for the thumbs-up, which Duncan quickly delivered.

"We can take the lid off here. You throw the fastballs as hot as you want. I'll ask for off-speed once or twice, but these guys can't hit you."

He was back behind the plate before the next batter was there.

"Thanks, Blue," he quickly retorted to the umpire.

"Don't you start nothing," the ump said right back to him.

Jack chuckled as he signaled for an inside fastball. Duncan grooved this one faster than any of the previous throws, and the batter was late.

"Strike one!" echoed throughout the park, and Jack fired the ball back to Duncan.

"Let's see," he said to no one in particular. "Let's try the fastball."

The second batter almost said 'what the hell was that last one?' That was what he was thinking. Jack signaled for the exact same pitch, and Duncan delivered. Only it was faster. Duncan was feeling it. The second swing was later than the first. Jack almost felt guilty as he called for the heater, low and to the outside. Same late swing - same result.

"Strike three!" never sounded better.

Jack stayed put for the third batter. He noticed the second batter stopping to talk to the next man up. Duncan's fastball had to be the topic of discussion. Jack modified the plan and decided a nice change-up would set this next batter's speed gauge back about a month. He remained in his crouch and waved three fingers. Duncan nodded and Jack could see a growing fierceness in his eyes. He delivered what started as a sure-fire fastball. Then it arrived about 15 miles an hour slower than the previous pitch.

The batter nearly dislocated his shoulder trying to adjust, but all it got him was "Strike One!"

Jack dispensed with any diversions. Duncan didn't need any help, not at this point. The maximum speed these guys had ever seen would be eighty-five, tops. Duncan had started there and was only going higher. Jack gave Duncan the shake, meaning, throw as hard as you want.

With a target in the middle of the plate, Duncan smoked it in for a swinging strike two. For the next pitch, Jack didn't even give a sign; he just smiled and held the mitt right in the middle of the plate. Duncan's pitch was faster than anyone in the ballpark could have possibly faced. The swing was in another time zone and Duncan had his first shutout inning.

Jack tossed the ball toward the mound and headed back to the bench. The team gave Duncan a pat on the back. They knew they had participated in something remarkable. Their rookie pitcher had just thrown nine straight strikes. Nobody had gotten a piece of the ball. Duncan was juiced, and Jack told him to keep it under control. Another inning would be good for him, and Randy agreed. He was enjoying the show, just like everyone else.

The Crushers roster was invigorated by Duncan's performance. They almost batted around, and put two more runs on the board. Jack used the time on the bench with Duncan. They discussed the other pitcher's mechanics. Jack had figured out very early that you can always learn something by watching other players. Paying attention was second nature to him. When the batter before Duncan was the third out, Jack was relieved. He hadn't planned on Duncan batting and maybe getting plunked. Working the other team over sometimes brings out their feistiness.

Except for two off-speed pitches, Duncan's second inning was a replica of the first. Jack relied on Duncan's fastball but framed them in a ladder fashion. He raised the target incrementally each time. That tested Duncan's control by moving the ball's placement, in successive pitches. It caused one of the Storm players to get a pop-up. If a batter's swinging level doesn't adjust to the slightly higher pitch, he'll get under the ball.

Duncan's control was exquisite. His pitches climbed each time as if they were on a miniature stairway. The performance was a perfect confidence-builder. It was imperative that Duncan gain poise and tenacity. A big-leaguer has to believe he can throw a fastball strike at any point in the at-bat. It makes all his other pitches that much more effective. For tonight, effective and confident perfectly described the debut.

In all, Duncan faced six batters. He gave up no walks or hits, obviously no runs, and no one reached first base. He was never in trouble. His last pitch was an absolute screamer, faster than anything he had thrown all evening.

Jack had held the mitt perfectly perpendicular to the pitch, so the ball crashed into the glove with an astounding crack. It sounded like a giant bullwhip, and the whole ballpark heard it. Jack was elated. He had hoped Duncan would perform acceptably, and the kid had delivered perfection. There was no fight left in the Sandusky team.

Joe Renihan completed the game. Three up, three down. The Crushers decided to celebrate the win at the Zone, and drifted toward the parking lot and their friends.

Sally and Danielle were waiting, along with Skip and the high school team. Patty and her friends lingered as well. The boys were boisterous, having seen their old teammate throw two monster innings to six batters. Their new 'coach' had demonstrated the swing he had been teaching them only yesterday, sending a ball farther than they had ever seen. They were having the time of their lives. Sally and Danielle hung back and watched the celebration. When the crowd began to thin out, Sally grabbed Duncan and gave him a happy hug.

"Sweetie, you were fabulous!" and she kissed him on the cheek.

She turned to Jack.

"Jack, I can't thank you enough. You were right all along."

Then she gave Jack a hug, and he also got a kiss on the cheek. At the same time, Danielle was gushing on her little brother.

"Cake, you smoked them! Unbelievable!"

She turned to Jack, using language she knew would add to her brother's celebration.

"Unbelievable! You were the bomb!"

Her wisecrack had Duncan doubled over. Jack immediately grasped the multi-layered humor. He smiled broadly, trying to say something appropriate. Danielle didn't wait for a response, and stepped forward. She reached her hand toward Jack's sweaty face, and gently laid her left hand on his right cheek. She leaned in, close to his ear.

"Thank you, Jack," she said, in a low voice. "Thank you."

And she kissed him lightly on his cheek.

Time and space were frozen. Jack was immobilized by something as casual as a friendly smooch. He thought that maybe Danielle was just celebrating; her brother had just succeeded wildly. Maybe she was simply carried away. But she had a look on her face that seemed serene and animated at the same time. Jack wanted to say the right thing, but nothing came out. He could only smile and hope she saw how he was captured by the moment. Finally, he thought of something to say.

"I hope I'm there for his first shut-out. I like your celebrations."

It came out corny; at least he thought so, but Danielle had a smile for him. Sally and Duncan were grinning as they observed everything. Duncan was amused.

"Break it up, you two. We're heading to the Zone to celebrate."

Jack was grateful for the diversion.

"Maybe Randy will be there, so we can see about tomorrow's game. I'll run by the room and do a quick clean-up, and meet you all there? The beer's on me."

He was looking to avoid the moment of deciding who would drive with whom. Danielle's little endearing moment had such an impact. If they were alone, he might say the wrong thing.

Jack grabbed his gear and practically ran to his car, not waiting for an answer. Feeling truly grubby after playing a full game, he needed a shower. Danielle had managed to fluster him. He wanted a little time to sort that out.

To top off Jack's discomfort, Duncan was shifting from the role he occupied only moments before. During the game, he had been responsive to Jack's slightest direction. But now he reverted to teasing brother. As Jack escaped, Duncan laughed at the reaction to his sister's affection.

"Jeez, Danny, you sure got him out of here in a hurry! I need that guy around, you know?"

Danielle only smirked at him. For some reason, she wasn't quite up to giving it back to her kid brother. Mother and daughter headed to their car with Duncan in tow. Sally smiled to herself. The universe was starting to return to its normal condition. Her kids were in benign harassment mode, and she was enjoying herself again.

It pleased her that the catalyst for her reverie was Duncan's baseball. David would have been tickled. There was no hurry to get to the Zone. Jack would be slightly delayed, but they had plenty to talk about. This was time to celebrate - no chores tomorrow. The fact that the barn painting was done was a huge load off Sally's mind. If they were on cruise mode for the entire summer, she'd still be happy.

They arrived at the Zone and ordered beers. Before long, Jack showed up, fresh out of the shower with his hair wet and glistening. Sally had never seen him spruced up. At the farm, he had been working and disheveled. Now, she thought his slicked-back hair made him look like one of those clothing models. The ones with the 'wet hair' look were all the rage in the ladies' magazines. Jack would have fit right in with the advertising. Sally was way too busy to know much about any marketing ploy, but she handed Jack a compliment.

"You sure clean up nice."

That got the discussion rolling. Everyone was still hopped up on Duncan's performance. Both he and Jack were animated. They replayed a few game moments and decided they had passed the test. Appetizers and sips of beer eased the conversation along. Duncan luxuriated in the family compliment moment. There's nothing better than a pat on the back from people you love and admire.

Once or twice, Sally noticed Jack and Danielle were smiling at each other. It might have been the beer; maybe it was the instant joie de vivre. Something was in the air.

The band had been playing, but Jack was too distracted to notice. Between sets, two of the musicians stopped by the table.

"Hey, man, you gonna play with us?"

Jack was so intent on talking to Duncan he hadn't realized his band buddies were there. He masked his surprise with his usual polite self.

"We just played a game and I'm beat. How 'bout another time?"

They were happy with that and said they'd see Jack again. Announcing that they were starting their final set of the evening, they launched into 'Mustang Sally.' Sally laughed and jumped up.

"Who's dancing with me?"

Jack demurred.

"Please, I'm worn out. Were you there tonight?"

Duncan was bubbling away, and was willing.

"C'mon, Mom, let's shake it!" and off they went.

Jack and Danielle watched them hopping around the dance floor.

"She's having such a good time," Danielle said. "It's because of you, Jack."

Jack was preparing to deflect the compliment when she continued.

"I mean it. We've all been in a funk this past year, and it's time to laugh again. It all relates back to you."

Jack was touched by her compliment.

"I'm glad to be part of it. It started out as just baseball, but this is such a neat family. I wanted Cake to get a chance to show his stuff, and we've got a great start. We're not done, and I'm having a blast. Everybody's so nice to me."

He was looking at Danielle throughout his little speech, and she was looking at him. She seemed about to say something, but the song had ended. Sally and Duncan were returning to the table. The band started playing the Clapton tune, 'Wonderful Tonight.'

"Last chance for that slow dance," Tom announced.

Whatever Danielle was going to say stayed unsaid, but she gently smiled when a slow dance was mentioned. Her look seemed to say that Jack should ask her, and he got the hint.

"I'm not too worn out for a slow one, if you don't mind a lousy dancer."

Danielle stood up and gave him a palms-up 'let's go' motion. Jack meant what he said. He had no idea what real dancers do, and he said it again.

"I'm really no good at this."

Danielle was being helpful.

"There's a song that says 'Teach me how to dance real slow,' right? Gotta start somewhere."

They ended up in some sort of a dance embrace. Jack barely knew the girl and was careful to not be too close. He also wanted to avoid looking like one of those clumsy robot dancers. They were swaying along, just shifting back and forth. But Danielle didn't seem to mind, and she leaned her head on Jack's shoulder.

Her brownish hair had light streaks in it. It had a silky feel on his face and her perfume made him light-headed. He didn't know what the scent was, but he knew that he would recognize it anywhere. It had been a very long time since he'd been this close to a woman. He'd forgotten how intoxicating it could be. She was a mixture of fragile and forceful that seemed to connect with his consciousness on a level he had stored far, far away.

The song ended and they both remained there for a few moments. Time was in slow motion as they returned to Sally and Duncan. Mercifully, Sally took things under control.

"It's getting late and we should be going."

Jack was grateful somebody else was talking. He needed to figure out what had just happened. Duncan stood up and agreed.

"You're right, Mom. We might be playing tomorrow."

Jack regrouped and attempted to return to familiar ground.

"I'll get with Randy and see what he wants, and let you know."

Dannielle didn't say anything at all. They all trouped outside and said a *pro forma* goodnight.

"Thank you again, Jack, for such a wonderful time," Sally said.

Duncan was still enjoying the evening.

"We got 'em, didn't we buddy?"

"We sure did," Jack concurred. "I'll get back to you about tomorrow."

He looked at Danielle, and only smiled. She did the same, with a dreamy aspect that took him back to the dance floor and his jumbled senses.

The three of them drove off and Jack wandered to his car in an unhurried daze. He could still smell the perfume on his shoulder. He wanted to hang on to the moment for as long as he could.

34

SHOELESS JOE WAS FRAMED

During the night, a steady rain arrived. It wasn't a loud thunder and lightning storm, so most folks didn't know the weather had turned. Instead, it was one of those long and murky showers that stay locked in the area. Its steady gentle sound delivered peaceful sleep, but it also delivered large amounts of water.

The early hours remained dark and overcast. With no morning sun, Jack slept soundly for over ten hours. When he awoke, he was surprised to see that it was nearly ten thirty. He figured that sometimes your body says 'time to do some regrouping.' It simply shuts down and waits for you to catch up. Last night's events returned and he exulted in the memory. Duncan could not have thrown better. As for himself, Jack's moments with Danielle's head on his shoulder were ethereal. He didn't care if it rained all week.

A look outside the window revealed that the edges of the parking lot were flooded. Jack noticed that his phone had a text message from Randy Powers. For a millisecond Jack flashed back to the message from almost a week ago. That had produced the hopeful lawman, and made Jack think his plans for Duncan were being derailed. The instant that thought faded, Jack feared there might be other bad news. How could last night's success have gone the wrong way?

Shaking the defeatist thought from his head, Jack figured the rain was going to cancel today's game. Probably Randy was just letting him know not to worry about showing up. What else could it be?

Texting was not one of Jack's favorite things. It caused people to lose the ability to simply talk to each other. Texting, to Jack's mind, was the great disabler. He'd seen people together at a gathering, in the same room, texting instead of talking. It was astounding. People were going to become robots, incapable of human communication. His rebellion was to avoid texting if at all possible. Jack hit the call-back button and Randy's phone started ringing. When the call went to voicemail, Jack left a message. At least Randy would know he'd responded.

It was decision time. If Jack got in the shower, Randy was sure to call. Sitting and waiting would ensure that the phone wouldn't ring. Jack stalled for a respectable ten minutes, while he checked to see if anything interesting was on TV. Then he gave up and headed to the hot water rehab center. There was no hurry, and a day like this was perfect for loafing and recharging.

The steam allowed a smooth, close shave and the clean-up was built-in. Jack was halfway through scraping his face when his phone beeped. 'It figures,' he said to himself. He hit the speaker button and simultaneously shut off the water.

"Hey, Jack, I guess the field is too wet," Randy's voice blared out.

"Yeah, the parking lot's half covered, so I figured the game's off."

"Yep, it's halfway under water. It's happened before. There's no way the field will be dry. It's gonna rain all day anyway, on and off. So you're off the hook."

Randy didn't sound all that disappointed about cancelling a game. Jack felt the same.

"Well, thanks for the heads-up. I sure appreciate getting the chance for Duncan to throw last night."

The response was quick.

"That's what I wanted to talk to you about. Can we meet some-where? I've got some things to run by you."

"I was going to grab some breakfast. Or lunch," Jack said, looking at the time. "You want to get together?"

Randy thought that was a great idea, and had a new location. Jack was in the 'bacon and eggs makes any day better' school of thought. Randy knew the perfect place. Jack wrapped up the shower and threw on blue jeans and t-shirt. He drove to the spot Randy indicated.

It was in a direction Jack hadn't discovered, past the highway turn-off. All the truckers visited the mom and pop operation - no frills with grits on the side. Its appearance gave Jack a feeling that good things had to happen here. The rain had paused temporarily. When Jack pulled up, Randy was leaning on his car. He wasted no time in walking over to Jack. He was pumped.

"Man, that was spectacular last night! I figured you had some-thing good going on, but that was amazing."

Jack snickered at Randy's enthusiasm.

"Glad it worked out for you. I was thinking he wouldn't need another night to show his stuff, so the rain doesn't break my heart."

"Let's get inside," Randy said. "You'll want to hear what's developed."

They walked in and found a quiet spot in the back. Randy headed to the restroom, so Jack had a moment to examine the surroundings. His gaze fell to the table top. It had photos of early 20th century ballplayers covered by a scratched plastic veneer. At first, Jack thought a table with iconic baseball players was a lucky sign. Pres-ently, he changed his mind.

These were faces that started the game on its path to becoming America's pastime. The names were so familiar even baseball haters knew them: Honus Wagner, who spent almost twenty-one years in a Pittsburgh Pirates uniform; Walter Johnson, a twenty-one year player for the Washington Senators. There were other illustrious names, but the one that caught Jack's eye was Shoeless Joe Jackson.

The guy was famous, or infamous, for multiple reasons. In a

twelve-year career, he held hitting and on-base records. As a rookie, hitting .408 gave him a record that stands today. Babe Ruth was quoted as saying that he had modeled his epic swing after Joe's. What other ballplayer has that sort of testimonial to commend his ability?

Every ballplayer knows Shoeless Joe's story. Sadly, the guy's legacy did not end happily. Seeing Jackson's picture made Jack think bad luck was on the horizon.

In the 1919 World Series, Joe played for the White Sox and led both teams with a .375 batting average. He committed no errors, and threw out a Cincinnati Reds runner at the plate. Somehow, Joe was caught up in a betting scandal. Notwithstanding a jury verdict to the contrary, the Commissioner determined that eight White Sox players had agreed to throw the World Series to the Reds. Joe was banned from baseball at the prime of his career.

Years later, the seven players who were involved admitted that Jackson was never present when they discussed the plan, and he had refused money that was offered to participate. Permanently banned, when he was blameless! According to some accounts, later in life, Joe played anonymously for nondescript teams. He just wanted to be part of the game. Jack knew exactly how Joe must have felt. He had done nothing wrong, but had been driven away from what he loved.

While Jack was musing about the similarity between his own situation and Shoeless Joe's, Randy returned to the table. Jack was deep in thought about the unfair treatment Joe received. The man never played for a big-league team again. The irony was not lost on Jack. Both of their careers had been cut short. For Jack, it launched a small cloud that had followed him for five years. When Randy saw the melancholy look on Jack's face, and followed his eyes to the Jackson picture, he knew exactly what was on Jack's mind. Before he could speak, his favorite waitress appeared.

"Molly's got the best omelets in the world, Jack," he said.

He hoped to get the food started. More importantly, he wanted to help get Jack's thoughts away from bad memories. There were more important topics to discuss.

"Same old for me, Miss Molly," Randy said to the smiling lady. Looking at Jack, he added, "Cheese omelet, bacon, toast and coffee. Yum!"

Jack was convinced and followed Randy's lead.

"The same, please."

"Got it," and Molly zeroed in on Jack.

"Hey, it's you! That was some game last night. My husband said that ball you hit hasn't come down yet!"

Her smile made Jack blush, and he bobbed his head at the compliment.

"Thank you, Ma'am."

He looked around for a rescue and Randy obliged.

"Molly, you're going to embarrass this guy right out of here. He's pretty shy, you know."

"Well, he's pretty," she giggled.

Then Molly snapped her order book shut and headed to the kitchen.

Jack's face flared at the remark, and Randy razzed him.

"You still got it, buddy."

He figured he'd take advantage of Jack's temporary laryngitis and put an idea on the table.

"Y'know, Molly wasn't the only one last night that liked what they saw."

Jack waited for Randy to continue the conversation. He had been dealing with a number of thoughts and emotions lately. Right now, he needed to observe, not talk. Randy collected himself.

"I didn't give you the full picture yesterday. I figured you had enough to worry about, what with having to keep Duncan tuned up, and all."

Again, Jack just listened while Randy explained.

"I told you Gordie had been in touch. It was lucky timing that he was passing through at the same time you had Duncan ready. Gordie was looking forward to coming, and I can tell you that he's interested. Real interested."

Jack had recovered enough from Molly's teasing that he joined in.

"So, that's a good thing, right? You said he was going to be here tonight. I guess with the rain we'll have to figure out another time."

"It's a real good thing, Jack," Randy smiled. "But there's more."

Emotionally, Jack was tapped out in the 'what if' department. He didn't care to speculate as to what the 'more' might be. Figuring Randy would bring it all together, one way or another, Jack waited. Randy had the feeling that how he framed his comments would have a definite impact on the outcome of the conversation. He knew that Jack was a tremendous baseball talent, and he also knew the story behind his fall from grace.

It didn't take a genius to figure out that Jack was conflicted over baseball in general. That was obvious to Randy, when Jack arrived to play scrub ball after disappearing for a couple of years. What Randy was balancing in his mind was a possibility for Jack to have some relief from his torment. Randy truly did not know the best way to go about bringing up the subject. He decided on a slow and easy approach.

"Do you remember when you showed up here to play some games a couple of years ago?"

Jack nodded, but did not comment on the memories the question evoked. Randy continued with his delicate delivery.

"What you don't know is that Gordie had stopped by a couple of times before that. Not like lately, when he's here more often, because his folks are ill."

Randy paused for a sip of water.

"He was aware that we knew each other, and he asked about you. I didn't have much to say until you appeared. The next time he came through, I told him you had played a couple of games."

Jack's melancholy gaze made Randy stop and regroup. He was getting to the difficult part. Rearranging the silverware didn't reveal an easy way to explain himself.

"What I learned from Gordie was that a whole lot of people in the organization felt awful about the way it went down. I mean, losing

Olivia was terrible enough, but it wasn't hard to see how that was connected to your situation. Nobody knew what to say or do. The front office was paralyzed. When the top guy sees things one way, there isn't a lot of room for discussion."

Both men were uncomfortable. Jack was being dragged back into the embarrassment of his life, and Randy was struggling with having to bring it up. The food arrived, and they took advantage of the lull in the conversation to collect themselves. Jack's appetite was gone, but he picked at the food so he wouldn't have to talk. Randy did the same. Halfway through the omelet, he tried again.

"Jack, I know this is rough. You got yourself into the whole thing for Duncan. After seeing him last night, I know why. I'm proud of you for going through it, for his sake. To me, that's one more big league play from you."

Keeping his eyes lowered was all Jack could do. He didn't want Randy to see what these thoughts and feelings could do to him. Those who love greatly, suffer greatly.

Randy took a breath and continued.

"After I told Gordie you were around, he always asked about you. People with the team wanted to reach out, but nobody had it in them, after the lousy deal you got. The whole thing was just...."

Randy paused, looking for the right word.

"Incomprehensible."

Jack felt sorry for the difficulty Randy was having, and he offered an escape.

"I understand," he said. "Nobody knew what to do, and when the boss is against you, you're trapped."

Randy leaned in closer.

"That's what I'm trying to tell you. Mr. Hutchens was off the tracks for over a year. Probably more. Losing his daughter just about killed him, and it screwed up his thinking. I have it that he spent six months thinking you had something to do with it, and it made him crazy. I mean, lock the doors crazy. They had him on medication - the whole nine yards. Everybody was afraid of what was going to happen next."

Jack had not heard this side of the story. His look must have told Randy that he needed to hear more.

"I mean it, Jack. Gordie doesn't want this out there, but there was talk of selling the team. Mr. Hutch just didn't care anymore. It took him a couple of years to begin to function again."

After all of his tumult, Jack was still a kind-hearted person. He still felt bad for Mr. Hutch's loss.

"I'm glad he got to feeling better. Losing Olivia was as awful as it gets."

Randy saw that he needed to put a finer point on the issue.

"Losing Olivia was beyond awful. But causing additional suffering made it worse."

Randy was searching for a way to explain what he meant.

"Have you ever seen an injured dog? One that's been really hurt and is suffering? If someone tries to help that dog, it will likely bite them, because the dog thinks that's the source of the pain."

Jack listened silently to the analogy. He could see where he was about to fit in.

"You see," Randy continued, "Mr. Hutch was in pain. He wasn't thinking clearly at all. Jack, I'm serious about what I said about emotional issues. He had lost someone he loved, and his reaction to his pain was to strike out at another person he loved."

Randy paused, putting the complex into words.

"That person was you, Jack."

Silence settled over the table as both Jack and Randy let the thought soak in. At twenty years old, Jack lacked the training or experience to sort through the difficult issues of Olivia's death. He had reverted to a time-honored reaction. When well-intentioned people face difficulties beyond their control, they blame themselves.

Suddenly, Jack saw that he was in a situation like the kid in the Good Will Hunting movie. He had been engaging in avoidance techniques to deal with his own pain, caused by losing Olivia *and* baseball. He had unwittingly blamed himself, and there had been no one there to help him. It was obvious now. Everything is simpler when it is explained to you in a way that speaks to your particular wavelength. Jack started thinking out loud.

"I was blaming myself, all that time."

And Randy spoke the words Jack hadn't realized were missing.

"It wasn't your fault."

Jack looked startled, hearing a long-delayed redemption.

"It wasn't your fault, Jack," Randy said again.

And like the kid in the movie, tears started to flow.

35

HAVE YOU EVER SEEN THE RAIN

Randy went to pay the bill while Jack got back on solid ground. Continuing their conversation in a public place was not what Randy wanted. There was more information to be delivered. He suggested that they head back to the veneer plant. No one would be in the office on a Sunday, and they would have all the privacy they needed.

"How about we drive by the field and make sure we've still got weather problems?" he asked. "The league needs details six hours before game time. That gives me about twenty minutes to make the call."

They both climbed into Randy's work truck, and left Jack's car in the restaurant parking lot. There wasn't as much water on the pavement, and the drizzle had stopped. But the grass was plemty soggy.

When they got to the ballpark, they walked to the diamond. Parts of the infield were under water. It was an easy decision, and Randy was instantly on his phone to report the poor field conditions. Jack didn't listen to the details. His thoughts were stretching back over five sad years. He'd been masking his emotions the whole time. Now he understood much more about what had transpired, but he saw no way he could have handled things differently.

Standing by the home team bench, he gazed toward the spot where he blasted the ball the night before. Of the twelve major league home runs to his credit, none of them had been that far. He wished he could have had the chance to hit a few more. Randy was off the phone. As he approached, he saw where Jack was looking.

"Holy Mackerel! That was a long shot. Maybe Molly's husband is right. That ball might not have landed!"

They both laughed at the idea. Jack was glad to play along.

"It can't stay up there with all that rain."

Randy shook his head and turned philosophical.

"That's probably what caused the storm. That darn thing busted up into the clouds and blew out some kind of reservoir."

Laughter started again, at the ridiculous image. At that moment, some rumbling thunder started, and Randy stayed at it.

"I told you! That ball is still rolling! Time to get out of here in case it starts up again."

Then he shifted gears.

"Let's scoot over to the office. I've got some more things I need to tell you."

They headed back to Randy's car. Sure enough, more light rain began to fall.

"I swear, Jack," Randy said. "From now on when I see a moonshot like that, I'm going to think of you and expect it to start raining."

They were in the truck, and Randy was still thinking about the monster home run.

"Seriously, Jack, I know that wasn't a big league pitcher. But it looked like an eighty-five or so fastball. You creamed it."

Jack agreed.

"That's about right. I got lucky."

Randy scoffed.

"Bull. You would have caught up to one at ninety-five. You still got it, buddy."

Jack smiled at the compliment, and realized that was the second time Randy said that. He was unsure where this was leading. They made the short drive to the veneer plant. Jack half expected to see the deputy sheriff there, explaining his latest theory of liability. Randy unlocked the door and punched in the alarm code. They walked past the reception area; Jack remembered that Samantha had said she was going to come to the game.

"Did Samantha show up last night? She was going to let me know if Suzy and her parents were there."

Randy hadn't seen her.

"She was feeling a cold coming on after work. Maybe she decided to lay low for the weekend."

They walked back to Randy's office and sat in the chairs in front of the desk. Randy propped his feet up and tried to remember where he'd left off in his story. He decided to approach things from a different angle.

"What are you thinking would be good for Duncan?"

He knew Jack would prefer to talk about Duncan's interests, rather than his own. Randy wanted to take the conversation to Jack's future, eventually.

Jack collected his thoughts.

"If he's brought along in the right way, I think he could stick with a major league team. Not right away, but time in the farm system would be good. I'd like to get him some type of try-out."

Randy was nodding at the thought, partly because he agreed with the idea, but he also wanted Jack feeling comfortable.

"Maybe you still have contacts that can make that happen," Jack ventured.

Randy thought this would be the right time to ease into the topic he'd been working toward.

"I think that's already in progress, Jack."

That comment caused Jack to pause and give Randy a sidelong glance.

"You remember what I said about Gordie Bowen?" Randy asked.

"How he had been passing through? I told him about you and Duncan."

Jack nodded, remembering that he'd been told Gordie was interested.

"Yeah, you said he was around. I figured down the road maybe we could follow up on that."

Randy hoped he could put his thoughts together in a way that made sense and didn't focus on Jack's past.

"That's it, more or less. I said he was interested, because he is. When I mentioned you were here this weekend, he was happy to come and take a look."

Randy decided to throw his cards on the table and see how they settled.

"Jack, if I'm not saying this right, just blame it on being hit in the head once too often, okay?"

Jack smiled. He didn't think Randy had any bad intentions. He'd proved that when the deputy tried to throw Jack under the bus. It was easy to meet Randy half-way.

"You're cool, Randy. What's on your mind?"

Randy just blurted it out.

"Gordie didn't wait for today to check things out. He was there last night. After you left with Duncan and his mother, we talked it all over. Gordie saw what Duncan can do. He wants to run it by the team. He thinks they'll want a tryout."

Randy hesitated slightly, based on what he wanted to say next. He pulled his feet off the desk, sat up straight, and jumped in.

"He also saw what you can do. Rather, he saw that you're doing what you always did. He wants to talk to you, too."

The words came flying toward Jack like a fastball shooting at his head. He was dumbfounded. A tryout for Duncan? And did Randy just say that Gordon Bowen wanted to discuss playing baseball? Did the people that killed his spirit want to revive him? Jack sat still, and let the words soak in.

"What I said about how things sorted out with the team was true,"

Randy added. "After Mr. Hutch got his head on straight, things settled down. I think they were trying to figure out how to make things right, but they didn't know what to do."

He sucked in a deep breath, and blew it out, building his resolve. While leaning toward Jack, he put his hand on Jack's shoulder. Condolences at a funeral would have looked the same.

"Gordie believes Mr. Hutch knows he did you wrong. It looks like Mr. Hutch is trying to figure out a way to make it right."

Jack was trying to deal with five years of disappointment, rolled into one sentence. He was shifting from blaming himself to thinking there was hope for something different. Maybe his loss would translate into Duncan's gain. Familiar ground was in sight, and Jack leapt past Randy's meaning.

"You said Gordie saw Duncan and wants a tryout. What's the next step?"

Glossing over Randy's intent was inadvertent. Jack jumped on the thought that his old team might give Duncan a look-see. He bypassed the fact that Gordie said he wanted to discuss more than one ballplayer.

Randy was working the issue on two levels, and saw a way to link them together. The lynchpin was Duncan's prospects.

"Gordie is heading back to the team. Tomorrow, or thereabouts, he'll be talking to player personnel. Looking at Duncan coming over sometime soon. Might even be this week."

Jack was nonplussed.

"This week? That's pretty close."

Randy was unruffled.

"From what I saw last night, and from what Gordie saw, Duncan is ready to show his stuff."

Randy paused for a closer look at Jack.

"Gordie is going out on a limb here, and I don't think he's out of line. He says Duncan could handle triple A. Right now."

This was a monster step in assessing Duncan's potential, and Jack savored the moment. Maybe his hopes for the kid, his mother, and maybe even his sister would meet with success. The entire proposition was insanely ambitious. Jack allowed a smile, and a tinge of optimism, to creep into his soul.

"That would be great, Randy. Let me know if they have a schedule in mind, and I'll have Sally follow through."

Randy smiled back. This guy was so good-hearted. He was thinking that his part in this scenario had played itself out. It was time for Part Two.

"Well, Jack, you won't have to run it by Sally," he said. "You'll be handling the details of Duncan's try-out your own darn self."

"How's that?"

Randy was grinning now, happy to be delivering this news.

"You'll be there for his try-out. Gordie wants you to handle the whole thing."

Jack couldn't believe his ears. He hadn't given thought to the possibility that he would play such a supporting role. He just sat shaking his head, not able to think what the next step might be. Randy took it from there.

"If you want me to contact Gordie, I will. If you're not ready to talk, that's okay. But he said to give you his number and you can call him to make arrangements to go to the ballpark. You remember the way, don't you?"

Randy was still smiling, pleased at how this discussion had developed. He'd worried that talking about a return to big-league baseball would dredge up demons for Jack. But they had tip-toed through the minefield.

With any luck, Duncan's tryout would pay off and Jack would get the catharsis he deserved. Randy felt like he was sending a child off to college.

"Pretty soon," he added, "I'll be calling you to get game tickets."

He paused.

"Old buddy."

Another pause.

"Old pal."

Jack laughed at the suggestion he would be part of any arrangements.

"I'm pretty sure we'll be calling Duncan for that."

Jack paused to regroup.

"I really appreciate what you're doing here, Randy. This is a good thing for Duncan, and you made it happen."

Randy gave him a pleasant shoulder shrug.

"Okay, let's get out of here. You've got things to discuss with Duncan and his mother; I'm sure the Boss at home has some chores for me. Call me this week and let me know what's up."

They headed outside for the ride back to Jack's car. Randy had deftly navigated the issue. He had been a good friend, and Jack would keep his eyes open for a chance to repay the gesture. They got back to the restaurant, and Jack opened the door to get out. He shook hands with Randy and let him hear his thanks.

"Randy, I won't forget this."

Randy grinned, and returned the sentiment.

"Neither will I, Jack. More ways than one!"

Jack eased the door shut and Randy drove off. Jack could still hear him laughing at his own joke, and it made Jack feel good inside. On the short drive back to the motel, Jack was thinking about how he'd approach all of this with Sally and Duncan. And Danielle.

At times he thought of them as a single unit, and other times he thought of them as individuals. The baseball connection with Duncan was easy to define. Sally was clearly a brave and noble mother who had weathered a storm, and came out proud. Capping it off was Danielle. Jack didn't know how to verbalize his thoughts about her.

Initially, he thought she was an obstacle to his baseball plan. Then she turned into a funny and caring supporter of Duncan's hopes. And then her sweet and amusing side began to show. There was a lot to like about that girl.

Jack decided to drive out to the farm and give all three of them a run-down on recent developments. It was pushing two o'clock, and

Duncan had to be told there would be no ball game tonight. It was just as well. They had bigger fish to fry.

Dang! They had a whale in a little bitty skillet. Reflection such as this called for music. Not motivational rock and roll. Music for the soul led to you-know-who.

Jack mused that not all opera ended with some fat guy holding a knife, singing about death and destruction. Figaro, for instance. It ends with reconciliation and forgiveness. Jack dared to hope, just for a moment, that he could find the same. He arrived at the farm, and saw Duncan walking from the barn to the house. Jack popped out of his car.

"Hey, Speedball!"

Duncan was laughing as he approached.

"We got 'em good, didn't we?"

"Sure did," Jack said. He looked around for Elvis, and then realized that the rain probably kept the dog holed up in the barn.

"Let's head inside. We've got some things to discuss."

Duncan was thinking about the game.

"We still playing? Or is the rain in the way?"

Jack answered as they walked into the kitchen. He saw Sally cleaning up some dishes and could see Danielle coming through the adjoining room. They had heard him pull up.

"Randy had to call in a no-go for tonight," he said. "The field's too wet."

There were quizzical looks all around.

"Don't worry; we did what we needed to do last night. If this is a good time, how 'bout we all sit down and let me run through a few things?"

All three of them edged around the table, waiting to see what merited a group meeting. There had been so much rejoicing last night; they wondered what could add to the news. No one said anything. They looked to Jack to set the pace.

"First of all, things could not have gone better. Mr. Cake here was pretty close to perfect."

Smiles started to blossom, and Jack tried not to dampen their spirits.

"There's a long way to go, so don't get too carried away. But it was a heck of a start."

He risked a small grin.

"I've been talking to Randy about a lot of details for us to consider. I was hoping we would be able to take the next step, but wasn't sure how."

He paused and rubbed his face, thinking of his next words.

"My idea was getting some exposure to shove Duncan along. Randy might have solved the problem."

Jack looked at each member of the family he had grown to like immensely. He hoped the door that was being opened would serve them well, beyond his ability to help.

After swallowing hard, Jack put his cards on the table.

"Explaining how it happened is a long story, but a major league scout was there last night. He wants to talk to us."

Each of them looked at each other for a speechless moment. Duncan shattered the reverie by jumping up and shouting.

"Yes!"

He started leaping around the room like a crazed ballet dancer. Sally seemed to be looking heavenward. Danielle gave Jack a joyfully serene smile and reached over to grab his hand. Her celebration was subtle but still powerful.

Jack realized that he had never looked closely into her eyes. They were a mesmerizing bluish-grey, with brownish flecks radiating outward from deep black pools. He was struck by their beauty, and didn't realize how long he had been staring.

Tears began to form in Danielle's eyes and Jack was jolted into politely looking away. He had been totally unaware that Duncan was still babbling, and Sally's joy had boiled over into full-blown crying. Her unabashed happy tears had Jack dabbing at his eyes for the second time in one day.

Sally got up and walked outside to sit on the porch swing. She needed to be alone. After collecting himself, Jack told Danielle and Duncan about his time with Randy. There was no need to go into specifics about his earlier life with Gordon Bowen, or what Randy had said about Mr. Hutchens. It was enough to say that Gordie wanted to learn more about Duncan.

The rest of the day was open. Jack mentioned that he had to head home to look after sports store details. He hadn't made up his mind about how he'd contact Gordie. If Randy set up a meeting, it would add another layer to the planning. Jack decided that he would talk to Gordie directly, and deal as best he could with whatever angst he felt about the team. If he stayed around tonight, he could head home tomorrow, and make the call somewhere in between.

"How 'bout we just do something fun?" he asked. "We don't have a game, so there's all afternoon and evening."

Danielle and Duncan were open to suggestion, so they went out to the porch to include Sally in the plans. She was still in the porch swing, and had a serene look about her. She smiled at her kids and the family's newcomer.

"Sometimes I come here to settle my mind on things. Your father and I would sit here together, and talk about family stuff. Lately, I come here and give him updates."

She paused and gave some faraway place a little smile.

"He's pretty cool, right now, with what's going on."

Then she stood up and drew all three of them in for a group hug. Jack tried not to think about the fact that Sally was pulling Danielle close to him. He held perfectly still and got a reprise of her perfume. Sally came up for air.

"Let's do something fun today. Or tonight. Or both!"

Danielle jumped at the chance.

"I have an idea."

Duncan was quick to interject.

"We ain't going to the mall!"

"Ha, ha, goofy! I was thinking of a picnic. The rain is over, and we could throw some sandwiches together."

The chance for an impromptu outing sounded appealing, and Duncan added his thoughts.

"That'd be fun. You old folks could take some wine."

Big sister looked at little brother and returned the volley.

"You could bring your sippy cup."

Jack laughed out loud. This family was so much fun.

They had a plan. A lunch basket was easy and everyone headed to the lake outside of town. There were picnic tables under a shelter where they spread out a cloth and dug into sandwiches. While they nibbled, Jack filled in some of the basic details about how Gordie came to be at the game. Sally thought Jack was the sly one.

"That was pretty smart of you, not saying anything about a scout being there."

Jack had to deflect the compliment.

"I didn't know anything about it. I guess Randy was the smart one, keeping it quiet. If I'd known, I might have screwed it up."

Duncan was thinking one step further.

"I bet he was impressed with the way you clobbered that ball."

Jack kept that card close to his vest.

"I doubt it meant much. No offense to the pitcher, but he was average for that league. Lots of guys could have hit that ball."

Sally thought Jack was being modest and said so.

"Maybe," Jack said. "It's never a good idea to brag too much over a good day. Things change soon enough."

He looked at Duncan.

"If you advance in this game, you want to remember that. Strutting around after a good play just makes you look stupid when the next inning goes the other way."

Danielle was observing the conversation, and finally chimed in.

"I think it was just amazing, from both of you."

She pulled a bottle of wine from the basket.

"We should celebrate. You, too, Cake. Mom, a little wine won't hurt."

Jack thought this was an interesting moment. He would never tell his mother that his underage sister was ready to start drinking. But Sally was unperturbed.

"One won't hurt. It's probably all the rules that makes some kids overdo it when they get out from under their parents. So, have some wine, Duncan, you're nineteen now."

Duncan grinned and deflected her concern.

"I've already tried that stuff. Don't care for it much," and he reached for a Coke.

Sally feigned shock while Danielle and Jack laughed.

"First booze, then wild women," Danielle joked.

Jack wasn't to be left out.

"You better stick to the baseball thing, my man. 'Wild women' will mess with you."

This was too big of a target for Danielle to ignore.

"So, you're dialed in with the 'wild women' thing, Jack?"

He just shook his head and ran his fingers across his lips.

Duncan started laughing mischievously, and Danielle gave him an evil look.

"Don't! Don't even think it, you...you...."

She sputtered, looking for a word.

"Try reprobate," Sally volunteered.

All four of them snickered and the conviviality continued. Jack was enjoying himself immensely. Sally and Danielle and Duncan had a genuine affection for each other. They seemed to naturally build each other up. Some people deal with loss by becoming bitter and disdainful, while others honor their lost loved one by embracing decency and rejecting antipathy.

This family was decidedly the latter. Their mutual support system was well-suited for helping them overcome their shared loss. Jack felt honored to be given a place with them. He considered himself blessed to play a role in advancing Duncan's interests, because any success would enhance Sally and Danielle's lives. Jack also reflected that he was feeling better about himself than he had in years. He attributed it all to his dealings with this wonderful crowd.

The lunch was winding down, and Sally suggested that they walk around the lake. There was a path that paralleled the shoreline, occasionally dipping close to the water and then cresting the hills. Jack estimated the entire circuit was no more than a mile and a half. It would be a nice little walk for all of them. There were a few spots where people were fishing.

"I've heard that the fish bite better after a rain," Jack said.

"Have you done any fishing, Jack?" Sally asked.

Jack admitted that he hadn't.

"Most people get into what their dads are involved in, and mine never had time for that. He worked a lot, and what time he did have, we spent on baseball."

"Well, he sure got results there," Sally was quick to say. "You are amazing with the game."

Danielle added her two cents.

"My dad was into a little outdoor stuff. I can't say we went fishing, but he did take us out camping."

She looked around the lake.

"There's a campground over those hills, and we'd go there and sleep in tents and cook over campfires. There's nothing like watching the stars at night, away from city lights."

"You're making a city boy look bad," Jack said. "I need to broaden my horizons. My mom says I need to learn to cook, so I'll add the outdoors to my list."

Sally had been waiting to mention Jack's mother.

"I hope to meet your mom someday, Jack. I think she raised an impressive son."

Jack smiled at this fine compliment.

"That's nice of you to say. I'll be going home this week to meet with some of the bankers involved with the store. I'll be seeing my mom, and you can bet I'll be telling her about you and your kids."

Duncan was feeling happily boisterous.

"It'll be easy to tell her good stuff about me, I know. Do me a favor, Jack, and make up some good things about my sister? She has so little to look forward to."

Poor Duncan was looking at Jack when he made this dangerous remark. Danielle came swooping up behind him and gave him a healthy shove down the hill. He slipped in the mud from the night's rain and slid down the path on his backside.

"Now you've done it!"

He regained his footing and clambered up the hill after his sister.

She ran shrieking behind a big sycamore tree and used it as a shield. They both were laughing and calling each other names Jack hadn't heard. Duncan was 'BabyCakes' and Danielle was 'Fanny.'

"Danielle, please don't hurt my prospect," Jack called. "He might have to perform pretty soon."

Danielle hammed it up.

"Cake, you are so lucky Jack is here to save you."

Duncan made his own vague threats, and Sally and Jack enjoyed the show. Jack turned to Sally.

"I have to ask about those new names. Where did they come from?"

Sally smiled her answer.

"Remember the Hines thing? When 'Cake' started, Danielle was only five. Duncan was her baby, or so she thought. So she called him 'baby' and 'Cake.' Sometimes they got combined. The other one happened when Duncan tried to copy his father when he called her 'Danny.' It came out 'Fanny' and that stuck, too. I haven't heard them used for a while. Sort of takes me back. It means they're getting along."

Jack was mesmerized by another glimpse into the inner workings of the family dynamic. There were so many nice aspects. He hoped he would be able to hang around and see more of them.

By now they had looped around the lake and were back to the picnic area. The mud on Duncan's clothes made him look like a real outdoorsman. They packed up their things and headed back to Danielle's hatchback. Jack had to add his part to the family teasing.

"Gee," he said. "I sure hope this mud that somebody got on his clothes doesn't end up in somebody's car."

"Keep it up, J.A.," Danielle said. "I'll figure out some trouble for you, too."

Sally jumped in.

"Now there's that one, again. J.A.?"

Jack liked being included in the family nickname battle.

"It starts with Jack," he said. "You'll have to ask your sweet daughter, who made it up. She knows what the 'A' stands for," and he patted his behind.

"Oh, you," Sally said, and gave a playful swat at Danielle. "Such a lady I've raised."

They voted to make evening plans. It would be close to suppertime, but lunch had been small. Sally suggested grilling out and enjoying the evening at home. Everyone agreed and they headed to the grocery.

Sally and Dirty Duncan stayed outside to avoid bringing lake mud into the store, while Danielle and Jack went in for steaks and salad. They looked like any young couple doing Sunday grocery shopping. As they cruised through the aisles, Danielle asked some low-key personal questions.

"What kinds of food do you like, Jack? I mean, Italian, or Asian, that sort of thing?"

"I'm not too good with spicy stuff," Jack said. "I guess I'm pretty bland, in the food department. I can go for the less hot items, if you're talking Mexican. But steak and potatoes will never steer you wrong. How about you?"

Danielle admitted to the same category.

"I think the Midwestern farm life starts you out with basic food tastes. I'd never heard of the more exotic stuff until I went to college. They had a sushi bar at the food court that I got into."

Jack made a face.

"You do know that's raw fish, right? Wrapped in some kind of seaweed? Yuck."

He made his best 'upset stomach' face while he grabbed his middle.

"We can't all be cultured," Danielle said.

They passed another couple with a baby stroller. Danielle couldn't resist.

"What a pretty baby!"

Some folks get uncomfortable when a stranger talks to them, but Danielle knew you can get away with complimenting anyone's baby. The couple smiled and the young mother pulled the baby's blanket aside so Danielle could get a better look.

"Oh, look at that face. Perfect for smooching!"

The new parents were pleased and asked if Danielle and Jack had any kids. Danielle fielded the question like a sharp grounder to second base.

"Not yet, but one of these days."

Both couples went about their business, and Jack gave Danielle a quizzical look.

"One of these days?"

"The real story would take all day. 'No, we're not married, I'm just here in the store with a guy who picked up my brother over a baseball game, and my mom kind of likes him and he comes over to paint the barn and have dinner, etc.' They'd know we're crazy and tell us to get away from their baby, real quick."

Jack had to agree with her logic. Quick, effective, and to the point. But Danielle did have a question.

"Since we're on the topic, Jack, what do you think about kids?"

It was a gentle probing, but she had a motive. Jack was enthusiastic.

"I think they're great. My mom has two sisters and they both have families. I like playing with their kids and being Uncle Jack. I think being a dad would be terrific. What about you?"

"Me, too," Danielle agreed. "Families are fun."

She had a pensive look on her face.

"What's the matter?" Jack asked.

She looked at him slyly.

"I was wondering which one of us has to go through morning sickness and wreck their body to get the job done."

She meant it as a joke, but Jack stopped in the aisle and looked at her. It was time for a brief but serious moment.

"I think the work and sacrifice in having a baby is astounding. Women don't get enough credit for what they do. If more guys understood how hard it is, half of the family issues in the world would go away."

Danielle didn't try to respond. She thought that Jack gave a perfect summation, and she filed it away for future use. Jack liked the ribeye steaks in the case, and asked if Sally and Duncan would approve.

"You can't go wrong with any steaks in this family. Duncan would eat fried baloney, and like it. So, yes."

Jack pointed out that the grocery had ready-made salad in to-go bags.

"That'd be great with steaks. I wonder where we could get sweet corn this time of year."

Danielle headed to the check-out.

"C'mon, clever boy. I'll find some, somewhere."

They were quickly back to the car and found Duncan explaining curve ball dynamics to his mother. Jack was amused that Duncan was now an instructor.

"Remember what Alexander Pope said, kiddo. 'A little knowledge is a dangerous thing.' Don't tell 'em all you know on the first day."

He was loading groceries into the car, and Sally perked right up.

"I did my thesis on Pope, Jack. And I am happy to inform you that most people misquote that one."

Jack played along.

"Do tell."

The teacher addressed her student.

"The correct quote, as taken from Alexander Pope, was 'a little *learning* is a dangerous thing.' He supposedly got it from Francis Bacon, who wrote something similar about eighty-five years before Pope was born. So, you're quoting a misquote of a misquote. Ha, ha."

Jack raised both hands.

"I surrender. Never argue with a word merchant!"

Danielle had to agree.

"I could have told you that. You don't want to get in a 'quote contest' with that one," indicating her mother.

Sally grinned at both of them.

"We're in the same world, Jack. You hit baseballs out of the park; I hit words out of the library."

Jack was still chuckling. Sally wasn't done.

"Pope had a few more. You ever hear 'to err is human, to forgive divine,' or maybe 'fools rush in where angels fear to tread'? Same guy, Jack."

They were halfway home and the kidding continued. Jack found the James family unpredictable. They had something intelligent to say on a multitude of topics and he liked the variety. People who wanted to talk only about one thing were hard to take.

Soon, the barbeque was fired up and the steaks were sizzling. Duncan had already gone inside to get rid of his muddy clothes. Danielle also needed a little clean-up.

"I'm gonna get out of these grubby jeans and wash my face."

Sally also took the opportunity to change. Jack wasn't going to be left out. He was alone so he headed over to the water pump and splashed off the lake dust. Dunking his head in the water was refreshing. It made him feel free and relaxed. Shaking his wet hair and smoothing it back was all he needed.

Rinsing off in the farm yard was completely natural and Jack did not feel self-conscious at all. He had a clean shirt in his car and was putting it on when Danielle appeared. She wore a cotton dress with undulating colors that flowed and shimmered. It was impossible not to notice how the dress accented her natural curves. Her image reminded Jack of pictures of women walking down some small back street in Paris or Florence. It landed Danielle in the same refined and innocent category. Jack thought she looked fabulous and perfectly feminine.

The timing was exquisite for watching the summer sun recede. Dinner was almost an afterthought. Between bites, they enjoyed the indigo light show as the sky faded into night.

Jack explained his plan for contacting Gordie Bowen.

"I don't know how the team will arrange the try-out, but they will need to see our boy here in action. It would be basic throwing, and they might have a couple of guys take a few swings."

Duncan looked a little flustered at the prospect.

"I'll be there the whole time," Jack said. "It might be a little intimidating, with new surroundings, and strangers giving you the evil eye, but it'll be just like throwing here. They want to see you succeed, Cake. Really."

Duncan was still unconvinced, but he knew that Jack had it all under control. It was time he put on his big boy pants and show them his stuff.

"Sounds great. We'll go when you say so."

Sally gave them all a lopsided smile.

"Jack, tell me how you do it. He doesn't fall in line so well for me."

The question called for Jack to give a philosophical answer: "The Good Book says 'a Prophet is never accepted in his home town.' And Sally, you are some kind of prophet."

No one made a clever retort, to Jack's surprise. They seemed to be thinking about his remark. Suppertime ended on that note and they did the dishes together, assembly-line style. The warm family feeling was enveloping Jack again, and he hated to see the night end.

"Jack, it'd be great to hear some tunes on the guitar, but I'm bushed," Sally yawned. "If it's okay with you kids, I'm headed to bed."

Everyone nodded, and she added her coda to the evening.

"Jack, let me know your travel details, and what we need for Babycakes here."

Danielle and Duncan liked the entertaining departure, and waved their mom off to sleep. Duncan was drooping as well.

"I'm ready to crash, too, so tell me tomorrow what I should be doing, okay?"

Jack nodded, and Duncan left. Jack turned to Danielle.

"I'll be taking off. See you tomorrow before I go?"

Danielle was agreeable.

"Sure. Let me walk you to your car."

When they got to the Mustang, Danielle hesitated.

"If you don't have to hurry, want to take a walk, and talk a bit?"

Jack couldn't say 'yes' fast enough. He wanted this night, with this beautiful woman, to go on forever.

36

NIGHT TIME IS THE RIGHT TIME

Danielle had a mischievous look on her face.

"Wait a second. I have an idea."

She motioned toward the house, and retrieved the half-empty bottle. She grabbed two plastic cups and poured in the rest of the wine. Then she handed a cup to Jack, as he approached.

"Here. Let's sit on the porch and finish this up."

The last twilight rays were filtering through the leaves. It gave the area an ethereal feel, with bits of soft light mixed into dark swatches. Jack basked in the moment.

"That looks kind of dreamy, doesn't it? Where the light mixes into the shadows and it shifts around as it all fades?"

Danielle nodded, as she looked out over the barn and surrounding area.

"It's funny you mention that. I've sat here hundreds of times with my dad. He said the same thing about the dreamy part. The light wafts around the trees and it reminded him of the time when you're sort of dreaming and not quite awake."

Jack stayed with the feeling and thought about a father using these peaceful edges to bond with his daughter.

"Was it a good time for talking?"

Danielle gave a soft shrug.

"Sure. We'd talk about the usual 'kid stuff' you go through. School problems; not getting invited to the popular party. Boy troubles. You know."

Jack gently smiled as he considered the distresses of youth.

"I have a hard time believing you had problems getting invited to the cool parties. Or, had boy troubles. I think you're pretty as all get out."

As soon as he said it, he cringed. 'All get out?' What was wrong with him?

Danielle was shaking her head.

"That's a new one for me. 'All get out.' Got any more?"

Jack actually covered his face with his hands.

"Good Lord, that came out wrong. What I meant was...."

He fumbled for the right words, and Danielle was amused by his struggle.

"Look at you," she said. "You're so calm when they're throwing baseballs at your head, and here you are bumbling around like a teenager."

That got her a soft elbow in the ribs.

"Thanks a bunch. You're making it worse."

Danielle took pity on the poor boy.

"I know what you're saying, and I think it's sweet. Believe it or not, I'll remember it as the first time someone said that to me. I like to remember 'first time' things. Maybe the first time my dad put me on the tractor. Or when I rode my bike without training wheels. There's the first time I went to school. It goes on and on."

Jack switched gears.

"Do you remember the first time some guy came into your driveway to see your brother?"

That prompted one of her delicate smiles.

"Of course I do. Seems like just the other day. God, he was such a pain in the you-know-what!"

Another gentle elbow resulted. The wine was gone, and Jack stuck the cork into the empty bottle.

"What about that walk you mentioned?"

They both got up, and strolled the same path they had walked the week before. The sunset had faded, but the barn had service lights on each corner. The fence line was easy to travel. They stopped by the spot where Jack and Duncan had been throwing. Danielle glanced around the area and gave a little sweep of her hand.

"This is the same place where my dad would play catch with Duncan when he was a kid. And they kept at it as he got older. It was the big thing they shared."

She shifted her gaze from the area and looked at Jack.

"And now he's throwing with you. Sorta fits, doesn't it?"

Jack was in his baseball comfort zone and his caution slipped ever so slightly.

"Danny, your brother...."

He froze as soon as he said it. Danielle was instantly aware that Jack had never called her 'Danny' before now. It signaled a shift in their relationship. She watched his face, looking for a sign. Jack knew he had crossed some sort of line, using the name reserved for her family. She didn't seem put off, so Jack gathered his courage and tried again.

"I didn't mean to...."

He searched for the right words.

"Maybe I'm getting too comfortable around your family. It just slipped out."

Danielle's soft smile kept him from feeling completely awkward.

"It's okay, Jack. I kinda like it."

She found his shy vulnerability disarming. With a slightly raised eyebrow, she encouraged him to continue.

"I'm trying to say that Cake has a gift," Jack finally managed. "I don't know how it works that way. Some guys just naturally have the right mix of biometrics and psychology. You have to have both, to really compete at a high level."

He paused to see if there was a chance she thought he made any sense. Danielle's deliberate look was a gentle nudge.

"I just saw this kid who could throw a baseball, and it seemed nobody was helping him. Everybody needs a little guidance and encouragement, at times. You know that, from teaching."

Danielle nodded pensively, and was still listening. They had reached the turn in the fence. Jack stopped and took a deep breath.

"I didn't mean to barge in on any family business, but it would be a sin to waste what he can do. And I'm feeling pretty good about the family being okay with it."

He hoped he was making headway, and Danielle seemed to be reading his mind.

"We love what you're doing with Duncan. Mom says you're an answer to her prayers. We always knew he had some kind of ability, but we didn't know what to do about it."

She paused and renewed her benign smile. The dim light could not obscure the glimmer in her eyes.

"Then you come along. And now Duncan's going to pitch for a major league scout!"

Her lighthearted laugh announced her unfettered joy.

"I think it's 'pretty as all get out,' don't you?"

Jack nodded and smiled happily.

"I sure do."

Something made him say it again, quietly.

"Sure do."

The walk continued along the next section of fence row. Danielle linked her arm with Jack's. She liked the warm feeling it gave her.

"Did you know I would hang out watching you work on pitching with Duncan?"

Jack was surprised.

"Really? How did you do that?"

"On the other side of the house, there's a clear view of that part of the barn," she answered. "You can hear what's going on there, because the sound bounces off the wall."

Intrigued by her sleuthing, Jack risked being teased.

"So, what did you learn?"

After a thoughtful pause, Danielle delivered a sedate answer.

"I learned you are a great baseball teacher. That you know a lot about the game, and you're very humble about your abilities. You are a good person who doesn't swear and respects people, especially women."

She stopped in her tracks, and locked eyes with Jack.

"I learned that my concerns about your motivation with my brother were unfounded."

Then she took her own leap of faith. All of the events of the past few days allowed her to trust this new kid in town.

"I learned that I was a jerk for doubting a good person like you."

Jack felt honored.

"Thank you, Danny. I just want the right thing for everybody. And sometimes it turns out the right thing for nobody."

He had been looking sideways at Danielle, but he turned to face her directly. They nearly touched as he leaned on the wooden fence.

"I get something out of it, too," he added.

Another raised eyebrow.

"Go on."

"I get to be part of this kid's success, even if it's only watching. It could be huge. And I get to be part of the family's happiness about it. I have to tell you, I was sort of wandering around for the past five years. Your little trio has helped pull me out of that. And I'm grateful."

Danielle smiled and patted his arm.

"I learned something else," Jack continued.

His smile turned impish.

"You're not a jerk. I'm almost sure of it."

Her pat on the arm became a swat, and she started off along the next fence section.

Jack was laughing, and called after her.

"Hey! Isn't that a compliment? Really, not being a jerk is a good thing, in my book."

Danielle was only a few steps ahead. Jack caught up with ease.

"Can we go back to 'pretty as all get out,' if that makes you happy?"

She beamed, the way women do when laughing isn't good enough. They continued their slow march along the fence. Jack switched to another subject.

"Tell me about Duncan calling you 'Dumbo.' Is that another family nickname?"

Her answer came with a wry grin.

"Yes, but it wasn't something my parents let him get away with. It was when I was ten or twelve, something like that. He was using it for the 'Dumb' part; sort of an extension of him calling me 'Dumyell.' You know, sounds like 'Danielle.' Just stupid kid stuff."

"All kids do that stupid stuff," Jack said.

"Yeah, but part of it was him making fun of my big ears. My folks really got on him."

Jack was confused.

"Big ears?"

Danielle gave him an exasperated look.

"You know, the Disney elephant? Dumbo?"

Jack was still looking lost, so she gave up. She lifted her shoulder-length hair so he could see her ears. Confused became amused.

"They're not big! They're kinda cute. What was he thinking?"

She rearranged her hair.

"I told you it was stupid kid stuff. And girls are sensitive to how they look."

She seemed vulnerable at that moment, and Jack wanted to rescue her. They had completed the fourth leg of the fence row, and were back to where the fence ended on the far side of the barn. There was a field light there, but the overhang cast a small shadow where the fence joined the building.

Danielle climbed up to rest on the fence rail, so her head was level with Jack's. She was sitting with her back up against the corner of the barn. When she commented about big ears, Jack picked this moment to boost her ego.

"Well, whatever it was, he sure thinks a lot of you now."

Danielle considered that remark.

"Actually, I kind of like it when he calls me 'Bo'. It means he's being nice. He's referring back to when he was hacking on me, but without the mean part. So, he's saying he has grown into liking me. Kinda complex, right?"

Jack saw the reasoning.

"I get it. And another thing. You were saying you were concerned about your looks?"

He didn't expect an answer. Her look told him she was waiting to hear what was on his mind.

"I think if anybody isn't sure how pretty you are, they're nuts."

Danielle's smile was the deepest yet, and she murmured her response.

"Do you think I'm pretty, Jack?"

He collected his thoughts because he wanted to get this right. Feeling slightly more confident, he dared to leap across the familiarity line.

"Hold that thought, Danny. You were talking about remembering first times. The first bike ride; all that?"

Danielle nodded. Jack wanted to weave this moment into his memory trove of happy first experiences. What he was feeling right now was at the top of his list of 'perfect firsts.'

"I'm big into that, too, because you only get one, whatever it is. It could be anything, hopefully good, but there are others. A bad thing could be the first time you got stood up, or something like that. But I'm talking about the good things to remember. Like seeing your first professional baseball game. You remember who you were with, the weather, and how green the field was. Or maybe you remember catching your first fish. The boat you were in, your dad helping you bait the hook, whatever it might be. Those are incredibly sweet moments, and they belong to you and no one else."

Pausing to see if she understood his point, he saw Danielle was listening intently.

"I hope I'm not rambling too much, but I think it's important. Duncan is going to remember his first major league strikeout. You and your mom will, too. I remember my first home run in the Show like it was yesterday."

Jack shook his head and looked off into the night.

"God, it was great. But private moments are just as good. I remember my mom buying my first guitar. It was a cheese-cutter that made my fingers bleed. That was great, too."

He glanced at Danielle, and then lingered by looking directly at her face. Her eyes revealed that he had embarked on new territory.

"Danny, there's only one first time, and when you know it's happening, you want it to be perfect."

She was still on the fence rail, leaning against the barn. A tiny shaft of light drifted down from the barn's overhang. It cast her face as a sublime portrait of contrasts, with shadows on her fine features. Her nose and cheekbones were perfectly silhouetted against the barn's fresh white paint. Jack wanted to freeze the transcendent image in his mind.

The light was too dim for him to see the fantastic color in her eyes. They were merely deeply entrancing in the shadows, and Jack realized he was staring. But Danielle didn't seem uncomfortable at all. She wasn't afraid to return the gaze. Maybe she was memorizing Jack's shadowy outline as well. Jack softly broke the silence.

"I'll answer your question now. And I want it to be a good 'first time' memory for you, Danny."

He caught his breath and spoke as evenly as he could.

"Yes, I think you're pretty. I think you are incredibly pretty."

Danielle didn't answer, at least not with words. Her look told Jack that she liked what she heard. He decided to swing for the fence. This girl was beautiful, and a chance like this might never come again.

"I think all that 'first time' stuff applies to a first kiss, don't you?"

Danielle nodded slowly, because she was also trapped in the moment.

"I mean, you want it to be perfect because it's going to last forever," Jack said. "You want to remember everything. Like what the girl is wearing. I'll remember that amazing flowing dress you have on. That perfume. It just about makes a guy dizzy."

He had moved from standing next to Danielle and now was in front of her. She slowly slid off of the fence rail and stood up straight. She was tall enough to easily reach her arms around Jack's neck.

"This is a good 'first time' to remember, right?" she said. "I mean, I think you had a 'baseball' hug before, and you got a smooch on the cheek, but this is different. What do you think?"

Jack was thinking he was having an out of body experience. Life since losing real baseball had been surreal. His emotions and hopes had been on hold, and the thought of stepping away from that sad endless loop made him dare to believe that he was feeling something reliable. So, he answered Danielle's question, sincerely and straight from the heart.

"What do I think? I think you're pretty as all get out. And the name 'Fanny' is cute and makes you sound sweet. I think that if I leaned over and kissed you, I'd never be the same. It would be a first kiss that I would remember more than any other 'firsts' in my entire life."

He paused and let her beauty wash over him. His heart was pounding, so loudly she had to hear it. He had never been this close, looking directly into her eyes. They seemed to draw him to her, in some magical way, as if they held answers to questions he hadn't thought of yet. Her mysterious smile made him answer her question with his own.

"What do you think?"

He literally held his breath. Danielle gently tightened her arms around Jack's neck, and slowly pulled him closer.

"I think you ought to find out," she whispered.

Then she kissed him gently on the lips, in a soft and slow first kiss that she would remember forever. She wrapped her arms tightly around him, and pulled him into a fierce embrace.

Again, she whispered.

"Pretty as all get out."

She kissed him passionately and time stood still for both of them. It would be impossible to forget, because for them, there had never been anything like it. They would have been surprised to know that they were both thinking the same thing. Both were wondering if it might be possible to somehow make this magic happen again.

37

A TRY-OUT WOULD BE NICE

Incessant knocking the next morning slowly penetrated Jack's consciousness. Last night's events reverberated in his mind. Finally awake, he thought that he had dreamed the two hours by the barn. Mostly, he and Danielle had talked, but there had been magical compelling moments which reprised their first kiss. His entire existence was still reeling from the feeling of Danielle's body close to him. She had somehow reached clear to his soul.

The night had been sweet and unforgettable, but it seemed shorter than a walk to first base. They met not long ago, connected by mutual concern for Duncan's welfare. That allied them on a level that effortlessly became physical attraction. But it would be inadequate to call it physical. Jack felt that each second with Danny revealed new aspects of his being. Her ability to see through life's clutter brought new meaning to everyday events.

When Jack walked through the memory of the crash that killed Olivia, Danielle was a perfect listener. She gently discerned that Jack had been medicating himself with periodic baseball games. Her calm and insightful manner gave Jack peace; a peace he had lost after grief destroyed his dream. Layers of disappointment were peeling away, solely because this young woman had such a depth of awareness, delivered by a kind heart.

Danielle also visited her disappointments. She told Jack about her college boyfriend, and how that experience hindered her thinking when Jack arrived on the scene. Her issues with a ball-player had prevented her from seeing Jack's true nature. Elements of her past that she hadn't faced seeped to the surface. There was the hurt of believing that she had a relationship that would last, which proved to be false. One item was particularly insightful: 'I was in love with the idea of being in love.'

It reminded Jack of the discussion he had with Sally, and he mentioned it. 'People tell you all the time who they are. You just need to listen.' Jack felt validated when Danielle told him that her mother had repeated that very thing to her. He felt even better when she told him that those words had guided her to listen – to what Jack was saying about who he was. Jack asked, a little hopefully, what she had heard.

She didn't say anything for a long moment. What happened next sent warm and gentle waves rolling over him. She reached toward him and softly put her hands on his face, and kissed him again. When she spoke, Jack felt part of him go to a place of serenity and happiness that he didn't know existed.

"What I heard was that you were showing me that you are a sweet, loveable guy that I want to have in my life."

Time seemed to stop. The world was reduced to only the two of them. Jack felt cherished and complete.

Somehow, they were able to say goodnight and Jack drove back to the motel. He was in some kind of trance – a place where he was invincible and could accomplish anything. He knew that there had probably been others who had similar feelings, but no one could surpass this. Blissful sleep arrived; the kind that comes to only the truly happy. Jack had to be in a deep slumber, because a noise that had been going on for some time slowly brought him to reality.

The clamor was distant and incomprehensible, but it grew louder and closer. At first Jack was confused and thought it was his phone. He fumbled for the cell and saw that the battery had died. At the same moment he realized what he heard was not a ringing sound. Jack recognized the knocking and managed to get to his feet. He could see through the blinds that Randy Powers was standing outside, rapping on the glass. Jack wrestled the door open.

"Your phone ain't working," Randy barked. "I've been trying to call you all morning."

"What time is it?' Jack croaked.

"It's about noon. You been out all night?"

Jack held the door open, and motioned Randy inside.

"I had planned to catch up to you today, before I headed home."

Randy didn't waste any time.

"Gordie Bowen called this morning, trying to reach you about Duncan. When I couldn't get you on the phone, I worried you were off in a ditch somewhere."

He was genuinely concerned, and Jack was grateful.

"Sorry, pal. I was up late. Did you give Gordie my number?"

Randy was happy to see that Jack was safe.

"Sure did, but he hasn't been able to reach you, either. He called me back forty-five minutes ago to say you were out of touch. He was hot to talk to you. So here I am."

Jack had gone into the bathroom to splash his face and pull on his jeans. Now was as good a time as any to contact Gordie, he figured, but renewing connections might be problematic. During Jack's brief stay with the team, Gordie had been friendly enough. But he had also disappeared when trouble arose.

"Let me call him now and see what he has in mind. My phone takes a while to charge before it works. Could you dial yours?"

Randy punched Gordie's number from his 'recent' list and hit speaker. He set the phone on the table and Gordie answered on the third ring.

"Hello, Randy, have you found Jack?"

"I'm here," Jack said. "You're on speaker with me and Randy. Nobody else is here."

It had been five years since they had spoken. Jack didn't know how this chat would unfold. He was relieved he had Randy as a buffer. They both heard Gordie's answer.

"Hey, Jack, I'm glad to get in touch with you."

Gordie sounded sincere enough, but Jack wasn't convinced. Randy jumped in, because he could see the conflict on Jack's face.

"Maybe I should step out so you two can talk business."

"That's Jack's call," Gordie allowed. "I don't have anything that you don't know."

"It's fine with me if Randy stays," Jack said.

He felt foolish for being uncomfortable at the thought of being alone on the call. But Gordie worked with the crowd that had pulled his heart out through his ribs. Jack wasn't being spiteful, just careful.

On his end of things, Gordon Bowen knew every aspect of the events Jack Ridley had endured. His sense of fair play had been insulted by the way Jack had been ostracized. In reality, there had been a large number of his co-workers with the same feelings, then and now. That feeling was at the core of the message he wanted to deliver to Jack, but this situation called for him to address other matters first.

"That's fine, Jack," Gordie said. "I've already given Randy the details. I understand you know that I came to see Duncan Saturday night. The team wants to bring him in for a tryout."

He paused to see if either Randy or Jack had a comment, but neither one of them spoke. Jack fixated on the phone, to hear what words were coming next.

"So," Gordie continued, "I was hoping you could make arrangements for Duncan to come to the ballpark; maybe this week, and throw a bit."

Jack was hearing words that, one week ago, he would not have thought possible.

"I can do that," he said. "Just give me a day or so to set it up."

Gordie was thinking logistics, as a good scout should.

"I'm told he's nineteen, so we'd love to have his parents along."

Jack met that uncomfortable moment head-on.

"He's only got his mother, but she'll be coming, too."

"I understand, Jack. Please let her know we are looking forward to meeting her, and we'll cover all expenses."

It occurred to Jack that Duncan might feel better with his mother and his sister along for moral support. He made a quick mental note that the women might want to bunk together. He'd make sure they were booked into the swankiest place there was.

"That's fine, Gordie, I'll go see them today and get back to you. Thank you very much for calling."

Randy tried to smooth the end of the call.

"I think you are going to like what you see."

Gordie chuckled.

"I already do. That's why I'm calling. By the way, an old friend of yours is looking forward to your visit, Jack."

Jack's warning lights started to glow.

"Who's that?"

"Mike Franz. He's our pitching coach, if you didn't know. I got to tell you, he's just about jumping up and down at the chance to see you again."

Jack was conflicted, and every misgiving he had about this contact was bubbling to the surface. Mike was not at fault for any of Jack's troubles. But the fact remained that Jack had been driving in the fatal accident because Mike had directed it.

Franz was a physical bookend to Jack's saga. He was the last player Jack had been around when he was a happy team member; and Mike was the last person with the club that Jack saw before the exile. It was still so very complicated.

Jack's pride had been devastated by people he trusted, and now he had to return and submit to their scrutiny. For a man of honor, having to endure those who previously wronged him is nauseating. What sustained Jack was his fervent belief that this was all for

Duncan. Jack had made a promise, and that was the end of the story.

"I'll make the call and get back to you," Jack said.

Randy clicked off his phone. He looked at Jack to summarize what had transpired.

"That went okay. You need anything on my end?"

Jack shook his head.

"I'll head out there now and talk to Duncan and his mother. I'll let you know how it goes."

Randy was comfortable with the results of the chat with Gordie.

"I'm real glad you got this going, Jack. I'm betting Duncan knocks the crap out of 'em. His dad would have been so happy, and it's because of you."

Jack was able to smile, just a bit, now that the call was over.

"It's about Duncan, but I'm glad I came along to see it. I hope he makes something good of it and can help his mom and sister. They are great people."

Randy nodded, and walked out. Jack climbed into the shower to get ready to go see the James Gang.

He was showered and shaved in no time, and did a little advance planning for the week. First up was how Duncan would go see Gordie. Then there would be arrangements to meet with the company lawyer and the bankers about the store.

Things were percolating a lot faster than they were last week. Baseball was the immediate issue, but then last night's images returned. Jack was dressed and walking to his car when the memory rippled to the surface. Slightly chagrined, he realized that the phone call with Gordie had stymied all other thoughts. Danielle's moonlit magic had been momentarily misplaced. The sweet picture reappeared, and he started to smile. A romantic reverie intertwined with baseball! Life was deliciously random.

Jack forced his mind to the task at hand. He'd prepare Duncan for the tryout. Somewhere in the planning, Jack would find a private moment with Danielle. He needed to tell her she was the most amazing person he had ever met. Thinking he probably delivered a similar message last night began another smile. Communication with Danny had encompassed many levels; some of them sweetly non-verbal. For today, she would probably appreciate it if he used real words. At least, while her mother was around.

38

MILES TO GO AND PROMISES TO KEEP

Before Jack left, he told the motel office he was checking out. They billed the store, anyway, so there was nothing to sign. He let the desk clerk know that he might be back later in the week. The Mustang fired up like it was new. It was behaving as if it never had issues. Jack started thinking the car had a mind of its own. Maybe it knew he had been wasting his time knocking around in small town baseball games, so it ran poorly. Now it was eager to go to the farm, where an optimistic future resided. The diner was just about to shut down the breakfast menu; he was lucky to grab an egg sandwich.

As he drove, Jack listened to the oldies radio station. A Neil Young song was playing: 'When the dream came, I held my breath with my eyes closed.' Jack didn't know the song, but he instantly knew the line applied to last night. Weren't dreams some sort of magical trance? Danielle easily had him holding his breath, because if he moved at all, the spell might disappear. He didn't know how he could manage it, but he resolved to find those moments again.

When he arrived at the farm, there was no one in sight. Jack pulled up next to the barn. If Duncan was inside he would hear Jack's car, but only Elvis appeared. Jack headed to the house with the dog wagging along. Sally came outside before Jack made it to the porch. At least somebody was home.

"Where is everybody?" Jack began.

Sally gave Jack a grinning, bouncy look.

"The kids went to the mall. Can you believe that? Duncan went to the mall with Danny!"

It was amusing. Sally was a slightly different person when her kids weren't around. That made sense, because the parenting role requires a different relationship, compared to regular interaction. Jack was a good people watcher; he knew too many people tried to be their kids' friends, instead of their parent.

Sally was a mother first, but when she stepped out of her parent mode, she was spontaneous and playful. Jack liked both sides - the mom *and* the fun person. He understood her point about Duncan going to the mall. It wasn't the first time he had expressed an aversion to shopping.

"So, she's going to shop 'till he drops?"

Sally let out a gleeful giggle.

"Nope! She told him if he was going to be seeing important people, he couldn't look like he just climbed off a hay wagon. So, she's picking out some nice things for him to wear when you take him to see your baseball buddies. He didn't put up any fuss."

Jack got the message.

"She has a way of smoothing things out, doesn't she?"

Sally gave no instant reply. Instead, she looked at Jack while trying to decipher this charming young man. He had decided to befriend her son, as a sort of baseball coach. Once that ball was rolling, she learned that Jack's motivation was a pure desire to see Duncan succeed. Stage One was complete.

When she found they had music and literature in common, Stage Two was a natural sequence. If they had met at a book club and delved into Edgar Alan Poe, they would have easily bonded on an intellectual plane. It was the hint of a Stage Three with Danielle that had her wheels turning.

Women are perceptive on a level that escapes most men. It might have come from primitive times, when males were straightforward hunters and females became keepers of the hearth. Close proximity with others must have caused women to become better observers of human nature. This talent allowed Sally to detect a nascent relationship between Danielle and Jack.

Originally, her daughter was mildly antagonistic toward Duncan's new friend. That feeling quickly eroded, mainly because it was simply wrong. But Sally had observed a subtle attitude shift. It began when Danielle saw Jack patiently teaching Duncan the finer points of baseball. She had clearly decided to accept Jack, if only as Duncan's mentor.

But Danielle's outlook changed again when she saw Jack's kindness toward a little girl and her spilled ice cream. Nothing was said at the time, but Sally saw the metamorphosis in full swing after Duncan played in the Crushers game. Her Danny Girl had treated Jack with a gentle affection that seemed to go beyond gratitude for kindness toward her brother.

This morning's demeanor got Sally's mind in full swing. Danielle mentioned that after Duncan and Sally went to bed, Jack had stayed and they talked. To Sally's thinking, Danielle seemed lighter and happier - more so than in a long time. If Sally had to guess, she surmised that more than talking had occurred.

Her mother's intuition told her that Danielle's uplifted spirits related to Jack. Sally was content to observe the upswing in her daughter's psyche, wherever it might lead. When Jack made his observation about Danielle's nature, Sally instantly processed all these intricate concepts. Still, she kept her answer low-key.

"She does have a way, that's true."

That sparse comment had Jack nodding in agreement, and mulling over all the possibilities. Sally thought it was time to shift the conversation to plans for Duncan.

"Have you decided on the next step for Cake?"

She asked the question as she turned toward the glider. Jack pulled his mind away from Danny and stepped up on the porch. Sally slid over and patted the spot next to her. She was asking about his intentions for her son, and he was just recently in another mode with her daughter. Life's randomness was working on him again. Jack collected his thoughts and dove in.

"Randy Powers came to see me this morning. He's been in contact with Gordon Bowen. Gordie's the scout I mentioned the other day - the one who came to the game when we didn't know he was there. He had gone back home to make arrangements for this week. He's already been talking to team management. Randy wanted me to know that Gordie was expecting to hear from me, to bring Duncan in for a tryout. So, I need to get it set up."

It seemed like a mouthful to Jack, and it involved a great deal of moving parts. It's not every day that some nobody gets to show his stuff at a major league facility. Sally was silent, trying to take it all in. She exhaled slowly.

"This is really it, isn't it, Jack? I can't believe I'm sitting here, talking about Duncan getting a chance to try out with a real baseball team."

She paused, and gazed at Jack for a brief moment.

"We're sitting in the exact spot where David talked about his hopes for Duncan."

She wiped her eyes with her sleeve, not awkward at all. Niceties mean nothing when you're dealing with raw emotion. Jack stayed silent and respectful. He knew this was a momentous time for Sally. She dabbed at her eyes a moment longer, and then she reached out and grabbed Jack's hand. She was trembling slightly and Jack was now lost for words. Gathering her composure was a tall order, and she was losing ground.

Jack thought he could show a little support by squeezing her hand. Sally still wasn't talking. She was looking far out over the fields while she wrestled with her thoughts. Letting go of Jack's hand, she stood up and walked to the edge of the porch. She briefly covered her eyes. Then she slid her hand down over her mouth and seemed to sag a little. Jack was relieved she could lean on the railing. Finally, she looked back to Jack and began to speak. Her voice was soft and guarded.

"I am afraid of what will happen if this doesn't work. It's one thing to think that maybe there's a chance out there, and maybe it will come or not. I feel weak in thinking maybe it would be better if Duncan didn't come to this crossroads. Because if you don't have to face up to it, you can always hang on to what might have been."

She stopped and looked away. When she looked at Jack again, her face was a frame of sadness and discouragement. Seeing her pain was difficult for Jack. Tears started to trickle down her face, and she made no move to stop them.

"I haven't known what to do since David died. I'm supposed to make decisions for my boy, and I have no idea what I'm doing. Baseball was his father's thing. Somehow, I started thinking it would drift away, and we'd never know what could have happened."

Sally turned to face Jack. The distress on her face was dramatic.

"Please don't think I'm not grateful for what you're doing."

Her voice was slightly above a whisper.

"I'm glad you have given this chance to Duncan. I just don't know what I will do if he fails. He'll have to come home and live with it."

Jack was nearly overcome. This woman was so brave and strong it just about broke his heart. He desperately wanted to say something that would ease her pain. He stood up and faced her. Important words should be delivered while you are on your feet.

"Sally, I want you to know how much I respect what you have done with your kids. They are kind and decent people. I am honored to know them. And you."

Sally gave him a weak smile. It almost put Jack over the edge. He paused to make sure he got all the words out.

"I played baseball for most of my life. It always made sense. It's just perfect. It's still a game, but it says something about being human that reaches your soul. You play as a team, but it allows you to win or lose on your own. When I was a kid, it was what connected me to my dad. When there were any problems, we could still play ball. We didn't have to talk. Just throwing a ball made everything okay. There's nothing like it."

Sally was listening intently. Jack didn't know if he was giving her what she needed to hear.

"I got lucky and played with some of the best ballplayers there are. And it made me even more positive about it: Baseball can heal what's wrong, even if you don't know what's wrong. Sally, have you ever seen a ballplayer give a baseball to a kid in the stands? The kid acts like he's been handed the Hope Diamond! And his parents are so happy it makes your chest hurt."

The picture of happy little kids at a ball game was one of his favorite memories, and he missed those images. He managed to continue, after a pause.

"That's what baseball is all about. There isn't a sweeter moment, anywhere, besides family. And I truly believe Duncan will have a place in that."

A wistful smile briefly grazed his face. It quickly vanished.

"I guess I had my chance, and I'm sorry it didn't last any longer. I've been trying to deal with that. Danny helped me figure out what was happening."

Sally intuitively understood the complex implications. Recent events served to reveal the multiple aspects of Jack's loss.

"When I saw your son throwing a ball, I knew he should have a chance of his own. I didn't care that my chance was over. Duncan deserves his. And I want you to know this: I'm not going to let anything get in his way. He has real talent. If he is brought along properly, I think he can become one of the best. I've seen them. It would be a crime to not give him a tryout. I can't promise it will all be perfect. But he has the goods to make it to the big leagues. Little kids are gonna want his autograph!"

He smiled at this revelation, and Sally smiled, too. Jack wasn't through.

"Please feel good about this. I'm going to take Duncan to the pro scouts, and they are going to see that your son has an extraordinary gift. I can promise you that. I'm not going to let anything bad happen to him. I promise."

Jack paused again, and had to blink back a tear, because the emotion of the moment was powerful. He looked Sally straight in the eye, and repeated the words that would help her face the unknown.

"Sally, I promise."

She left the safety of the porch railing, and walked the three steps to Jack. Sniffling into his shirt, she gave him a fierce hug. He could feel her shaking and he waited until things settled down. Remembering a bit of history, he brightened the moment.

"Hey, you know that the Crushers play for the veneer company? And that makes them an industrial team, right?"

Sally nodded.

"I guess."

She wasn't sure where this was going.

"And Duncan is nineteen years old, right?"

Sally nodded again, knowing that Jack had some poetic logic behind all of this. Jack grinned at his inspiration.

"I was reading about guys who were signed at a young age. We could be on the right track! There was a kid who played for an industrial league over a hundred years ago. He was signed to a pro team in Boston. Would you believe he was nineteen years old? And a pitcher! He did pretty good. I think it's a sign for us."

Giving Sally a sly smirk, Jack headed off the porch toward his car.

"I'm going to head back home and take care of some store business. And I'm going to get with Gordie Bowen and set up the tryout. Then I'm going to come back here, and we get to celebrate again. Sound like a plan?"

Sally was standing on the porch, sorting through all the emotions she had just explored. Jack was jetting off on the Grand Adventure, and she was going to keep the home fires burning. She supposed things were proceeding as they should. Jack was fastening his seat belt, and Sally called after him.

"Wait! How does that guy fit in with this?"

Jack still had a foolish grin on his face.

"It's easy! Duncan played in an industrial league. He is nineteen years old. And he's gonna be signed as a pitcher. Just like the other guy. He's gonna do great, just like the other guy!"

Sally was perplexed. What the heck was Jack talking about? She yelled her question, over the engine noise, as Jack started the car.

"What other guy?"

Jack was practically giddy that he had distracted Sally. She was no longer in the grip of desperate emotion about Duncan's future. Jack had teased Sally perfectly – to arrive at a frivolous moment. The timing was perfect, for the best angelic smile he could muster.

"Oh, that. Just another ballplayer. A nineteen-year-old industrial league pitcher. His name was George Herman Ruth. But everybody called him 'Babe'. I'm thinking 'Cake James' has a good ring to it!"

Clever Jack was down the driveway and gone. Sally laughed and cried at the same time.

39

THERE'S ONLY THREE LAWYER JOKES

During the drive home, Jack had plenty to consider. On top of the list: meeting with the 'men in suits' to discuss the store's future. Next was Duncan's future. The best scenario would be a minor league contract. Once Cake was in the capable hands of big league coaches, Jack would step aside. He'd have years to watch his Project prosper. Duncan would become a star in the Show, and Jack was enough of a poet to see a fitting epitaph for his own career.

It was time to move on, and be the businessman the sporting goods business dictated. Jack reconciled himself to this outcome. It wasn't what he had dreamed about, but the money would be good. He couldn't possibly be unhappy with the financial rewards of entrepreneurship. It wouldn't be a storied career in baseball, but it would be comfortable. Would that be enough?

Jack's mind mulled over the word - 'comfortable.' He hadn't been looking to be merely complacent. Sometimes he felt he could be a Rudyard Kipling poster child. Hadn't he 'watched the things he gave his life to broken and tried to build 'em up with worn out tools?' He wasn't the first guy who saw his plans go off the track. That put him in good company with the rest of the world. And if it fit into a category named 'comfortable,' there were only about six billion people in the world who would be glad to switch seats.

One baseball career was getting started, and another was ending. Jack resolved himself to that concept, and shifted his thinking toward Danielle. He had to put his feelings into some kind of focus. If something permanent between them was developing, he'd better figure out what it was he could offer. The good news was she already knew he wasn't a baseball guy anymore. If she would consider getting involved with a business owner, he'd better make sure the future was on solid ground.

Safety dictated that Jack pull off the road to call Michael Teal, the lawyer for the sporting goods store. Mike had helped get the store rolling five years ago, using Jack's signing bonus. Twenty-five percent equity was a good start, while the rest of the ownership was spread among five different banks. Mike managed the arrangement and had set up a plan where Jack could buy the banks out. He called it a 'buy-sell' agreement.

Once a year Jack could exercise the option to buy more shares in the store, and the banks were obligated to sell. Most of the money made during the first five years of the store's operation did just that. Jack had bought roughly two percent back from each of the other owners, and now owned close to thirty-five percent of the business. Expanding to more stores interested the banks, because the first store's success was remarkable.

Jack thought expansion was a good idea, especially because he needed to transition from baseball to dedicated businessman. Working through the planning was his reason for going to see the lawyer. Jack expected to go along with whatever Mike proposed. He hadn't been wrong yet.

The firm Mike worked with represented Jack when he signed his first pro contract. They had been very fair then, and Jack stayed with them for the business arrangements for the store. The firm had a bunch of partners, but they used only the original two founders' names to identify the outfit.

The first was named Edmund Rich, the same name as one of the country acts. The other was Jeremy Peebles, so when the phones were answered, you heard 'Rich Peebles, may we help you?' It always made Jack laugh.

Pure truth in advertising! The lawyers were looking for rich people, and seemed to be finding them. When Jack was feeling perky, he'd say "I'm with the poor peoples, what can you do for me?" One or two of the receptionists knew his voice, and would give it right back to him.

That's what happened on this call, except caller ID betrayed Jack. When the firm answered, he spouted his clever line. Then he heard, "You've reached the boring jock's hotline; go ahead, caller." Jack burst out laughing.

"Did you say 'boring Jack' hotline?" I've come to the right place!"

The receptionist was laughing, as well.

"Hold on, Jack, Mr. Teal's expecting your call."

Mike clicked in almost immediately.

"Jack, are you coming this way? I told the banks we'd be hearing from you soon."

'Good old Mike. Always on the ball,' Jack told himself. Speaking to Mike felt encouraging.

"You bet, I'll be in town within the hour. When do you want to meet these guys?"

Mike had a ready answer.

"They're meeting at the State Bank this afternoon. Your option is coming up; we need to decide if you're increasing equity."

Jack had no problem sticking to the plan.

"If the cash flow is there, we should do the same as always, right?"

"Probably," Mike answered. "But we might want to package it with plans for expansion. The meeting's at three p.m. Can you come to see me about one-thirty or two and look at some ideas?"

Jack thought the timing was good. It would give him time to talk to Gordie.

They clicked off and Jack punched in Gordie's number. During Jack's brief time with the team, they were cordial, but they hadn't been close. Jack had no expectations. He only wanted to make the necessary arrangements for Duncan to be seen by the team management. Any contact with his old team required losing some pride. When Jack heard 'hello,' he took a cautious tone.

"This is Jack Ridley, calling for Mr. Bowen."

Jack always reverted to politeness when he felt embarrassed. Unbeknownst to Jack, the number Randy had given him wasn't for support staff. The call went straight to Gordon's desk.

"Hello, Jack, it's Gordie. I've been waiting for your call."

Jack didn't know what to say, so he waited.

"I wanted to tell you how much I enjoyed watching young Duncan throw last week," Gordie said.

He realized that Jack was in a difficult position, and came to the point.

"I was wondering if you'd like to set up a time to bring Duncan in. You know Mike Franz, our pitching coach, and he's ready to see him."

Jack was still wary, and his answer was brief.

"Yes, sir."

Gordie continued his pitch.

"Mike and some of our coaches could see Duncan in action, and the team would take it from there."

Jack wanted to be helpful, but the old feelings of dread and disappointment were sweeping over him. He managed a slight concession.

"If you pick a date, I'll have Duncan ready."

Gordie already had the next weekend in mind. The team was at home for a Saturday night game, and Mike Franz would be available. Gordie also knew it was not the right time for any other topics. Jack agreed to noon, the following Saturday, at the ballpark.

The call was mercifully over; Jack was relieved. He got back on the road with time to get some lunch and then go to see Mike Teal.

Sometime during the day, he needed to check in with his mom. During her school year, she was immersed in her teaching duties. It was next to impossible to spend any time with her. What little socializing she did was usually with her gal pals. Now that summer had started, Jack figured she'd squeeze him in. Ashley should be home from college, as well. It was time to catch up with the Ridley girls.

His home town had a converted train dining car that was a popular eating spot. Jack had been stopping there since dirt was new. He wondered if Mr. Ackelmire still owned the place. The diner had sponsored Little League teams as far back as Jack's Pee Wee days. Everybody knew Mr. Ackelmire, and everybody liked him.

Jack had seen him slip a young fellow a few bucks, on the sly, so the kid didn't come up short on a date. When Jack signed with the Reds, Mr. Ackelmire had a small party at the diner. It was impossible to think of him without smiling.

So, Jack pulled into the parking lot and looked to see if Mr. Ackelmire's old station wagon was parked there. He didn't see the car, and went inside to search further. Jack didn't know the lady at the counter, but she looked apprehensive when he asked for 'Mr. A.'

"I'm sorry," she began. "Mr. Ackelmire has been out sick for about a month. He's pretty much at home these days."

Jack was concerned.

"Not serious, I hope."

The lady was noncommittal. Jack couldn't tell if she didn't know Mr. Ackelmire's condition, or she was being circumspect with a stranger.

"I'll drive by his house and look in on him."

She smiled, and took him to a booth in the corner.

While Jack was seated, he saw a few people he knew. They said hello, as if he showed up every day. A lady from his high school asked about his mother, and Jack tried to conceal the fact that he had no new information. To add to his problem, he couldn't remember the lady's name. He was embarrassed on both counts, and escaped as best he could.

"I'll tell her you said hi."

Jack had gotten used to summer traveling where he didn't know everyone. Now he would have to adapt to remember details about people he ran into. He ordered his all-time favorite, a BLT. This diner wasn't shy about piling on the bacon.

While he was waiting for the sandwich to arrive, Jack called his mother's number. She didn't answer, and he figured she was either out with her pals, or digging in her flower garden. He left a message.

"Mom, I've escaped from the kidnappers and made it home. Let's have dinner."

Short and sweet would do. He'd save the details for when they got together. The rest of the lunch was uneventful; it was soon time to see Mike Teal. Anything his lawyer was planning was the least of Jack's worries. This was one guy who had put Jack's interests ahead of his own. Jack figured Mike had been absent on the day the professors talked about how to cheat clients.

An Abraham Lincoln quote Mike had on his wall caught Jack's attention: 'The Lawyer has a superior opportunity of being a good man.' It gave Jack comfort. In the midst of the issues he faced, he could always count on Mike. When he got to the firm's building, everything looked the same. The friendly lady on the phone was at the receptionist desk. She sent Jack directly to Mike's office, who met him at the door.

"Man, it's good to see you. I think you'll like this proposal."

Jack was ready for the details and Mike started in.

"The banks recommend that we expand. They like the store's ratios."

Jack deadpanned.

"Sounds great, Mike. Who's Horatio?"

The lawyer grinned at the lame joke.

"Numbers that say you'll make money, big guy."

Jack knew that his lawyer buddy was about to explain how this deal was a good idea, but he liked messing with him.

"You had me at proposal," Jack said. "Go ahead and do your legal thing."

Mike went through the details that showed the store was performing ahead of projections. Sales and earnings were strong. That was the reason Jack was acquiring a larger part of the store. Mike's opinion was if things continued on track, in ten or twelve years, Jack would be the sole owner.

"So, that's good, right?" Jack asked. "That's what you mean by 'expand'?"

"Not quite," Mike answered. "It's either let the store stand alone, or start adding a new one. Or two. Or more, if all goes well."

Jack got the idea.

"Sort of like a franchise."

Mike gave a 'so-so' hand motion.

"In terms of additional stores, yes, but not in terms of new owners. You and the group would own the new stores. The difference is, because the banks are investing new money, they get the buy-out deal you have in the first store. You'd stay at twenty-five percent equity on any new properties."

Jack liked the idea.

"What's the downside?"

The question netted a small shrug.

"None, to my thinking," Mike allowed. "If you do nothing, you stay with one store. If you agree, you end up with part of a new store, and part of more stores, down the road. What's cool is, your first store is not part of the financing. No matter what, it stays yours. I did that by agreeing to let the banks have your equity growth position in the new stores."

Jack patted Mike on the back.

"You always were the smart kid in school. So I can do nothing and keep the one store, or let them do something and I still own the one store and part of another, right?"

Mike grinned, happy that Jack understood the plan.

"That's about it. The bank guys will run through the details. But that's what you'll hear."

Jack and Mike walked the few blocks to the bank. Jack was comfortable with the proposal, but he wanted Mike to do the talking at the meeting. Mike reminded Jack that the bankers could proceed without him, but they wanted to maintain Jack's presence in any new ventures to continue the branding image. Mike had leveraged that to Jack's advantage, with no additional risk.

The bank reps were all there for the meeting, and Jack enjoyed seeing Mike in action. He went through the particulars with the bankers and everyone agreed in principle. The bankers would finance the construction of a new store. Jack would own twenty-five percent with the same deal for any future builds.

There was additional discussion of advertising and product lines, with annual review of any new plans. Jack grew tired just watching Mike at work. He had all the bases covered. The meeting concluded with handshakes all around.

Mike had just presented the final stages of a plan that he'd spent months putting together. With any luck, Jack was on a financial arc that would solve any future problems. Impressed with the effort, during the walk back to the car, Jack told Mike how much his work was appreciated.

"Just another day in legal land," Mike joked. "Don't forget, I get to help run the stores and keep billing you until I'm old."

"That'll be fine, pal. And I'll quit telling lawyer jokes, just for you."

Mike feigned seriousness.

"There are only three lawyer jokes, buddy. All the rest are true stories."

Jack laughed all the way to the parking lot. The irony of the situation didn't escape him. He now had a chance to make a living through a baseball connection, but it wasn't from actually playing. Jack figured this was a solid indicator that the end of his playing days was ordained, and he could live with it. With that settled, he called his mom. She answered immediately.

"Jackie boy, you're back in town! Are you coming over, or what?"

He told her he was on the way. Just hearing his mother's voice always made Jack feel good. She was on his side, no matter what. When he had been shoved out of professional baseball, he'd been in a dark funk for months. She didn't try to talk him out of it, but stayed close by and let him work through the issues. She knew her son would come to terms with his loss, without any pep talks.

Sometimes the best help is just being there, and Jack was able to slowly get back on his feet. He was lucky at the outset, because he had his mother and sister giving him emotional support. Plus, he had Mike Teal to get the store launched. It took a year or so, but Jack was able to eventually become part of the store operation.

When that stabilized, he began his baseball therapy. He slowly edged toward life as a permanent entrepreneur. As he drove to his mom's, Jack sorted through all the details that needed updating with her. A lot had happened in the past two weeks.

The Duncan Project topped the list. A subpart of that outcome would be putting baseball behind him. Jack was pretty much at peace with that. Floating around in the mix was Danielle. He started to run through what he would say about her, and Jack realized he didn't have that figured out. Was he on the road to a relationship with her? Would she be interested in him beyond her brother's needs? Would she enjoy the prospects of a sales career? The 'would be' total was mounting.

Jack arrived at his mom's condo, and simultaneously banged on the door and let himself in. Her small-town habits included leaving the door unlocked. He always ribbed her about it, only partly in jest.

"Mom, some mugger is here!"

Jack's mother, Elizabeth Ridley, was a hugger. She bounced into the room and squeezed her boy with a vengeance. Elizabeth had an intriguing ability. When you were with her, she made you feel like you were the most important person in the world. Usually, whatever you said to her became her focus and nothing else mattered. But when Jack tried to steer the talk toward important details, for once she hesitated.

"Let's wait until Ashley is here. We can start supper first. Then we'll all know what's up."

That made great sense, so Jack and his mom prepared her famous pasta dish, with bacon and veggies. Ashley had just started some type of summer job, and she arrived home to supper on the table. Plus, there was a surprise guest! The three of them ate and talked through the evening.

They discussed the entire spectrum of what was happening in their lives: the end of the school year, summer plans, Ashley's new job, sporting goods store growth, and Jack's departure from baseball - with a small detour into Duncan's tryout. Jack casually mentioned that Duncan had an interesting sister. The Ridley women were intrigued with this development. They went into full-blown 'girl talk' mode and wanted to know all the details. When Jack edged away from the topic, they didn't sense any significance.

Familial warmth enveloped Jack. He was startled to realize that the peaceful feeling he was enjoying was very similar to what he experienced in a farm kitchen during the past week. He'd gotten too used to running on empty for too long, and he cautiously welcomed the change. An emotional desert had become a happy oasis, and Jack decided he needed to keep it that way.

40

WHEN CUTE GOES THE DISTANCE

Elizabeth Renie was a newly-minted teacher when she attended a local July 4th festival with her parents. It was organized by a coalition of churches to celebrate Independence Day and honor veterans, past and present. Patriotic events are gateways to gentle echoes that are shared by those who served. Old soldiers and sailors, airmen and airwomen come to tend to their individual memories of the dawn's early light.

Many different groups were present, scattered around tables set up adjacent to a small stage in the park. A bluegrass band was starting to play, and Elizabeth noticed an older couple approaching. A good-looking young man was with them, and he busied himself situating chairs. Everyone was seated; he brought the older couple food from a buffet line and made sure they were comfortable.

"You can tell a lot about a man by how he treats his parents," Elizabeth's mother said.

The remark seemed to be directed to no one in particular. Mrs. Renie headed to the table next to the couple and their helpful son. Before long, there was easy chatter about the festival and the music, and that's how Elizabeth met John Ridley.

He had recently left the Army and was returning to civilian life. While the 'old folks' talked about the weather and current events, Elizabeth and John discussed their school experiences, music, and anything else that popped into their heads. They agreed to get together at the church picnic the next day. There were games and activities, but the new couple spent the entire time talking about family, plans, and dreams. By the end of the day, Elizabeth had decided that John Ridley was the fellow she'd been looking for.

She went home that night and told her mother she had met the man she was going to marry. One month later, she included the lucky guy in her discovery. The ceremony was held the following Christmas.

One year later, a baby boy was born, and they named him after his dad. However, his grandfather's nickname settled on him quickly. Baby Jack was strong and determined, and showed himself to be very athletic. The Ridleys doted on their child, while they pursued the usual family goals. Five years elapsed quickly, and Jack was in kindergarten when Elizabeth found she was expecting a second child. Jack was old enough to appreciate the arrival of a new baby. He decided the child had been procured exclusively for him. Ashley was his to protect and love, and no little girl ever had a more fiercely devoted defender.

The family advanced through the years with the usual bumps and scrapes. Jack became an outstanding athlete, and Ashley tended to more academic endeavors. College baseball was on the horizon until John Ridley suffered an unexpected stroke. The tight-knit family clung even closer to each other. When John passed on, Jack remained with his mother and sister, instead of leaving for school. Entry into minor-league ball allowed him to stay relatively close to home. The family bond grew stronger.

————

When Jack returned home from time to time, it was as if all three members of the Ridley family had never been apart. The current reunion was no different. During dinner his mother and sister took up where they had left off. They chattered past a respectable bedtime and Jack promptly passed out on the couch. He didn't care where he slept. His mom and sister were a pleasant exhaustion.

Before going to bed, they agreed that Jack would stay through the next day, so they'd have another family dinner. Then Jack would return to Jason to help get Duncan ready for the coming Saturday. Both Ashley and Elizabeth wanted to see Jack's Project in action. Ashley had been too young to know much about her brother's previous life in professional baseball. Jack didn't see any problems with her coming along to the tryout.

He took pains to explain to both of them that he was acting only as Duncan's mentor. Revisiting the team, with all its bad memories, wasn't particularly high on his bucket list. He kept those negative thoughts to himself. Jack wanted to endure only what was necessary to get Duncan on the path to big league baseball. After that, he'd be on his way.

In the morning, they made plans for dinner that night. As Ashley left for work, she told Jack she was looking forward to the next weekend.

"Tell me, Jack," she teased. "Is this Duncan fellow cute?"

Jack would not be outdone - not by his kid sister.

"He's not going to be interested in girl stuff, Ash. It's all about baseball. Now, if you could develop a curveball in a few days, maybe you'd have something to talk about."

She left with happy anticipation of the coming visit. Jack's mother knew Ashley's motive.

"She's pulling your chain, Jack. She's got some fellow at school she's been talking about. In fact, she's been worried about you meeting him."

Jack gave his mom a knowing wink.

"I guess I'll have to check out this guy, sooner or later. But she's a sharp kid. I doubt she'll bring home some knucklehead."

Elizabeth chuckled.

"She doesn't think there's anybody you'll approve of."

Big brother status was familiar ground for Jack.

"She's probably right. We'll just have to trust that she makes it easy for us."

Jack made an ominous face for his mother's benefit.

"When she shows up with some poor devil I'll give him the once-over."

The two of them had plenty to do during the day, including grocery shopping for the evening meal. Jack enjoyed hanging out with his mom. She was funny and well-read. He could bring up any topic or author, and the chances were she had read something on point.

Elizabeth had started Jack on his wide range of music and literary tastes, and she wasn't finished yet. Her reading interests covered a broad spectrum, from Tom Clancy to Danielle Steele; from David McCullough to J.K. Rowling. Jack liked to dig up a new author for his mother. By the time they met again, she would have read the book and have questions ready. She'd even read a couple of the Jack Reacher novels. She teased her son about the loose similarity she saw in the stories.

"Are you wandering around playing baseball or saving the world? It's the same first name, isn't it?"

She delivered the line with a straight face and Jack howled. Her inane humor appealed to his psyche. It occurred to Jack that his mother had a lot in common with Sally James, personality-wise. Both of them were smart, funny, and vivacious. After grocery shopping, with discussions of literature and current events, they headed home to make dinner. Ashley arrived and they enjoyed another family evening. The time passed quickly and it was bedtime before they knew it.

The next morning, the women prepared to go about their day. Jack got ready to head back to Jason. He needed to work with Duncan to clue him in to what Saturday's tryout would bring. After protracted goodbyes, Jack drove to the farm to put Duncan through his paces.

During the drive, he started making a mental list of the pitches the team would want to see, and how to present them. As Jack drove on, he wondered why he hadn't expanded on any details about Danielle with his mom and sister. He answered the question with another: 'What would you have said about her?'

From the outside looking in, it had to appear odd. He was trying to promote a young ballplayer, who just happened to have a sister. She was a person of interest; Jack was quickly finding her irresistible. He didn't even know what was going on between them. With Jack's luck, while he was gone, she may have decided the whole thing was insane. She was probably going to tell him that they'd had a few laughs, but he needed to focus on Duncan. It was entirely possible that once again, he had thought he was winning when he was losing again.

Jack stopped at the diner on the highway where he'd eaten with Randy. Then he went straight to the farm. When he pulled into the gravel driveway, all the thoughts from home were rolling around in his head. In addition, he wondered what reception he'd get from Danielle. 'First things first,' he thought to himself. That meant preparing Duncan for the test of his life.

Jack could see the tractor, far away in the field to the south of the barn. Guessing that Duncan was the operator wasn't a stretch. Danielle's car was gone, so she was away somewhere. Sally would be in the house. Jack bounded up the two steps and hit the porch.

"Hey Sally, I'm back."

His heart skipped a beat as Danielle appeared in the doorway.

"She's in town, will I do?"

She glanced toward the field where Duncan was at work. He was heading further south, away from the farmhouse. More importantly, he had his back to them. Danny gently tugged on Jack's shirt and pulled him inside. She wrapped her arms around him and kissed him with a vengeance.

"I'm not going to say that I missed you," she said.

Jack was elated. His concern Danielle might have changed her mind was off-base. Perhaps they could assess their feelings about their romantic reverie, but the topic was too large for small talk.

Details of Jack's family visit would suffice for now. Danny was cleaning up after lunch, so Jack pitched in while he talked.

It wasn't long before Duncan made a north-bound swing with the tractor and saw Jack's car. He made a beeline to the house and bolted through the door. Danny and Jack were sitting at the kitchen table with glasses of lemonade.

"Jeez, Jack, I thought you might have dumped me!" he exclaimed.

Danielle laughed at his angst.

"Your bromance is safe, Cake."

Jack relished simply being around these two. He belonged, somehow. Their sibling teasing and general wacky behavior tickled him. His mind jumped toward how much his outlook had changed in the past weeks. A month ago he was depressed and failing, but didn't really know it. Now, he had two families to boost his spirits, and a baseball project to boot. Life's randomness was dragging him into new territory, and this time he liked it.

Sally pulled in before long, and the circle was complete. Jack filled them in about his mom and sister, and general details about the store. He was glad he could present himself as someone with real prospects. It was time that he got down to business, literally and figuratively. He could still have a hobby called baseball, but serious men needed a career. At the very least, Jack wanted Sally and Danielle to consider him a serious man.

Duncan's tryout would be Jack's final chapter in organized baseball. He was determined to make it a success. How they would approach Saturday was fixed in Jack's mind, so the boys excused themselves and headed outside to talk it over.

"What they are going to need to see is your ability to throw basic pitches, with control," Jack began. "Nothing new here, buddy. Placement, movement, and speed."

Duncan nodded, saying nothing. He was paying rapt attention. Jack wanted a relaxed and fluid approach.

"It's going to be a different experience. I don't know where they'll put us. It could be just a warm-up area. I doubt they'll have us in the bullpen. That's past the outfield wall. Maybe on the regular field. They'll get better views there, and they could have some guys take a swing or two."

Jack reflected back to his first time in the stadium. For a rookie kid, it was huge, impressive and intimidating. And that was when it was empty. The first game in front of a mammoth crowd is something you never forget.

"Simply walking out onto the field can be overwhelming, but we'll go slow. There's gonna be some serious eyeballs on you, no matter where we're throwing."

Jack felt as if he were reading from an instruction sheet for rookie players.

"Being prepared for that feeling, and expecting it to happen, will make it easier to handle. I'll know beforehand where we throw, so that will calm us down a bit. The bottom line is, we treat this like we're just throwing here at home. Nice and easy. You've got the stuff they want. All we have to do is let 'em see it."

Jack gave Duncan a light punch on the shoulder. Duncan responded with a boxer's stance and feinted a return punch. The look of determination on Duncan's face, and his confident demeanor, were all Jack needed to see. But in the back of his mind, Jack knew there was a baseline truth in all of this. Duncan had the goods, but he was going to have to bring it on Saturday.

It was only midday. They decided a little light throwing wouldn't hurt. The normal four to five day rest needed for a game didn't apply. Jack would rest Duncan on Friday, but he wouldn't be working that hard during the tryout. They had Wednesday and Thursday to fine-tune. All they needed was about an hour each day, to reinforce mechanics and approach. They returned to the work zone by the barn and loosened up for a while.

"Nice and easy, Cake," was all Jack said.

They had the routine set by now, and after a regular warm-up, Duncan was in the groove.

"Let's just go with five or so with each one," Jack called. "I'll keep it in the middle of the plate. Let me know when you're throwing something else."

The fledgling pitcher stood, ready to throw. He was zeroing in on his target while he adjusted his grip on the ball. Jack couldn't immediately describe it, but there was something new in the young man's bearing. There was a higher level of confidence, a discernibly enhanced attitude. Then Duncan gave the standard forward motion of his glove, fingers down, indicating that the first pitch would be a fastball. He was the picture of determination.

After five or six heaters, Duncan signaled he was going to throw a curveball by sweeping his glove in an arc. He threw five curves, and then gloved a flat punching motion toward home plate. The change-up was coming. The next group came floating in as scheduled. Jack was satisfied, and called a halt. He took a seat so he could evaluate the throws.

"You're exactly where you need to be," he said. "What we just did is what they want to see on Saturday. They might ask you about injuries."

That was something that Jack and Duncan hadn't covered.

"I haven't seen anything in your throws that tell me there have been any problems there. Am I right?"

Duncan nodded, somberly.

"Never had any issues. My dad said he thought I just had a naturally strong arm. Plus, he didn't let me pitch because he was afraid the coaches would get me hurt. He said that was the way some big leaguer did it."

Jack agreed, and remembered a particular player.

"Trevor Hoffman. A strong arm, like you. His father had him play infield, because he had the same injury questions. Pitching started *after* he was in the pros, when they found out he could bring it at ninety-five."

Duncan was fascinated by Jack's knowledge of baseball lore.

"So, he did good after that?"

"Well, yeah, if you consider 601 saves doing good. When Hoffman retired, he had the record. But he hit 500 and 600 saves faster than anyone. So, yeah, we'll call it good."

While Duncan let that soak in, Jack added more.

"I'm thinking your dad did the right thing. You've got a cannon arm, with no injuries, and we show it off this weekend."

Duncan wanted to talk about the tryout process, so Jack turned the education in that direction.

"This thing for us on Saturday is unique. Usually, it's a group. Three or four hundred kids, at all positions. Major league baseball holds group tryouts every year. It's pretty rare to get signed then, but it's a start. They use tryouts to get names in the system. But, we got lucky last week. Gordon Bowen had a hunch, I guess, and stayed to see you in action. That took about six months off of the process, if we'd gotten a tryout at all."

Jack paused for a small introspection.

"Gordie might have been there to see what kind of a mess I was in, because he was there for the bad old days. Hard to say, but I'm going to chalk it up to clean living and good karma, Cake. It's about time something good happened to both of us."

Duncan somberly took it all in. He shifted his attention to the tryout itself.

"So, will I be dealing with anybody there or do I just throw?"

Jack liked the way Duncan was facing the event, head-on.

"I'll be talking to anyone who wants to say anything. Most likely, they won't say much beyond 'hello'. They don't want to get into a personal thing at a tryout; they want to see what you've got. You're not there to make friends. They'll like you plenty if they decide to sign you."

Duncan was surprised.

"They sign guys from these?"

"It's possible," Jack replied, "but that's not your issue. You just keep your game face on. If you're looking at somebody, make it look like you think they're trying to steal your girlfriend. Pitchers need that 'stare down' look."

Jack was pretty sure he wasn't putting any scare into Duncan. He continued with tryout details.

"You're starting with a clean slate. They have things in mind they're looking for, but they don't have any notions about what you can do. You are under the radar, because you weren't in college ball. You'll be fine, Cake. We dance in there and show 'em your stuff. End of story. They sure as shootin' are going to know who you are after Saturday."

Jack decided to gravitate toward a more comfortable spot on the porch. He motioned with his head in that direction, and Duncan followed. The rookie returned to the lesson as they walked.

"You said they have things in mind?"

Jack nodded, and started reciting the list.

"They start with general physical stuff. Things I've already processed. We've talked about injury questions. They'll ask height and weight. I see you as about six-two and around one ninety, right?"

Duncan nodded.

"Mom says I'm still growing."

"They'll like that," Jack continued. "Probably will ask if you wear glasses or contacts. I've decided your uncorrected vision is fine. You didn't have glasses in the theater, and while throwing you picked up some pretty fast and weak signals."

"I thought you were just trying to trip me up. Didn't know it was a test."

Jack shrugged.

"All part of the evaluation, buddy. They might want to know if you've had family members in the pros. Blood lines, and all that. I've seen kids asked about their parents' marriages. Something to do with temperament. If you're the nervous type, they don't want you. Again, I've observed all that. All good."

Duncan was looking at Jack as if he had a bug on his face. This was amazing new stuff.

"We're just getting started, Cake," Jack said. "They look at body structure. They're not interested in a couch potato. But, they know that already, too. They'll look at your hand size."

Duncan was rolling his eyes at the body information. Jack laughed at him.

"Hey, you might see them pulling out a tape measure, so don't get too shy. There are intangibles, like how you handle yourself on the mound. That's part of the confidence thing. This is stuff they already know, in general, having seen you last Saturday night. Remember, this whole thing springs from what you showed them, at least one of them. I'm going out on a limb and guessing that Gordie has already told them his rankings. They like what he's saying, or we wouldn't have the invite. They just need to see it, up close and personal."

Duncan inhaled, and blew out his cheeks like he was preparing to throw.

"What do they look for, pitch-wise? I'm hoping I got that part covered."

Jack was quick to be supportive.

"You sure do. It's what we've been working on. They want to see what kind of fastball you've got, and what kind of movement you have with off-speed pitches. You remember when I talked about ball placement?"

Duncan nodded, still deep in the moment.

"Don't be surprised if they have me put the glove in a specific area. There's another thing I've just thought of. Have you learned zone numbering?"

Duncan tried not to look stupid.

"I've heard of it."

Jack laughed inwardly. Answering like this would get a rookie 'haze mauled' in camp.

"The zone is divided into nine squares. The bottom inside is one; low middle is four; bottom outside is seven. That's where placement is analyzed. I've told you about how hitters have areas that they have trouble hitting the ball, right?"

Duncan nodded.

"When the coaches call for a ball in a zone, they do it because they're working on a perceived weakness," Jack noted. "So, we're gonna show them you can put the ball wherever you want. Don't worry about the numbering. I'll just yell 'hit the four", or 'hit the eight' and I'll hold the glove in the right spot. That'll make 'em think you've got the zones all figured out. Cool, huh?"

Duncan realized this little sleight-of-hand was yet another indication that Jack was pulling hard for him. He grimaced, and revealed his misgivings.

"I sure hope I don't let you down."

Jack didn't want any load added to whatever burden already existed. By now, Sally and Danny had joined them. They had listened to the 'numbering system' portion, with looks approaching amazement.

"Cake, don't even think that. You won't be letting anybody down. Everybody here wants what is best for you. If it's not coming Saturday, that changes nothing."

Sally and Danny smiled at this show of support. Jack wasn't through.

"I'm not just whistling Dixie, kiddo. I know with absolute certainty you have what they want."

Jack paused to collect his thoughts - summarizing the large amount of information they'd covered.

"If they start talking about your training regimen, let me handle it. You haven't been in a body strength program. That's what they're after. I think you're strong from farm work, but they don't have a metric for that. The truth is, big league pitchers spend a lot more time *preparing* to pitch than they do actually pitching. You know, leg and arm strength. They want to know about your inclination toward weight room work. You don't have that yet, so let me take care of that question, if it comes."

Duncan stood up, and reached over to give Jack a pat on the back.

"Thanks, man. You've got this all figured out."

Jack wanted to end on the best note possible.

"Duncan, I've saved the best part for last."

All three members of his audience leaned in closer.

"I know I've said that speed is the least important part of pitching. That's in a game, over the course of a hundred pitches. But on Saturday, we're going to show them what got me over to that high school game. They want to know about movement and placement, for sure. But what's going to grab them is 'velo.' A kid at one of those four-hundred person tryouts who throws eighty-five miles an hour is going home. Give them ninety-five, and you've got their undivided attention."

Jack took a breath, and looked one more time at all three of his new-found baseball allies. They were bonded on many levels, but the immediate concern was the youngest member of the clan.

"These guys want to see you throw strikes. Walking people loses games, faster than allowing a hit. And you *will* throw strikes. But, when I tell you it's time, you are going to 'light up the gun' like nobody they've ever seen at a tryout. Then we're gonna have 'em."

Jack punctuated his remark with a fist jab. Duncan looked resolute. Sally looked pleased. Danielle looked pretty.

Sally finally weighed in.

"Jack, I have a couple of questions. First, since you're here tomorrow to work with Cake, why don't you stay in the guest room? You don't need the drive into town, and there's no need to spend money on the motel."

Jack smiled his agreement.

"Sure, Sally, that's fine. I've got my clothes and stuff in the car. I like being here, anyway. What's the second question?"

"What's 'lighting up the gun' mean?"

Jack started chuckling.

"That's a perfect topic for the next lesson. Does the room come with dinner?"

Sally was laughing as well.

"It's on the table. Time to eat, kids!"

They all went inside for another great family meal. Jack reflected that he'd had three family nights in a row. That was a rare trick, and he wasn't just whistling Dixie. During supper, Jack explained how baseball analysts use a radar gun to gauge pitch speed.

"It's the same technology police use on highways. You point the gun at the pitch, and the read-out tells you the speed."

Sally's eyes widened.

"I've seen them do that on TV! They use that hair-dryer thing behind home plate."

Jack kept his response to a wry comment.

"That's right, Sally. A hair dryer."

Danny and Duncan exchanged furtive smiles. They knew Jack was going easy on their mom. After the dishes were dried, they all went out to watch the sun go down. To Jack, it was a picture-perfect postcard evening.

The sun's rays touched the top of the trees on the western edge of the farm, and silhouetted the barn. There was even a rooster weather vane on top. Sally asked about Jack's trip home and he revisited the details about the store expansion. He went farther than he intended.

"They tell me the money's going to be good. Good enough to not have to worry about anything."

He wanted Sally to know that he wasn't going to be a baseball bum forever. Sally filed that information away and got up from her seat on the porch. She wordlessly went inside and returned moments later with the guitar and handed it to Jack.

"I guess this means play for your supper."

They sang a few old songs. Jack decided a song about the sunset would be about right, so he started 'You Are My Sunshine.' They all joined in the sublime moment.

"My mother used to sing that to me when I was little," Sally said. "It sure brings back memories."

Danielle joined in.

"It's nice how a song can take you to a time and place. Maybe who you were with when you heard it."

She was looking at Jack and he wondered if that meant she'd be thinking of him when she heard the song in the future. Then he wondered if he'd do the same. Jovial banter continued and then the lightning bugs arrived. They put on a spectacular show out in the fields. Sally had another dreamy look on her face.

"Did you know the males flash their light to attract females? If the female likes what she sees, she flashes some kind of code, and off they go!"

Danielle started giggling.

"Maybe we could get Cake a real cool flashlight and he could go out and start flashing!"

The 'flashing' joke got Jack into a laughing fit. He was still at it when Sally called a halt to the party.

"I'm cruising off to bed. You kids don't stay up too late."

Sally walked through the door and Duncan stood up. Jack handed him the guitar.

"Could you put this to bed for me?"

"Got it," Duncan answered. "Right before I do the same. The lady bosses here worked me pretty hard today."

He left and Jack and Danny were alone on the porch. A few moments passed; they watched the remaining fireflies fade from sight. Danielle returned to what Jack had said about his business prospects.

"I take it you'll not be playing much baseball, if you're working the store?"

Jack exhaled through pursed lips.

"I guess so. I finally figured out what I was doing, with your help. Playing with these teams was just hanging on to the past. Some kind of therapy, and I think it all led to getting Duncan a tryout. After that, it's time to grow up and get a real job."

Danielle was leaning back on the porch railing, looking directly at Jack. The quizzical look on her face told him she was wondering if there was more to be said.

"I mean, I should get serious about a real future," he continued.

"The right girl isn't going to be interested in a bum who plays weekend baseball."

A philosophical observation arrived with a half-shrug.

"She might," Danny ventured, "if the bum spends his weekdays building a business. Lots of guys play golf on the weekends, so maybe a little baseball isn't so bad."

Her appraising eyes were on Jack, and she gave him a furtive smile.

"You thinking of finding the right girl, Jack?"

Her impish look reminded him of the Mona Lisa. Jack's analytical mind leaped to a new insight: Maybe the famous painting depicted a girl who wasn't sure how a guy fit into her world. He decided to meet Danielle's question with a flirtation of his own.

"You thinking of being the right girl, Danny?"

She leaned off of the railing and sat next to Jack on the glider. She kept her gaze out in the distance, and her hands were folded on her lap. Her words were halting and careful.

"When you're a kid, you think you'll grow up and know what's going on. At least I did. During high school, you date somebody and think they're special. And then you realize that the people you thought were cool weren't really cool at all."

She paused to examine her hands.

"I guess my mom told you a little about my college fiasco. I thought I was the right girl then, but I was wrong."

Jack wanted to set her mind at ease.

"Everybody gets it wrong, once or twice. I'm thinking the guy was major stupid for playing you."

Danielle glanced up with a pained expression.

"It shouldn't have to be this difficult. I just don't want to be lied to."

Jack gave her what he thought was a helpful smile, and tried to defuse the situation.

"How 'bout if I fib only a little? Like when you ask 'do these pants make me look fat?' *Never* anything important."

Her slight grin was disarming, but also thoroughly charming.

"I took a psychology course in college, and one of the topics was 'can there ever be a good lie?' It's called 'lying for the greater good.' The gist of it all is that if you're lying to protect someone, it's probably okay. So, go ahead with the white lie about the pants."

Then she gave Jack a little shove in the ribs.

"How are you on more important things, like being faithful?"

Jack didn't know where the conversation was going, but he wasn't going to dodge this candid moment.

"It probably makes me look stupid, but I've never been in a full-time relationship. When it happens, I want to be like my parents. They were the kind of people who meant it when they said 'til death do us part.' I can't figure out how people can get themselves to a wedding, and two years later, they're done. Unbelievable! When you tell someone you love them, you ought to mean it."

Danielle shifted her gaze from the darkened fields to Jack's face.

"My folks were the same way, Jack. I've thought that very same thing. I always figured they would be one of those forever married couples. They would have, too. Your folks sound the same."

She leaned her head over onto Jack's shoulder. It seemed as natural as breathing; to put his arm around her and draw her close. She put her hand up over his heart and held it there.

"It's like the song that goes 'Can't you feel my heart beat.' I like that one," she murmured.

Jack started humming the tune.

"My mom loves that sixties stuff. There were so many cool songs. That same band also did one of my favorite tunes."

Danielle was in snuggle mode.

"Sing it to me."

Jack started softly singing, 'I'm Into Something Good.'

Danielle perked up.

"Mom sings that. I didn't know it was a real song."

Jack almost choked.

"Good God, Danny, it's Carol King! You have to know her stuff."

Danielle sniffed.

"I probably do. My mind is elsewhere right now."

Then she went back to heartbeat analysis.

"Are you into something good, Jack?"

He teased right back.

"I dunno. I'll ask Carol."

Danielle used her free hand to smack his chest.

"Nice one, buster. Just when I think you're telling the truth."

But she didn't return her hand to where it had been. Instead, she reached up to hug him closer. They stayed like that for a long time. She broke from the reverie with a question.

"Did you have anyone to talk to after Olivia died?"

Jack was slightly jolted. He had avoided any real thoughts about Olivia. The unfairness of her loss was beyond description. When he dreamed of that night, he always found himself trying to save her. He always failed. Jack collected himself and gave the best answer he could.

"I guess not. There was no one from the team around. Nobody else knew the story. Nobody would get it."

Danielle sighed.

"You went through that alone, and it's been the same for the past five years?"

Jack opted to treat that as a rhetorical question and stayed still. They both sat there for several minutes, each mulling over the import of Danielle's last comment. Then, she stirred again.

"Would it be too much like twenty questions if I asked more?"

"Go ahead," Jack said.

He was hoping for a bit of levity, so he added a caveat.

"Your mother said I can stay here, so you can't throw me out."

She ignored the remark.

"Have you ever been in love?"

Jack was slowly shaking his head.

"No. I've never really been that involved before."

Danielle processed that answer for long moments, and took the next step.

"Are you ready for the hard question?"

It was dark on the porch, but Danielle felt Jack shrug his shoulders. He had no idea where she was going with this, but he wasn't afraid of what she might ask. Danielle took the shrug as a signal to continue. She breathed deeply, and started in.

"I want to get to know who you are, Jack. I feel like I could be close to you. A lot about you, I know already. I like what I know. You're sweet to my mom and you're good to Duncan. I'm not sure what you and I have going here, but I'd like to take a long time to figure it out."

The one million dollar question had to be asked.

"Are you the kind of guy who tells a girl he loves her as just a part of dating?"

Jack sat up straighter so Danielle's head was off of his shoulder. He turned so they were face to face, dark or no dark.

"Danny, I've never told any girl I loved her. I think that guys who do, when they're just playing around, are jerks. When that happens, I'm going to mean it. Is that enough truth for you?"

Danielle smiled.

"Yes, Jack. That's enough truth."

Then she returned her head to Jack's shoulder, and they resumed their silent visit. Jack thought it was his turn.

"So, now it's your twenty questions, okay?"

She nodded, silently, and Jack began.

"Tell me what kind of guy you like."

Danielle had been waiting for her chance to get even for his previous joke.

"Why, are you going to fix me up with somebody?"

Jack gave her a light tap on her head.

"Oh, you're funny. It so happens I know a couple of nice guys on work release, so I'll do what I can."

Danielle laughed and snuggled closer.

"Okay, okay, you win. I've already told you. I like a guy who's honest and respects women. Who's not into himself 24/7. I like a guy who wants to help people, and likes kids. Who makes me laugh. He has to be smart. And have a good heart. It would help if he's kind of cute."

Jack untangled himself and stood up.

"Dag nabbit! You were talking about me, 'til that last part!"

Danielle chuckled as she stood up from the glider. She reached up, and put her hands on Jack's shoulders. Pulling him closer cast a little light from inside the house on his face. She looked into his eyes as if she were examining the fine print on a winning lottery ticket.

"Haven't I told you before that I think you're cute? I mean, this isn't how I treat just anybody."

And she gently kissed him on the lips and tightly wrapped her arms around him. She raised up on her toes so her lips were close to Jack's ear. He heard her whisper, and the words jolted right through him.

"I mean really cute, Jack. *Really* cute."

41

NEW PERSPECTIVES & NEW PROJECTIONS

Stealing good-night kisses brought sublime moments to the young couple. Jack finally managed to pull himself away and lie about getting some sleep. He grabbed his bag from his car while Danielle waited. She closed the door after he returned, and silently went upstairs. Jack used the downstairs bathroom to brush his teeth and prepare for bed.

He looked at his reflection in the mirror and said to himself 'she thinks you're cute, buddy.'

Jack quietly climbed the stairs. He knew the way to the guest room. Danny's bedroom door was open when he crept past. She stepped into the hall and gave him a silent hug.

"Good night, cutie Jack," she whispered.

She retreated into her bedroom and Jack saw the light go out. He turned into the guest room and closed the door behind him. He slipped under the sheets and let the night's surreal moments sweep over him. Drifting off to sleep, with the smell of Danny's perfume to guide him, Jack dreamed peacefully.

He awoke the next morning to Ludwig van Beethoven wafting through the house. Ode to Joy is a fine start to any day. Jack knew that the piece came from Beethoven's ninth symphony and he considered the number a lucky omen. Nine was his number in the Show. Somebody had the stereo fired up and he could smell breakfast. Beethoven and bacon. It can't get any better. Jack raced through his morning routine and was quickly downstairs. He was slightly embarrassed that the James Gang was already there.

"Okay, I'm a failure at farm life."

"Relax, Jack," Sally grinned. "You're not here for your farm skills. We're working you hard enough with this kid."

She nodded in Duncan's direction, and Jack was gratified to see that he didn't look too terribly awake, either. Danny, on the other hand, looked terrific. Jack had to speak up.

"You look ready to go so early in the morning."

"Silly boy," Danielle replied. "Men have no idea what women go through to get ready. And you! Just fall out of bed and brush your teeth and off you go."

"She's just going for sympathy," Sally intervened. "The girl gets up and brushes her hair, and here she is. No make-up. Only wake up. Life isn't fair."

Jack wasn't inclined to comment further on Danny's appearance, not in front of her mother. Certainly not first thing in the morning. But he did think she looked fabulous. All of them enjoyed a farm breakfast and Jack pounced on clean-up duties. Sally noticed his happy effort.

"I'm going to have to meet your mother. She raised you right."

Jack was looking forward to getting them together.

"She'll be coming Saturday, I expect. Ashley already said she'll be there. They're great; I know you'll like them."

He bypassed the thought of introducing a girl, at least indirectly, to his mother. There was more. He was introducing the girl's mother, as well. That was too much to handle at this stage. He needed to remain in baseball mode. After the dishes were dried and stacked, he and Duncan headed outside for some light throwing. The ladies decided to tag along.

"How much warmup do the pros need?" Sally asked. "Do they spend a lot of time getting ready to throw?"

Jack was getting into position with Duncan.

"It depends on each guy. Some take longer. You need to be loose, so you're not hurting yourself when you throw hard. You'll be sweating when you're ready."

He put the girls over to the side with Elvis, away from any errant throws. Duncan started with easy pitches, and Jack brought up a technique they would need.

"We need to spend a little time throwing from the stretch. That didn't happen Saturday night, and we got lucky."

They discussed the rules requiring a full stop before the throwing motion. Because Duncan threw right-handed, keeping an eye on a runner on first required extra effort.

"Sometimes the pitcher can make the pick-off, because the third baseman tips the throw," Jack added. "It's a timing thing, but when it works, it's great."

After Duncan was heated up, the pitching began in earnest.

"Same as yesterday, okay?" Jack called.

They did the same three-pitch pattern and then a few from the stretch. Jack had a point to make.

"We'll make sure your motion and positioning keeps you away from any balk questions. But we're still going to finish with heat."

When Duncan had gone through the cycle, Jack asked if he felt ready to throw hard.

"Show your mom what a big league fastball looks like!"

He was certain that Duncan was completely warm, and there was no danger to his arm. Plus, it was a good idea to have him perform on demand.

"We will probably end like this on Saturday," Jack added. "Don't do anything stupid and get hurt. Just stay within yourself and speed up when you feel it."

Duncan was willing and his response was brief.

"Sure."

He gave Jack the glove signal for a fastball, and did a regular windup. The ball came in at medium speed, directly into the glove Jack held over the middle of the plate. Jack silently returned the ball, and Duncan repeated the process. He made successive throws, increasing the speed with each pitch. Jack counted fifteen total pitches. The last third topped out over ninety, and Jack estimated the last two were approaching ninety-five. Jack stood up to assess the progress.

"I like the speed. How much you got left?"

Duncan shrugged.

"I can throw harder. Just trying to keep it under control."

Jack was pleased. He'd set up a system to protect Duncan's progress, and the kid was sticking to the plan.

"There'll be time for more heat later on. Right now, that's all we need. Save it for Saturday."

Jack turned to the only two fans they had.

"What do you think of our boy?"

They both had been silently watching, with wide-eyed looks. Sally was impressed.

"Duncan, I don't think I've seen you throw that hard. So intense!"

Danielle was enthusiastic.

"Cake, you are really bringing it!"

Glancing at Jack, she had to razz him just a little.

"I *guess* Jack knows what he's doing."

She had a teasing grin on her face that Jack couldn't ignore.

"You're right, I'm just standing around. You could do the same. Here, use my mitt. See the heater from this end."

He was joking. Letting Danielle get on the back end of a baseball thrown that hard was dangerous. Getting hit by such a pitch could alter your life permanently. So when Danielle jumped up to call his bluff, he caved.

"Just kidding. I can handle only one at a time with this family."

Sally observed it all with happy amusement.

"Okay, you kids, let's get a few things done around here."

Danielle and Duncan headed toward the house.

Sally lingered while Jack dumped his baseball equipment in his car. She began a bit haltingly, not sure how she would say what was on her mind.

"Jack, I mean it. I'm no expert, but Duncan is throwing faster. And I know it's because of you. You've done wonders for his confidence. He's acting more grown up since you've been here."

Jack smiled and tried to deflect a bit of her praise.

"Thank you, Sally, but don't put too much on me. I meant what I said. He's got real talent, and mostly I just get out of his way."

She wouldn't be denied.

"I hadn't been on track enough to think it through. After David died, we all just fell apart a little bit. I guess you sort of go on autopilot to get through the rough times. I'm realizing now that Duncan needed to have baseball in his life. It was slipping away right under our noses. And then you came along."

She paused for a benevolent moment, and then she put her hand on Jack's shoulder.

"Don't think I'm crazy here, but you've got me thinking about something the priest said at David's funeral. He told us that there would be a time in the future when we would know that David was still with us - that he was acting to help us. I thought they were nice words, to console us. Later on, I asked him what type of thing he thought might occur. He said I'd have to figure that out for myself. The event would be something that had meaning for us, individually."

Jack was listening, perfectly still. Perhaps she would reveal something that would apply to his own life, and his own father's passing.

Sally continued, slowly and thoughtfully.

"I kept thinking he was saying words that were comforting, but they didn't mean anything. Then, out of the blue, here you are, saying that Duncan could pitch. I didn't know what to think, at first. I was just being polite. But Duncan liked you, and I thought it wouldn't hurt for him to have some kind of baseball happiness."

She stopped and wiped away a tear.

"I'm sorry," she sniffed. "Thinking of David makes me cry sometimes. I guess I've been staying away from that, to keep things together for the kids. He used to quote the line from 'Field of Dreams' where the writer says 'baseball reminds us of all that was good and could be again.' It made me start thinking Duncan's pitching was a return to good."

She was looking directly at Jack.

"The priest would say this is David acting through you."

She smiled through tears.

"I've been praying for some good out of this, so I guess you're the answer to a prayer."

Jack felt humbled by her comments.

"I think a prayer would find someone better than me, but it's nice of you to think that. But this is going to work because Duncan has huge talent."

Sally smiled at Jack and linked her arm in his. Then they walked to the house.

"My little boy," she mused. "Hard to believe."

Duncan headed out to the barn, and Jack went along to help. Sally and Danielle busied themselves with bookwork required for farm expenses. They continued on various chores for the day, and gathered for lunch and dinner.

The next day, Thursday, was a repeat of the day before. The boys went through a light pitching drill, and Jack declared that Duncan was ready for Saturday's test. He would rest on Friday. Chores were completed, and Sally told everyone they should all take the day off with Duncan. They agreed to sleep late, have lunch in town, and generally goof off.

Jack offered to showcase his barbeque skills for that night's supper, so they stopped at the grocery. After a nice cookout, they discussed the coming tryout and the trip to the ballpark. Jack continued his calm analysis of the throwing plan.

"Cake, there are no surprises tomorrow. We've done what we need to be ready. All that's left is run through the sequence we've practiced."

He let that thought settle, and then switched to the aftermath of the tryout.

"After you show them what you can do, I hope they will want to talk about signing. Probably not right then, but if they're interested, they'll let us know. I'll get a feeling from the people there. Mike Franz is coming, as the pitching coach. There could be other big shots. Makes no difference. If they say they want to meet, I'll tell them you'll talk to your lawyer."

That got a quizzical look from Duncan. Sally wasn't far behind, but Jack was ready with an answer.

"Don't worry; I know you don't have a lawyer. You can talk to Mike Teal's firm with no obligation. They helped me, and that should buy a little time for you and your mom to make a decision. And your sister," Jack added, looking over at Danielle.

Sally was the first to bring the topic back to Jack.

"What about you?"

Jack shrugged.

"I figure this is a smooth way for me to put baseball to rest. I've had my run. I was telling Danny about the sporting goods business picking up, and that's where I should be spending my time. Maybe I can play a little for fun, but this weekend will be the 'for real' beginning of Jack Ridley's business career."

The others looked a little glum. Jack didn't want his situation to throw a shadow on anything this family was thinking.

"It'll be a good thing. It has a good future and I would've been leaving baseball sooner or later. Sooner is okay."

He smiled as best he could. This was the most he had ever talked about life after baseball, and this farm was a safe place to do it. Sally was right. Duncan's baseball was a way for all of them to get back to good. It was just that Jack's version of good was something different.

Danielle took another angle for Jack to consider.

"So you'll be going home and Duncan might be off to God-knows-where with some baseball team? It's going to be different around here with just me and mom."

Something in the way she phrased it told Jack she was asking about his personal plans.

"Well, shoot, I'd be coming back here to visit, if I haven't worn out my welcome," Jack said. "It's not that far."

Sally was contemplative.

"We hope you're always close, Jack. You're a part of this family, now."

She finished this comment with a glance at Danielle. Jack wasn't sure what her look implied. He felt that some type of relationship was starting, but he doubted whether he or Danny could explain it to anyone. But you never know what a girl might share with her mother. Jack decided to gloss over the possibility, for the moment.

"I'm going to have to be around, to see how Cake is doing in the Show, right?"

He hoped this little curveball would shift them back to less serious ground. Nobody said anything, and they watched the dying embers in the barbeque pit. After a while, Sally brought them back to reality.

"I guess we all better hit the hay, so we have a good start tomorrow."

The clean-up began. Everyone picked up items from their supper and trooped inside, except Danielle. She was still gazing at the smoking coals. No one asked if she was coming along. She must have sensed the unspoken question, and spoke to the retreating backs.

"I'll clean up what's left and be right in."

So she did. There were napkins and silverware, which she took to the kitchen. The plates and silver were quickly placed in the dishwasher. She announced that she'd take the trash outside. Jack had gone to retrieve his overnight items. Danielle tossed the bag in the container and walked to Jack's car. She leaned on the fender for a moment, and then stated what was on her mind.

"Mom had a good question, Jack. After Duncan gets to try to be a baseball player, what happens to you? What happens to us?"

She paused.

"Is 'us' part of the deal?"

Jack was holding his travel bag. He dumped it on the car's hood and moved next to Danielle.

"I was hoping. I hadn't planned anything like this. Originally, I figured you thought I was just an idiot ballplayer."

He felt a little helpless, because he didn't know how to explain himself. Danielle was silent, waiting for him to put his cards on the table. Jack had a sudden premonition that the next moments would have a significant impact on a whole list of things: his outlook, his decisions, and his future. He had decided he was tired of the emotional limbo that had captured him for the past five years. Now was the time to admit it. So, he jumped past inhibition.

"Danny, if you could stand it, I'd like 'us' to be a part of it. I'm not trying to drag you into forever, but it sure would be nice to see if we can make something work."

She was listening intently, and Jack couldn't tell whether he was losing ground.

"I'm not very good at this sort of thing, but I haven't felt this way about anybody."

He paused once more, trying to make sense of it all. He started again.

"So..." and Danielle reached over and put her finger to his lips.

"You had me at 'hoping,'" she said, and she kissed him, long and completely. "You have yourself a girlfriend, Jack. Think you can handle that?"

He was holding her close, and he wanted to savor this first moment of official relationship status. He waited a long time, with just the feel of her body and the smell of her hair soaking into his consciousness.

Then he spoke, very quietly.

"Yeah, Danny girl. I think I can."

The stars were twinkling and the night was perfect. For just one second, Jack thought he'd see a shooting star in the distance, to complete the storybook picture. Then his poet's soul told him he didn't need to see a shooting star in some distant heavens.

There was one racing through his heart.

42
_____

THE BIG LEAGUE BECKONS

Planning for the trip to the ballpark was loose and flexible. All that was needed was to get to the stadium, and have Duncan ready to go at noon. Jack figured if they arrived by eleven, he could have the warm-up rolling by eleven-thirty. Duncan would be heated up just fine. A few minutes getting acclimated wouldn't hurt. Anybody could be intimidated by the try-out, coupled with the size of the ballpark. To ease the tension, Jack had a little trick from the movie 'Hoosiers' in mind. He'd show Duncan that today's process was no different from what they did at home. The tryout was merely a seamless extension of their routine.

All four of them were up and moving by seven. A nine o'clock departure would have them there with time to spare. Jack wasn't a huge worrier, but he didn't want a flat tire to cause any problems. They had breakfast and everything seemed uncharacteristically relaxed, at least to Jack. He remembered his first tryout. He had been all nerves until things got going. Just as he was getting used to Duncan appearing unflappable, Sally rearranged his thinking.

"Jack, this would be a mess if you weren't in charge."

Then it hit him: He was the difference. Duncan didn't feel the pressure, because his support system was with him. Whatever it took to keep this kid on track was fine with Jack. There were so many variables in the mix today. Duncan had the goods, but things could go wrong in a hurry.

Jack maintained a light and breezy attitude throughout the morning. He suggested they relax and take their time at breakfast. They cleaned up afterward, leisurely washing and stacking the dishes. Everything was ready by eight-thirty, without any rush. Jack contacted his mother and his sister, and arranged to meet them at the ballpark. He went outside to enjoy the morning air, and soon everyone joined him to stroll around the property. Jack sought the bucolic zone, as a buffer against the coming test.

"I know this is all a huge amount of work, but it has a nice relaxing feel about it. There's something about being connected to the earth that settles you down, isn't there?"

His remark met with silent assent. They were walking together and savoring the peaceful country aura. The farm's energizing aspect motivated Jack to say it felt like they were easing off to some sort of happy rendezvous. It didn't seem as if a life-changing event was looming. Sally agreed.

"Being raised on a farm gives you a great foundation, but kids want to get away to something exciting. Then they realize that the farm is the only place that feels normal. When people have to move from their farm, it just kills them."

The comment reminded Jack of another facet the James family possessed. They had a centered aspect to their lives, due to rural living. Their solid down-to-earth background would help carry Duncan through the challenge. Jack was counting on it.

At around nine-fifteen they loaded the SUV. Jack thought Danny would be driving, but she handed the keys to him.

"You know the way, Jack. You get to be in charge for a while."

Duncan and Sally piled in the back, and Elvis watched the load-in. Jack gave him an ear-scratching for good luck, and climbed in the car.

"Keep an eye on the place, buddy," Jack said, and off they went.

The drive on what Jack called 'blue highways' was uneventful. He explained how the term applied to road maps. Smaller roads are blue to distinguish them from interstates. Of course, he had once read a book by the same title.

Danielle amused them with stories about her college days. Jack's favorite was about her twenty-first birthday, when she tried serious drinking for the first time. It explained why she found no romance in alcohol. She had assumed that orange juice negated vodka, and drank beyond human limits.

"You don't want to know the mess I woke up in," she confessed. "Haven't touched one of those since!"

She looked back at her brother.

"Are you listening, Cake? Your twenty-first birthday will arrive, and I hope you're smarter than I was."

Trips seem shorter with great conversation, and the group soon arrived at the ballpark. Jack parked in the players' lot. It hadn't changed much. The current players wouldn't be arriving for the night game until two or three. Jack and the James Gang would be long gone by then.

They were in luck, because Jack's mother and sister arrived at that moment. Jack introduced everyone, but there wasn't time for conversation. They walked to the players' entrance. It was unmarked, just off the parking lot. On game days, with a team representative just inside, only authorized persons entered. Jack opened the door and stepped in. A young fellow Jack didn't know was seated in the hallway. He began with a question.

"You're Mr.?"

Jack recognized the tactic. You had to give the correct name to be allowed in.

"Ridley," Jack answered.

"I'm Nick Farmer," the gatekeeper said. "I'm supposed to take you and your guests to the clubhouse."

Then he locked the door behind them, and led the group down

the hallway. Jack thought it was a good omen. Mr. Farmer was leading a young farmer, on the first step to baseball's farm system. Random events in action.

No one else appeared on the way to the clubhouse. When they entered the large room, they were alone. Duncan was looking at the players' uniforms hanging in the individual cubicles. There were some famous names, and he seemed a bit awestruck.

"No big deal, Cake," Jack said. "Every one of them came in here once, for the first time, just like you are right now."

The door from the manager's office opened and a familiar face appeared.

"Jeez, Jack, it's good to see you."

It was Mike Franz. They hadn't spoken since the day Mike told Jack that the team wasn't going to re-sign him. It seemed like a hundred years ago to Jack, but Mike acted like they had just parted last week. He quickly closed the distance between them and grabbed Jack in a giant bear hug.

"I can't tell you how happy I am you're here. That whole thing was so messed up. I'm glad we got this chance to straighten it out."

Jack was confused as to what was being straightened out, but he remembered his manners.

"This is Sally James, the mother of our prospect here, Duncan. And this is his sister, Danielle. I think you remember my mom and my sister."

Mike was his old gregarious self.

"I'm glad to see you all. I can't wait to see what this young man can do. Gordie has told me all about it."

The ladies exchanged pleasantries, but Duncan was nervous and kept silent. Mike was the first big leaguer he had ever met, up close and personal. He didn't include Jack in that rarified company. Jack was just a guy he knew.

"Let's get the women comfortable," Mike addressed the group. "Jack and Duncan can get loose."

The boys got their equipment ready, cleats and all. Mike led Sally, Danielle, Ashley and Elizabeth down the tunnel to the dugout.

"Would you like to watch from here, or grab a seat?"

They opted for seats bordering the field. It was a beautiful sunny day and a few of the groundskeepers were out with water hoses. They had just finished mowing the outfield, and the smell of freshly cut grass wafted toward home plate.

There was no need to walk to the outfield bullpen. Jack knew there would be plenty of eyes already on them, regardless of where they warmed up. So, after some light stretching, they just started throwing in front of the dugout. Jack's guidance was barely minimal.

"Nice and easy, Cake. No hurry."

After the first couple of throws, they got into a rhythm. The smack of the ball hitting leather echoed throughout the silent stadium. Nobody was talking. Duncan followed the regimen they had established on the farm. They gradually increased pitch speed during an intense half-hour. The Rookie was ready. Jack called a halt, to regroup in the dugout and get some water.

Duncan had a nice layer of sweat going, and an intensity that Jack liked. There were several people arriving on the field, and Mike was in conversation with them. From the dugout steps, Jack recognized a couple of faces, but couldn't connect any names. He assumed they were part of the team's scouting corps. He delivered his final thoughts.

"Okay, Cake, it's about time. We've got this covered. We go with the same routine as home. Let's start about medium speed, and work our way through the pitches. We end up with the heat."

Duncan nodded, and kept his eyes on the field. He was ready. Jack saw a familiar face standing at first base with Mike.

"Wait here for me here a second," he said to Duncan. "I need to check out some details. Stay warm."

He walked over to where Mike was standing with a guy named Tim Lyons. Tim had been a clubhouse attendant Jack knew in the old days. They had gotten along well, as they were about the same age, and both were new to the club. Tim was smiling as Jack approached and shook hands.

"Glad you're here Jack," he said. "I hear you've got a prospect."

Jack was smiling, too. Lyons had nothing to do with the bad times five years ago. Jack was genuinely pleased to see him.

"I'm hoping, buddy. Good to see you still here with the team. Looks like you're running the gun today?"

It was a question based on the fact that Tim had the radar equipment set up behind the plate. Tim nodded. Jack had expected this part of the evaluation. He thought it was a stroke of luck that Tim Lyons was the operator.

"Do me a favor?"

"You bet."

"When we get heated up, can you tip me off on speed? I'd like to know if my guy is hitting the numbers."

Tim nodded once more, and held up one finger, then two, then three.

"Like this?"

Jack grinned and turned toward home.

"Perfect. Thanks, man."

He walked toward Mike, who had shifted to the group at the plate. Tim wasn't the only equipment operator on hand, Jack could see. There was a camera at the backstop, and Jack assumed there were more around the field. Duncan was going to be recorded from every angle. His performance would be analyzed and graded on every possible aspect. That was a good thing, Jack knew. If Duncan delivered the goods, they'd have it on undeniable video. When observers said he was amazing, no one would be able to claim otherwise.

"How 'bout I introduce you to these guys afterwards," Mike said. "You've got enough on your mind."

Jack agreed, and he and Mike separated from the others.

"Everybody's pulling for you, Jack."

The way Mike said it made Jack pause, just for a moment. This was about Duncan; Mike's meaning was ambiguous. Jack guessed that his old battery-mate was merely offering encouragement. If the catcher did well, so would the pitcher. Jack stated his intentions.

"I figure we'll roll through standard pitches, so you can see what he's got. About thirty? Then we finish with heaters."

Mike nodded his assent.

"Gordie got us here because he liked what he saw last week. If your boy has the same stuff, you'll be fine."

Jack headed back to the dugout to retrieve Duncan. He expected to see him pacing nervously. Amusingly, Duncan was swinging a bat he had taken out of the rack.

"Maybe they want to see me hit a few, too," he said.

Laughing at Duncan's youthful exuberance took a little pressure off Jack. The kid was too young to realize what they were up against.

"Let's just be a pitcher today, Rookie. You can switch to home run hitter next week."

They headed out to the mound. Jack saw that a few more bodies had arrived to see the show. He didn't focus on any faces. He lasered in on Duncan.

"You look at me, Cake. Nobody else. I'll tell you what's next. Same as home."

Duncan nodded, and locked his gaze on an imagined strike zone. Jack decided it was time for his 'Hoosiers' comparison.

"Notice anything familiar out here?"

Duncan looked blank. Jack pointed toward home plate.

"I think it's still sixty feet and six inches. Just like home. Don't hurt me when you start throwing hard."

Duncan didn't say anything, but his nose crinkled. Arriving at the plate, Jack nodded at Tim. He was stationed off to the side, radar gun at the ready. Jack turned and got set.

"Give me a few easy ones."

Duncan started his windup, and threw a medium speed pitch across the plate. Jack wordlessly returned the ball, and counted five more of the same. Then he stood up.

"A few a little faster, maybe three-quarter speed. Then switch to the change."

Duncan showed no reaction, just signaled another fastball with his glove. This pitch was quicker than the previous throws, just like they had practiced. Jack knew his boy was feeling it.

"A little faster. Hit the one."

He held the glove low and inside. Duncan nailed the target, with a bit more speed. Jack estimated he was in the mid- eighties, and glanced toward Tim Lyons to see if he might get some kind of confirmation. Tim quickly held up five fingers. Eighty-five is a good start, Jack thought. He resumed the drill.

"Faster, in the six."

Duncan delivered again, high middle in the strike zone.

"Faster, in the seven."

This would be a low outside corner pitch, and Jack held the glove on the edge of the plate. The ball hit the spot at a speed Jack guessed to be about ninety. Another pitch was on the way, and Jack guessed they were now past ninety. A glance at Tim showed two fingers.

Ninety-two should get the team brass starting to pay attention, Jack reckoned. It was time for part two of the plan. Jack stood up and called loudly to Duncan, so everyone would hear.

"You're warm now. Switch it up."

Duncan flipped his glove to indicate he'd be throwing a curve. Jack saw that Mike and the other team reps got the signal. They were edging closer to the plate, to get a better view of the ball's movement. The first curveball came in on a huge arc. It started toward what would have been a right-handed batter's chin, and snapped down low to the outside of the plate. It had perfectly bisected the strike zone. Jack wordlessly fired the ball back to Duncan, and rolled his right hand in a circular motion. It meant more of the same.

Duncan appeared machine-like. He delivered six more curves, with the same result. Jack noticed the approving looks being exchanged. He didn't have to speak very loudly this time.

"Show 'em the change."

Duncan gave the signal, and the ball was on its way. He looked like he was ramming a fastball down the pipe, when the ball was actually going about eighty miles an hour. Compared to a fastball, it had a parachute slowing it down. Jack signaled for more, and another half-dozen change-ups were delivered.

"From the stretch," Jack directed.

Duncan signaled a fastball and switched to his side stance. He brought the glove to his chest for the required pause and fired the ball home. After five more throws, Jack stood up and walked toward first base.

"Show them your pick-off."

When Jack arrived at the bag, Duncan was already in his stretch. He whirled toward first and fired the ball to Jack.

"A few more," Jack ordered.

Same throw. Same results. Jack had seen better pick-off moves, but that was by more seasoned pitchers. Duncan's technique was more than adequate. They had thrown for about half an hour and Duncan had already shown himself as a legitimate prospect. The only thing he hadn't showcased was a really hot fastball. Jack knew that Duncan had made all the required pitches. More importantly, he was performing well.

He caught Duncan's eye as he left first base, and gave the kid a quizzical look. Duncan knew what was coming, and he nodded, with his high-intensity stare. Jack continued walking back to the plate, and then he paused by Mike and his crew. It was time to unleash the dragon.

"Okay, boys. Now it's going to get *interesting*."

He dropped back behind the plate and called to Duncan.

"Finish like we always do. One at a time."

Duncan was standing on the mound, turning the ball over in his throwing hand. He had an almost defiant look about him. Briefly, he snapped his glove, fingers down, toward the plate. Every baseball eye in the place knew that a fastball was coming. Jack held the glove dead-center. Duncan rolled through his windup and whipped the ball home, right down the middle. Jack guessed it was a low nineties throw.

He didn't need to look toward Tim Lyons for the speed. Not just yet. Jack threw the ball back to Duncan and did the circle motion with his throwing hand. Duncan signaled a fastball again, and another pitch came roaring home. As they had done at the barn, it was faster, and Jack knew the surrounding coaches knew it, too.

Another pitch was on the way. Duncan was on a roll. After the next pitch, Jack glanced toward the radar gun. Tim was holding up five fingers. Jack knew Duncan had plenty of speed to give. He had a look on his face that Jack had seen in major league games. It was beyond competitive. It said, 'I'm going to take your girlfriend *and* your lunch money.' Jack was smiling behind his mask. He signaled for more, and Duncan delivered several more burners.

When Jack stole a glance at Tim, he was tapping on the readout with an odd look on his face. Jack didn't have time to wait. Duncan was winding up and another screamer came in. Jack let it slam into his glove so it made the loudest crack possible. He stood up and looked toward the coaches and scouts.

"He's got more boys, but that should do it for now."

Jack motioned for Duncan to come in off the mound. As the rookie prospect walked toward home, Jack took a final glance at Tim. He had put the radar gun down, and was showing Jack seven fingers. Jack knew that Duncan had passed the test. He gave Sally, Danielle, his mom and Ashley a thumbs-up. Happy and expectant faces greeted him.

Duncan had arrived at the plate. He was sweating, but completely unruffled; not breathing hard at all. He appeared to be the calmest person in the group. Jack spoke first.

"Gentlemen, this is Duncan James. He can throw harder, but I think you've seen enough."

He looked at the assembled faces, and they were believers. Jack stepped aside, and handed the moment to Mike Franz.

"Want to handle the introductions?"

Mike walked through the list: Will Hinkle, bullpen coach; Kevin Schiewer, third-base coach; Jim Obergfell, assistant scout; Frank Kelly, manager; Gerry Weimer, player personnel. As the pitching coach, Mike made it a six-man group. Jack saw Gordie Bowen arrive to make it seven. Gordie greeted Jack warmly.

"We watched it all from the owner's suite. Very nice, Jack."

Jack slapped Duncan on the back.

"Well, Cake, if they don't like you now, they should all retire."

Mike shook Duncan's hand and spoke encouragingly.

"I'm pretty sure they're going to like you, Duncan."

Mike turned to Jack.

"I'm recommending they sign your boy. Can you visit with legal this afternoon?"

Jack hesitated. He wanted Duncan to have all possible leverage.

"He's a minor, but his mother is here. I'm not his rep, but I was thinking of calling Mike Teal."

Sally and Danielle had arrived to give Duncan a hug, with Elizabeth and Ashley right behind. Jack introduced them all.

"Of course," Mike agreed. "I don't think they expect to sign; they will just want to put an offer on the table. Mrs. James can consult with anyone. How about you get cleaned up and you all have some lunch on the team? We can meet - say around two or three in the admin office?"

Jack glanced at Sally and Duncan and Danielle. He knew they would accept whatever he decided.

"We'll go eat and talk about it, and I'll get back to you."

There were nods everywhere, and Jack and Duncan headed to the clubhouse. Tim Lyons followed.

"I'll look after the ladies until you get back," Mike said, and he took both families on a stadium tour.

As soon as they were alone, Jack couldn't resist cornering Lyons.

"What was the deal? I saw you tapping the gun."

Tim grinned and smacked Duncan on the shoulder.

"Dude, I think you hit one hundred! I thought the darn thing had stopped working, because it was showing zeros."

Duncan laughed and thanked Tim.

"Cool, buddy, thanks a lot. Never did throw as hard as I could. Guess I was amped."

If Jack wasn't convinced before, he was now. Duncan had just quietly said he could throw harder. His top end was going to be extraordinary; maybe a little frightening. The realization renewed Jack's commitment to delicately nurture this raw monster talent.

A quick shower got both of them out of the clubhouse before any players arrived for the night game. Jack wasn't ready for any team discussions about the tryout. However, there was another avenue to keep them close by the team brass. Mike suggested they eat lunch at a restaurant which was part of the stadium complex.

Many fan amenities had been added since Jack had played. Fine food was one of them. Mike walked with all six guests to the restaurant and arranged the billing. He handed Jack a business card.

"Call me when you're ready. I think this could be good for you and Duncan."

Jack watched him walk away and joined the group at the table. While they perused the menu, Jack decided two things. He would make sure they all ordered the most expensive meals possible. Then he would figure out what Mike meant when he said 'good for *you* and Duncan.' For the immediate future, the steak and lobster appeared acceptable.

43

BASEBALL'S REDEMPTION

At lunch, Duncan was exuberant. His performance had been spectacular. Sally and Danielle were giddy, as well. Spirits were running high. The ladies were gabbing away like old friends. Jack joined in the celebration, but he also kept things in check. He'd wait until there were signatures on a contract before he got excited. It was time to explain to Sally what the team might do.

"I expect they'll offer a three-year contract," he said. "That's the undrafted rookie term. They are usually the league minimum. The kicker is spending time on the minor league team on a split contract, which I expect he will. They get paid less."

Sally eased into her question.

"There's no way of knowing how long you're in the minors, right? I've read most of the minor league players never get to the big leagues."

Jack nodded.

"That's true. Plus, life in the minors is a grind. You might make up ground with a signing bonus, which they might offer to keep Cake from shopping another team. Just the fact that he's had a personal tryout increases his chances elsewhere, and they know it."

There was much to consider. Jack counseled waiting until the club made an offer. For now, lunch was outstanding, and all of them enjoyed every minute of it. Jack wished it were a late dinner, so they could really celebrate. He'd order an expensive bottle of wine; maybe two.

They wrapped up just after two o'clock. Jack signed the check as Mike had directed. Then he called the number Mike had given him. The lady who answered told them to come to the executive offices when they were ready, and Mike would meet them.

The happy gang walked to the stadium elevators and punched the proper floor. The door opened to an office area Jack had never seen. A young lady at the reception desk saw them approaching. She was all smiles, and asked them to follow her to a meeting room. Jack walked in first, and he saw Mike and Gordie Bowen. They were accompanied by the manager, Frank Kelly, and a lady in a suit. Mike introduced her as the club's lawyer, Jessica Miller. Other team personnel were scattered around the conference table, but there was room for Sally, Danielle, Duncan and Jack to sit side-by-side. Elizabeth and Ashley sat right behind them. Mike assumed control of the meeting and began the discussion.

"Let me start by saying how happy we are that Duncan was able to come today and show us his outstanding pitching. We owe Jack many thanks for getting Duncan ready for his tryout."

He indicated the two newest members in the meeting with a small gesture.

"Frank Kelly, our manager, and Ms. Miller were not part of the organization when Jack played here. For them, I say that Jack was a terrific player and member of the club. I am very pleased to say that by bringing Duncan to our attention, Jack is demonstrating what a valuable team asset he still is."

He had been looking at Duncan and his family, but now Mike paused to look at the other organization representatives. Jack wondered where Mike was going with this line of thinking. Mike didn't give him very long to dwell on it, because he spoke directly to Duncan and Sally.

"Duncan, with your mother's permission, we would like to offer you a contract to play baseball for the Reds. You are in a unique position, as an undrafted player. As Jack can tell you, draft order affects signing bonuses and contract terms. He will also tell you that it's hard to assign a draft value to a non-college player."

Mike then shifted his attention to his old catcher.

"Jack, we like Duncan very much. If he had a consistent college career with what he showed today, he would be a first-round pick. As it is, we see him as a possible second rounder."

The representative for the Reds paused to let that sink in. He doubted that Sally and Duncan realized the significance of what he just said, but he knew that Jack did. Jack's look toward Sally and Duncan told Mike he was right. He hoped that Jack's personal relationship with the family would help with the explanations.

Mike shifted his attention to Sally, individually.

"Mrs. James, maybe you would like Jack to explain to you and Duncan the contract basics for rookies in major league baseball."

Mike was using Jack's relationship with the family to keep things smooth. Jack swallowed hard, and turned to the family he had brought to this event; to this critical moment. He had to recalibrate his thoughts, because the second-rounder talk was unexpected.

"I know second-round salary and bonus money is around a million a year. They aren't guaranteed. You have split contracts for the minors. Then the pay goes way down. A signing bonus is an inducement the team offers to keep the player from going somewhere else."

Jack said this last sentence while he was looking at the team lawyer. He wondered just how much coaxing the team planned to do to get Duncan. Then he switched to Mike.

"Am I about right?"

Mike jumped in immediately.

"Just about right, Jack. As I recall, you told me your signing bonus got you into a sporting goods store. Maybe Duncan will have the same type of opportunity."

Mike looked toward Ms. Miller, and the lawyer knew it was her turn to add to the meeting.

"Hello, Mrs. James; hello, Duncan. Mr. Ridley gave us a nice perspective, and I hope to follow-up on that. The team is offering Duncan a three-year undrafted rookie deal. Two things make this contract special."

Jack was on full alert. The next few sentences could make all the difference. The team lawyer continued.

"We are very interested in Duncan playing for us. We believe this offer demonstrates that."

Ms. Miller looked directly at Jack.

"First, this is not a split contract."

She paused to let that sink in. Sally was confused by the contract term.

"What does that mean?"

Jack felt a tremor of satisfaction in his bones, as he responded.

"It means that when Duncan plays in the minors, which he will, he still gets paid under a major-league contract."

Sally and Duncan and Danielle looked at each other. It was Danielle who spoke up.

"That's a good thing, right?"

"Yes, Danny, that's a good thing," Jack said.

He looked at Ms. Miller for her follow-up.

"Second?"

"Mr. Ridley, would a guaranteed contract be a sign of good faith?"

A warm rush filled Jack's body.

"Yes, ma'am. A guaranteed three-year contract is fine."

Ms. Miller smiled slightly, and took out a pen to make a notation on her legal pad. Then she looked up at Jack.

"You're welcome to check the figures, but the most recent second-round average was around nine hundred thousand, give or take. How about we say this: three years, guaranteed, no split, salary and bonus at one million per year?"

Jack closed his eyes and let a breath of relief escape. He felt a wave of satisfaction, because Duncan would get his chance. Something good had come of baseball purgatory. He could move on, knowing that he had a small role in the happy ending. His own baseball life was over, but Duncan's would begin with a vengeance. The lawyer stood to depart. She looked at each member of the family in turn.

"Perhaps you would like some private time to talk this over?"

The rest of the team management took their cue, and stood to leave the room. One by one, they left Sally, Duncan, Danielle, Elizabeth and Ashley with parting good wishes. Before his exit, Gordie stopped to see Jack and shake hands. Jack offered his best wishes regarding Gordie's parents. Gordie had something else on his mind.

"Let me say one thing before leaving, Jack. After Randy told me you were in town, I wanted to see you in the Crushers game. I always hoped you were doing okay. I was glad to see you played so well."

He paused and put a hand on Jack's shoulder.

"Duncan was an unexpected bonus, but I came to see you, Jack. I saw the same great kid I saw five years ago. That guy you threw out at second was an NCAA college sprint champion. He has major league speed, but you nailed him by five feet. And you hit a ball about four hundred and fifty feet. You've still got it, buddy. Big time. I hope you come back."

He hugged Jack and left. Jack was asking himself what did 'come back' mean, coming from Gordie? Ms. Miller had her papers stacked and ready to go.

"One more thing, Mr. Ridley. I understand you are very close to the James family?"

Jack nodded, silently.

"There's something I'd like to address, and you can be alone or have the family here, if you'd like."

What the woman was getting at, Jack had no idea, but there was nothing his mother and sister didn't know. Of course they would stay with him. Jack opted to keep Sally, Duncan and Danny with him as well. He doubted a personal embarrassment was coming. All of them knew the story about his time with the team, if that was what Ms. Miller was driving at.

"I'm happy to have them here," Jack said. "They're sort of my adopted family, anyway."

Ms. Miller nodded, and pressed a button on her cell phone.

"There's someone else with the team who wanted to speak with you, if you don't mind."

———

Moments passed and no one spoke. Jack had no idea what was about to happen. A cruel sense of foreboding engulfed him and he couldn't stop it. Was this recent happiness about to be snatched away? He helplessly wondered what new calamity was upon him. His hands were shaking and his eyes were resignedly closed. Approaching footsteps forced him to pry them open and face whatever callous fate waited.

The door was still open. Jack was astounded to see Mr. Hutchens framed in the opening. He looked older and beaten down from how he last appeared. Jack managed to get to his feet. He tried to speak but his strangled voice produced only two words.

"Mr. Hutchens."

The man just looked at Jack for a long, sad moment. Then he shuffled forward and reached out to shake hands. Jack was practically in shock, but he tried to be mannerly.

"Sally James, this is Mr. Hutchens, the team owner."

Jack indicated Danielle and Duncan, and introduced them. Before Jack got to his mother and sister, Mr. Hutchens spoke. His voice was barely audible.

"I remember Mrs. Ridley and Ashley."

He gravely shook hands with each of them. Then he turned to

Jack. His face was the definition of melancholy. When he spoke, his speech wavered and seemed to come from a distant place. He slowly and deliberately mouthed his words. There was indescribable pain in his voice.

"Jack, I've wanted to tell you, for a very long time, how sorry I am about how things happened after Olivia died. I was so distraught, and I said and did things that were wrong. I blamed you, and it took me a couple of years to see clearly. It wasn't your fault. You had nothing to do with that accident, but I acted in a way that drove you away from the team."

By now, tears were coursing down his face. He made no attempt to hide them. Jack was still motionless, frozen in place. It was Danielle who approached Mr. Hutchens, holding out her handkerchief. He took it and dabbed his eyes. He reached toward Danielle's face, and gently touched her cheek. Then he turned to Jack.

"I am so sorry, and I hope you can forgive me. Olivia's memory deserves better than what happened. You had the last five years taken from you. You should have been with the team. I'm hoping you will come back."

His quavering voice could say no more. He put his hand on Jack's shoulder for a moment, and tried to collect himself. He choked out his final words.

"Ms. Miller has an offer for you," he whispered. "Please consider it."

He gave the others a small, weak smile, and then he slowly left the room.

Jack was aghast. He could not have been more overwhelmed. Having never expected to see Mr. Hutchens again, an abject apology from him was beyond belief. Jack crumpled into a chair, and waited for Ms. Miller to finish what she had to say. The lawyer came right to the point.

"Mr. Hutchens has directed me to offer you a no-split contract to play for the Reds, or within the organization, guaranteed for five years. It is a midlevel average of current salaries for the eleven to twenty highest paid catchers. It's in the five million per year area, Mr. Ridley. I have the numbers in the contract here for you, to take to your agent."

She slid the contract across the table to Jack, who was absolutely stunned. Trying to compose himself took all he had. He hoped his doomed struggle wasn't too evident. Everyone in the room, except Ms. Miller, looked at him in frozen amazement.

"I don't have an agent," Jack mumbled absently.

He was familiar with basic contract terms, and turned to the 'supplemental' page. The critical numbers were there. His eyes locked on the figures.

"Ms. Miller, there's a mistake. You said five years, at the midlevel average. This has ten years written in the 'term' portion."

The lawyer gathered her papers once again, and stood up. She looked at Jack with a small sympathetic smile.

"May I call you Jack?" she asked.

Jack could only nod, and Jessica continued.

"I've been here for three years, Jack, and your name keeps coming up. Everybody says how good you were for the team, and how bad they felt when you went away. They all hope you'll come back. Me, included."

Jack looked at Sally, Danielle, Duncan, Elizabeth and Ashley for support. They all were watching him as if he had suddenly appeared from outer space. Jack was slowly finding his way toward comprehending all that was happening. He had his hands over his mouth, covering his shock.

"But you said five years, and this contract says ten."

Ms. Miller had started edging toward the door, but now she stopped. She gave Jack a look that was sad, but somehow benevolent. She spoke very quietly.

"The ten years is back-dated, Jack. You'll be under contract for five; you get paid for ten."

Jack was slowly crawling toward realization, but he needed to clarify what he was hearing.

"So, this means....?"

He had to search for the right words.

Jessica Miller paused and looked at the soul of astonishment revealed by Jack's face. She didn't know Jack Ridley, but she could sense that he deserved absolute kindness.

"Mr. Hutchens said he was sorry, Jack. I think he means it."

The lawyer left the room. Jack's hands went from covering his mouth, to covering his entire face. It was just as well. Years of frustration, shame and disappointment were rebuffed. Redemption had arrived.

Jack Ridley, big-league ballplayer, began to cry. He didn't notice that everyone in the room did the same.

44

A NEW TOMORROW STARTS TODAY

L ife is so random. Moments arrive, unannounced, that have seismic impact on the rest of your days. The day began with Jack expecting he would need to summon all the grace and elegance he possessed, to bravely accept a new chapter in this life. He would launch Duncan's baseball career, while he parted with his own. But Mr. Hutchens altered time and space by making an offer Jack couldn't refuse. There would be financial reward beyond anything he ever contemplated, and there would be unexpected redemption.

A subtle demon had been following Jack after he exited baseball. It wasn't failure; it was rejection. Mr. Hutchens had created the demon, and now he was destroying it. Jack's mother and sister excitedly grasped the moment, and their joy nearly smothered him. His new family of Sally, Danielle and Duncan also joined in the celebration. The marriage of opportunity and renewal suited perfectly.

After a quick consensus, the happy group traipsed out of the meeting room to find Ms. Miller's office. Jack told her that he and Duncan would accept their offers. He didn't need to consult with an agent to know that the team was being generous to both of them. The lawyer called Mike Franz to let him know of the decision. Mike happily bounded into Miller's office, shaking hands all around. He was especially effusive towards Jack.

"Man, I always hoped you'd be back. We've missed you around here."

Mike corralled the bevy of coaches and managers who were arriving for the night game, and informed them that the team's fortunes had just improved dramatically. Those who had known Jack were enthusiastic. The newcomers were quickly made aware that their team had just signed two impact players. The news reverberated throughout the clubhouse. When the blogs lit up, long-time fans rejoiced that Jack Ridley had returned.

Mike Franz and Jessica Miller huddled briefly to talk about how soon the signings could be scheduled. The lawyer proposed a media event.

"I can have all the documents ready before today's game is over. Do you want to sign and have an announcement before tomorrow's game?"

Mike looked at Jack.

"We play at 2:10 tomorrow," Mike said. "We could have the reporters here before the game starts. The timing would be good, right?"

Jack agreed with the rough plan.

"How about we look over the contracts tonight, and come here tomorrow about one o'clock for signing?"

Heads were nodding, and Miller added her thoughts.

"The contracts will be messengered to you, and you let me know about any issues."

"Jack, you all can hose the team for hotel rooms tonight!" Mike chortled. "Make sure you find an expensive restaurant."

Jack grinned at Sally and his mother.

"We order that wine, after all."

Duncan was laughing and indulged his youthful exuberance.

"Mr. Hutch is going to be sorry!"

Behind them, Mr. Hutchens was approaching. He heard Duncan's remark. The older gentleman walked toward Jack and Duncan, and stood between them. He put an arm around each shoulder.

"Boys, there is never going to be anything about this day that makes me sorry."

He lingered for a long moment, with his arm draped around his newest players. The team photographer snapped a picture. It appeared on the front page of the sports section the next morning, with the caption 'Ridley Reunites Reds.'

The boys and their families weren't staying for the night game. Jack and Duncan needed to plan with the team brass, so Jack suggested that the ladies visit the shopping mall.

"How about we meet back at the hotel in a couple of hours and we go to dinner from there?"

They were easily convinced. Danielle walked with Jack toward the door. She had a devilish grin on her face.

"I've never dated a millionaire before. I wonder if the shopping is better."

Pulling Jack's chain came easily to her. Sally laughingly pulled her daughter through the door, as Jack pretended he was worried. Danielle's subtle humor was one of her attractive traits.

Frank Kelly thought there was a way to maneuver Jack and Duncan onto the roster, at least temporarily. There were tickets to sell, and the team could capitalize on Ridley's return.

"We've got a couple of guys about to go on IL this week."

He was using baseball shorthand for 'injured list.' It meant that two players currently on the major league roster would be medically unable to play. They would normally be replaced by temporary call-ups from the minor league team. It was the bane of a minor league team's existence. Lower level clubs exist solely for the benefit of the big league team. A minor league manager's reward for developing a stellar player is ironic: The player is taken from him.

Thus, a major-league player who was removed from the team via injury could be replaced by a minor leaguer, or by a recent acquisition. That maintains the team's twenty-five man roster.

Duncan inadvertently showed the team bosses that he had an analytical mind.

"I always wondered why they used to call it 'disabled' when it's really 'injured.' That had to confuse some folks."

Mike Franz and Frank Kelly exchanged thoughtful glances. This kid was a thinker.

The coaches agreed that Jack and Duncan would take those two positions, if only briefly. They might see some game action during the IL period. In the interim, the team could decide where the players ended up within the organization. It was a never-ending chess game and the ballplayers were the game pieces. For the moment, Kelly was the chess master.

"Gordie Bowen tells me that he thinks Duncan could give us a couple of innings right now," Kelly said to Jack. "You think that might work?"

Jack was tentative. He was going to protect his protégé.

"I guess it might sell tickets, putting a rookie in like that. But we'd have to really control the situation. If he gets shelled, it could screw him up."

They agreed to monitor the situation and make a determination later. Duncan could practice during the week and see how well he faced the team's hitters. If he held his own, he might see some game action. As to signing the contracts, the club requested media coverage, so the team's past and future would be announced to the fans. The usual outlets were contacted to schedule a news conference before the Sunday game, but Jack and Duncan would not play just yet.

The team put the media machine in motion, and Duncan's introduction to major league baseball was underway. Jack knew the event and the surroundings could be intimidating, but he also knew that Duncan's temperament would keep him on solid ground. Plus, Jack would be with him throughout. Together, they would keep things in perspective.

Jack made hotel arrangements and told Duncan the signing would require more than blue jeans and a sweatshirt. One call got the ladies in on a suit search for both boys. Sally was about to see her son transform into a big-league player.

The celebration was not particularly raucous. Jack's mother and sister were in the initial stages of getting to know the James family, so they maintained a slight reserve. Sally and Danielle were happy to get to know Jack's family, but they kept their emotions in check. Everyone was contemplating how Jack and Duncan were about to embark on a media maelstrom. Both of them would be rich, by their family's standards, so the moms were quietly thankful. It's not every day your son achieves financial independence. After the dinner, all six of them walked to the hotel to let the day's events settle. Jack was planning for the coming week.

"After the signing announcement, we'll practice with the team. They'll decide if they want to put Duncan in a game. It'd be short relief."

The ladies announced they would be returning home Sunday evening to tend to their own schedules, while the boys took care of team business. The women could easily return if the coaches decided to put Duncan to work.

Jack could have gotten away with booking private rooms for each of them, but the moms opted to bunk with their daughters. Jack didn't mind pairing up with Duncan. When and if they were assigned to the minor league club, they would probably be rooming together, anyway. They received the room cards and parted ways in the hotel lobby, but Jack and Danielle lagged behind.

"This is probably the last time you'll be sitting in a hotel lobby without baseball fans hanging around," Danielle noted.

Jack agreed.

"It can get messy. On the road, you pretty much stay in your room."

He nodded in the direction of the hotel bar.

"How about we finish the night with a drink? The team can afford it, right?"

Instead of a laugh, Jack got a somber look from Danielle. He waited until they were hidden in a corner booth before asking what it meant.

"C'mon, Danny, that was funny. You look worried."

The barman walked over for drink orders. Jack directed a suggestion at Danielle.

"Two glasses of Pinot Noir?"

She nodded, and they were alone again. She had both hands flat on the table, palms down, gently tapping her fingers. Jack waited for her to sort through her thoughts.

"Okay, Jack, it's like this. A couple of days ago I was falling for a guy who had a future selling baseball equipment. Tomorrow, before the day is over, he's going to sign a baseball contract and get millions of dollars. I'm wondering if he's the same guy. Does he still want me around?"

Jack avoided his natural inclination to smooth over a rough spot by making a joke.

"Danny, the thought never occurred to me. You should realize I'm nuts about you. If they called the whole thing off tomorrow, I'd still be at your door the next day."

That seemed to give her a moment's reprieve, so he continued.

"You said you were my girlfriend before any of this started. I'm all in. Does that sound good to you?"

She reached both hands across the table.

"It sounds perfect to me. Now, I'm going to get you drunk and take advantage of you before the other girls find out what a hunk you are."

"Too late! I've already booked you with your mother."

He'd gotten a joke in, after all. As they sipped the wine, Jack wanted Danielle to know that he was sincere. He wasn't ready to make a commitment, but he knew he wanted this woman in his life.

About that time, a piano player went to work, playing soft standards. Jack stood up.

"You started a dancing lesson, I recall. How about another?"

Danielle stood and they danced right on the spot. She laid her head on Jack's shoulder, and her perfume worked its magic once again. The piano man played one of those slow swaying numbers for the only two people in the bar. Both of them just enjoyed the alluring moment, and when the song ended, they stayed in their embrace.

"Jack, that was a dream," Danielle murmured. "I'm going to need about five thousand more of those."

Jack smiled and gave her a gentle kiss.

"Start the meter, Danny. I'm in."

They finished the wine and headed up to the rooms. Danielle and Sally were next to Elizabeth and Ashley, and Jack and Duncan were further down the hall. Jack thought he could afford another teasing moment.

"You're protected by the moms," he smiled at Danielle.

She giggled and jabbed him in his side.

"I was going to say the same thing about you."

They made plans for breakfast and ended the night with a quick kiss. Jack walked to his room thinking that this was a season of surprises.

It looked like he was falling hard for Ms. Danielle James. And, he was about to return to major league baseball. Neither of those prospects had been on the horizon a few short weeks ago. If this whole thing were in a movie, he would have to indulge in a whole lot of suspension of disbelief. It would take a true romantic to accept this happy kismet.

When Jack let himself into the room he found Duncan playing a silly video game on the TV. Jack reminded himself that he might have a future Cy Young award winner on his hands, but the kid was also a nineteen-year old goofball. Life was so random. There was a surprise waiting for Jack in the room. Duncan directed his attention to the closet.

"Look what the team sent over."

Hanging in the closet were several new baseball uniforms. Jack saw one with his name and his old number. There was also one bearing the name "James" with the number twenty-four.

"How'd they manage that?" Jack asked.

Duncan shrugged.

"They said they figured you would want your old number. I had my pick of about five of them. I thought twenty-four might be good because that's my birthday."

Duncan grinned at Jack.

"It's also how old Danny is, but I ain't counting that."

"Buddy, we'll take anything we can get," Jack smiled.

He fell asleep thinking he would enjoy having anything from his old days back again.

———

Jack awoke the next morning certain that he had been talking to Danielle. Sometimes he woke up and didn't know where he was or what was real. In the small dreaming seconds before wakefulness, Jack was reliving a romantic moment.

He quickly checked to see if Duncan might have overheard anything, but his roommate was sound asleep. A hot shower helped Jack clear his head, and Duncan was up and moving when Jack finished. He waved Duncan toward the bathroom.

"Your turn for cleanup. I'll find out what time Mike wants to see us."

Jack called his mother's room and found that all four ladies were getting ready. They had time to meet in the hotel restaurant for a ten o'clock brunch. He also called Mike Franz, to see when they were expected at the team office. The team had already arranged a one o'clock press conference announcing the signings, in time for the game. The big wheels were already rolling.

The women checked out of the hotel, as they'd head home after the game. At the restaurant, everyone was quiet. The gravity of the event was sinking in. Jack remembered that the sports news cycle can be intense, so he talked to Duncan about staying calm under the bright lights. As noon approached, the ladies re-arranged their make-up, and Jack and Duncan retreated to their room to put on their suits. Jack demonstrated the fine art of a Windsor knot.

"Don't use a lot of these on the farm," Duncan joked.

When they all re-convened in the gift shop, Jack pointed out some team jerseys on display.

"One of these days, that'll be you. Maybe we'll get you a 'merch' deal."

Duncan gave Jack a blank look.

"It means merchandise. Guys cut deals for jerseys and t-shirts. Some college help for Duncan, Jr."

It was time to make the short stroll to the ball park and the team offices. Franz and Kelly were waiting. Jack and Sally had looked over the contracts and were satisfied with the black and white details. The signings were quick and private, and the families posed for photographs with their newly-minted stars. Mike gave them a run-down on his announcement for the assembled sportswriters, and told them that the reporters would then ask questions.

"Nothing you haven't seen before, Jack," Mike said. He gave Duncan an assist.

"Just tell them you're happy to be here and can't wait to be a part of the club. Stuff like that."

It was time to introduce the team's two newest signees. Everyone trooped toward the media room. Jack paused at the door. He wished he could think of something appropriate to say. 'Let's get 'em' seemed weak. Sally saved him by stepping between him and Duncan. She pulled both of them closer.

"I've been praying for this," she said. "I didn't realize what it was, but this is where we're supposed to be."

She kissed her boy on the cheek, and did the same to Jack. She didn't say any more; only hugged both boys. Her face radiated happiness, and Jack knew he would remember this moment as another all-time favorite 'first.'

The door opened, and Duncan James stepped into the next chapter of his life. Jack Ridley stepped into his past, and the strobe lights ignited.

45

THE RIDLEY RETURN

Jack had forgotten how tumultuous sports news could be. As he walked through the door, there were shouts.

"Over here, Jack! Jack's back!"

There were faces from the old days; Jack was surprised at the size of the Sunday crowd. Genuine happiness radiated in the room.

Sportswriters who were accustomed to seeing careers crash and burn were glad to see that one of the good guys was getting a second chance. The fact that this return was conjoined with a phenom's arrival was a bonus.

The team had 'Ridley' and 'James' uniforms displayed behind the podium. Jack's analytical mind took over. Nine and twenty-four share the same numerical factor: The number three is critical in baseball. Three outs each inning. Three strikes. Three bases. It had to be a harbinger of good things to come. Jack was amused by his oblique thinking, as Mike Franz read a short statement.

"Guys, I'll make an announcement and then we'll take questions. Our first signing today needs no introduction and...."

Mike went on about Jack's prior time with the team, and launched into details about Duncan. Jack wasn't listening. He reminisced about the first time he came to the team and how bright the future had looked.

So much heartache had occurred between then and now. Grateful for a new beginning, Jack was distracted. He didn't realize one of the reporters had asked him a question. Luckily, it was a face he knew.

"I'm sorry, Tom, could you repeat?"

That was Jack's first comment as a second time big league ballplayer. The reporter, Tom Rivelli, was smiling at Jack.

"I was asking about what you've been up to since you were here last."

Jack played it straight. In the old days he always had good press from Rivelli.

"I've been in sporting goods, Tom. Be sure to tell all your friends about our great store."

The Ridley Return was complete; the baseball repartee from five years ago came full circle. The reporters were mainly interested in Duncan's story. He answered their questions with a bucolic shyness that whetted their appetite.

"When will we see you in action?" one reporter called out.

Duncan smiled and played along.

"You'll have to ask Mr. Kelly. I only work here."

The media loved it. They could see quotes coming from this kid for years.

Frank Kelly jumped in.

"We'll see if we can get Duncan in a game as soon as we can, folks. You'll have plenty to write about. We have to break now to get the game started."

The conference was exactly what the team wanted. Jack and Duncan exited the media room and the reporters headed to the field.

"That went pretty well," Mike said. "You guys can sit in the dugout and there are box seats for the ladies. Or, maybe you all want to watch the game in the owner's suite."

Jack thought they'd do better meeting the players at a practice and Duncan agreed. The suite would give them more family time together. The six of them traipsed to the elevator to the box level. A buffet lunch was waiting. Sally had never seen this side of professional baseball.

"Jack, aren't you supposed to get me a hot dog? Buy me some peanuts and…. Hey!" she joked. "Are you the Cracker Jack guy, too?"

Her lame comedy suited the moment perfectly.

The game progressed and Jack huddled with Duncan, discussing pitch selection and strategy. The ladies were impressed that Jack could predict a particular type of pitch before it was thrown, or when a runner would attempt to steal. He told them that a certain batter approaching the plate would probably be walked. When he was, they thought he was clairvoyant.

"Guys, it's just knowing the situation," he laughed. "It ain't magic."

Explaining the moment to his mother and Danielle took him into their classroom background.

"Have you ever known that a particular kid was going to act up in class? It's the same thing. Just comes from experience."

Toward the end of the game, the door opened and Mr. Hutchens walked in. What might have been awkward became enjoyable. He was initially timid, but warmed to Duncan and Ashley's youthful exuberance. He was particularly taken with Danielle. Jack realized Olivia would have been about the same age.

As Mr. Hutchens spoke with Duncan's sister, a bit of healing began. Danielle told Mr. Hutchens how happy he had made her family. He quietly stated that Duncan was going to be a star, and seemed to intuitively understand that she and Jack were meant for each other. He shyly put his arm around them both.

"You two will be great together," he said.

The game ended with a Reds win, and everyone watched the fans celebrate. Mr. Hutchens departed with a cordial invite.

"You all come here anytime to watch Jack and Duncan."

Sally, Elizabeth, Ashley and Danielle hugged him like a long-lost family member. He acted like this sort of thing happened all the time.

Jack hoped for many future gatherings, where each event would slowly chip away past negativity. They left the suite and walked to the parking lot. Jack and Duncan said goodbye to the ladies, with a reminder.

"You might be getting a call to scoot right back, if Kelly brings Duncan in. The Giants arrive tomorrow for three days. We're off Thursday, and then we're at home for the weekend with the Red Sox."

He told Danielle he'd make plans to retrieve his car later on.

"Maybe you could drive it, if you and your mom come to a game?"

Danielle gave him a furtive wink.

"Anything you say, Jack."

As the ladies drove away, the boys were smiling. They retreated to the hotel room and rested. Jack knew the drill, and told Duncan what to expect. There would be batting practice before the next game. Jack outlined what he remembered of game day procedures, and reminded Duncan to keep a low profile.

"We had a 'big splash signing' today. You can bet guys on the team are talking about it. There will be questions, so just stay quiet and let things develop. We'll figure out if anybody has issues."

It was Duncan's first experience with room service.

"Live it up while the team's paying," Jack laughed. "You get a couple of weeks to find your own place. We've got plenty of time to look for an apartment."

With no reason to go anywhere, they stayed in and watched late night TV. Jack stuck the 'Come Back Later' sign on the door, because there was no need to wake up early. The Monday game was scheduled for 7 p.m.

Since neither one of them would be playing the next game, Jack decided to call Mike around noon to see what time they should be at the ballpark. There would probably be a team introduction before batting practice, around three for the home team. Before dozing off, Jack was caught up in the magic of the whole process.

"How cool is this, Cake? You report to your first day of work, and it's a 'noonish' show-up! Beats the heck out of a real job."

Around ten the next morning, Jack stirred from a dead sleep. Duncan was still out cold; Jack had no idea how late the kid was up. He ambled down to the lobby for coffee and a newspaper. The sports section had a small story about their signing and temporary assignment to the big club. There was plenty of time for a shower and breakfast. By the time Jack was toweling off, Duncan was awake.

"If you want food, I'm ready to go," Jack said. "Or, you can shower first."

Duncan was starting slowly.

"Go ahead," he mumbled. "I can eat later."

Jack left Duncan to his own pace and headed to the hotel restaurant. Over breakfast, he finished reading the paper and called Mike a bit earlier than he'd planned.

"How about you guys come in around two," Mike suggested. "That gives you time to meet the guys and get a little BP."

He meant batting practice. They wouldn't be playing, but it was a solid plan for getting started with the team.

When Jack returned, Duncan had left on his own. Jack stretched out on the bed to wait. There were two hundred TV channels and nothing he wanted to watch. A nice meal is a good excuse to snooze, and soon Duncan shook him awake.

"Time to get to the park, Sleeping Beauty."

There was no need to hurry, as they would not be going through the usual pre-game ritual. Normally, there would be stretching and loosening drills. Jack liked to spend fifteen minutes in the whirlpool, to get his muscles moving. Another fifteen minutes using a foam roller on muscle groups to help blood flow and mobility was a good idea. All of that occurred before any batting practice or throwing drills. But today, the two new team members would meet teammates, and use temporary spots in the clubhouse.

Jack expected that sometime in the next week he would need to have Duncan ready to pitch a relief inning. Then they'd probably be sent to the triple A team. Duncan would be returning, with age and experience, to a long stint as a marquee pitcher. One day the kid could inspire quotes like the one Reggie Jackson made about Tom Seaver: 'Blind people come to the ballpark to hear him pitch.'

It sounded awkward, but Jackson had the sound thing right. Jack had *heard* Duncan before he ever saw him, and knew that great things were possible. Jack wasn't sure about his own future, but he knew people would hear the power and majesty of Duncan's pitching.

On the short walk to the ballpark, Jack was having flashbacks about his initial impressions in the big leagues. The whole experience had been overwhelming. The facilities are first-class, and the stadiums and crowds are enormous. The first time he encountered autograph seekers, part of him wondered why they were interested in him. He was nervous about reentering the world that had once discarded him. All sorts of rumors had circulated back then, and Jack had no idea what he would be facing.

When they got to the clubhouse, he discovered there were only two players who were even on the team when he had been there. They hadn't been particularly close, and they didn't seem to have an inordinate interest in Jack, anyway. Once again, he had been paying a debt to worry that wasn't due.

Duncan was just happy to be part of the team. He and Jack moved around the clubhouse and spoke with individual players. Some of the older ones were nonchalant. They had seen newcomers before. A few of the younger players were enthusiastic and wished both of them well.

In all, it was somewhat clinical. Professional athletes are aware they are part of a business, and their basic interests are finding out who can play. Personalities enter into the equation, but a team member's production is what's important. The initial focus would be solely on Duncan's contributions as a player. Later on, the fact that he was an attractive and interesting kid would be noticed, and he would achieve magical heights in sports orbits.

What was intriguing was that Jack knew that Duncan wouldn't

have to do anything special for this to happen. He would simply have to display his pitching skills. Eventually, his exuberance and generally loveable human qualities would bubble forth, and the icing on the cake would be revealed.

Occasionally, such a player comes along and the combination lights up the sports page. Loping along just under the surface was the reality that the same template applied to Jack. His athletic arc had simply been disrupted, but was now on the verge of being reestablished. That part hadn't quite sunk in to Jack's view of the world.

The team was drifting to the field for more loosening drills and BP. Mike Franz suggested that Jack and Duncan get into their practice gear and hit a few balls. Afterwards, being in the dugout for the game would generate interest among the sportscasters and was sure to get Duncan media exposure. That would translate into ticket sales when he did become a permanent part of the team.

No one expected much from Duncan at the plate. But Jack was another story. Batting practice was fun for him, and he had always been an outstanding hitter. When his turn came, he was his old self. He bounced a few into the deep outfield seats. His BP habits remained, and his new teammates got a glimpse of what Jack was bringing to the game. They would soon realize what he had behind the plate, and they would know that the team had improved overnight.

Jack had Duncan warm up for a few throws to his teammates. There was no need to throw hard in batting practice. Jack did use the opportunity to showcase Duncan's ball control. He called Mike Franz over to kibitz. Jack decided to grandstand just a little.

"Tell Dunc where you want the ball," he said nonchalantly.

Mike started calling locations, and Duncan nailed them all. Some of the players gathered at the plate. Heads were shaking in disbelief. Mike understood the totality of Duncan's perfection.

"Holy cow! Does he always put it where he wants it?"

Jack was elated and rubbed it in.

"Yep. And it gets better when he heats up."

They all headed to the clubhouse. The players who had witnessed the display were silently observing the rookie. Jack knew that their demeanor conveyed respect. The rest of the team prepared for the game. Jack and Duncan knew they wouldn't be playing, so they enjoyed the clubhouse meal and cleaned up after the light practice. They suited up and were on the bench that night.

————

The TV broadcasters were able to get shots of the team's newest acquisitions sitting together. The announcers mused about when Ridley and James would appear in a game. Jimmy Hyde, the color analyst, was enthusiastic.

"The return of Jack Ridley, who played here five years ago, would be enough on its own to get the fans fired up. In his short time with the team, he batted over .350 and was phenomenal behind the plate. There's been speculation about why he left, but that's all downstream, now."

The camera shot zoomed in for a close-up of Jack and Duncan. The announcer had more.

"What's even more exciting is the talk I've heard about the newcomer sitting with Jack, whom you see right there. My sources tell me Jack discovered this young pitcher, Duncan James, and he is a flame-thrower. We're talking Nolan Ryan rolled into Sandy Koufax here, folks. The organization won't publicize it, but they are over the moon about this rookie."

His sidekick was playing skeptical for the audience.

"I'm going to hold off on notifying the Hall of Fame before I see him pitching, Jimmy. For an old guy, you're pretty excitable."

The second announcer's name was Bobby Bintner. Jimmy occasionally called him 'Bitter' when he was in one of his acerbic moods.

"Now, don't be getting bitter about it, old buddy," he wisecracked. "I'll be glad to take bets on the game these two bring to the team. The sky's the limit, everybody is saying."

Both were doing their part to entertain viewers. They knew exactly what was being said about Duncan's potential, and everyone knew that Jack had been a game-changer. With any luck, the new guys would give the announcers plenty to talk about.

As the game progressed, Jack concentrated on strategy and signs. He was giving Duncan a tutorial on the flow of the game, and helped him see the signals being sent to batters by the third-base coach. When the team was on defense, the manager sent pitching signals to the catcher, who relayed them to the mound. Duncan had never operated under those terms before, and he listened intently to Jack's guidance. The television coverage got great shots of Jack explaining the finer points to the young protégé. The announcers noticed as well.

"What you're seeing there, folks, is a master of the game explaining the craft to a rookie."

Jimmy Hyde was practically gushing, adding commentary.

"Young Duncan James is getting a graduate course in baseball theory from one of the most knowledgeable players around. What he's learning from Jack Ridley is going to help him deal with game situations and decision-making. As I've said before, understanding the moment helps you react to what's going on. And Jack Ridley is the perfect guy to help a young pitcher get on the right track."

The television producer cut to a booth shot. The viewers saw Bobby Bintner pulling out his cell phone and pretending to look for a telephone number. When his partner gave him a quizzical stare, he deadpanned.

"I'm just making sure I've got the number for the Hall of Fame ready. You've got the kid packing his bags right now."

Jimmy Hyde was not to be deterred. He had found a good way to stir up viewer interest.

"I'm thinking we should start a fan competition right now. When James gets into the regular rotation, we can have a contest for the closest projection of when he wins twenty games. The winner gets game tickets and dinner, courtesy of Bobby Bintner."

Just like that, a way to generate attention for the newest player was born. Jack's situational assessment with Duncan continued throughout the game. His instruction was not wasted on Kelly. The manager positioned himself close enough so he could hear Jack's running commentary. The depth of Jack's analysis was impressive and on-point. There were moments when Jack observed nuances beyond what Kelly had contemplated. He realized that when Jack was in the game, the team would have another coach on the field.

The game wound down to a 4-2 Reds win, and Jack and Duncan celebrated with their teammates. As the players headed down the tunnel to the clubhouse, Kelly took Jack and Duncan aside.

"You were getting the good stuff from Jack today," he directed at Duncan. "Pay attention to what he's telling you. It'll make a difference when you get in."

Duncan was smart enough to just nod and keep his mouth shut. Kelly had seen Jack in action during batting practice, and was thinking of putting him to good use.

"Jack, I don't know if it's time to put you behind the plate, but I think you'd be fine to pinch hit tomorrow. If the situation's right."

Jack gave his manager a silent nod, but added something just for fun.

"It'll be a Fogerty moment, Skipper," he said, using baseball slang for the team's leader.

Kelly raised an eyebrow for the explanation. Jack smiled.

"You know, 'put me in coach; I'm ready to play' is how the song goes."

All three of them grinned like babies with a new puppy as they arrived at the clubhouse.

46

NOW BATTING, NUMBER NINE

For the next game, Jack's preparation was more purposeful. If there was a chance he would pinch-hit in a game, Jack wanted to be ready. He arrived at the ballpark early and did light running and loosening exercises. Duncan noticed a subtle attitude change. His buddy was friendly and outgoing, as always. But his build-up to the game had an edge to it. He was more focused, if that were possible.

Jack had lavished maximum effort on Duncan to get him ready to pitch in the Show. That effort was now being directed toward Jack's own needs. It was an important lesson for Duncan. He was being shown how a professional applies himself to his craft. An athlete must nurture and protect the only real asset he or she has.

That asset is the physical talent necessary to become a professional athlete. Such natural talent must be jealously safeguarded. Duncan was aware of a painful example of physical gifts being neglected. Mickey Mantle possessed baseball skills in towering proportions. But his lifestyle subtracted years from his playing days. Mickey ruefully admitted that drinking and poor training habits led to injuries that shortened a stellar career. Once the gift is wasted, it is gone. Duncan promised himself that he would adhere to a proper diet and training regimen to stay in professional baseball as long as he could.

By game time, Jack had stretched and loosened every muscle he had. Whirlpool time was extended to clear out residual lactic acid, and avoid any post-exercise burning sensation. It was part of his program to let his body completely relax. One of Jack's strengths at the plate was his ability to stay calm and composed. Other batters got excited and 'expanded the strike zone' by swinging at pitches that would have been called a ball. Not Jack. Things seemed to slow down for him during stress moments. There was no reason to help the opposing pitcher.

Jack played baseball using the old adage 'when your opponent is making a mistake, don't interrupt him.' But Jack changed 'don't interrupt' to 'don't help' and it worked quite well for him. His only concern was whether he still possessed the skill level that had propelled him to the top of the game.

The game proceeded without incident. The Reds pitcher, Harold "Joe" Dorsey, got a strikeout and two ground outs to complete the top half of the first inning. He also threw only ten pitches, so he hadn't been over-extended. Jack always felt that a good start required getting past the first three batters with no damage, which included his pitcher not throwing too much. The pitch count is always running. Throwing twenty or thirty pitches in the first inning makes it hard to stay in the game for the long haul.

The Giants returned the favor and held the Reds scoreless in their half of the first inning. It turned into a pitching duel, and both clubs came up empty for seven innings. The Reds had three hits, and the Giants had two. Each had stranded runners. The lineups had batted around three times, and no one appeared on track to break the game open.

When the Giants were threatening in the top half of the seventh inning, it looked like things were about to change. Joe was starting to struggle a bit, and the Giants' lead-off man got a cheap single to center field. The second batter failed to advance the runner, with an easy fly-out to right.

The next batter hit a screamer down the third base line, which would have scored the runner on first. But a spectacular grab by the Reds third baseman helped end the inning with a double play. Dorsey survived, but the announcers were speculating that he might be done for the night.

They were right. Kelly figured it was about time to throw a new variable into the mix. He ambled over to Jack.

"Dorsey's up third this inning. I figure to pull him and you'll be hitting."

Jack nodded and headed to the bat rack. He generally preferred a thirty-two ounce, thirty-four inch bat, but the supply he had ordered hadn't arrived yet. Fortunately, his choice was popular, and the team had plenty. He found one made of birch that felt nicely balanced. New birch bats were avoided, because the wood took time to harden and deliver the best punch. But this bat had been knocked around and felt great.

Jack was in the tunnel doing a few stretches when the first batter looped a ball over the shortstop's head for a clean single. Jack grabbed a batter's helmet and headed to the warm-up circle. He heard a collective intake of breath from the crowd as he exited the dugout. The TV viewers were informed immediately.

"Looks like we've seen the last of Joe Dorsey, folks," Jimmy Hyde announced. "Jack Ridley, just signed to return to the Reds, is heading out to pinch hit."

True to form, Bobby Bintner added his part.

"You've probably jinxed him, with your great buildup. He's been out of pro ball for what, five years?"

Jimmy took the bait.

"The older the violin, the sweeter the music. I'm saying Ridley will get a piece of the ball. Frank Kelly must know something positive, or he wouldn't be putting him in with a potential game winner on base."

Jack was taking practice swings when he saw the third base coach give the sign for a bunt. It made sense. A successful bunt would advance the runner on first to scoring position, and give Jack a chance to drive in a run. Of course, the Giants knew this as well as anyone, and the entire infield drew in to field the attempt.

They hoped to quickly play the ball and get the lead runner at second. With luck, they could get both the runner and the batter. The third baseman was standing about halfway to home plate when the batter dumped one down the first-base line. The pitcher had to make the play and barely made the throw to first base.

There was no play at second, and Jack found himself in familiar territory. He was coming to bat with one out and a man on second. Scoring a potentially winning run, on his first major league at-bat in five years, would be a perfect return to the game.

Then came the old announcement: 'Now batting, number nine, Jack Ridley.' A rolling cheer swept over the crowd. There were plenty of people who remembered him from before, and they were pulling for him. Jack could hear the familiar voices: "C'mon Jack!"

It was as if he had never left. There was something new, and it took a moment for Jack to focus on it. He could hear Duncan in the dugout, screaming at the top of his lungs.

"J.A., make 'em pay!"

It was an entirely new cheer, and Jack laughed in spite of the lung-crushing tension of the moment. He didn't know the umpire or the Giants' catcher, so he gave them only a polite nod as he settled into the batter's box. They had never seen a pinch-hitter enter the game with such a relaxed and smiling attitude.

Jack had been watching the opposing pitcher all night and thought he was starting to tire. There were the usual signs. His delivery had started to lower, and his fastball was imperceptibly slower. He'd had to hustle to make the play on the previous bunt attempt, and had taken his time getting back to the mound. Jack was betting that his fastball wasn't going to get any faster.

The pitcher's name was Rick Chatmon, a right-handed gangly kid who had pitched well tonight. Jack had never faced him, but had seen him on TV. He had detected that Chatmon tended to throw off-speed stuff after a successful fastball. Not every time, but enough to make it worth considering. Plus, he would know that Jack was a recent addition to the major-league roster. A pinch-hitting new player could be expected to be a little anxious. Jittery batters would be more susceptible to off-speed pitches, and Chatmon had to be thinking Jack just might be a bit antsy.

His wiry, long-armed delivery helped disguise the true nature and speed of his 'change.' Jack was betting that the first pitch would be either an inside fastball or a curve. The intention would be to drive Jack away from the plate, to set up an outside fastball. Chatmon pitched from the stretch, glancing at the runner on second. At this exact moment, Jack decided Chatmon would be throwing a curve. There was something about the way he was readjusting his grip inside his glove. If he had the fastball in mind, he'd easily have the seams in place.

Chatmon wanted to intimidate what he thought was basically a rookie. His curveball started at Jack's head, and most new players would have backed away. They'd helplessly watch the pitch dive down and left into the strike zone. Jack was ready and immediately saw that the pitch was too far inside. He was in no danger of being hit. He simply leaned back and gave the ball room to pass harmlessly in front of him. It was a good three inches off when it passed the plate, but was closer to the zone when the catcher brought the ball into his glove.

The umpire fell for the catcher's repositioning of the final location, or he wasn't going to make it easy. Either way, he called it a strike. Jack resisted the temptation to even look at the ump, choosing to concentrate on his bat's label. Jack figured that Chatmon would expect him to overreact to the bad call, and respond with aggression. He parked his fastball off the outside corner, inviting Jack to go fishing. Jack made it look like he was starting to swing hard at the pitch, but held up in time. The pitch was too far off the plate for the umpire to rob Jack a second time, and the count was 1-1.

Jack could afford to get creative. If he guessed wrong, he'd have strike two against him. Guess right and he'd have a hit with a run batted in. Smart money would say that the change was coming. The pitcher would try to make it look like he was taking a second stab at getting his fastball over the outside corner. He'd bet that a newly-arrived pinch-hitter would be overeager and aggressive. It was solid thinking. Chatmon would have been right ninety-nine percent of the time.

But not tonight. Jack was expecting Chatmon's fastball delivery, disguising the off-speed pitch. The throw appeared, for a half-second, to be a fastball headed toward the outside of the plate. But Jack knew it was going to arrive a heartbeat late, and delayed his swing ever so slightly. He timed it perfectly and lashed at the ball with vicious coiled power. He caught the ball squarely on the barrel of the bat.

The huge, unmistakable crack of a baseball meeting hardwood reverberated throughout the ball park. People leaving their seats for the restroom or concession stand stopped in their tracks. The ball arced toward the leftfield wall, and the outfielder barely moved from his position. He could see immediately that he had no chance to catch this one.

Jimmy Hyde jumped to his feet and knocked coffee all over his notes.

"Holy Mackerel!" he shouted. "That ball is headed to the upper deck! Holy, Holy Mackerel! It hit the scoreboard!"

Jack's smash had gone over the second level in left field and hit the electronic scoreboard behind the seats.

"That's a light-bustin' rocket," Jimmy howled. He'd seen balls bounce into the screen, but never one hit on a direct line.

By now, Jack was touching second as he trotted around the bases. He kept his head down, but inside he was fired up. Meeting the ball solidly was what he wanted; he hadn't planned to crush it. The ball's speed, combined with his swinging power, launched it out of the park. Jack was just happy that his return to the plate had been successful.

Jimmy Hyde and Bobby Bintner watched the Reds team meet Jack at the dugout. He'd given them a 2-0 lead with one inning to go. Rick Chatmon was able to regroup and get the Giants out of the inning. Joe Dorsey's relief, a lefty named Bill Hermann, was able to get three outs in the top of the ninth. Dorsey got the win, Hermann got the save, and Jack Ridley got the press. Every TV and radio and newspaper outlet wanted to interview Jack. He tried to deflect the attention.

"I got lucky. Chatmon threw a heck of a game. I was able to get around on one ball."

One of the reporters tried to elicit a comment about the distance the ball had traveled, but Jack wasn't gloating.

"It was just one pitch. You saw how Rick regrouped after that, which is the mark of a great pitcher."

The old-time reporters noted that vintage Jack Ridley was working his magic. He was going to make everyone look good, on both teams. The newspaper had a picture of Jack's home run swing with a caption reading 'No Ego - Just Jack.' The story referenced Jack's initial stint with the team, and speculated on whether he would remain. Jack hadn't intended any of it, but a controversy over who would be the catcher for the Reds was brewing. Duncan was ecstatic over Jack's performance.

"Man, I knew you could play, but that was a killer home run!"

Jack was circumspect about the whole thing.

"There'll be plenty of times it doesn't go out, so I wouldn't get too excited."

He wanted to keep Duncan on an even keel, and locked in on Chatmon's calm recovery.

"That's how you respond to getting hit. You'll get rocked, and you have to hit the 'reset' button and get through it."

Still, it was something to celebrate. They called Sally and she put them on speaker with Danielle. Both of them had seen the game and Danny was in a teasing mood.

"There was lots of cheering for you, mister. Do we need to keep an eye on you?"

Danielle was keeping it cool in front of her mother and brother. Jack was willing to play along.

"Yeah, you both better show up and keep me in line."

He wanted to spend some time with Danny on the strong chance he'd soon be traveling with the team or be assigned to the minor league. Jack also related what Frank Kelly had told him: There was a possibility Duncan would be soon pitching in relief.

"If it's all the same for you, show up for the next couple of games. Duncan might get an inning or two."

The boys also called Jack's mom and were happy to learn that both families would be returning to see the next two games. The coming few days held lots of promise for all of them.

47

RIDLEY TO THE RESCUE

Returning to the big leagues revived Jack's game day pattern. He resumed his usual post-game ritual, starting with a late supper. Some guys like a workout after a home game, because the routine is familiar. The equipment is topnotch, but for Jack, a heavy workout meant no food. In the old days, he opted for one big meal after a game and weightlifting in the morning. Just as he remembered the great spreads the clubhouse manager used to prepare, Jack got a nice surprise. Rick Ross, his old clubhouse buddy, was still with the team. He had an enthusiastic welcome for his returning friend.

"Jack, I can't believe you're back! I've got your favorites ready for you."

Counting his blessings that Rick was still around, Jack weighed his options. Weight rooms would always be there, but a great meal wasn't always waiting.

Big-league clubs delicately manage nutrition. They ensure a solid meal each day for the players. In addition, they have cereal and fruit available for breakfast, and various types of sandwiches for lunch. Tonight was no exception. Rick had arranged for steak and roasted chicken, accompanied by vegetables, salmon with rice. There were also plenty of salad choices. To complete Jack's welcome, Rick added ice cream to the menu, with an assortment of syrup flavors.

To celebrate his spectacular pinch-hit, Jack decided to indulge in steak, veggies and salad. He figured he'd earned vanilla ice cream, slathered in chocolate syrup. The chocolate reminded him of Little Suzy, and their 'chocolate collision' a couple of weeks ago.

After stuffing his face, Jack liked a marathon shower - the hotter, the better. Hot water is perfect for the circulation tired muscles need. Some games get you all juiced up, and you need time to settle down. Adrenaline might keep you awake after a night game, until one or two in the morning. The combination of food and a shower usually helped Jack doze off. That's how he worked it after playing the Giants. He was amped after his home run secured the win, although he did a good job disguising it.

The routine helped. He was in bed by one and a hibernating bear could not have done better. The deeper the sleep, the fewer the dreams. When Jack's body was settled, his subconscious mind didn't bother him with past troubles. During the bad old days, he'd dream about the car crash and wake up agitated. But things were on the mend now, and everything was peaking at the right time.

After the game, Kelly had some manager's guidance.

"Do what you need to get Duncan squared away. The timing might be right, and everybody is interested in the new kid. If it works out, we might call him out of the bullpen for an out or two. Maybe an inning, if he's up to it."

Jack was quick to concur.

"Sure thing, Skipper. I'll give him a light prep and you let me know if he's coming in."

Jack went out on a limb and left a message for Danny. He alerted her to the chance Duncan could see game action. The manager's words were still on Jack's mind when he woke up around ten-thirty.

Duncan was already awake, playing one of those games that seem to make video addicts out of the kids. Jack climbed out of bed and headed to the bathroom, while croaking recognition at his roommate. The kid returned the greeting by briefly lifting the game controller in Jack's direction. His eyes never left the screen, and his fingers didn't pause as he pounded away at the keys.

"Let's wrap up here and get some breakfast," Jack said. "We have some planning to do."

He wanted to ease Duncan into the notion that 'sooner or later' might be this week. Facing a few batters was a possibility. Overemphasis had to be avoided. There was a chance that Duncan would freeze up the first time he realized he was up against big-league hitters. After all, a few months ago he was messing around with a high school team, with no idea that professional baseball might take an interest in him.

Coming into a game as a relief pitcher meant that Duncan was literally going to be thrown to the lions. These lions might not eat him, but they sure could chew him up and spit him all the way back to the farm. Jack jumped in the shower and thought about a plan to keep Duncan relaxed and effective. Hot water got his brain going and he ran through various strategies. He toweled off and threw on some jeans and a t-shirt.

"Let's see if the hotel restaurant has eggs the way I like 'em."

He figured he could use breakfast time to slowly bring Duncan to the finer realities of major-league pitching. Jack planned to play it like a magician, distracting his subject with one hand while he managed the trick with the other. The maître d'hôtel saw them approaching and exclaimed "Great homer, Jack!" He received a smile and a thumbs-up in return. It was a teachable moment for Duncan.

"You'll have people pop up all the time like this when you're playing. But they aren't all friendly, depending on winning or losing."

Duncan nodded. He had learned to pay quiet attention when Jack was talking. Duncan's thoughtful and calm responses appeared purposeful and controlled. Jack knew that this habit would serve his rookie well in the contests to come. If you're calm and collected on the mound, it doesn't matter if you're about to have an internal break-down. The batter sees only what you allow him to see.

Jack had read somewhere that ordering the same menu item as your dinner companion is a subconscious way of getting on the same wave length. Salespeople do it all the time. So when Duncan ordered an omelet, Jack asked for the same thing. It allowed him an opening remark.

"We're thinking alike. Next, you're going to want to ask me about girls."

Duncan remained silent, but Jack saw a suggestion of a smile. He couldn't tell where Duncan was going with the thought. Before long, breakfast arrived and they both dug in. When they reached for the syrup at the same time, Duncan laughed.

"We're on the same track, alright. Comes from thinking about how to pitch in certain situations."

Jack saw his chance to go to work.

"That's exactly right. When the pitcher and catcher both under-stand how to approach individual batters, it's that much easier."

Explaining how some pitchers get jumpy when a guy gets a hit, or walking a guy, was a place to start. Jack wanted Duncan to see those occasions as an opportunity, not an obstacle. The youngster got the point.

"You can't get a double play unless there's somebody on base," he said. Jack grinned his approval.

"Exactly! If somebody gets on, that's when you get even calmer. Don't be the guy who gets flustered because somebody got on base. You just pick the guy off the bag, or get two from the next guy."

Jack spent the rest of the meal stressing that returning to the basics was the way to work out of a jam. He explained that the batters Duncan would be facing were there for one reason.

"They're professionals. Even the worst hitter on the team can take you out, if they get the right pitch. Believe me, Cake, over the course of a season, it's going to happen. You might be able to handle the top six or seven batters in the lineup, and along comes number eight. You'll struggle to get him out."

Duncan was silently absorbing the lesson. Jack wanted the kid's confidence in his abilities to be unshakable, even after he got rocked with a homer.

"One bad pitch will get knocked out of the park. It ain't the end of the world. You keep making your pitches and you'll get outs. It's a statistical probability."

Duncan wanted to accept the concept, but he voiced his concerns.

"It's kind of unreal, pitching to these guys. I guess I can do it, but it's still hard to believe."

Jack wanted to intercept any negative thinking immediately.

"If you go into it thinking you can't, you'll be right. A lot depends on what you believe you can do. Name any Hall of Fame pitcher. The best they did was winning two out of three games. If you look at it that way, they failed every third time!"

Jack liked the competitive look on Duncan's face.

"Because there's *real* hitters over there!"

"And you're a *real* pitcher! Not a complete one yet, but you're gonna get there. And you don't have to be perfect. Look at Sandy Koufax. He *never* pitched as fast as you can, but he's one of the greatest of all time. Because if he lost a game, that didn't keep him from winning the next two. And that's gonna be you, Babycakes."

Duncan grinned, and Jack felt like he had him headed in the right direction.

"You know they're gonna put you in a game one of these days, right?"

Duncan nodded, only slightly apprehensive. That was Jack's cue for a bit of confidence-building.

"Nothing to worry about. That's why I'm here. It'll be just like home. We'll take it one pitch at a time, and we'll put it where they can't hit it. And if somebody smacks one, we'll get the next guy."

Breakfast ended. Jack signed the check and they headed back to the room. He saw he'd left his phone on the bed, and text messages were waiting.

"Look, Cake, your mom and Danny are coming to see the next couple of games. They might get a chance to see you in action."

Duncan looked like he was trying to decipher a secret message.

"I sure hope I don't screw it up in front of them."

Jack saw his chance to put another spin on what was to come.

"Doesn't matter to them. They're happy to see you sitting on the tractor. Or, falling off the dang thing."

That got a chuckle going. Jack saw that having Duncan on an even keel, where his mother and sister were concerned, would keep him mentally on track. Letting side issues creep in would be a distraction.

"Somebody might hit a pitch or two. It happens," Jack continued. "It'd be nice for your mom and Danny to see you burn through an inning. It might be this week; it might be down the road. But them showing up ain't part of it right now. You just do what you do. I guarantee you'll like what happens."

They had an hour or two to rest, so Jack let the peaceful morning soak in while they watched an Andrew Chaikin space documentary on TV. Baseball could wait, but there was one truism lurking. Just like the space travel pioneers, Duncan was eventually going to have to dig himself out of a jam. His mental state was going to have to make the difference.

Their reverie was short-lived, and around two o'clock they headed out the door. Jack circled back to game thoughts.

"You know, there's one thing you've got going for you. We haven't really touched on that."

The strategy was working, because Duncan was in a playful mood.

"Besides good looks and charm, you mean?"

Jack had a 'keep it up, rookie' glance for him, so Duncan doubled down.

"I can't see how that helps a fastball, but you would know."

Jack gave his best patient smile.

"Good one. And being a bit of a wiseguy can help. But I'm talking about your teammates. You're going to be surrounded by some of the best ballplayers on the planet. They will take up the slack. I've seen outfielders climb the wall and turn a home run into a spectacular out. An infielder is going to grab what should have been a double and get you an out at first."

Duncan nodded his understanding of this baseball reality.

"What I mean is, you don't have to be perfect," Jack said. "They will get the bat on the ball plenty. That just means the ball's in play."

The reasoning was sinking in. Duncan's thoughtful look said so. Jack finished the lesson.

"No need to start thinking you're out there alone. You'll love the help you're gonna get."

They had reached the ballpark and entered the clubhouse. Other players were in various stages of preparation. A few of the pitchers had a poker game going and stopped to give Jack a welcome. There's nothing like a clutch hit to make a guy popular.

The pitcher scheduled to start was named Steve Patrick. An unknown quantity, he had arrived during Jack's absence. He threw in his cards to leave the game. Taking Jack to one side for a chat was more important. He was upbeat and friendly from the get-go.

"I saw you here when I was in college and loved your game," he said. "It's great that we get to play together."

Jack appreciated the support, but told Steve he doubted they'd see action.

"They're probably going to be sending me down soon. I'd like to get in a game with you, but I don't think I'll be around that long."

He was grateful for the kind words from the pitcher. There was brief small talk about family and background, and Jack decided that he liked the guy. He couldn't tell, but Steve seemed slightly older. That made sense, if he played four years of college ball before playing professionally. Jack was about to politely let Steve return to his card game, when Mike Franz ambled their way.

"You guys get the news on Aaron Holden?"

Jack knew that Holden was the Reds' regular catcher, but hadn't heard anything about him. Steve Patrick spoke first.

"I was over here talking to Jack, and was just about to see what he knew."

He glanced at Mike for more information. Franz had a dour look on his face.

"Is Aaron going to be able to go?" Steve asked.

Jack had no idea what they were discussing. Mike Franz shook his head and grimaced at both of them.

"We haven't made an announcement yet," Mike said. "Holden has some kind of bug or food poisoning. He's been puking all morning. The doc gave him something to settle him down but he's gonna need a miracle. We have to change plans."

Mike looked at Steve and jerked his head toward Jack.

"You get a chance to talk this over?" Steve shrugged while shaking his head.

"About to get to it when you showed up."

Jack was completely lost. It felt like chemistry class, and he couldn't catch up. Steve took the reins.

"If Holden can't go, we need another catcher. I haven't worked with Pete Spikes, who's backing him up."

He looked at Jack with raised eyebrows.

"Haven't worked with you either, so it's two unknowns."

It was Mike's turn to speak up, and his gaze at Jack was telling.

"I'm thinking that you might be a better choice, Jack. Nothing about Pete; he's a solid player. But he's been struggling lately and you're hitting right now. I already know you can handle it behind the plate."

Jack had to conceal his surprise.

"You want me to jump in the lineup and catch Steve instead of using Spikes."

He said it as a statement to mask his concern.

"Is Kelly okay with that? I mean, I just got here."

Mike nodded somberly. He was assessing whether Jack would rise to the occasion. Jack was trying to give Steve Patrick a graceful way of opting out of this crazy idea. Patrick had other plans.

"I know you're just returning, Jack," he said. "But you can flat-out play. I've already told Kelly I think your bat is stronger right now."

He paused for one second, to add the kicker.

"One more thing. Spikes told me he isn't feeling too good himself. If it's because of some bad food, it's all from the same joint last night. He's voting for you, as well."

Jack could see that the deal was already in motion. He shrugged, and gave Mike and Steve his most encouraging grin.

"Fine with me. I've been there before, right?"

He looked at Steve Patrick.

"I guess we'll be getting loose together."

Steve clapped him on the back.

"Don't take this the wrong way, Jack. It's a break you're here. It'll be a blast playing together."

Jack got down to business.

"Okay, we'll get warmed up and get our signals straight."

Jack admitted to himself that he was having a small jolt of butterflies. In about six hours he would be a starting catcher in the major leagues, once again.

———

The stretching and loosening rituals were complete. Jack had corralled Duncan during batting practice, and told him about the switch in the lineup. That got Duncan pumped.

"Holy cow, they're gonna put you in! This is so cool, and you said your mom is coming."

Jack tried to bring it back into perspective.

"It's your mom, too. With Danny and Ashley. Don't forget about tickets for them. I'm going to be busy."

He paused and had another item for Duncan.

"Remember, they're coming because they figured there's a chance they get to see you get in a game. And they still might."

Duncan gave Jack a quizzical look.

"You're thinking Steve Patrick will need relief?"

Duncan seemed unconvinced. Jack rolled out his analysis.

"It isn't likely he'll go the distance. If he's got a no-hitter going, he might stay in. But lots of things can happen. He might wear down and they get a couple of guys on. In that situation, Kelly goes to the 'pen.' It could be you."

Jack was saying that, if needed, a relief pitcher would finish the game. In the modern game, that's what usually happens. He wanted Duncan to be in the right frame of mind, if he got the call.

"I'm not sure what the bullpen strengths are right now. If Kelly thinks you can match up with a batter, he might put you in for that one guy. If you get outs, you might stay for the whole inning. You just need to be ready."

Duncan nodded and kept quiet. Jack took it as a good sign. The kid was getting his game face on. But if the manager brought Duncan into the game, he'd have to be ready. There wouldn't be time for any cheerleading. Relief pitchers spend the game in the bullpen, away from the team's bench. In other words, Jack had a message for his Project: His main support would not be close by to help him.

"When the game starts, I'll be behind the plate and you'll be in the pen. The next time I see you, if you pitch, will be on the mound. In front of God and everybody. There won't be a lot of talk. We'll probably be in some sort of jam, and they will be asking you to dig them out of it."

Duncan got the point.

"I'll be warmed up and ready to go. Don't you worry."

"The bullpen coach will get a call for you to get ready," Jack advised. "You get heated up with the bullpen catcher. If it's the middle of the inning, Kelly will be on the mound 'cause he just took Steve out. I'll be there when he hands you the ball. That's the keys to the big leagues, Cake."

Jack thought that parents must feel this way when they send their kids off to school, or to start a new job.

"Maybe it'll be the start of the inning, so then it'll be just me. Either way, you show up and do your thing. Everything will be fine."

Out in the ball park, things were under way. The home team vacated the field to give the Giants their warm-up time. The club-house was loose. Everybody felt good about last night's win, including Jack's part in it. Word got around that he was catching, so the players came with encouraging words.

He fell back on the old routine. The warm-up jersey and pants were discarded, and Jack took a shower before getting into a clean uniform. He'd always preferred the home whites. For some odd reason, they made him feel like a real ballplayer.

All players have their own pre-game rituals. Card games might get a second look; some players have their headphones pumping out favorite music; others get a bite to eat while a few just rest or read fan mail at their cubicle. For all of them, today was just another game. But for Jack and Duncan, it was shaping up to what would define the rest of their days.

Jack kept talk with Duncan low-key. Motivation wasn't an issue because the rookie was excited. His usual quiet demeanor remained about the same, but Duncan *was* nervous. Jack would have been concerned if he wasn't a bit skittish. Ballplayers experience the pre-game anxiety spectrum, from stone-faced nonchalance to nausea. Jack knew it was best that his novice stayed somewhere in the middle.

They spent the half-hour before game time reminiscing about painting the barn and other farm details. Jack thought the overall feeling was about right, and then it was time to head to the field. Half of the stadium seats had warm bodies in them, and more were trickling in. A Tuesday night game wouldn't be a sell-out, but Jack figured a crowd of around twenty-five or thirty thousand would witness whatever happened tonight.

If Duncan launched a successful career, there would be plenty of fans who claimed they were on hand. When someone becomes a star, many people say they saw his first game - more fans than the stadium holds. Jack hoped that plenty of baseball fans would someday be telling their kids that they had witnessed Duncan's arrival in the Show. It would mean that he succeeded.

It was time for Duncan to join the gang of relievers in the bullpen, where Steve Patrick was heating up. Jack grabbed Bill Hermann, who had pitched in relief the day before.

"Keep an eye on my boy, would you?" he asked. "Kelly might bring him in before this thing is over. Make sure he gets warmed up right, okay?"

Bill Hermann wasn't clued in on Jack's history with the team, but he knew from last night's performance that Jack was a player who deserved support. He was happy to help Jack help the team by helping Duncan. Plus, his job was supposed to be team play.

"Sure, Jack, no problem," Bill said. "I'll keep his head in the game. He'll be ready if they call."

Giving Jack a hard time was too easy for him to resist. "You're the one I'm worried about. It's been a while since you've been behind the plate, buddy. You sure you know where to stand?"

The ribbing made Jack feel right at home.

"I can probably save the passed balls for when you're throwing," he lobbed back. "If my walker doesn't get in the way."

Jack watched Duncan and Bill walk to the outfield bullpen and had the 'first day of school' feeling again. It was as if he were sending his child off to face the world, except this was a world where hitters could send a ninety-five mile an hour fastball into next week. Jack had to comfort himself with the knowledge that he had done all he could for Duncan. The hard part was yet to come, and Duncan was going to have to handle that mostly on his own.

The umpire and both team managers were already meeting at home plate, to exchange lineups. A baseball ritual Jack really liked was about to begin. Teams invite local military units, American Legion Posts, or VFW members to present the colors for the anthem. Jack had not been in the military, but his father and grandfather were veterans. He had ultimate respect for those who had served, and allowed him to play a game.

Jack made it a point, no matter where he was playing, to meet with the service members in the color guard. When he was a rookie, he had seen a veteran player named Micah Hofner go over to some soldiers and introduce himself. Micah had acted as if the soldiers were his heroes and he was the fan. Jack asked him what he was up to, and got an answer he never forgot.

"Kid," Micah said, "each one of those soldiers was willing to fight for this country. They had friends who didn't come home from doing just that. Fans want our autographs, when they should be asking for the soldiers'. If I can't respect what they've done, I shouldn't be here."

From then on, Jack always visited the color guard and told them he was honored to be there with them. He asked their names and their hometown, and it tickled him when one of them would tell him how they admired him as a ballplayer.

"It's the other way around," he'd say, and get their autograph instead. No color guard member who talked to Jack Ridley ever forgot the encounter.

The home team took the field and Jack paid his respects to the flag-bearers. The Reds stood at their positions for the anthem while the Giants lined up by their dugout. The music faded, and Steve Patrick threw his warm-up pitches. After the eighth pitch, Jack fired the ball to second base; the umpire yelled "Play ball!" The reborn catcher readied himself for the first batter, simultaneously reclaiming his past and his future.

Jimmy Hyde and Bobby Bintner were calling the game for the TV audience, and Jimmy keyed in on Jack's appearance behind the plate during warm-ups. Jimmy clued in his viewers immediately.

"Folks, our old friend Jack Ridley is making his first appearance behind the plate in five years. After putting up some impressive numbers as a rookie, he left the team under a cloud that was never fully explained. To my knowledge, he hasn't played professionally since then."

Bobby Bintner wasn't going to be left out. He thought the road to broadcast notoriety was through bombastic commentary. It had worked for Howard Cosell. That was good enough for him.

"We're about to see what Ridley has left and if he can still compete at this level," Bintner chirped. "Frank Kelly is known for taking chances as a major league manager. But this maneuver might require some explanation when the game is over."

At that moment, Jack was reacquainting himself with his old position.

"Seems like old times," he grinned at the umpire. Then he checked for the pitch call from the dugout.

Jack was grateful that Mike Franz was doing the thinking today. Jack didn't know anything about the opposing team. Mike signaled for an inside fastball to start against the first Giants batter, and Jack relayed the call to Steve Patrick. Leading off for the Giants was their shortstop, a speedy kid named Felipe Diaz. He threw off waves of energy as he stepped into the batter's box. He'd be a tough out all night.

The Reds' third baseman was a relative newcomer named Scott King. Strong-armed throws to first were what got him to the big leagues. Any ball he snagged would be a sure out. As Steve Patrick was unloading his fastball, Jack realized that King was opting for a deep position at third base. He was back in the grass.

A lightning thought flashed through Jack's mind. A bunt down the third base line would never be fielded in time. Almost on cue, Diaz squared to bunt. Jack had already started coming out of his crouch to chase the ball. The pitch was on top of Diaz before he got in position, and was tipped barely outside the baseline toward first base.

Diaz had intended to dump the ball in the grass and his speed would have easily placed him on first. Instead, the ball floated in a tight arc about head height. Normally, it would have fallen harmlessly as a foul, but Jack was moving before contact. He dove and caught the ball at the last possible second. With one pitch, the Reds had their first out, because Jack had made a spectacular heads-up play. The crowd loved it, and so did Jack's teammates. They fired the ball around the infield with an intensity that told Jack they had come to play. There were twenty-six outs to go.

After the gift of a one-pitch first out, Steve Patrick methodically retired the next two Giants on ground-outs. To face the Reds in the bottom of the first inning, the Giants had a young fireballer on the mound named Miguel Izquierdo, nicknamed 'Izzy.' Jack intended to watch him closely to prepare for his own at-bat.

Kelly had put Jack in the sixth batting spot, so there was time for Jack to go to school on Izquierdo's pitches. True to his name, Izzy was a lefty with a terrific record against left-handed batters. Generally, batters perform better against opposite-handed pitchers, which was one reason Kelly was comfortable with Jack batting. The Reds line-up had five righties tonight, and one switch-hitter. They had a numerical advantage, at least on paper.

First up for the Reds were three right-handed batters, so Jack got a good look at how Izzy planned to pitch. His fastball was decent; he used it to set up his movement pitches. The curve started away from a righty batter, and dove down and in. Izzy's changeup was deceptive. It seemed to slow right at the plate, and simply fall to the bottom of the strike zone.

Predictably, the first three Reds batters set the tone for the night. The first struck out swinging; the second blooped the ball to the shortstop; the third was caught looking at a curve. The game was going to belong to the pitcher who could keep opposing batters off-balance.

In their half of the second inning, the Giants hitters fared no better. Steve Patrick was able to work the corners, and all three batters went down in order. Jack hoped for a workmanlike outing for Steve. In order for that to happen, he needed to keep the pitch count at a reasonable number.

The bottom of the second showed a pattern for the Reds, when the two batters ahead of Jack grounded out. Izzy was getting movement on the ball, which made it difficult to get solid contact. Down two outs, Jack came to the plate thinking long-game strategy. A hit right now was less important than game planning. The Giants would certainly remember yesterday's homer, and Jack wanted to convey an aggressive attitude. Maybe Izzy would adopt a pattern that would be useful later on.

Hoping that Izzy would misinterpret his demeanor, Jack's warm-up swings were wild and threatening. It appeared he was swinging for the fences, and Izzy tried to take advantage with off-speed pitches. Jack made sure his tactic worked, by repeatedly swinging early.

No one knew it, but striking out was part of Jack's plan. Swinging early on every pitch, Jack appeared to stab at the ball with no strategy. He even trudged to the dugout looking as dejected as he could. Jack was going to face Izzy in exactly eight outs. He wanted the Giants pitcher to think that the new guy playing for Reds was one-dimensional.

The game proceeded as an even duel between Patrick and Izzy. Occasional batters reached first base, or even second, but neither team could produce a timely hit to bring the runner around to score. There were signs that Steve was beginning to tire. His fastball was beginning to tail off, and his ball movement began to flatten out. Sooner or later, Steve was going to get into a jam that he couldn't fix.

At mid-game, there had been no scoring. Jack's second at-bat in the fourth inning was a repeat of his first. Izzy was relying almost entirely on fastballs to retire him. Jack was ready to spring his trap the next time he came to the plate, which would be about the sixth or seventh inning.

While the Reds were batting in the bottom of the fifth inning, Jack noticed that Steve had an odd look on his face. Thinking his pitcher might be having arm problems, Jack eased a little closer on the bench.

"You look a little rough, buddy."

Up close, Steve appeared distressed.

"Your arm giving you trouble?"

The pitcher was sipping on one of the lime-infused water bottles the trainer prepared.

"It's not my arm, although it feels a bit tired," Steve said.

He looked around to see who might be within earshot.

"My stomach's starting to feel queasy. I wonder if I got the same bug that Aaron did."

Steve put both hands on his midsection and gave a small groan.

"This ain't good. But I didn't eat what Holden did."

Alarm bells started going off in Jack's head.

"You were at the same restaurant with Holden?"

Steve had a helpless look on his face when he answered.

"Well, sure, we always get together before I pitch. He had some fish thing and I had a steak."

Jack struggled to keep his voice down.

"At the same table?"

When Steve nodded, Jack nearly choked.

Jack was sure he heard odd rumbling coming from Steve's general direction. While Steve headed down the tunnel to the restroom, Jack went to find Kelly. The veteran catcher came right to the point.

"You need to get your relievers ready. In about twenty minutes Steve's going to be puking all over the mound!"

Kelly didn't respond as he reached for the bullpen phone. Jack heard him telling Mike Franz to get the left-handed Herman ready to go. As usual, Jack was thinking ahead.

"Skipper, the three batters due up are righties. Then there're two lefties and I don't know what pinch hitters they've got."

Jack paused to sort it out.

"You need to decide if Steve can get past the first three. That'll get us to the bottom of the seventh, if it works, and then you can bring in Bill for the lefties."

Kelly was thinking it over. It would allow him to avoid going into his bullpen too deeply, if it worked. The second Reds batter had just popped out for out number two. The decision needed to be made quickly. Patrick was out of the tunnel and Kelly wasted no time.

"Jack says you're sick."

It was a question and a demand.

"I'm starting to feel queasy," Steve answered. "But I'll be okay for a while. I can get another inning."

Kelly looked at Jack for some kind of confirmation, and Jack closed the loop.

"You get Bill ready for the lefties," he said to Kelly. "I'll keep an eye on Steve and try to get us through the bottom of the sixth. Then bring Bill in for the seventh, and you decide if he stays or you want Duncan or some other right-hander to handle the rest."

At that moment the third Reds batter grounded out to short, and Jack headed out to the field. He grabbed Steve by the shoulder.

"C'mon, dude, let's make this fast."

Jack was convinced his pitcher wouldn't last past the third batter - fourth batter, tops. They hustled through quick warm-up pitches and Jack rifled the ball down to second base.

'So far, so good,' Jack hoped. This was something new.

For this inning, Steve was on a very short pitch count, and an even shorter 'batter count.' The top of the Giants batting order was up again, with Felipe Diaz leading the trio of right-handers. Jack had correctly assessed Diaz as a contact hitter, which made him a good lead-off batter. The bench called for a cutter heading toward the outside of the plate, and Steve delivered.

The good news was Diaz swung at the first pitch, but the bad news was he connected and pushed a little floater into right field. Another batter on base would guarantee the end of this inning for Steve Patrick, Jack had no doubt.

The second batter up was the Giants' right fielder, Brian Ivey. He was playing more for the strength of his arm than his batting prowess. The scouting report said that Ivey had trouble with pitches high in the strike zone. He tended to chop down on them, and that resulted in ground balls. The bench wanted high fastballs so Ivey would either miss or top the ball into a double play. Steve wasn't wasting any time. Jack knew he wanted the inning to be over, one way or another. He called out, mainly so Ivey would hear him.

"Nice and easy, Steve. Brian likes curves."

Ivey glanced at Jack, trying to figure out what he was trying to pull. Steve's first pitch was as good as it was going to get, tight at the top of the zone. For an eye-blink Jack was afraid the ump wouldn't give him the strike, but his right arm shot out to signal strike one. Jack was muttering, as if to himself.

"Supposed to curve."

Ivey had Jack in his peripheral vision, and Jack wanted him to see what happened next.

"C'mon, Steve," Jack called out, louder this time.

He simultaneously made a bouncing motion with his glove, low and inside. He hoped Ivey would see the location and fall for the misdirection. But low and inside wasn't where the ball was headed, because Jack simultaneously signaled for a repeat of the first pitch. Steve was quickly into his windup and the ball came sailing into the top of the strike zone. Ivey couldn't resist, and chopped at the ball.

It bounced twice on its way to the Reds' shortstop, Rico Rivera. He vacuumed it up and rammed it to the second baseman, Freddy Stout. Freddy neatly dragged his foot on the bag, to force Diaz at second. In the same motion, he fired the ball to Hank Stafford, the Reds' veteran first baseman. Ivey was out, completing the double play. Smiling to himself, Jack relayed the pitch call to Steve, who by now was staying as motionless as possible. He had only one batter left in his tank, Jack was certain.

Batting third for the Giants was their catcher, a quarrelsome character named Gardiner. To Jack's thinking, Gardiner's antics had worn out his welcome. He wasn't overtly confrontational, which would get him thrown out of the game, but he tended to yap about calls. Such behavior would eventually lose you a close one or two. Jack had to take advantage where he could, under the circumstances. He began with a comment to the umpire, which was really intended for Gardiner.

"We'll keep it in the middle, Blue. Don't want to upset anybody."

Jack knew the batter got the point, because he glanced back at the ump. There was a chance Jack's foolery would disrupt his timing. Calling for a curve, Jack hoped he had riled the guy into an early swing. Gardiner missed the curve completely, for strike one.

Jack prayed for two more quick strikes, because Steve Patrick was looking green and pale at the same time. Deciding that the batter was still fuming, Jack called for a changeup. Steve overcame his malady well enough to float it in, dead center. Gardiner was way ahead of the pitch and tried to slow his swing.

He got under the ball for his trouble, and popped up sky-high to Rico Rivera at shortstop. Jack didn't watch the ball. Instead, he watched Steve. What he saw made him burst out laughing. The pitcher didn't wait for the ball to reach the top of its arc. He bolted as the ball was rising. Rivera made the catch, and the whole team wondered what was happening to Steve. He was off the field, almost in the dugout when Rivera caught the ball.

Mercifully, the TV cameras didn't get a view down the tunnel to the clubhouse. Steve had made it as far as a large cooler the trainers kept full of ice. The cooler would see no game action because Steve was barfing in it. He had the tunnel all to himself; even the worst practical jokers on the team wanted no part of the event. Every last one of the players in the dugout busied themselves elsewhere.

Steve Patrick was through for the night, having pitched six innings of shutout ball with only one throw-up. Even Jimmy Hyde and Bobby Bintner were discreet about Steve's departure, and no one was the wiser.

The last third of the Reds batting order was due up in the bottom of the sixth inning. Kelly had his choice of pinch hitters to replace Patrick. Izzy was still on the mound for the Giants, but he was running out of gas. The Reds had a chance to jump on him before he was replaced.

Batter number seven was Scott King, the third baseman. He took an outside fastball for ball one, and calmly waited for Izzy to get one over the plate. Scott guessed that Izzy would try to sneak a curveball by him. It didn't have the snap of Izzy's earlier pitches, and Scott lashed it to short left field.

Kelly played it safe with a man on first and ordered a bunt, to advance Scott to scoring position. Freddy Stout, the Reds' second baseman was up, and he dropped a perfect bunt down the third base line. Freddy nearly beat the throw to first, but King was safely on second, looking like he owned the place.

For batter number three in Steve Patrick's spot, Kelly had elected James 'Jay' Brown, or 'J.J.' to pinch hit. J.J. platooned in the outfield, but his strength was clutch hitting. He also had the advantage of having watched Izzy all night, while he himself was an unknown quantity.

It didn't take long. J.J. fouled off the first pitch, a fastball. Izzy must have figured he'd have success with a second heater, but J.J. was expecting just that. He hammered the ball to deep right center, and it nearly went out. Brian Ivey came close to a circus catch by climbing the wall, but the ball ricocheted toward the center fielder.

J.J. got an RBI double and Scott King scored the go-ahead run. The Giants bullpen was immediately in action, but Izzy was able to get a grounder for out number two from Rico Rivera, at the top of the Reds' lineup. The Reds left J.J. on second when the next batter popped out. The Giants had escaped, only one run down. Jack figured that Izzy was done for the night and his grand design for batting against the left-hander was wasted.

Hoping to mask his intentions, Kelly had waited until the top of the seventh inning to reveal his relief pitcher. He called Bill Hermann in from the bullpen, and the Giants opted to keep their left-handed batters in the game, which Jack expected. It was a bit early to make big changes. Bill could usually be called on to secure three outs, and he didn't disappoint.

He repeated the previous night's performance by getting a quick strikeout, a ground out to Rivera at short, and another strikeout to end the inning. The Reds were batting in the bottom of the seventh, and were six outs away from a win. Jack headed to the dugout to map out the remaining part of the game with Kelly.

The Reds' fourth through sixth batters were next, including Jack. The others were usually good hitters, and they were all due. Mildly surprised that Izzy was returning to the mound, Kelly considered his defensive options for the next two innings. The Giants' right-handed batters Jack had mentioned were coming up. Hermann was done. He'd worked two days in a row. Kelly had called for a second right-hander to warm up, a fellow named Marvin Lowe, along with Duncan.

With only a one-run lead, which pitcher to use was a huge decision. Kelly wanted choices. He decided to wait to see how his batters did for now, in the seventh. He was not inclined to bring in an untried rookie with such little breathing room. The front office had hyped Duncan pretty well, but calling on an unknown kid was a big gamble. It would make for great press, but press wouldn't do him any good if the decision went off the rails.

Hank Stafford, the first baseman, was batting fourth. He was already in the batter's box. Izzy was on the mound and ready to go. Hank was a first pitch fastball hitter, and Izzy made the mistake of leaving one in the middle of the plate. Hank ripped the ball right past Izzy's head for a clean single.

Kelly repeated his earlier tactic and called for a bunt. The Reds' leftfielder, Richie Rodríguez, would have preferred to swing away. But he followed orders and bunted Stafford to second. Jack watched it all from the warm-up circle, and quietly congratulated himself for the trap he was about to spring. It occurred to him that the Giants might have delayed pulling Izzy because Jack was batting next. Perhaps they had fallen for the deception; they were betting Jack was outmatched and was a guaranteed out. Mrs. Ridley's son planned to show them otherwise.

Calming himself was easy. Jack knew he had the upper hand. His intent was to swing wildly at whatever Izzy threw first. That would further convince Izzy that Jack was out of his depth. Just as he had done previously, Izzy threw a fastball and Jack swung noticeably late. The announcers saw their chance to say something provocative and insightful.

"It's beginning to look like Frank Kelly has reached too far this time," Bobby Bintner said. "He's got a player who seems to be able to handle catching duties, but is past his prime as a batter. He wasn't even close on that last pitch."

Jimmy Hyde was slightly more generous.

"Ridley did launch one yesterday against Rick Chatmon, but he seems to be struggling with the fastball tonight. He's playing catch-up right now."

Of course, Jack heard none of the criticism. Focusing on Izzy's every move consumed him. Only a changeup would alter his plan, and Jack knew he had Izzy thinking his fastball would net a strikeout. The next throw was on the way, and Jack could tell from the spin he had the pitch he wanted. He delivered the same swing that had caught Gordie Bowen's attention.

The ball rocketed off his bat on a majestic arc over the left field fence and Jack had his second homerun in two games. Hank Stafford stood at home plate to congratulate him. At the same time, the Giants manager was headed to the mound to call it a day for Izzy. Jack hurried to get with Kelly to determine whether Duncan would be pitching.

"Tell me what Marvin can do," he began. "I'm confident Duncan can get us an inning, so you decide which one to use."

Izzy's replacement had rolled through his allowed eight warm-up pitches. Scott King was ready to bat. Kelly was ambivalent.

"If we get more runs I'd put the kid in. If they score a couple on him, I could still bring in Lowe. I'd rather keep Marvin fresh."

Kelly was thinking out loud and Jack tried to help him along.

"I can't promise, but if Duncan is on his stuff, you'll be glad you put him in. But, if they get a couple of runs, Marvin is still good insurance."

Kelly's mood brightened when King singled off the new Giants pitcher. Jack had more strategy to offer.

"Whoever you put in, use our last batter's spot this inning. That way, there's little chance he'd be batting."

Kelly liked the reasoning, but grimaced when Freddy Stout hit into a double play to end the inning. The manager considered his options and listened to his inner gambler. Baseball strategy is supposed to be fun. Kelly looked at Jack for a long moment. The manager had an odd expression on his face. It was part dare and part affinity. Then he swatted Jack on the back, and invited the baseball gods to smile.

"Let's roll the dice."

Kelly grabbed the bullpen phone and uttered three words that would change Duncan's life.

"Send in James."

Sally James' little boy was going to pitch in a Major League Baseball game for the Cincinnati Reds.

48

A WALK ON THE WILD SIDE

rupting from his seat behind the microphone, Bobby Bintner was nearly apoplectic. He wanted the viewers to know he was the smartest guy watching events unfold. Duncan James was jogging in from the bullpen to the pitcher's mound, where Jack was headed to meet him. Bintner gave full voice to his inner critic.

"Holy Mackerel in Never-Never Land, I can't believe what I'm seeing!" He glanced at his game notes to get his details correct.

"Frank Kelly has been walking on the edge of reality all night, and now he's jumping into Crazy Town!"

Jimmy Hyde let him go on, if only for entertainment value.

"You are seeing something that may never happen again, folks. The manager of the oldest professional franchise in major league baseball history is bringing in an untried nineteen-year old kid to pitch against the Giants! This is unbelievable."

Bintner had more.

"This youngster has never thrown a pitch in professional base-ball, at any level!"

Jimmy Hyde thought he'd temper the analysis with a kinder, gentler approach.

"It gets more interesting, Bobby," he said. "Young Duncan James never played in college, either. A real feel-good story is unfolding right here. His father passed away right before he graduated from high school. He didn't go to college so he could stay home and help with the family farm. Jack Ridley, who was out of baseball, discovered him and got the Reds interested. They signed him for a reason, and we're about to see why."

Bobby Bintner preferred his 'shock and awe' approach.

"It's not more interesting, Jimmy, it's worse," he crowed. "The kid didn't even pitch in high school, according to my sources. We could be seeing the ultimate train wreck, right here and now."

Jimmy Hyde remembered that he was employed by the Reds, so he attempted to inject something positive for the fans.

"Or maybe we're seeing the start of a stellar career. Never pitching before getting to the big leagues isn't a disqualifier. Ask Trevor Hoffman. His stats are pretty outstanding."

Bintner had Hoffman's career to think about as Jack walked to the mound to meet Duncan. As Duncan approached, an intriguing thing happened. Kelly left the dugout and joined Jack. During an inning, if a pitcher is to be removed, the manager comes out to retrieve the ball from the departing pitcher. He subsequently hands it to the reliever. Because this was the start of the inning, there was no pitcher to replace. There was no reason for the manager to be there. Still, Frank Kelly came to welcome Duncan and give him the ball. No one could remember seeing such an exchange. Jack was elated. He saw Kelly's appearance as a unique blessing on Duncan's first moment in Major League Baseball. Fans would remember this forever.

There were no speeches or inspiring commentary when the Rookie got to the mound. Kelly was low-key and simply handed the ball to Duncan, in baseball's time-honored tradition. Jack reveled in the pure beauty of the experience. The manager was handing a new pitcher his opportunity to compete at the epitome of baseball. Then he gave the youngster the best send-off Jack had ever heard.

"Go get 'em, kid. I've been looking forward to seeing this."

Leaving the details to Jack, Frank Kelly headed back to the dugout as cheerfully as a beach stroller. He had already informed the umpire of his double switch. Duncan was taking Freddy Stout's spot at second, because Freddy had just batted. With any luck, Duncan wouldn't bat and face any pitchers. The Reds utility infielder, Marcus Carroll, would slide into Steve Patrick's batting spot, but play at second. The substitution strategy was complete.

'Keep it simple' Jack told himself. It was time to hand the stage to Duncan. Jack hadn't rehearsed his precise delivery. The two of them were bound together in this epic moment by a flood of thoughts, hopes and emotions. Jack hadn't decided on what to say when the announcer's booming voice filled the stadium. His exact words had never been heard before.

"Now pitching for the Reds, number twenty-four, Duncan James."

Two spectators practically came out of their skin, they were so excited. Sally and Danielle jumped, screamed, and pounded on each other as the announcement echoed through the ballpark. Jack just wanted to savor the moment with Duncan. It was a 'first time' that would never happen again.

"Awesome sound, ain't it?"

Jack couldn't resist smacking Duncan on the back.

"Let's get 'em, buddy. You set?"

Duncan nodded, with the same intensity Jack had seen at the try-out. It was time for Duncan to do what he was born for, and Jack was psyched to be the one to open the door.

"Okay, Cake, it's you and me, just like we always did. We'll probably need mostly fastballs and a little off-speed. If one of these jokers gets on, we just get him doubled up, okay?"

Jack didn't know what Duncan might say, but the youngster only nodded again and kept his focus on home plate. Jack had one more strategy in mind.

"Don't show them a lot of speed in the warm-ups."

His point was pitchers who appear out of nowhere get only one 'first time' with big league hitters. There's no need to clue them in as to what's coming. If Duncan did what Jack knew he could, after tonight the entire baseball world would know about it. Jack wanted the Giants to discover Duncan's fastball the hard way.

Marching back to home plate gave Jack an odd feeling. He was always invested in his pitcher's success, but tonight was different. Duncan was here, in this ballpark, because Jack had set the wheels in motion. He didn't want to admit how desperately he wanted Duncan to succeed. This was for Sally. And Danny. Jack didn't know where they were sitting, but he knew their eyes were riveted on their boy.

Rolling through the allowed warm-up pitches was easy for Duncan. Jack kept the glove in the middle of the plate for the medium-speed fastballs. Each pitch arrived straight and true. The entire Giants team watched Duncan, just as lions observe their prey approaching a watering spot. Usually a guy has some kind of track record when he throws his first major league pitch. No one had ever heard of this kid, much less seen him throw.

Duncan would be facing the first three batters in the Giants lineup. Up first once again was Felipe Diaz. It wasn't likely that he'd be bunting this time. Jack just wanted Duncan to throw strikes and let his fielders do the rest.

Diaz had come close to getting hits all night, but had only the one blooper to his credit. He didn't know who this rookie pitcher was, but he was determined to show what 'El Bateador' could do. That was the name he'd earned in Cuba, playing at Estadio Tropical en La Habana. Everyone on the island knew he was a dangerous batter, and he meant to keep it that way.

Jack signaled for an inside fastball and Duncan put it right on the edge. Diaz must have been looking for a pitch toward the middle, because that was where all the warm-ups had been. He reacted quickly and got a piece of the ball, fouling it back into the screen for strike one.

Repeating the same pitch was good strategy, but Duncan brought it a bit inside. Ball one gave Diaz a slight edge at 1-1. Jack declined creativity, because he wanted Duncan's velocity. These guys were going to have to prove they could hit the heater.

Jack gave his finger waggle, indicating more speed, same location. Duncan overcompensated for the prior pitch, and left the ball a little too much toward the middle. Diaz was not going to let a fastball get by him, and he was swinging early. A change-up would have fooled him, but he was in front of the ball and drilled it tightly down the third base line. Most balls would have dipped inside the bag for extra bases, but Scott King was hugging the line. He dove to his right and snagged the ball as he landed in foul territory.

A basic big league throw would have gotten the out, but Scott was trying too hard to help the young pitcher. He drilled the ball to first, but the throw went over Hank Stafford's head.

Luckily for the Reds, Diaz was intent on getting to the bag. He didn't immediately realize Stafford had to retrieve the ball after it bounced off the groundskeepers' rolled-up tarp. Scott was charged with an error, and the Giants had a runner on base.

The game's intensity didn't stop a quote from popping into Jack's head. 'Adversity doesn't develop character, it reveals it.' Duncan's major league career was only ten minutes old, and the world was going to get an intimate glimpse into his character. Jack didn't react at all, but he prayed the error would not take Duncan off into the weeds.

Barry Ackerman, batting in the Giants second spot, strolled up to the plate. He acted as if he had been getting hits all night. The guy was almost as petulant as their catcher, Paul Gardiner. Jack was determined to show Duncan's ability to control the edge of the plate. If Duncan got the impression Jack had any doubts, they could forget about developing the confidence needed to succeed at this game. Plus, the fastball was starting to heat up. Jack was counting on it.

So, he defiantly signaled for an inside fastball. His look told Duncan that they would get through this little setback. On the other end, Duncan gingerly controlled his emotions, because he knew he should have an out to his credit. He resolved to do exactly what Jack had said: Use the runner on first to get a double play. But somebody would have to hit the ball for that to work. The little self-generated irony made Duncan smile ever so slightly. It gave him a look of confidence that had Barry Ackerman wondering what was happening.

Duncan pitched from the stretch, after keeping the runner close to first. The ball came roaring in exactly on the inside corner, for a called strike one. Jack knew the kid was still in control and aggressively snapped the ball back to the mound. Duncan grinned slightly once again, as if at an inside joke. Jack could feel the kid's gutsy attitude clear from home plate.

Seeing the opposing pitcher and catcher sharing a humorous moment seemed to anger Ackerman. They were disrespecting him, somehow. They had the audacity to paint the corner when they should have been going for safer pitches. He decided he would be ready for another inside pitch, and crowded the plate to see if that would disrupt this kid's delivery.

Duncan saw what the batter was doing and knew what it meant. 'Buddy, I can put the ball inside a five inch box,' he said to himself. The next pitch was an exact duplicate of the first, only faster. Ackerman didn't even try to swing. He had something else in mind.

There are people in life who play by the rules. They are offended by those who cheat, or try to cut corners, or bend the law. Others advance by their ability to cheat, cut corners, and take advantage of everyone else. Barry Ackerman was the poster child for the latter.

His motto had been developed long ago: 'If you ain't cheating, you ain't trying.' Crowding the plate hadn't disrupted his opponent's ability to throw a perfect strike. No matter. Barry had another option up his sleeve. In fact, he had his sleeve as an option.

A hit batsman is awarded first base, but the rules require a batter to 'attempt to avoid' a pitched ball. Barry leaned forward into the pitch, and the ball grazed his uniform. The umpire should have ruled that Ackerman caused the contact. Instead, he awarded the batter first base. Intentional contact is illegal, but Jack's protest was ignored.

It was hard to ignore Frank Kelly. He came roaring out of the dugout and nearly got ejected. The deed was done, and the Giants had runners on first and second with no outs. The fact that Kelly came out on the field to bellow at the ump provided the only benefit. Jack was able to quickly tell his manager not to bail on his pitcher. Everybody has to work their way out of a mess, sooner or later. Duncan's 'sooner' was right now.

The charming Mr. Gardiner was coming to the plate, and he represented the tying run. Predicting his strategy was easy. He'd be swinging hard for the fence, and he saw this faltering rookie on the mound as roadkill. Jack decided to use his aggression against him, and called for a curve. Getting the ball in the infield would yield at least one out, and bring the inning back into a controllable situation.

Pitching from the stretch didn't seem to bother Duncan, and he looped his curve in perfectly. Gardiner had been expecting another fastball, and his swing was early. Most pitchers would choose speed for the next pitch. Jack hoped the opposing catcher's instincts would bring him to the same conclusion. A changeup would disrupt the batter's timing, just enough to get a second strike, or put the ball in play. Duncan took the sign and appeared to be burning in a fastball. At least, it looked like a fastball.

Paul Gardiner was a testy individual, but that didn't mean he couldn't hit baseballs. When he got his first view of the pitch, he was swinging to blast it perfectly. But his skill was enough to recognize that the ball was coming in slower than he anticipated. He delayed his swing just enough to make contact.

He was still in front of the ball, and he pulled it sharply toward third base. That was where Scott King was stationed, to protect against any extra-base hit down the left-field line. He was still kicking himself for his earlier error. Fate was about to give him a chance to redeem himself in spectacular fashion.

The ball rocketed to King on one hop. It was in his glove almost instantly, and Scott's natural motion toward the ball positioned him perfectly at third. Kicking off the bag gave him superb leverage *and* out number one as he whipped the ball to Mark Carroll at second. Mark fielded the ball as he swept his foot over second base in one smooth motion, for out number two. He fluidly zoomed the ball to Hank Stafford at first. Gardiner was a half-step away when Hank snagged the ball for out number three. The crowd erupted in a deafening frenzy.

The Reds had just executed a perfect 5-4-3 triple play, and the inning was over. The disaster waiting to happen was averted. Duncan was in near-shock as he walked off the mound. It had all happened in less than four seconds. Jack joyfully met Duncan at the baseline. The ecstatic catcher couldn't resist busting on his rookie.

"Just like I drew it up!"

He joined his teammates in high-fiving their new pitcher.

"I told you there was help out there! Jeez-o-Pete, that was great!"

The whole team celebrated the rare event while the next three batters prepared for their at-bats. Jack sat with Frank Kelly to discuss the pitching strategy for the top of the ninth. Three more outs would give this close contest to the Reds. Jack wanted the save to go to Duncan.

"Skipper, he's throwing strong. That was a freak jam we got in, and getting out of it was a great confidence-builder for everybody."

Kelly seemed noncommittal, and Jack didn't want to spook him. Maybe he had gambled enough.

"Keep Marvin ready to go if you want. I'm saying Duncan can get three outs."

The manager was still silent. Jack put in one last word.

"You need to let this kid know you believe in him. It'll pay off in the future."

Kelly said nothing, but gave Jack a tight grimace and a quick nod. They watched Izzy's replacement take their next three batters down in order. It was 'go time' for the last inning. Adjusting his catcher's equipment, Jack corralled Duncan.

"We're going to put the heat on 'em. You feeling good?"

Duncan nodded, his usual stoic self. Jack needed to put the last inning in perspective, and strengthen his pitcher's attitude.

"We just had two weird things happen. That's over and done. You're the man now."

Two guys on base with no outs was scary, Duncan had to admit. But he was getting his game face back in place. Pitcher and catcher headed out to their positions. Duncan was all business as he completed his warmups, and Jack resolutely sent the ball to Mark Carroll at second. The top of the ninth was about to begin.

Glancing at the opponent's dugout, Jack saw that the Giants manager had a surprise for Duncan. He wasn't going to be facing the right-handed batters Jack had anticipated. The heart of the batting order was due up, but 'last chance' logic was at work. The Giants skipper was down to his last three outs; it was time to score runs or the game was over. He decided to play the odds and see how the rookie right-hander handled left-handed pinch-hitters.

Advancing to the plate was a journeyman outfielder named Dean Wahl. He was perfect for the situation. Defensively, he was merely dependable, but he was a strong left-handed batter. Jack had seen him before, and knew he was a monster fastball hitter. Expanding the strike zone by swinging at bad pitches was not part of this hitter's game. Still, Duncan needed to work the edges. Pitches in the middle of the plate would get a Wahl ride to the wall.

Knowing that Dean tended to take the first pitch, Jack risked a fastball. He wanted to get ahead in the count, so he called for inside heat. Initially, the pitch straddled the corner, but it tailed slightly inward. The call could have gone either way, but rookies don't get rewarded on close calls. Pitching from behind at 1-0 was something Duncan needed to learn to handle; Jack was patient. He decided Wahl would be sitting on another fastball. Time for a changeup.

Duncan got lucky because Dean was way out in front of the pitch. The count was even at 1-1. It was time to try the edge again, and Jack shifted to outside and low. Duncan's throw was tracking outside the plate, but it stayed too high. Wahl slashed at it, and his broken bat plopped the ball just over Mark Carroll's diving attempt at second base.

"Here we go again," Bobby Bintner commented for his TV audience. "Frank Kelly needs to sit this kid down and bring in Marvin Lowe, before this game gets away. The tying run is on deck, sports fans."

Jimmy Hyde liked to push his broadcasting partner's buttons when he acted as if he were the manager.

"Let me get Kelly on the phone here. He probably hasn't realized that the Giants have more batters."

Secretly, Jimmy was worried that this young pitcher would get slapped around and not recover. He had seemed like a nice kid at the signing ceremony.

Another pinch-hitting lefty was on the way. The Giants reserve first baseman, C.J. Wozniak, was an unknown quantity. One thing was obvious: His large and bulky frame would deliver a powerful swing. Jack resisted the urge to get cute and ask what 'C.J.' stood for. He'd save that for another time, perhaps when his pitcher wasn't teetering on the edge of disaster. What he knew about the opposition, or more accurately, didn't know, was enough to urge caution.

Duncan was going to have to ramp up his fastball to get the job done. Jack signaled for heat on the inside corner. C.J. must have thought the ball was headed off the plate, but Duncan got the call. Jack did his finger wiggle calling for more of the same. He had a feeling C.J. would have trouble getting in front of Duncan's heat. He decided to up the ante for the next pitch.

"Wait 'til you see one of his fast ones," he muttered.

The nearly imperceptible eye shift from C.J. told Jack he'd touched a nerve. Duncan brought a smoker to Jack's outside corner target. C.J. tried to catch up to the pitch, but was only able to foul down the left field line.

Up in the count 0-2, Duncan was looking like a big leaguer. Jack tried to outguess C.J. and figured he would expect something off speed. Velocity had netted two strikes. Sometimes reverse psychology works, Jack hoped.

"Hmm, let's see," he said in a weird conversational tone. "Maybe you'd like a look at something slower."

But he was signaling for the exact same fastball Duncan had just thrown, now inside. C.J. did not bite on Jack's bait and switch. Duncan's fastball roared toward the spot Jack had selected. C.J. managed only weak contact, and plopped the ball toward first.

It was up to Hank Stafford to make the play. He bolted toward the ball, snapped it up, and with a single motion threw to Mark Carroll to get Wahl at second. Duncan's inexperience hurt him. He was late getting off the mound to first base, to field the return throw for the double play. C.J. made it safely to first and the Reds got only the lead runner for the first out. Bobby Bintner wasted no time in cackling about Duncan's faux pas.

"That's a rookie move from Duncan James, not getting over to first in time," he said smugly.

Jimmy Hyde was beginning to wonder what angle Bintner was chasing, with all the negativity directed toward the newcomer. He let his dry sense of humor state his case.

"Well, Bobby, you might be on to something. Chances are you'll get a rookie mistake from a rookie in his first major league ball game."

The off-camera producer laughed, as Jimmy continued.

"That should be the title of your book, Bobby. 'Why Veterans Aren't Rookies' or something else super clever."

Then he returned to his duties of calling the game.

"We're in the top of the ninth with the Reds holding on to a three-to-nothing lead. The Giants have one out with a runner on first. On the mound for the Reds is nineteen-year-old Duncan James. He is appearing tonight for the first time in major league baseball. It's been flirting with disaster so far, but the rookie has shown promise."

Down on the field, Duncan was kicking himself for not making the play at first.

'You had two outs, idiot,' he said to himself. He directed his frustration at the ball, and signaled to the umpire for a replacement. Jack took advantage of the pause to give Duncan a subtle hands-down motion, meaning 'keep it calm.' It was time to focus on the next batter, third baseman Armour Ellsworth. Jack didn't see another left-handed pinch hitter at the ready. The Giants manager was either running out of lefties, or he was underwhelmed by Duncan's performance.

Jack knew Armour from the old days and liked him. The Reds had played in San Francisco and Jack met Armour's family. Their grandfather had been part of the famed Tuskegee Airmen. They were a highly decorated group of aviators who fought in World War II. Jack had bonded with Grandfather Ellsworth, who regaled him with stories of the pilots' exploits. It was another chapter of Jack's fervent admiration for veterans.

At one time, Armour had been a fearsome power hitter. After ten years in the league, his bat speed had eroded slightly, but he was still a dependable contact hitter. He would be able to get the bat on off-speed pitches; Jack was betting that Duncan's speed would make the difference. As Ellsworth approached the plate, Jack greeted him as if they had spoken just the other day.

"I was wondering when you'd show up," and got a grin in response. Armour considered Jack a member of his family, and was in a playful mood.

"Go easy on an old man, Jack."

He took a couple of warm-up swings.

"The old folks think I can still play."

He was referring to a conversation from years ago when Armour's grandfather pretended Jack was his favorite player. Armour and Jack had a bond that was easily retrieved. Both of them were smiling when they returned to the matter at hand. Jack was in his element; it was honest competition with a worthy opponent.

He decided to start with an off-speed pitch. Then he'd see if his old friend could adjust. Duncan delivered a first-pitch curve and it arced in perfectly. Armour was fooled and took strike one.

"Pretty nice. Where'd you find this kid?"

The umpire was intrigued at the friendly exchange between these two competitors. Some ballplayers are chatty at the plate, especially if they are old teammates. There are basic greetings, and then each player gets down to business. There's work to be done. So the ump figured these two knew each other from way back. Jack continued the easy banter.

"You know me, Arm. I just wander the countryside finding kids who can throw some heat."

This was ironic, because a fastball down low was exactly what Jack was ordering.

Armour must have thought Jack was using misdirection, because he wasn't looking fastball at all. The ball clipped the bottom of the zone, and whammed into Jack's mitt with a terrific crack for a second strike. Duncan was rolling now, and Jack wanted another screamer climbing the ladder.

Angry with himself for allowing two called strikes against a rookie pitcher, Armour had the bat moving almost simultaneously with Duncan's release. He was going to 'go down swinging' no matter what, and the chips could fall where they pleased.

The good news was he got under the ball and hit a long out to right field. The bad news was Marcus Crane misjudged the ball off the bat, and actually started in before he realized his error. Over in center field, Roger Pruitt had a better angle to judge trajectory and was shrieking for Marcus to get back on the ball. It was too late. Jack was aghast to see Crane jump for what should have been an easy second out. He was only able to bat it down.

Anticipating the fly-out, C. J. had advanced halfway to second. The muffed catch allowed him to jog to the bag, and Armour was standing on first when Crane retrieved the ball. Jack wondered what else could go wrong in this inning from hell. His young pitcher should have been out of the inning, game over, but bad luck had runners on first and second with only one out.

The answer was quickly upon him when he saw Mike Franz come out of the dugout on his way to the pitcher's mound. It was the first step in Duncan being removed from the game. Jack noted that Brian Ivey, the Giants' right fielder was on his way to the batter's box. At the mound to meet with Franz, Jack knew the first questions were always directed at the catcher.

"How's he look to you?" Mike asked.

Jack could be direct with Mike, because they had participated in this exact type of exchange many times before. Except in the old days, Mike was the one trying to get out of trouble. Franz knew if Jack thought his pitcher was having issues, he wouldn't try to bluff his way through it. Professionalism required a pragmatic approach.

"I think he's fine, and getting stronger. We're in this mess because of a couple of freak events. We'll get through it."

Both Jack and Franz were thinking that Duncan was looking remarkably impassive during the exchange. The pitching coach turned his attention to Duncan.

"You feeling okay?"

Duncan nodded.

"You seem to be putting the ball where you want to."

Duncan bobbed his head and gave a quick answer.

"Yes, sir. We'll get two more outs."

He wasn't about to throw anyone under the bus, but all three of them knew his defense had let him down. Franz liked the positive attitude. The kid sure looked as if he had plenty of fight in him.

"Okay, then, let's get two more. Ivey is always ready to expand the strike zone."

Franz gave Duncan the customary swat on the behind and headed to the dugout. A second visit would require Duncan's removal, and Jack wanted to forestall that event. He turned away from Duncan and spoke briefly with Franz.

"Mike, I want this kid to finish the inning. He's not at fault here.

Let him know this team believes in him. I don't care if they get a couple of runs, we still win. The worst that can happen is Ivey hits a dinger, and ties the game. You can pull Dunc then, and I'll go along with you. But you need to let this kid fight."

The raw sincerity of Jack's words resonated with Franz. He remembered when Jack had gone to the mat for him in similar situations. It had made him a stronger pitcher, and Franz hoped it did the same for Duncan.

As Franz left the mound, the umpire approached to break up the meeting. Jack spoke quickly.

"Cake, these guys can't hit you if you do what we've practiced. Strong and hard, just off the plate for this guy. You'll get him swinging."

Jack gave Duncan a fist pump for emphasis and headed back to home. Brian Ivey was taking confident warmup swings and Jack threw a little curve of his own.

"Your chance to be a swinging hero, Brian."

And he grinned mischievously at Ivey. The unspoken dare just might tip the batter toward aggressive swings at the pitches Jack was planning: Too close to ignore but not close enough to allow any damage. Jack dared to hope for a ground-ball double play, but the miracle in the previous inning cast the odds against that. He settled in and called for heat off the plate.

Duncan delivered perfectly, just off the edge, but Ivey had planned to take the first pitch to see if the rookie had the heart for this conflict. The 1-0 count did not deter Jack from the same call, only slightly closer to the plate. Ivey pulled the string but did not catch up to the fastball. It floated foul, just out of reach for Hank Stafford. Jack would have traded his car for an out on that pitch.

All three of the combatants were feeling confident in their positions. Ivey thought he could handle what this kid had to offer; Duncan and Jack knew their best was yet to come. Jack decided a pitch in the same location, faster and slightly higher, would elicit a swing that would miss. It almost happened that way.

Ivey was guessing fastball and swung early enough to make contact. He did misjudge the placement, and hit a looper to shallow left field. The ball was too deep for Jack to hope for an infield fly ruling, and Rico wasn't going to get there. But Rodríguez hit an extra gear, and somehow made it in from deep left to make a miracle diving catch. Jack's heart climbed back into his chest, and he prepared to get the final out.

————

Invariably the spectators at a ballgame will include someone who believes they know baseball's finer points. These persons regale the fans around them with their insight into the nuances of the game. They give their opinion on what strategy the coaches should be pursuing. This game was no exception.

Just behind home plate sat a fellow named Melvin Koven. He had achieved financial independence in computer sales. People bought lots of computers, and to his thinking, he had an indispensable role in the process. He was rich. As day follows night, it made sense to him that his success was inextricably related to his unique personal traits. Someone with such enviable qualities had to have knowledge that should be shared with others.

True to form, Mr. Koven had spent the evening telling everyone what was really happening in the game. His audience included his date from his office staff. Melvin was full of insight. He knew what pitches should be called, what substitutions should be made, and what strategies should be employed.

When Duncan entered the game, Mel informed everyone that the youngster was ill-prepared and should not be playing. He went so far as to say that this poorly-equipped neophyte would shortly disappear from major league baseball, and never be heard from again.

As Duncan's troubles worsened, the disparagement increased. At any moment, Mel told the assemblage, the interloper would be knocked out of the game. The guru's omniscience would be validated.

His self-appointed clairvoyance was, in his mind, about to be demonstrated.

Having garnered two outs, Jack felt better about life in general. He cheerfully greeted the next batter, Carlos Mejía, the second baseman for the Giants. He wasn't a formidable hitter, hence his eighth spot in the batting order. But he was a flawless fielder and a speedy threat if he got on base. Jack resolved to treat him to Duncan's fastball, which was hovering in the ninety-five mile per hour range.

Jack knew that if Duncan pumped it up to his maximum, Carlos would never see the ball. The first pitch duplicated what Duncan had thrown to Brian Ivey: a tantalizing fastball on the edge of the plate to see if Carlos would go fishing. But Carlos had adopted the same mindset of the previous batters, and waited out the first pitch.

The umpire had called the same pitch a strike when Jack was batting, but Duncan didn't get the call. Ball one. Jack resisted the strong urge to complain and called for the same pitch. He brought the glove inward, so the pitch would be undeniably in the zone.

Duncan had been pitching from the stretch since there were men on base, and Jack was happy to see that his velocity was not impacted. They hadn't spent a lot of time perfecting his technique, but Duncan was performing well, technically. Jack had discussed the rules of pitching from the stretch, and had emphasized that Duncan could always 'reset' by stepping off the rubber.

After a pitcher comes to a 'set' position, disengaging the pivot foot is essential before any other movement, besides throwing to home. Duncan had shown he understood the basics. He hadn't stepped off yet, but Jack knew the moment might come, especially with active runners on base. After taking the sign for the second pitch, Duncan delivered another fastball. Jack watched its path and happily saw the ball bisect the black edge of home plate. It meant that a third of the ball was clearly in the strike zone and the call would be even at 1-1.

During the previous innings, Jack had been having doubts about the umpire. He was inconsistent with his strike zone. Earlier, he had called a strike on Jack for a pitch that had been further outside than the one Duncan had just thrown. Jack's doubts became dislike when Mr. Blue called a second ball.

The computer replay showed a clear strike, and the crowd erupted with lusty boos when they saw the pitch on Diamondvision. Jack allowed himself the silent catcher's protest, by hanging on to the ball in his crouch position for as long as he dared. He straightened up and took a step toward the mound and returned the ball in a lazy arc.

"Good pitch, buddy," he called to Duncan.

Then he turned back to his position and shook his head all the way. He didn't say a word to the umpire, but the meaning was clear. The ump was wrong, again, and everybody knew it.

He signaled for the same pitch. Jack was daring the misguided idiot to cheat Duncan again. The rookie gunned a strike to the identical spot and the ump exacted his revenge. Ball three. Jack decided enough was enough, and he spoke directly to the batter.

"You're going to be famous, Carlos. You'll be on millions of views on how to call strikes."

The comment wasn't made directly to the umpire, and did not specifically criticize the call, so Jack wasn't risking ejection. But it was a clever way of saying the umpire was making bad decisions. It probably wasn't the best thing to do.

Jack dropped into his crouch to give the next signal. He moved the target inside. Carlos probably wasn't swinging anyway, and the umpire would *have* to call a strike when the ball was in the middle of the plate.

A bit of apprehension crept onto Duncan's face as he went into his stretch. That was understandable, because he had just been absolutely *robbed* on two pitches. He paused in his stretch and then began his throw. Immediately, the umpire jumped from his position behind the plate and waved his arms. Duncan was already in his delivery. Startled by the sudden movement, he bounced the next pitch.

"Balk!" the umpire screeched.

Then he yelled "Ball four!"

Jack was stunned and Frank Kelly came shooting out of the dugout for the second time.

"What the hell was that?" he screamed at the umpire.

Without any explanation, the umpire gave the 'toss' signal and Kelly was ejected. It didn't stop Kelly from demanding why a balk had been called. The call had caused ball four. The umpire had created a walk and Carlos went to first base. The bases were loaded.

The crowd hooted unmercifully when the replay showed that Duncan had properly paused in his stretch. The timing was close, but there had not been a balk. But even if Duncan had stopped his throw, a balk call would still advance the runners. The rules allowed the pitch to be counted as ball four. The damage was done and the Reds had to deal with the winning run coming to the plate.

The Giants pitcher was up, but was pulled for a pinch hitter Jack recognized. It was Louis Parrish, a former teammate. He could hit, but Jack remembered that Louie had one notable weakness.

———

In the stands, Melvin Koven was in his element. There was a multitude of explanations to be made, and understanding the balk rules requires exquisite knowledge. He had been providing his analysis of the pitch selection, and regaling everyone with his breakdown of perceived flaws in Duncan's mechanics.

The balk call allowed him to switch into professorial high gear. His date was mightily impressed. Old Mel seemed to know everything. It was at that instant Jack started out to the mound. He first extended his hand, palm out, to make a 'stop' motion toward the dugout. No one else was coming to the mound. If the replacement manager came out, Duncan was done because it would be a second visit.

Jack approached his young pitcher gingerly. Duncan looked like he had just been shocked by electricity from a poorly wired lamp. Taking the kid's mind off his troubles was job number one. It wasn't his fault the umpire had memory issues. Apparently he'd forgotten the strike zone, the rules, and probably his mother's name.

Melvin's date was properly inquisitive. She wanted to know what the boys might be discussing.

"Mel, what's he doing out there?"

Koven knew the answer, of course.

"I figure the catcher is making sure they've got the signals right. They're really in trouble, and they need to be on the same page."

Glancing around expansively, he made sure the nearby fans got the benefit of his analysis.

"Probably talking about getting past the balk call, which was wrong, by the way. Then, what to pitch to the next guy. He has to calm this young guy down."

Computer genius Koven settled back in his seat to let the significance of his wisdom sink in.

"Oh, Melvin, you're so smart," his date said admiringly.

By now, Jack was standing with Duncan. Most catchers would have encouraging words for their pitcher, but Jack knew focusing on the dire situation would make it worse. His baseball acumen was in full stride, and he shifted gears entirely. He eased Duncan into another reality, as far from the game as possible.

"You know, Cake, I've been hanging out with Danny a little bit."

Jolted by the comment from left-field, Duncan looked at Jack as if he had pulled out a recipe book and started talking about baking. Jack ignored the stupefied stare from the youngster, and delivered a second off-beat comment.

"We're sort of getting together. Kind of dating, I guess you'd call it."

Duncan was looking sideways at Jack, not quite believing what he was hearing. He'd expected some sage advice about pitching, but this was sounding like a bizarre visit to the high school malt shop.

"I've seen you two out by the barn, Jack. Mom has, too. Ain't no big news."

Jack affected a relieved look and exhaled slowly.

"Oh, good. I guess I'm saying it's kind of a boyfriend and girl-friend thing. I was wondering if you're okay with it."

Duncan actually started to smile. Jack's concurrent grin made the two of them look like co-conspirators. Even Jimmy Hyde and Bobby Bintner commented on how incongruous the meeting appeared.

"I'm not sure what's going on out there, but somehow Jack Ridley has convinced Duncan James that having the bases loaded is funny," Jimmy said.

"Ignorance is bliss," added Bobby. "The rookie must be too young to know what a fix he's in."

"Or maybe they know something we don't," Jimmy mused. "Kind of hard to figure out what it might be, though."

The umpire was coming out to break up the meeting and Jack started taking backward steps away from the mound. He was still facing Duncan.

"I'm okay with it, Jack, but I've got a question." Duncan had a totally mystified look.

"Aren't we supposed to talk about the batter?"

"Oh, yeah. I forgot about that," Jack laughed. "I know this guy from Triple A. Can't hit anything low and inside. Smoke it."

And with that, Jack was back to the plate. Duncan was standing on the mound with a foolish grin on his face.

'Danny and Jack together,' he thought. 'And she didn't like him. Weird.'

Louis Parrish had been observing the mystifying exchange on the mound. He received a Ridley reception as if they had visited only recently.

"Louie, you are one lucky guy. You get to be a hero if you hit one out of here."

It was possible Parrish would let desire interfere with good judgment. Jack had every intention to put the ball in a tight little spot where Lou had difficulty finding it. He pounded his glove and dropped into position to give a sign that Duncan already knew.

"Let's get one more," he yelled to no one in particular.

Jack held the glove low and inside, and Duncan delivered it perfectly on the edge. Of course the umpire called a ball. Jack was starting to wonder if this problem child would call a strike even if the batter was swinging at a pitch.

He resolved to bring the ball in slightly and gave Duncan the sign for the same pitch with his finger wiggle for more speed. Duncan had just hit ninety-five with his fastball, and it was time to bring even more. Parrish would have to swing at this one.

The next pitch was straight and true, just above the batter's knees and running inside the corner. Parrish swung but was late and above the ball. His old malady was still there for Jack to exploit. Jack knew that two more pitches, exactly the same, were all Duncan needed to survive his baptism of fire.

He wiggled his fingers and made a bug-eyed face at Duncan, feigning surprise at the speed his pitcher was bringing. Duncan could see Jack's grin inside the catcher's mask He smiled ever so slightly at the sign for a fastball. The next pitch was on the way.

The Pitchcast computer showed a ball in virtually the same location, and Jack knew it was faster. Parrish swung mightily, and missed.

'One to go' Jack thought, and asked for a repeat. The crowd was on its feet, screaming for a final strike. Duncan took the sign and completed his stretch. He sent his fastest pitch yet rocketing to the plate, still low and inside. Louie Parrish tried to swing but he had hardly gotten the bat in motion before the ball ripped into Jack's glove. No one heard the umpire shout 'Strike Three!' because the crowd had erupted.

Jack didn't run to the mound with the rest of the infield. He watched the bench empty and surround Duncan. Jack wanted to savor the moment. Pitchers get only one first save, and the longer it lasted, the better Jack felt. While standing on home plate, he jammed the ball into his pocket for safe-keeping. Duncan's first big league souvenir was secure.

The tumult was deafening, but Jack was enveloped in a graceful serenity. He was where he belonged. After all the disappointment, frustration and uncertainty, Jack had found peace. He had gambled on rediscovering baseball through nurturing Duncan's talent, and had been vindicated. The kid was going to be a major league pitcher.

After the team had finished pounding Duncan on his back, he and Jack headed to the dugout. A boisterous crowd was gathered nearby. In the middle of it all, Sally, Danielle, Elizabeth and Ashley appeared. Duncan jumped over the gate next to the dugout and bear-hugged his mother and sister.

Jack wasn't quite as demonstrative, but his face hurt from all the grinning. Viewing his mother and sister celebrating, with Duncan and his mom and sister, was all the reward Jack needed. He was happy to let the excited vortex subside. Then Danielle reached over the wall to give him her congratulations.

"You did it, Jack," she said in the midst of hugs and tears.

"I knew it all along!"

Jack had to call her on that one.

"Really? All along? C'mon, Danny, I was there. Remember?"

Danielle gave Jack one of her cutest crinkly-nose smiles and a bone-crushing hug.

"You're right, J.A. I was a bit slow at first. But I'm bringing the heat from now on."

The game was over, but the best part was about to begin.

EPILOGUE

Willa Cather wrote of "Something entire, whether it is sun and air, or goodness and knowledge. At any rate, that is happiness; to be dissolved into something complete and great. When it comes to one, it comes as naturally as sleep."

For Jack Ridley, baseball was entire, complete and great. Excelling in a game had come to him as naturally as sleep, and it had been taken from him by cruel fate.

Connecting with Duncan and his family gave Jack random events to help him rediscover his happiness. 'Repairing his losses,' as envisioned by Walt Whitman, had sprung from helping another find his own path. Throughout his days of exile, Jack had naturally helped others. In doing so, he had healed himself. Exorcising the demons that came to him five years before was the culmination of the redemption.

He and Duncan would enjoy years of baseball success and security. Best of all, they had the blessings of a man who escaped his own torment, by welcoming them back to the game that embraced them all.

———

The families celebrated Duncan's first professional save with raucous abandon. The youngsters were boisterous while the mothers were quietly thankful. Jack and Danielle let it be known that they were now a happy couple, to no one's surprise.

Duncan contemplated his immediate future as a ballplayer, and the veteran told the Rookie to expect to hone his skills at the minor league level. Eventually, he would become a permanent part of The Show.

Whether Jack and Danny progressed to a permanent relationship remained to be seen. For now, Jack was content to retire from discovering prodigies - to focus on baseball, business, and Danielle.

It was fitting that everyone owned a part of the happiest of days, as they had been part of the days that made the success possible. Something great and complete had happened, and it was as natural as sleeping.

TEASER

Preview the next book by Alex Murphy

Available in 2021

LAWYER'S LUCK

See No Evil

Hanging around the courthouse is a great way to keep your eye on what's going on. In smaller areas, such as Templeton, Indiana, it's even more effective. The easy pickings tell which perfect couple filed for divorce, or whose kid is in trouble. There's drinking, or shoplifting, to tempt the adventurous youth. Small town gossip is fueled by juicy details about who got arrested over the weekend. What job the work release crowd is handling this week might bubble up.

The reporter for the Templeton Gazette got a lot of information via an occasional stroll through the courtrooms. That very thing paid dividends many times over for Stan Burke. Besides finding plenty of stories, Stan got the dirt on everybody who occasionally swerved off into the weeds. It's a good idea to stay on the good side of a guy who

447

knows town secrets. It so happened that Lawyer John Luck was on the writer's good side.

His real name was Stanley Bukowski; Stan Burke was his news-paper byline. The name had caused him trouble ever since he started school. An off-beat name will usually get noticed by a school bully, and Stanley attracted his share of unwanted attention. During the first week of high school, one of the older tough guys decided to push him around.

School bullies focus on victims who are weak, less capable, not inclined to fight back, or some combination of all three. Young Stanley was a slightly-built freshman and Gerry Hicks played his part predictably. Stanley Bukowski was the first target of the year. After ridiculing the smaller boy's name, Hicks cornered Stanley in the bathroom. The time-honored 'swirly' was about to be demonstrated. That's when the smaller boy is held upside-down and his head is dunked in a toilet.

Enter John Luck, a recent transfer to the senior class. He was a good-sized kid with several older brothers. If a youngster is lucky, he can learn a lot from older siblings. The topics can range from acade-mics to basic life lessons. John leaned toward academics, but one brother in particular leaned toward delinquency. He taught John a useful concept. There is a trick to getting a fight over quickly: imme-diate and brutal aggression. Many troublemakers think throwing a weaker person to the ground is a fight. They've never met a real puncher. The reality shift is noticeable when their nose gets shoved back toward their brain. It's even more effective if they get their first sight of their own blood.

John was not particularly prone to fighting, but his older brothers had provided him with two things. First, he wasn't derailed if someone hit him. Second, he was stronger than most folks realized. If a boy started a fight, John wasn't shy about keeping it short and sweet. Gerry Hicks was in full bully mode when he felt a tap on his shoulder. He instinctively turned toward the tapper and saw a fist screaming toward his face. Gerry thought he was a capable fighter, but John hit him in the nose harder than Hicks had ever been hit in his life. The blood foaming on his face stunned him as much as the pain. The bad-ass moment was over. Gerry's brief thought that he'd get even some day quickly disappeared. Something in Luck's eyes told Gerry there was plenty more where that punch came from.

Qualifying as a bully doesn't necessarily make one stupid. Gerry got the message in one easy lesson. He had no intention of engaging someone who could fight back. John's introduction was short and sweet.

"Leave him alone."

Those three words caused three things to happen. One: Stanley never had another problem from Gerry, or any of his friends. Two: Word got around that John didn't start fights, but he sure knew how to finish them. Three: John had an ardent admirer and supporter for life. When Stanley got older, he caught up in size and was as capable as the next guy. But he always remembered the day John Luck came to his rescue. He was prepared to return the favor many times over.

By the time John finished law school, Stanley had graduated with a journalism degree and a new pen name. A series of reporting jobs culminated in Stan Burke becoming a well-respected journalist. He was the 'man about town.' He knew who had skeletons in their closets. Sometimes he knew when people were planning to get a skeleton. Anything Stan uncovered about local comings and goings was available to Lawyer Luck. From referrals to evidence tips, there wasn't anything Stan wouldn't do for John Luck.

Trial lawyers have to be part hustler. This is a many-faceted description. Not all hustlers are bad. Athletes, known to expend total energy, are known as the good sort of 'hustler.' But every coin has an opposite side, and there is an opposite 'hustler' type. Those are the lawyers who incline to play fast and loose with clients' cases - or their money. Attorney Luck was familiar with the benign and brutal spectrum. But he didn't have to control an evil streak that would cause him to misuse the wrong guy. When the bad boys and girls discovered that they got a fair shake from John, his street cred grew accordingly. It's true that there is honor among thieves. It's just a different type of honor - separate and distinct from board room platitudes. When 'Slamming Sam' promises to give you what he owes you, you can bet you're going to receive something. Good or extremely bad, payment is delivered.

Hustling in John Luck's orbit meant working hard to serve a client. It also meant looking out for others' interests. Early on, John asked an older and well-respected attorney for his best advice on lawyering.

"Tell the truth, and show up on time," was the simple guidance.

It sounds simple, but its application takes effort. You have to physically show up. It's as simple as keeping appointments, or doing the groundwork necessary to do a good job. Telling the truth means being honest with clients, judges and lawyers. You never have to keep track of any alternate message. Reality is always on your side. The simple formula would save Mr. Luck many times over. That's exactly how the Barrington case got started.

The Barringtons were the wealthiest family in the state. In fact, they ranked at the top of national incomes. They attracted multiple levels of attention. The well-to-do circled Luther and Camille Barrington, as moths find a flame. Unfortunately, the Barringtons were also visible to hopeful criminals. When the more ambitious lawbreakers targeted the family, Luther responded as would any law-abiding citizen. He immediately called the police. But intricate problems require inventive solutions. Mr. Barrington needed a back-up plan, because even the law has limits. He called John Luck.

ABOUT THE AUTHOR

Alex Murphy is a teacher and lawyer from Indiana. After retiring from the U.S. Army JAG Corps, stories he had accumulated along the way became novels. "The Lost Innings" is his first published work. He and his wife have three grown children and two grandchildren. He lives in Indianapolis and is happy to visit your organization, especially veterans' groups.

Contact with him at www.MagicBearLLC.com.